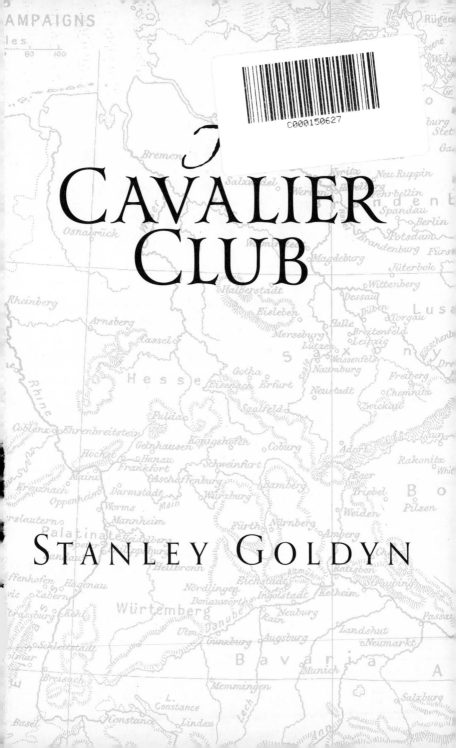

CAVALIER CLUB

STANLEY GOLDYN

The Cavalier Club
Stanley Goldyn

Published by Classic Author and Publishing Services Pty Ltd.
Imprint of JoJo Publishing.

First published 2015

'Yarra's Edge'
2203/80 Lorimer Street
Docklands VIC 3008
Australia

Email: admin@classic-jojo.com or visit www.classic-jojo.com

JoJo Publishing Imprint

Editor: Julie Athanasiou
Designer / typesetter: Working Type Studio (www.workingtype.com.au)
Printed in Singapore by KHL Printing.

National Library of Australia Cataloguing-in-Publication entry
Author: Goldyn, Stanley, author.
Title: The Cavalier Club / Stanley Goldyn
ISBN: 9780987144737 (paperback)
Subjects: Historical fiction.
Dewey Number: A823.4

For Irene, Damian and Mark,
and to Ricky—naughty to the end.

ACKNOWLEDGEMENTS

As an avid reader of books and one who enjoys a good novel, the desire to create my own tale lay like a dormant kraken hidden within the watery depths of my subconscious being. Aware of my insatiable curiosity with history—especially the fading Renaissance period—the urge to write steadily strengthened and I was prodded, gently and quietly, by Irene, my wife, whose unfailing encouragement ultimately persuaded me to pen this story of a romantic time in Europe's history that had captivated me since I was a boy.

Eventually, the factual maypole around which my fictional characters danced, took shape, and my gratitude goes to my publisher whose belief in my manuscript launched this process. Thank you to my friends and family whose excitement and profound support spurred me on with their positive criticism and optimism. Special recognition must go to my brother, Michael, whose military knowledge and technical adjustments assisted me throughout this lengthy task. I will continue to look fondly forward to our continued debates.

Kind appreciation to my readers and editors, Julie

and Mona, who silently coaxed commas into their rightful place and brought order to text that was ill and in need of medication. They meticulously corrected errant punctuation, straightened syntax and reformed prickly grammar into the regimented and readable final form. I am also indebted to Luke whose magic mouse conjured images and designs worthy of blessing the cover of any tome.

And finally, I am abundantly grateful to the real characters that lived and graced those incontrovertible moments in history with their desires, failings, deeds and adventures. I thank them for lending me their lives around which I was allowed to weave my yarn.

SG

Melbourne.

EUROPE 1618

English Miles

0   50   100

Rügen

Gdańsk

Pomerania

POLAND

Szczecin

Rv Noteć

Brandenburg

Rv Wisła

Berlin

Rv Warta

Warszawa

Łowicz

Rv Odra

Lusatia

Radom

Silesia

Kielce

Dresden

Kraków

Rv Elbe

Hradec Králové

Rv Ohře

Bohemia

Prague

Pilsen

Moravia

Netolice

Týn nad Vltavou

Lomnice nad Lužnicí

Záblatí

HUNGARY

Budějovice

Lower

Krems

Linz

Vienna

Upper

Austria

Salzburg

Rv Danube

OTTOMAN EMPIRE

Chapter 1

The cavernous void of silence engulfed him. Jack was aware of movement everywhere around him, yet his ears registered nothing—as if he lay in a soundless vacuum. It was more of an irritation, like bumbling his way around a dark and unfamiliar room, than a distressing concern. Jack was an experienced officer and battle-hardened physician; as such, a sober nature that was immune to panic and optimism owned his mind and soul like the marrow trapped within his bones. He believed his deafness was temporary and would pass.

Raising his eyes to the dust that hung in the stillness like a translucent layer of fog, Jack was reminded of the frequent damp mists that cowled the country roads back home on wintry mornings—soothing, serene and just as starkly quiet as now. Through the gaping rift blown away from the crenellated battlement, he could make out cavalry soldiers cantering in orderly lines down in the distant southern valley.

They were the enemy; he recognised their regimental colours despite the distortion of smoke-fogged air.

Jack was distracted by a movement—visible but blurred by the dust—across the yard, inside the walls and watched with detached, mild curiosity as an old pikeman threw his pail of water to stifle flames stubbornly burning from a wooden cannon-wheel, the veteran's pike cast temporarily aside on the cobblestones. Beyond him, a handful of muske-teers fired randomly at targets hidden from view past the city walls, biting at their powder charges with blackened lips and reloading their guns in turn. He could tell from the recoil and spasmodic wisps of smoke—a scene saturated with commotion, yet eerie and cocooned in a powdery haze and confound-ing silence. Loath to move, Jack followed the line of ramparts further across to his left with his gaze. A soldier in a broad-brimmed hat stood taking aim from behind a merlon while his comrade—battle-dented morion strapped to his belt—struggled to push a siege-ladder away from the walls with his halberd.

The deafened officer blinked, trying to clear the gritty dirt from his eyes, and realised that he had lost his hat. He felt naked without its protective shade. Damp strands of hair clung to his face like rivulets of wax running down a candle. He gazed methodically around him, taking in his immediate silent world and realised that he lay unceremoniously sprawled on a pile of rubble, head resting uncomfortably on a bent, upright musket. His neck was as taut as a bowstring and inflamed with pain. His sword was saddled on stone and half-hidden under a smoking wooden beam inches from his reach, and his pistol, still cocked, had been knocked from his hand. It lay where it had fallen, muzzle pointing safely down the temporarily abandoned parapet, its grip nestled across his forearm. He frowned as his memory tussled with what had happened.

The first, distant, pockets of sound began to invade Jack's consciousness as he started to stir. He felt as if stubborn wax was being cleansed from his ears, becoming aware of his pulse throbbing in the back of his head like a tedious pendulum. His thighs, buried under dusty planks, were sore. Jack kicked timorously, flinching with each dart of pain as he knocked some of the boards aside and sat up slowly. He leaned on his arms and surveyed the scene around him. A scowl modelled his face. He was covered with a canescent layer of dust and surrounded by litter. Broken masonry lay strewn about him like the remains of a village that had been shattered by a wild storm. The nearby pyramid of stacked cannon balls had miraculously escaped untouched, but

Jack's companion was not so fortunate. Jack's cold smile evaporated as he recognised the fawn-gloved hand. The arm, motionless and only partially visible from above the elbow, protruded upright from under a pile of rocks and bricks like that of a puppeteer. The curled, lifeless fingers were parted, beckoning as if frozen by Medusa's petrifying glare.

"Goodbye, my friend," Jack muttered, as much to himself as to his dead compatriot, slowly rising to his feet with a groan. Loose planks of timber slid off him. Brushing his curls from his eyes and wiping sweat and dust from his forehead, he looked around for his hat. He collecting his pistol and pulled his sword out from under the debris, struggling to wedge both into his broad belt. His head ached, and he grimaced as he loosened his left arm, pain stabbing at his shoulder, which he realised had been bruised from the fall. His elbow was throbbing misery.

Tugging off his companion's glove Jack removed his ring whilst miming a silent promise to return it to his friend's wife in Hradec Králové when opportunity next allowed. A brief smile spread across his lips as he recalled the day of their wedding—all the joy that two young lovers could pray for bound by vows symbolised by polished bands that glinted fleetingly as he passed them to the groom. Jack dropped the golden band into his pocket and noticed his hat, dusty and crushed under a stone, yards away from where he had been thrown by the shell blast. He recalled all now—vividly.

The full sounds of war struck him like rumbling echoes of thunder. Silent, chaotic activity was replaced by a frenzied, raging siege that inundated him as if swamped by a deluge. Protestant Bohemian regiments had advanced and struck the walled defences of Pilsen with a well-planned and remorseless ferocity. Inside the fortifications, the Catholic inhabitants were defending the city with equal resolve despite being significantly outnumbered by the rebels.

Jack's eyes momentarily glazed over like kitchen-window glass frosted by winter's breath. His mind was not yet ready to accept the violence to which he had just awoken. He leaned against a massive timber post for support and allowed his mind to wander away from the chaos around him. He was once again a carefree boy of seven, assuming command of an army of noble cavalrymen and valiant musketeers scattered around the sand mound overlooking the fields that ran endlessly towards the distant unseen borders of the family's estate. He was a fearless and seasoned commander, loved and respected by the motionless toy troops stationed about him. His father's people, who tilled and worked in the surrounding rolling paddocks of wheat and rye, were the make-believe enemy. Safe in his puerile and perfect world, he slipped away into countless conflicts and endless hours of playful stratagems and bloodless campaigns. His silent and fiercely loyal men went where he dictated without question. The heavy, battle-scarred helmet belonging to Jack's father covered the boy's milky curls as he manoeuvred his troops into positions of the greatest advantage among the folds of sand in which he sat. He would adjust the helmet as it frequently slipped down over his striking blue eyes. He had never lost a single battle. He was invincible. He could not die.

Nearby, oppressive musketry fire eventually shook Jack rudely and reluctantly away from his halcyon nostalgic reminiscence and dragged his mind back to brutal reality. His glassy eyes slowly focused on the scenes of war engulfing him. He smiled surreptitiously, mouthing the words he had often repeated as a young general in the sandpit: *I cannot be beaten.*

Their first assault had come shortly after initial light. Repeated cannon shots ruthlessly battered the thick and obstinate walls, the gunners probing for weaknesses. Defending troops had been ordered to occupy the battlements, and a company was assigned to protect each of the three main gates, which had been immediately barred and heavily braced. The guns on the walls continued to return fire, but the main body of the enemy's cavalry and infantry had been installed safely beyond range. The obdurate defenders were like granite, as dogged as Pilsen's walls. Smoke wafted across the intervening countryside, carrying with it the smell of acrid gunpowder and sulphur. Eventually the cannon fusillade gave way to sporadic volleys of musket fire, the guns' barrels cooling in the chilly autumn air as the attacking force advanced in preselected squares. Drummers sounded the beat, and pikemen, supported by musketeers, marched forward in lines with scaling ladders. There was clearly no point sending in a cavalry charge; the infantry units were given the responsibility of taking the city.

It was now early afternoon on 20 September 1618. The attackers, beaten off repeatedly, had earlier withdrawn their main force to a safe distance to allow an initial sequence of gun bombardment to dampen the Imperialists' spirit. Jack had been knocked senseless and his comrade crushed during the barrage. A cannon shot had clipped the roof of the corner tower on the south-eastern city wall, raining masonry and heavy timbers down around them. Jack had been taking aim at an enemy soldier on a ladder, but the exploding debris knocked the pistol from his hand and showered him with detritus, a tile hitting his shoulder and knocking him unconscious to the ground. The splintering of the disintegrating structure had temporarily deafened him.

Dusting off his tunic and breeches, Jack made his way to a small group of defending musketeers intent on their fight from the battlements a short distance away. Their intermittent shooting, although deadly and accurate, had little effect in staunching the approaching enemy's rush. Senior in rank to all of them, Jack barked at them to muster to his side. The musketeers were confused at first, but they bustled to congregate around him when he raised his rapier, holding it above his head like a rallying beacon, and repeated his intentions with a peremptory roar, his commands booming over the chaos.

Checking his drawn pistol as he ran ahead, Jack led them to a section of the defences where the wall embrasure had been pounded partially away, leaving a yawning gap. He shunned complacency and always considered the impossible. This would be the perfect emplacement, he judged propitiously, to make an initial stand. Ordering the musketeers into two ranks of four, Jack directed them to reload. He pointed with his outstretched sword to a designated score of attackers advancing about thirty paces away from the base of the wall and commanded the front rank to aim and fire. Before the pungent smoke cleared away, he yelled for the front rank to move behind the second row and reload, the rear rank now taking the firing line with another effective volley at the oncoming group. Jack had no time for fear. As always, his fear quickly wore away into resolve.

Although Jack's throat was hoarse from shouting and dry from the choking smoke, his orders to fire resulted in the decimation of the advancing party. It was a simple, logical manoeuvre, yet devastatingly effective. He took aim himself at one point, firing his pistol and hitting the leading officer in the shoulder. Finally the demoralised group scattered like disorderly rabble, with only two enemy soldiers managing to escape unhurt, nursing three others with them. Yet there was more to be done. Ignoring the nagging ache in his head and buoyed by his group's success, Jack directed his squad of eight to reload while assessing their next action and seeking the most effective striking position. Aware of sporadic enemy fire, the band took advantage of whatever cover was available.

"What is your name, soldier?" Jack asked, shouting over the din at the man closest to him after studying the group.

The old, craggy soldier adjusted his grey cap and turned his argentine eyes to face him.

"Chauvin, sir. Corporal Alain Chauvin," the man replied respectfully in French.

"Well, Chauvin, take this fine crew of lads to where that broken wooden buttress spans the rampart," Jack engaged the man's attention with a pointing finger. "Scatter them into four tight pairs around that segment of wall, making sure that they remain concealed behind the merlons to maximise their cover. You may be aware that the enemy has muskets as well, and a few know how to shoot them," he beamed with a broad, cheeky grin.

"Have them fire at those who are closest and advancing towards the scaling ladders, and ensure that every shot finds its mark. I'll go back down to the bailey and return with every available bandolier and shot pouch as soon as I can," Jack continued, blaring above the furore and stared into the man's face until Chauvin nodded confirmation. Still smiling, Jack added loud enough for the whole group to hear, "And Chauvin, as you're in charge, don't get yourself killed, or I'll shoot you myself!"

The corporal smiled back agreeably and warranted in an emphatic tone, "Yes sir. I'll be here when you return."

"Then go!" shouted Jack, jerking his head involuntarily as a musket ball suddenly whistled within inches of his ear and struck the nearest tile above. The group members, bent to provide the smallest visible target, moved off in a single line to the nominated point with Chauvin encouraging them from the rear.

Jack treaded gingerly to the nearest parapet staircase and glanced back at his little band before descending the rubble-strewn steps one at a time from the rampart to the yard below. As he looked up, he could see that the French musketeers had taken squatting positions behind the cover of the broken battlements and had begun firing carefully at menacing targets beyond the walls. He sheathed his sword while shoving his empty pistol into the back of his belt and moved methodically from one body to another with his baselard, slashing or pulling the leather bandoliers free and draping them over his shoulder. He also searched the dead for pouches containing lead shot, filling his pockets. He found an unfired musket and two pistols and pocketed a collapsible, leather telescope that he'd discovered from inside the tunic of a dead officer. His mouth was like parched sand, and his bladder pressured him although he'd emptied it minutes earlier. Calculating that he had been away long enough, Jack returned at a steady trot up the steps to his little band on the walls, the pain in his legs and shoulder now a distant memory.

The group was firing progressively, although Chauvin pointed to one dead Frenchman, who had taken a lead ball in the eye, when Jack reached him. The now unrecognisable, charnel face—recently young and comely—gaped open-mouthed at nothing, fragments of bloodied brain splattered like a handprint on the bastion behind him. Jack nodded grimly in acknowledgement at the motionless soldier slumped against the stone embrasure and laid his retrieved treasure on the battlement pathway. There would be time for sentiment and reflection later tonight.

"Distribute these amongst the men and move that last pair along this alure to the third crenel from the corner turret," Jack said, pointing out the tall, stone structure to avoid ambiguity. Sweat stung his eyes. "Have them harass that advancing party over there."

Chauvin followed his gaze and confirmed with a nod, adding "aye sir," as he moved off on his hands and knees to relay the order.

Jack knelt on one knee as he surveyed the scene through drifts of smoke. Artillery balls whistled above them. The musketry group had now drawn the attention of the enemy, and with it, a more concentrated fire—a direct result of the musketeers' diligent and effective shooting. They had clearly become a threat. Jack saw the slaughter that they had caused below and smiled broadly. Just beyond the outer curtain wall in front of their position, the

Protestant gunners had set up a small number of artillery pieces.

Jack peered cautiously from behind a stone bracing and scanned the line of cannons more definitively with the telescope he'd found. He could discern a gunner shielding his infant flame from the persistent wind that had arrived from the northwest as he touched the bowl of his pipe. Smoke wafted from the fired, recoiling gun many seconds before the rumble reached his ears. The ball dropped low on the wall, which the enemy gunner rectified with elevation adjustments. Further shots, however, were proving equally ineffective. Jack guessed that the calibre was inadequately light. Their cannons could splinter the merlons if they clipped the top of the battlements, but they barely grazed the main body of the wall. Their cannoneers would need to be particularly ardent with their accuracy if they were to significantly impact these robust defences.

Reloading his pistol, Jack set it beside his knee, examining the field closer to the walls. He was impressed and proud of the efficiency with which Chauvin's band had implemented his tactics. The enemy infantry's nerve had evaporated, and eventually soldiers ceased to advance towards the deadly pocket of muskets. The main east gate, however, was now under full attack as the assailants shifted their focus there. Jack hurriedly prepared to follow Chauvin and pass on his next order.

An enemy corporal had slowly crept to the right of their position and squatted at the base of a nearby ladder. Leaning on the body of a dead comrade, the soldier sat perfectly still, vigilant like an alerted stag, his eyes darting covertly along the battlements. The posture caught Jack's attention; it was odd, unnatural—the body in an unlikely pose in an attempt to feign death. The corporal was within range, and Jack was a good free-hand shot. With a gelid smile, he mouthed the favoured question quietly to himself: *Have you ever ridden beneath a Hunter's Moon and kissed the prettiest maiden before the autumnal equinox?* As a boy who initially struggled to manage the weight of a musket, or steady his outstretched hand while holding a pistol, his father had taught him to recite a short poem, hold his breath, aim and fire. This had been his first shooting lesson and he now knew from experience how the words sharpened his aim. His eyes centred in on the target in an unwavering, tunnelled focus. He snatched up and aimed his pistol, held his breath and fired. The trigger obeyed, and when the smoke cleared, the corporal lay dead, slumped on his right shoulder with blood pooling at his elbow and his foot twitching in lifeless spasms. The field below their fragment of wall was littered with many more corpses than before Jack's systematic involvement with Chauvin's small company of musketeers.

"Fine shot, sir," the old Frenchman praised loudly from a distance, with warm approval in his voice. He sealed those words with the open grin of a veteran who recognised the note of a true marksman as one special grain of sand on a windswept beach.

"The sneaky, inimical bastard got too cocky, Chauvin," Jack sneered, tilting his head as he yelled back over the din. "And it cost the idiot his life. They're throwing considerable force against our main gate now and harrying the two gate towers. Their cavalry is sitting and waiting patiently on that distant hill, watching their infantrymen perform in this spectacle. They'll cheer in unqualified support if our gate collapses." Jack had moved up and knelt beside his corporal. He still had to shout to be heard.

Somewhere in the distance, a trumpet sounded distress. Chauvin followed Jack's gaze and solemnly nodded in agreement as they both stared in the direction of the horn. The musketeers continued firing but less frequently now as their target's numbers thinned.

"We need to move across to reinforce the gate's defences. We'll give them a long wait." Jack's grin was as infectious as a clown's laughter at a circus. "I don't know where your men learned their trade, but I haven't seen such accurate shooting from French musketeers since the king was a boy."

Jack continued smiling appreciatively as he bathed the corporal's grey eyes with approval. "Leave that last pair where you placed them with two additional bandoliers. They can continue to pick off the stragglers and any others who try to advance on this section of wall. They must continue to hold and consolidate this position—cover our flank." He emphasised his point by separating his outstretched hands. "Tell them to join us in about half an hour, but remind them that it's vital to make their powder count."

Searching through the shifting smoke, Jack looked around, re-appraising the scene, and added, "Gather the remainder and follow me." After a brief pause, he asked, "Are you missing anyone?" He was momentarily confused, remembering that there had been eight in their group earlier.

"Legard is dead," Chauvin replied morosely, reminding Jack of the comrade shot earlier on the wall. Their eyes met briefly—Chauvin's blunted with sadness and loss and Jack's subdued, sharing sympathy for the corporal's struggling sense of perdition.

The musketeers made their way along the battlements towards the main gate, occasionally stopping to fire at easy enemy targets. Jack was a good shot with the pistol, but the group's accuracy continued to astound him. One musketeer in particular took more difficult, longer-range shots and seldom missed. Jack simply nodded his head in amazement. They travelled slowly and hid sporadically behind cover, moving forward cautiously.

Jack finally halted his little group about 50 paces from the main gate. They were breathing hard. Below, the Protestant troops had clustered their numbers in a swarm and fallen on the barbican like locusts. They were firing steadily up at the towers skirting the eastern entrance to the city. The scene was anarchy. Corpses, piled up to three bodies high in places, concealed the mammoth timbers of the lowered drawbridge. It was a quilt of limbs and lifeless torsos. Blood dripped into the moat below, where the number of floating human carcasses steadily grew as the dying fell from the embrasures above, staining the water in the fosse the colour of rust. If not for the breeze, the opaque and etiolated scene of misery would have been totally obscured in a thick fog of smoke. Splintered airborne debris rained on those below. The ground shook. The stench of blood wafted in eddies, mixed with the stink of scorched flesh and the malodorous reek of sewage, sweat and vomit. The smell of fear was unmistakable.

The battle screamed in Jack's ears. He wondered

why they hadn't brought their guns forward, recalled their men away to safe ground and bombarded the gate with their artillery. A concerted effort would have brought them a genuine opportunity to destroy the gate. *A squandered chance*, he mused.

Nevertheless, this situation gave Jack's marksmen the opportunity to advance on their attackers, and he ordered them to disperse once again into pairs and fire independent volleys. This time, he sent Chauvin to retrieve more ammunition from the dead whilst he took the two spare pistols and musket and fired at the advancing infantry men. As the span proved too great for the pistols, he reloaded and placed them to the side, concentrating his attention on the musket. It was close-range work for the firearm, and he just couldn't miss. Although slow to reload, the harquebus proved to be accurate at this short distance as the enemy soldiers massed their numbers in a wide, confronting arc around the gate and missing one resulted in invariably hitting another. The musketeers' presence assisted the other defending soldiers in stemming the attackers' thrust, and when Chauvin returned with the additional scavenged ammunition, he helped distribute the bandoliers and lead shot to the others.

In an attempt to minimise their mounting losses, the Protestants brought up two small-calibre leather cannons, which although light and manoeuvrable, were really only effective over a short distance. Although their gunners were out of musket range, both guns were soon destroyed when the defenders deployed their artillery, merging their fire on these targets. Before this, however, the eastern gate had been hit a number of times, producing two weakened gaps in the timbers that motivated the enemy to rush forward again. As they moved into musket range, the advancing infantrymen were steadily picked off from the walls. Shrieks of pain from wounded and dying men added to the cacophony of pistol shots and musket fire.

The French pair that had remained behind eventually rejoined the group. They had exhausted their ammunition. Their heavy musket barrels were too hot to touch, so Jack sent them off in search of drinking water. Like the others, he had not eaten or drunk since morning, and fresh water would partially sustain them until nightfall. Chauvin had found two bags of grape shot, and they launched these simultaneously into the thickest enemy ranks, causing devastating carnage. Water was soon distributed to the men as they continued firing. It was now almost dark, and the defences, they guessed, would hold for another day.

"What do you think will happen tonight, sir?" the

Frenchman asked above the commotion as he fired his musket, grazing one soldier past the temple and striking the one behind him through the neck.

"Tonight, it appears that we shall survive," Jack replied with untethered optimism, ramming his rod into his musket as he and Chauvin took cover behind the battlements. "At no point in the day have the Protestants hit the city with sufficient, puissant artillery, and this ill-fated infantry attack of theirs is proving to be a minor massacre. Their men stand on open ground and continue falling like pheasants and ducks out of the sky. Death loves those brave infantry ranks. They must have a significant-sized force to squander lives this way or are building a second bridge to our portcullis with the carcasses of their dead. Their cavalry is of no use either in such a siege. They remain idle, useless unless the defenders mount their own assault. It's possible that our defences are simply being put to the test. They may be counting our number and the strength of our guns. It's impossible to scry. If they review and change their tactics, I doubt that we'll be able to hold." Jack turned, aimed and fired and then hid again to reload. His eyes were as sharp as a kestrel hawk. "Thank the Lord in heaven that it's getting dark. I have five musket balls left," he continued evenly after several moments.

The odd enemy shot struck occasionally into the

stone wall beside them, but they were well protected. "There are so many of them," Jack added, his smile icy, "that their continued surge may eventually crush us by sheer numbers and firepower. Despite their losses, all they need is larger, well-placed cannons, and they'll take the city in a matter of days." His measured tone was grim, his frown cold. He was not ordinarily someone who allowed insecurity to contaminate his mind.

"We'll move away from here when it gets too dark to shoot." Jack looked up to gauge the sky as it loured ominously. "How many shots have you left, Chauvin?"

The Frenchman counted out 14 and passed half of them over, dropping them into Jack's hand. "That's all I have," he coughed out a raspy reply. "These Protestants have little stomach for fighting after nightfall. I do not know who is leading Pilsen's defence, but I expect the main regiment will stay to protect and repair this gate and brace the others overnight. I agree with you, sir, that with heavier guns, the city will ultimately fall. That only leaves the element of timing of a relief column, assuming there will be one," he added, raising a quizzical eyebrow.

They remained silent, firing until their ammunition ran out. Before complete darkness veiled the grim and bloody landscape, Jack ordered two from the group to replenish the powder and shot supply a final time. They all met at the well in the main square a short time later, and Jack led them to the steps outside the cathedral in the centre of the city, within which a large kitchen had been provisionally established to feed the defending soldiers. This place would be safe and far enough away from cannon shots and the odd sniper fire. They would all get some sleep.

Chauvin formally introduced his men to Jack. They were the remnant musketeers from a French regiment that had become separated from the main force a week ago in Radčice. They were well-equipped, Jack noted, each carrying a musketeer's sword, dagger and pistol as well as a woollen blanket. They wore excellent, above-the-knee leather boots and broad-brimmed felt hats, each one with a gaudy feather much like Jack's and bore uniforms closely resembling those of King Louis XIII's royal guards.

The evening lapsed into tranquillity as darkness quelled the fighting, the moon having disappeared behind heavy, malevolent clouds. Other defenders, drained and smeared with powder and grime, had come to congregate at the church. Some of them sat smoking pipes while a few cleaned and polished their muskets. Others drank wine and talked quietly. Some lay asleep. Jack and Chauvin were relieved to have lost only one man today, especially as lengthy and tempestuous periods during the day had seen precarious, intense fighting.

The group shambled wearily into the church, encouraged by an invitation from some of the locals to eat at the kitchen. Although tired, Jack waited patiently for Chauvin's men to go ahead of him in a sign of respect to the seven fine, reliable, professional soldiers. As the corporal passed him and entered the church, the flinty veteran crossed himself out of habit and murmured, "The cathedral is always open to sinners and repenters alike."

Mounting the steps to follow the musketeers, Jack looked up at the dark, starless sky and turned around at the cathedral porch door to gaze back toward the myriad enemy campfires dotting the distant hills. *They are indeed a large force,* he appraised, suddenly feeling cold beneath his tunic. In retrospect, he could have chosen any number of different routes to travel to Prague to meet with his friend, but the small, local family breweries in Pilsen had established an excellent reputation, and he had never before been presented with such an opportunity to pass through this celebrated, ale-brewing city. Yet he could not have foreseen that this would happen. The besieging of Pilsen had caught many others unaware. With a pensive shrug, Jack turned and slowly stepped inside the cathedral.

Chapter 2

Finding a couple of empty chairs by the fire in the large presbytery, Alain Chauvin and Jack settled comfortably a little way from the others. Chauvin studied Jack's face with smiling eyes.

"With all due respect, sir, you're obviously of a higher rank than a mere corporal like me despite your youthful appearance," he began coyly but in a tone tinged with open regard. "You took charge of my disparate band this afternoon like a natural leader, or perhaps like a non-commissioned officer? There is no mark of a rank displayed on your doublet. You carry that air of bravado."

Jack wore no uniform and, despite his grimy face and dusty clothes, looked younger than his 28 years. He was fashionably dressed in stylish breeches and a slashed tunic with paned sleeves, and his plumed, broad-brimmed hat was of the finest felt, typical of that worn by noblemen. His clothing was a lustrous, raven black in contrast to his sweeping plume, which

25

was a stark white—the shade of Arctic snow—matching his whisk and sleeve cuffs. He was tall and slender, with attentive eyes that were intelligent and as blue as a tropical morning sky. His strong, regal nose and broad shoulders gave him the bearing of an aristocrat—handsome and elegant—and his long, masculine fingers were well-suited to gripping a blade. Curly, medium-length, sable hair hung in waves under his hat, and his face was clean-shaven aside from a long, flowing, straight moustache. Jack was active in his military duties as an officer, and the sun had turned his complexion the colour of honey. The gorget at his neck, a gift from his maternal grandfather, was stamped prominently with the family crest and on the reverse an inscription reading, *Quae Quaere Sursum Sunt—Seek the Things That Are Above.* He treasured his knee-high ebony boots with broad, turned-over tops made of the finest Spanish leather—a gift from his king—and his scarlet sash, a proud memento of his graduation from university.

"For a foreigner, you speak French very well," the corporal continued. "Your accent reminds me of the genteel culture of northern France and is certainly not provincial."

"Quite right. A foreigner, indeed, and a lieutenant by rank. You have a perceptive ear." Jack toyed with the tip of his moustache. "I was born in Kraków,

actually—the former capital of Poland—and educated in medicine at the local Uniwersytet Krakowski.
My mentoring professor was German and taught me
his language."

Albrecht was an erudite and saintly man, and
Jack's memory of his professor hung fondly in the
deep reaches of his mind like incense wafting about
the heads of worshippers.

"I was also tutored in French and English as a child;
my father emigrated from the Scottish highlands
and spoke something akin to the King's English."
Jack's face brightened suddenly in a broad, sponta-
neous grin at the recreation of the heavy, guttural,
mountain brogue in his head. "Our family believed
that these skills would be most useful in later life."

Jack smiled back at the Frenchman, and reaching
for his belt, withdrew his rapier from its leather scabbard. He began sharpening the blade in long smooth
strokes from hilt to tip and back again with a small
stone partially wrapped in an oiled cloth. Chauvin
studied the sword's complex, swept hilt. Jack glanced
up and noted his interest.

"It's an Italian designed, three-ringed rapier. It
belonged to my father. He wanted long, stout quil-
lons, straight and exquisite, and a wire-bound
handle to afford a firm grip. Although designed for
his hand, it has partnered mine most agreeably." Jack

followed each part of the rapier with his finger as he spoke as if caressing a familiar lover. "The pommel is a practical size, and the knuckle-guards are simple but discerning. It's a most graceful yet functional weapon. I wrap my forefinger over the front quillon for greater control and flexibility, and this is protected by the three rings. The forte of the blade is almost an inch wide at the hilt, and for a rapier of this length, it has excellent balance and supple manoeuvrability."

He proffered the weapon to Chauvin for closer inspection and asked, "Tell me about your group of men. They shoot their muskets extremely well, like well-trained snipers."

Chauvin picked up his mug and swallowed a mouthful of ale. Stubborn droplets of froth lined his upper lip. Still fondly examining the sword and turning it in his hands, he began speaking.

"Armand Besson, Emile Garreau and Guillaume Maguiere are seasoned professionals whom I've known for over 30 years. We are all from the same region in the provinces and joined the army within a few weeks of each other." Chauvin ran his thumb lightly down the front of the blade and tested the point with his fingertip. A log crackled in the fire, scattering sparks around their boots. "We've seen action in campaigns at Fontaine-Française, Ivry and the Château d'Arques. Learning to shoot efficiently and accurately became a simple matter of survival at Vimory in the harsh autumn of 1587. Some of us were only boys. We became veterans overnight."

"Tristan Paillard and Guy Vasseur were neighbours," the Frenchman continued. "They've carried muskets since they could lift them and honed their skill shooting at running hares and foxes on the farm."

"Julien Roberge is a loner," the old corporal nodded in the direction of a man lying alone on the floor some distance from the others, puffing pensively on an old briar pipe. "He likes to be on his own. Roberge is an excellent marksman—easily the best in the group. He was born with a harquebus in his hand. Unique. He can consistently kill a man at 80 paces. Always aims at the head." Chauvin leaned back in his chair and scratched at his stomach. He gently laid the rapier across his knees. "And he reloads quickly before his target can move 12 steps." His exaggeration to prove the point was obvious. "He prepares his own charges using a slightly heavier load of powder, and I've seen him polishing his musket balls, filing away surface imperfections."

Jack listened intently, totally absorbed by the picture the old soldier's description was painting.

"Deadly accurate, Roberge is a pleasure to watch in action—a steady and unhurried maestro. He prefers to shoot from higher ground, more often from a turret or bell-tower than a rampart or a street. I've watched him dispatch 22 enemy soldiers with as many consecutive shots. The count would have been higher, but he exhausted his powder supply. There are few who can match his marksmanship, and the ungifted question what I have witnessed. They all died instantly, bleeding red stains from the skull onto the snow. Apart from that, I know little about him. He is a private man who is difficult to get close to."

Both men sat pleasantly content, bathed in the delightful warmth of the fire, as Chauvin went on. "Today we lost Jean Legard on the wall. He's in heaven now, still killing rebels with his musket. I did not see him die but found him lifeless against the wall. At least his death came instantly. I closed his mouth and covered what remained of his face."

"Hopefully his smoking musket had found its last target," the Frenchman spat, momentary anger flaring in his eyes and replacing the dancing flames reflected there. "I have asked that he be buried with the other defenders. We shared our valedictory on the battlements."

Jack grasped his sword as Alain handed it back. He swallowed another thin slice of cheese as he returned the rapier to its scabbard.

"And finally, we come to Michel Arbois," the

corporal continued in a hushed tone, his eyes haunt-ingly distant. "The youngest of my men—only a mere lad, really. He joined our regiment only three years ago after his young wife took her own life. She had apparently blamed herself for a miscarriage. It was to be their first." He cleared his throat and sipped on his beer, wiping his mouth clean with the back of his hand. His downcast eyes studied the floor at his feet. "Michel would have been 22 last week. I had tried to pair him with Roberge, but Julien wasn't happy. The lad's presence bothered him. He claimed that it distracted his concentration. I wanted the boy to learn from a real master."

Chauvin rubbed the middle of his tanned brow, pausing briefly. "Vasseur and Paillard taught him to fence and fire his musket, and the lad had learned quickly. He was growing into an excellent soldier. Last month we were with the regiment in Klatovy, some 12 leagues south of Pilsen. Musket shots fired by some drunken idiots had startled a draught horse pulling the munitions cart. The horse reared and trampled Michel, crushing his head. We recognised him from his uniform and ring. Most of his face was missing. Now there are only seven of us."

The two men sat in companionable silence for some time. Jack studied the corporal unobtrusively by the light of the fire. Chauvin was sinewy and of medium height, an alert and agile man with greying, wavy hair—nearing 50. A good eye with a musket, he would probably flounce like a ferret when forced into a swordfight. A short scar ran over his right eye, bisecting his eyebrow. His argentine eyes could be as hard as the metal of his blade and a match to its shade. His sleeves were rolled up to the elbows, revealing deep, dark blue veins that ran like rillets of wine down his arms. He had a habit of walking slightly stooped, belying his fulgurant reflexes. A grey Monmouth cap covered his head when it was wet or cool, and a crimson scarf was knotted loosely around his neck. He was a thoroughly experienced and shrewd military man—possibly one who had known no other life. Most importantly, Jack felt that he could confide implicitly in the corporal.

Jack prodded at the fire with the toe of his boot, too relaxed to reach for the poker. Chauvin finally raised his cup and whispered hoarsely with a sleepy yawn, as if each word carried the weight of an anvil, "A votre santé, monsieur. I'm off to bed."

"Na zdrowie," Jack replied ruefully as both men drained their mugs.

After his friend had shuffled away, Jack leaned back in his chair and drew out each side of his luxuriant moustache between his index finger and thumb as was his habit after eating. His eyes rose towards the dark, lofty reaches of the rafters and the vaulted roof. *A decent round of direct strikes from the enemy's heavy guns would bring this sacred church down*, he mused silently to himself. Thankfully the cathedral occupied the very heart of the city, which effectively placed it beyond their normal range. He scanned the coloured glass windows, admiring the beauty of their scenes. The grand windows easily stood four or five body lengths high, each a masterful example of the artisan's talent. The glass tiles were a mosaic of beauty, telling a compelling story of God and his creatures. He was attracted by one, in particular, that depicted a pious-looking man with white hair and beard crossing a stream with a staff in hand and carrying an infant. There were serenity and conviction captured in the old man's face, and a bird—a sparrow, perhaps—watched him from a nearby branch just above his shoulder.

Jack imagined how brilliant the window would look with daylight shining through. A spark of recognition suddenly touched him. He realised that the figure was that of St Christopher, the protector of pilgrims and patron saint of travellers. Jack was impressed. He could have seen it as a beacon of hope and safety had he been a superstitious man. Yet he was religious, and the thought crossed his mind that he had conceivably discovered a protector that night in the tranquillity of the cathedral that contradicted its own presence in this battered and beleaguered city.

The stately Roman Catholic Cathedral of Saint Bartholomew was one of many Gothic cathedrals that had burgeoned across Europe between the 13th and 16th centuries. Notre Dame de Paris was arguably the most famous example of such imposing architecture. A specific innovation of Gothic structures included the pointed arch, which originated in India and was adopted in European churches around the 11th century. Unlike classic round arches, which rested their entire weight on the columns that supported them, pointed arches did not require these pillars to carry the full load as they were self-supporting to a large degree. With the added introduction of exterior flying buttresses and rib-vaulted roofing used by medieval masons, fewer and more slender supports were used in the creation of capacious Gothic churches, allowing for more uncluttered space within the buildings. Jack had learned this during his university days and recognised the Cathedral of St. Bartholomew as a magnificent example of Gothic-style edifices.

He did not know exactly when he fell asleep, but the noises of general movement in the room woke him the following morning. The fire had burned itself out, leaving a pile of black and grey powder. As people bustled quietly about, the group of musketeers settled to eat at one of the few remaining tables that had been placed in the nave. There was little interest in conversation as the cavaliers concentrated on their broth and bread. Garreau had scored another block of cheese, which he passed down the table to be shared equally amongst them. It added a new perspective to the otherwise uninspiring soup.

"We won't hold this place," volunteered Maguiere, breaking the silence. Resignation was evident in his eyes. "Their inferior cannons lack the firepower to break down the walls, but the word is that they have sent for heavier artillery. When that arrives, they'll pound the gates and eventually raze them like the walls of Jericho in a cloud of dust and splinters." He swallowed audibly as a number of grunts endorsed his opinion.

"If it hasn't already, word must be sent to Emperor Matthias," retorted Jack, "and with some urgency," he added with conviction. "Additional outside support will preclude the city's fall."

He received nods of silent agreement around the table. The men sat in pensive silence, contemplating the fate of the city. Chauvin cut two slivers of cheese and passed one to Jack, who swallowed it with a mouthful of water. Paillard lifted the jug, offering him the local brew.

"No thank you, my friend. If it was wine, it would complement the cheese, but I have no taste for beer so early in the day," Jack explained, smiling. "We'll celebrate properly another time. For now, eating the broth will be our penance this morning."

The rural fortress of Pilsen and its outlying settlements lay at the confluence of four rivers, the northern Mže and the Radbuza in the south, which joined to become the Berounka beyond the northeastern corner, and finally the Úslava River that flowed from the southeast. Situated some 20 leagues southwest of the Bohemian capital of Prague, Pilsen thrived commercially. It was well-known by the surrounding districts for its superb local ale brewed from recipes originating back to the 15th century. Farmers would venture into the many taverns to sample and enjoy the fermented brews before returning to their farms after selling the produce they had brought to market.

The surrounding hills were mostly covered with forest. The vast, heavily-wooded areas to the north of Pilsen lay in contrast to the romantic rural character of the immediate southern precinct. Fortified by a wall surrounding the large central cluster of buildings, a secondary defence, curtain wall had been erected along the southern and western sides. A chessboard of agricultural fields occupied the intervening space between these two walls. The Radbuza

River was diverted into a moat to protect the city's northern and eastern sides and provide the inhabitants with water for drinking as well as brewing the all-important golden beverage. St Bartholomew's church had been constructed to be the sanctifying hub of the citizens' lives and was Pilsen's most imposing structure. The gallows and cemetery, in stark contrast, shared prominence in the main square surrounding the church.

Entry into Pilsen was through two main gates, one on the eastern wall from a bridge over the moat and the other from the south. Both entries were designed for defence, and Pilsen was regarded by many as a place where stubborn, efficacious resistance could be established against a strong assailing host. A third smaller western gate, streaked with a patina of accumulated rust, could be adequately defended by fewer guards. Its approach was much like the pass at Thermopylae, making it less vulnerable to attack. The inconsequential fourth gate facing the Mže to the north was seldom used and almost inconspicuous from outside the walls. Barely wide enough to allow a mounted horseman to pass, its massive rusty hinges supported a heavy steel portal, studded and green with age.

Some four months earlier, on the 23rd of May, an event occurred in Prague that ushered in the genesis of a terrible and bloody war that would last 30 years and devastate most of central Europe. Roman Catholic King-elect Ferdinand II and Habsburg Emperor Matthias imposed significant restrictions on Protestant parish ownership and finances, resulting in a slowly evolving situation wherein the continued existence of Protestantism was perceived to be under threat. In response, a band of Protestant burghers and nobles met at the Hradschin Royal Castle in Prague and threw two Catholic regents out of an upper window. Luckily both survived the fall. Jack, returning from France as an envoy sent by his king, Sigismund III Vasa, had inadvertently become embroiled in the situation at Pilsen on his way to meet one of those regents, his good university friend, Vilém Slavata of Chlum.

As a result of the defenestration, Catholic nobles and clergy began fleeing Bohemia. Farmers and labourers, fearing for their lives, abandoned their isolated dwellings and fled for refuge into the cities. Unfortified villages and estates, together with many monasteries and abbeys, were evacuated, the fugitives converging on Pilsen. The swelling city remained loyal to the Emperor and was reportedly well-prepared to sustain a lengthy siege. The inhabitants believed that a victorious defence could be coordinated within its walls.

Graf Ernst von Mansfeld had been appointed lieutenant general of the Bohemian Protestants army. The illegitimate son of the governor of the Spanish fortress in Luxembourg, he was brought up as a Catholic. Taken prisoner by the Dutch in a battle with Spain, he remained in captivity, awaiting the payment of a ransom. Receiving no offers to settle the requested sum, he gave his word that he would return to the Prince of Orange and rode to Brussels seeking the required amount. He returned empty-handed but honouring his word, he resubmitted himself to internment. This principled action earned him his release, and he joined the service of the Duke of Savoy as a mercenary and sided with the Protestants.

An ambitious and mature 38-year-old when he arrived to lead the siege of Pilsen in September, Mansfeld found that his guns lacked sufficient calibre to breach the city's walls. He disagreed with the inhabitants' optimism and believed that the city could be broken—either its walls breached or its occupants starved into surrender. He rode to Prague himself and was reluctantly given two larger cannons in October to penetrate the city's stubborn defences. Disinclined to advance and jeopardise his army of 20,000 men, he positioned his camp on high ground around the southeastern corner of the city's outskirts, well past the range of the defenders' guns. His army was steadily growing, with new volunteers arriving daily. Mansfeld decided that a siege should be instigated to starve the inhabitants of Pilsen. He would call on his large cannons later if necessary. He was a patient man.

Receiving a nod from Jack, Chauvin looked down the table at his seated comrades. "Gather your weapons and load the muskets. Arnaud, you and Guillaume distribute the powder belts equally, and all of you move outside. Fill your water flasks and wait for us beside the fountain." He looked at Jack for further orders while the group began moving out.

Jack had slept well. He looked up from studying his dirty fingernails. *My mother would scold me*, he thought, smiling to himself.

"Alain," Jack waited for a brief moment. "A quiet, quick word if I may." He traced a finger across an eyebrow as the pair sat alone.

"In answer to your question last night, I am officially a lieutenant in the king's guard but spend much of my time away from the Royal Palace in Warszawa with my family at home in Kraków. My primary role is to be available at any time to act as an envoy of the king. I am now returning home from such a duty." Jack hesitated before continuing, his face unreadable. One hand rested next to his hat on the table, the other on his knee. Vacillating fingers tapped the table. He glanced at the honest, unshaven face staring back at him. He briefly reconsidered taking the wiry corporal he had so swiftly warmed to into his confidence, but the veteran's grey eyes returned an unwavering sincerity that trumped his heartbeat of indecision.

"My full name is Andrzej Hiacynt Channing. Rather an odd mixture, I know." A mischievous smile spread slowly across Jack's face.

"Yet it all rather does make sense when I explain a little more about my family." He looked the corporal directly in the eye. "You're a good, honest soldier, Alain. Your men like you and more than that, they trust in you and never question your decisions. I respect you for that. You're an old, salty, gritty bastard that gets the job done. No issues and without delay. And as none of us knows how things will go today, I wanted to share a little about myself with you. There may not be another evening together by the fire again tonight. That's in God's hands."

Chauvin bowed his head slightly, embarrassed by the praise, and picked at an imaginary splinter in his thumb. His face was sombre; he listened intently as his companion continued.

"I am returning from a diplomatic mission in Paris and was on my way to meet an old friend in

Prague when I got caught up in this. Like you, I guess, neither of us believed that Pilsen would fall under siege, trapping us here. We are in strange and troubled times. I feel increasingly uneasy. There is an atmosphere of chaos growing gloomily around us. More than that, I felt it in France, the Palatinate regions and especially here in Bohemia. Rumours of war—many believe it to be inevitable. The whole of Europe may be affected. People are worried, scared. There are provocation and mistrust between the Catholics and Protestants." Jack scanned the vastness of the nave around them. Women were washing plates and bowls, sorting blankets, and hushing children. Most of the men had left to relieve guards on the walls.

"I *must* meet with my dear friend, and the sooner, the better. He will be able to update me with intelligence that I need to relay to my king and his council."

The Frenchman stared back gravely, keenly listening to the officer. Jack summoned another cheeky smile, needing to lighten the topic. "My father fought in Poland as a Scottish mercenary paid to protect the king in the royal regiment. He was known as 'Jock' to his comrades, a common enough name in Scotland, I understand. Retired now, he stayed in Poland after meeting my mother. He was also an accomplished swordsman and eventually became the royal fencing master, teaching me—and others—many subtle skills and tricks with a sword.

"I was named after my mother's brother but was commonly called Jack, particularly as a child. And eventually it stuck, being a variation of John and, of course, my father's name. My military colleagues referred to me as nothing else, but my university tutors preferred 'Jacek', the Polish version. I received my middle name when I was christened. My mother loves flowers, and the priest obliged. For obvious reasons I never use it." Jack's smile widened. "So now you know a little more about me. In fact, more than most, my friend," he added jovially. The two men laughed aloud, attracting curious looks from some of the closer women. Chauvin relaxed, absorbing the trust shared in him.

"I was fortunate, however, Alain, with the turn of events some years ago," Jack continued evenly. "In the spring of 1612, the king's trusted envoy was scheduled to meet with an ambassador from Brandenburg at an inn in Poznań, selected for being more or less equidistant between Warszawa and Berlin. The clandestine assignation had been arranged well in advance, and my father and a small group of cavalrymen travelled as an escort to protect the diplomat.

"My father intervened in an attempt on the life of our ambassador, and although badly wounded, he saved the ambassador's life. My father's timely inter-cession was generously rewarded by the king, and in retirement, he received significant lands and estate plus a very comfortable and handsome pension. With my education and knowledge of languages, my name was forwarded to the palace as a suitable ambassadorial replacement. And here I am—a royal envoy in dusty and crumpled clothes. A shabby cava-lier!" Jack leaned back with out-stretched arms and grinned like a jester.

The pair laughed heartily again as they rose to gather their belongings. Jack buckled on his belt and inserted his pistol and dagger. Chauvin reached for his musket and cap. Their attention was abruptly drawn by the calling of an approaching figure, a portly man who revealed a bald pate as he pulled off his hat inside the church. He hurried to them with quick, small steps.

"Gentlemen, gentlemen," the man hastened, short of breath. "My lords, I understand from reports provided by my troops that you assisted in defending our walls yesterday. I believe that a handful of your men had made quite an effective impact against our enemy. Remarkable shooting, I've heard." He stopped a few paces from the pair and looked, with mouth open, from one to the other. He had spoken in a local Slavic dialect, and Jack understood most of what he had said. He was unarmed and neatly dressed as a civilian. He did not possess the bearing of a military man. Of medium height, he was clean-shaven and carefully groomed. His small eyes blinked nervously, and his puffy cheeks moved like a bellows sucking in short breaths. He looked like an anxious butcher with an empty gambrel and no meat to sell. Jack guessed that he was a man of position due to the deference shown him by the townspeople in the nave.

Reading their blank expressions, the visitor introduced himself and bowed contritely. "Hritek, Jaroslav Hritek. Burgomaster of Pilsen," he announced formally, punctuating his words with a faint smile. "My apologies!" His ruddy cheeks glistened in the light streaking through the arched windows.

Jack's eyes danced over him. "I am honoured," he responded and bowed slightly, with Chauvin imitating the gesture. The two waited for the burgomaster to continue.

"Gentlemen, I was told that I would find you here and have come with the wish to express my gratitude, on behalf of the residents of this illustrious and fair city, for your brave actions. I fear, however, that your continued assistance may be required at, let us say, a more elevated level." Pausing to give his words more effect, Mayor Hritek appeared to be constantly short of breath and shifted his hat fretfully between puffy fingers from one hand to the other.

Jack began to translate, but Chauvin confirmed with a raised finger and a lazy nod that he understood most of what was being said.

"I have just now left a meeting at my chambers in the Radnice with the captains of the guard. We have been in discussion for many hours this morning, and I have been informed that the majority of our defenders have been preferentially posted onto the three main gates leading into the city." Hritek wheezed slightly as he spoke.

"To date, artillery damage has only been slight, and we suspect that the enemy's guns are underpowered against our walls. Repairs have been made during the night to one of the gates that sustained some minor abuse. There has been no major assault, and their inconsequential attempts have been successfully repulsed by our musketeers, and thankfully, your excellent marksmen. Gentlemen, perhaps we can sit down," Hritek extended an arm to invite the two soldiers back to the table. "The Protestant forces, camped on the hillsides southeast of the walls, appear to totally outnumber us. Nevertheless, we have sturdy walls and sufficient food and munitions to hold adequately for five—perhaps six—weeks against a sustained siege, including a limitless supply of fresh water from the well," he added as an afterthought.

Hritek spoke quickly, again paused for breath and looked at each man in turn. His expression was grave, and he could barely shroud the fear in his eyes. His furrowed forehead glistened with beaded sweat. "We understand that Mansfeld is leading the Protestants and that their bombardment has ceased temporarily until heavier cannons arrive. Our guns are small and lack the distance to be effective at this time. We will wait, however, to hit back hard when they move in force, closer, against us."

The mayor's mood lifted somewhat as he said this, adding, "We will wait for the Empire to send reinforcements. As Catholics, we stand together. Undoubtedly Emperor Matthias will be gathering troops to march to our aid. In the interim, we must remain strong," he offered, his tone momentarily patriotic and vibrant. Jack looked steadily at Chauvin, expressionless. He then turned back to Hritek to respond.

"Sir, we thank you for your most gracious praise. By way of introduction, this is Corporal Alain Chauvin," Jack nodded towards his friend, "and I am Lieutenant Jack Channing. We remain at your service! We will help, of course, where we can. May I humbly suggest that we first find an appropriately high vantage point from which to accurately assess our current situation, and then we can reconvene to discuss the most appropriate ongoing defence strategy for your city?" He spoke in broken Slavic, adding Polish words where he had to.

Echoing these sentiments, Chauvin added in a formal and diffident tone, "We are experienced campaigners, sir, and I am confident that we can add the odd tricky tactic or two to harass our hostile friends on the hill and stimulate further confidence amongst our defenders." There was conviction in his voice as he made an effort to emulate Jack's suggestion.

The mayor hastened to agree, nodding his head repeatedly in rapid jerks and pleased to hear their supportive proposal. "You will have an excellent, unobstructed view spanning many leagues, gentlemen, from the spire of St Bartholomew's. God has given us this cathedral, it seems, for more than one purpose. May I suggest that we assemble again, with my captains, here in this nave in approximately half an hour?" He dabbed at his brow with a wrinkled handkerchief.

The two nodded in agreement and were led away by their nervous, corpulent guide to the staircase that would take them to the cathedral's tower. "These stairs will lead you to the bell landing, from where you will have a clear outlook over the city and surrounding countryside. Forgive me for not accompanying you, but I am, of course, familiar with the environs and will go to gather my officers," the mayor affirmed, still fidgeting with his now badly crumpled hat.

Hritek was a man who had been born and reared in hot water. This reflected his rapid, sporadic speech and nervous disposition. The youngest of five boys, he had been raised in the shadow of his domineering brothers in the staunchly devout and comfortable croft that had belonged to his family for seven generations. Coming from a line of respected bakers, his grandfather recognised the lucrative potential in the brewing trade and abandoned his flour and ovens in favour of a cooperage that flourished on the back of the mushrooming local ale industry. While retaining the hamlet cottage, Hritek's astute father managed the successful and thriving business with acute churlishness, moving his craftsmen and equipment into larger, newly-leased premises in Pilsen. Shrewd and parsimonious sagacity were the red platelets that coursed through his paternal forebears' veins, augmented by a hint of avarice. Hritek's blood contained this same inheritance. As the family gained civil recognition and provincial prominence, unlike his brothers, Hritek excelled in following his father's mayoral footsteps. He subdued his agoraphobic demons with an ostensible show of judicious bluster, and the family business continued to prosper. The siege was simply another financial opportunity.

"Half an hour, gentlemen?" the burgomaster repeated firmly with raised eyebrows as they mounted the stairs.

Chapter 3

Departure

The climb up the stone steps proved wearisome. They had been worn by centuries of regular pedestrian traffic and eventually took Jack and Chauvin to a partially enclosed, square platform high above the cathedral's slate roof. Their thighs pulsed. The tower with its spire continued even higher but from this landing they were presented with an unhindered, panoramic view in all directions. A pair of ravens cawed as they flew off, disturbed by the sudden presence of the two men. The cavaliers indulged the autumn wind, which was cool and gusty at this height, by removing their hats. Fortunate to have a relatively fine day, they were blessed by a vast expanse of cyaneous sky that was marred only by distant, billowing clouds strewn across the far northern horizon.

They had reached the level of the bell tower that contained two brass bells, one larger than the other. Less ornate than the majestic icons installed at Notre

Dame, these bells were nevertheless impressive. A series of ropes had been attached, allowing the bell pealers to ring either or both bells at the required times. The platform had been built to allow for the maintenance and cleaning of the bells and their cable mechanisms. Standing higher than any other structure in the city, their unobstructed plangent tolling would carry well beyond the fortifications to the nearby farms and small clusters of surrounding hamlets, calling the inhabitants to Mass.

"Alain!" Jack called in a loud voice so as to be heard over the wind. "What a pity that this landing is so high. It would have been an ideal position from which your Monsieur Roberge could fire at the attackers should the wall be breached." He peered out at the spectacular landscape.

"My thought exactly," Chauvin responded incisively. "Did you notice the many windows that we passed climbing up here? He could position himself further down in the stairwell and knock out the glass from those nearby on all sides. Roberge would be very comfortable, I'm sure, sniping from that height with such an open, unimpeded view. Shooting the enemy like lambs in a yard," he laughed wistfully.

Jack made use of his telescope, silently thanking Galileo for its timely invention a few years earlier. The rest of their party could be seen gathered below, near the fountain in the square. They were smoking while waiting, as ordered, for the officers to return.

Resting against the corner column to steady his view from the buffeting wind gusts, Jack first scanned the view to the north. The pretty countryside featured predominantly undulating, wooded hills stretching into the distance. The northern periphery of Pilsen ran parallel to the Mže River, which was wide and fast-flowing just before its confluence with the Radbuza River to the east, effulgent in the morning sun. The city's outer curtain wall closed the gap between the north bank of the Mže and the formidable Berounka River, encompassing a small cluster of buildings beyond the main wall. Their inhabitants had recently relocated inside the city for safety, leaving the buildings empty. Jack could see no sign of enemy movement in this direction.

Moving his attention further east, Jack saw wide stretches of cultivated fields between the two walls. Two Protestant companies had bivouacked outside the outer wall, their role to secure and patrol these open paddocks and the adjoining sparse woodlands beyond. Mansfeld had plainly issued orders forbidding the burning of crops and destruction of buildings outside Pilsen's perimeter. His unreserved belief in victory meant that he recognised the value in saving the harvests for the use of his own soldiers, their mounts and the wagon animals.

Jack proceeded to the diagonally opposite column, and continuing to explain to the corporal all that he saw, peered intently through the telescope to the south. Here, beyond the expansive, proximate stretches of open farmland, he observed the main body of the opposing army. The lightly wooded hillside was inundated by their agminate camp, confirming the extent of the campfires that he had seen during the previous evening. He could only guess at their number, estimating about 15,000 troops but not knowing how far the encampment stretched out of view beyond the ridgeline.

"I can see Graf von Mansfeld's quarters, Alain. A few banners, adjutants and guards, but, in general, all is quiet."

Just beyond the outer wall, six companies had been stationed near the eastern corner of the city. They had apparently gathered their dead during the night and were waiting beyond effective musket range for further orders. An air of complacency pervaded the enemy camp, presumably instilled by the belief that their vastly superior numbers were undefeatable. Jack panned further to his left, now looking at the main gate and beyond, towards the northeast wall. More infantrymen had been positioned across the river and had occupied the abandoned village past the bridge. This was their main outlying force—muskets and pikes, together with cannons, trained onto the main gate. Clapping a hand on the Frenchman's shoulder, Jack passed the glass to Chauvin so that he could appraise the situation for himself.

"Not much activity out there," the corporal commented in a gravelly tone after some minutes. The wind was beginning to chill him. He blew on his cold fingers as he returned the telescope and gloved his hands.

"I believe they're waiting—perhaps wanting to starve us into submission—and why not? Yesterday's attempt cost them dearly. Their supply lines are fully open and are being replenished daily, unopposed, while we're shut up in here, surviving on what we have in the granary," Jack spat into the wind. His gaze swept over the eastern vista one last time, and he replied sombrely as he snapped his glass shut, "We should descend. It's time to report to Mayor Hritek."

A small body of officers had gathered in the nave as agreed. They nodded briefly as the pair appeared from the stairwell.

"Well, gentlemen," asked the mayor cordially, "did you observe all you wished to see?"

"An illuminating view from the bell tower, sir; I would refer to it as most stunning under different, more peaceful circumstances," Jack confirmed, shaking his head.

Standing in a comfortable circle, Hritek smiled fleetingly in agreement, his eyes blinking rapidly. "Please allow me to introduce my officers."

Pointing to each in turn, the mayor presented Captains Emile Horvat, Zdeněk Svoboda and Miroslav Kovar. Jack and Chauvin bowed to each. The two men were afforded respect despite their lower rank and were treated as equals in recognition of their valorous conduct on the parapets.

"Monsieur Hritek, may I suggest that we adjourn to the presbytery and continue our discussions in a little more privacy?" Jack nodded to the door on his right. He stood next to the mayor and caught the sour, nervous smell of the man's sweat.

"Absolutely; quite right," the mayor agreed and pointed the way ceremoniously with his puffy hand. "After you, gentlemen!"

The six men entered the smaller room in which Jack and his group had spent the previous night. It was still comfortably warm despite the fire not having been rekindled. Jack looked up at the window of St Christopher and was impressed by the scene when lit by daylight.

"We don't want misconstrued or idle rumours being spread by our hard-working kitchen staff,"

Hritek stated, looking back into the nave while they seated themselves comfortably around the furthest table from the door. Chauvin was invited to join them.

"My officers, Messieurs Channing and Chauvin, have collected intelligence. Captain Horvat will present his report. Please add whatever facts from your own reconnaissance you deem important to complete our appraisal." The mayor pronounced Jack's surname as 'Sharning', having misheard the original introduction. He looked at his senior officer with expectant, raised eyebrows, signalling him to begin.

Horvat, winsome and amicable, spoke slowly and clearly, looking frequently around the group of faces to impress each point. He commanded respect and respected authority in equal measure. "Gentlemen, we have 2500 soldiers, including 30 cavalrymen. Our infantry consists of approximately 1500 musketeers and 1000 pikemen, although the latter have been trained to use the harquebus. An additional 400 able-bodied men who are not soldiers but include farmers, shopkeepers, nobles and so on have been utilised as sentries to periodically relieve those on the walls." He paused to clear his dry throat. "Even those in the dungeons could be called to duty." These were desperate tactics.

"There are 15 small-calibre cannons deployed primarily on the northeast and southeast ramparts protecting the two main city gates with the majority of our men. A small contingent of muskets has been placed at the third gate as a precaution. Every other postern gate is guarded by a pair of sentries. The cannons are mobile and can be positioned where necessary. We have essentially proportioned our defences to counter that of the capricious enemy.

"We expect Ernst Mansfeld's attack, when and if he decides, to push through the northeast gate. There, we have the moat and the most solid defence gate towers, with cannons and marksmen heavily concentrated along both adjoining sections of the battlements. The moat is deep and precludes the enemy from tunnelling under the fortifications and barbican."

Horvat hesitated, looking around the group for questions. When no one spoke, he continued cogently. "The state of our provisions, under rationed distribution, leads us to estimate that we have sufficient food for four weeks." There was an audible murmur around his audience. "Although we are happily blessed with more than enough muskets and hand weapons, our finite powder supply may be exhausted early, but this totally depends on the frequency and need for retaliatory efforts to repel enemy advances. Musket balls, cannon balls and grape shot are in plentiful supply. The powder will be the limiting factor." He purveyed a grim atmosphere with this unexpected and unwelcome news.

Chauvin looked around the table and asked politely to speak. Receiving numerous nods of approval, he continued slowly, pausing between each word to ensure that his accent was not an obstacle. "And what of morale, sir?"

Captain Horvat glanced enquiringly at the mayor, who gestured back at him to respond.

"The city folk and majority of our army believe that the arrival of reinforcements is imminent, and for that reason, spirits are high."

"Have messengers been sent seeking military assistance?" questioned Jack, assuming that such a fundamental action had been one of the foremost tasks to be completed by the city's leaders.

"Most definitely, sir," Hritek replied incisively, blinking quickly. "Two riders left for Prague and another pair to the Duchy of Bavaria. We believe that Emperor Matthias may be on his way to Munich from Vienna."

"When did they leave?" Chauvin interjected, smiling thoughtfully at the mayor.

"Five days ago," Hritek confirmed.

"How secure are the granary and water supply?"

Again the mayor responded, "The granary was built near the western gate, positioned there to be close to the farmlands southwest of the city. It is an old, inconspicuous building with extensive cellars. The fact that Mansfeld has not bombarded it with his guns implies he is not aware of its location." The others concurred with nods and brief mutters as he continued. "There are two wells within the city precincts. The primary well is about 200 paces inside the main gate, and the smaller ancillary water well lies just outside this church in the square. They are both fed through a number of filtering traps from the river. The quality of our water is excellent—fit for the finest brewing," the mayor concluded, his remark bringing about a dulcet spark of subdued laughter.

Faces turned from the table in response to a cautious knock at the door. A couple of women from the kitchen had brought in a tray with cups and two steaming pots of tea. Jugs of fresh milk were placed next to a neat stack of spoons and sugar. Some vodka and glasses were requested, and these soon arrived as well. Captain Horvat wasted no time in pouring out a healthy round and passing a cup to each person at the table. The women curtseyed as they left.

Jack leaned back into his chair and echoed Horvat's toast. "Salut," he responded, downing his drink in typical Slavic style. In a pensive tone, he added, "I am sure that both wells would be visible to the Protestants from their elevated encampment on the southeastern hills. They may turn to bombing the water supplies or poisoning their source. I do not know General Mansfeld's mind, but if he is preserving our crops and fields, he may do the same with our water. Nevertheless, we should validate its quality daily by having a dog or cat drink from it."

In response to this authoritative and welcomed proposal, Horvat glanced at Miroslav Kovar. "Can we rely on you to take responsibility for water inspections, captain?"

Kovar raised his finger deferentially, confirming agreement. His face was a shadow.

"And what can *you* add, Monsieur *Sharning*, from your earlier observations?" the nervous mayor asked, mopping his brow. Actions were very clear in Jack's mind. He had formulated them while in the bell tower. He pursed his lips with the composure of a pregnant gust of wind that would spark glowing coals to flame.

"I would like to suggest the following to assist the city's cause for your consideration, gentlemen and, of course, I am not aware of your own preparatory analyses." Jack removed his handkerchief and blew his nose, offering an apology. He gently wiped his moustache.

"Firstly, as the view is excellent from this building's tower, we should gather intelligence about the enemy during daylight hours every day. I suggest that we install alternating pairs of men at the top of the tower, each pair covering two periods of the day. One will remain on the landing to act as observer. Should there be a need, he will alert his companion— the runner—to report to these officers whenever there is a conspicuous change or major movement outside these walls. Each team can be fed from the kitchen below, and as the landing is sheltered, observation can continue even during inclement weather. Provision of a telescope would be most beneficial. I approximate the enemy's number to be between 15,000 and 20,000 men. This should be verified."

"Excellent; approved!" confirmed Hritek, tapping the table. "I agree that St Bartholomew's is the overtly obvious choice. Pilsen's footprint is a rough square, and if we draw a cross within that square, the cathedral blesses its intersection." He raised his eyebrows and traced geometrical shapes in the air with his stubby fingers. "Each of my officers has a glass. One will be made available."

"Next, we should gather information from under Mansfeld's very nose. This requires a pair of experienced and nimble men to leave and return secretly every night with updated bulletins on armament number and placement, weaknesses in defence and troop movements—in fact, any information that will assist us in hampering the enemy. We must convert any one of Mansfeld's forfeits into gain as an alchemist transmutes base metal into gold! "

"Done!" Hritek agreed vigorously. "Will you please see to that, Captain Horvat?" The burgomaster felt less troubled now, no longer burdened by a Calvary of despair. The lieutenant was an intelligent officer who crackled with ideas belying his youth. Hritek viewed him as a singular hero—one who possessed a perspicacious eye; an arm of granite, and an omniscient mind.

"Thirdly," Jack continued. "Our store of munitions needs to be scattered about the city, especially the precious powder."

"An important observation, if I may add," Chauvin interposed animatedly. "I personally witnessed the gunpowder magazine disintegrate totally after a shot exploded in the storeroom during the battle of Fontaine-Française."

"We currently hold our gunpowder in two separate storage cellars but will further disperse it around the defences to ensure that we don't lose it all in a single and hapless direct hit," Horvat retorted. "Captain Svoboda, will you ensure this happens?"

"Additionally," Jack spoke with a tinge of levity.

"Medieval history has taught us that a popular form of defence was to assault the enemy with flaming balls of tarred hay. Despite our current advanced modes of battle with gunpowder and cannons, this old yet effective technique may be worthy of consideration if the city holds sufficient stocks of hay and tar. In light of our potential powder shortage, torched bales could be launched from the walls onto the advancing rebel ranks." Despite the immediate reaction of subdued laughter, Horvat and the other captains speedily recognised the simplicity and practicality of Jack's suggestion. He sipped his tea before speaking again, allowing the others to settle.

"And finally," Jack came to his most substantial item of the morning. "We observed earlier that the main Protestant force is camped in the hills to the southeast of the city and that the small gate opposite their watchful eyes—the small gate on the north wall—appears to be unguarded. In fact, totally ignored."

Jack stood up from the table, pushing his chair back slowly and clasped his hands behind his back. He stared at the group for a moment before continuing, wanting to impress his point. His eyes sparkled like the waters of the river outside the city walls.

"As envoy to the Polish king, I have urgent and important business in Prague, after which I must return to Warszawa to report to the king's council. I have news from France for my king's ears. It is imperative that I leave Pilsen after dark tonight for your capital. I further suggest that at least two more riders be despatched to make contact with Catholic forces to plead the city's plight. We must ensure that word gets out in case those who left five days earlier were not successful. With your approval, gentlemen, our party can leave through this gate around midnight and disperse once we have crossed the Mže."

The mayor considered the proposal for some time, digesting the gravity of the Polish officer's words, and then gazed around the table. "Are we all agreed with this, gentlemen?"

The congruent approval was unanimous. Jack smiled and thanked them for their trust and support. His conscience was at ease. He regarded Horvat and quietly asked, "Captain, may I speak with you separately concerning arrangements for a good horse, some minor provisions and guidance for an alternative route to Prague? Travelling the main road would be ill-advised these uncertain days and in these circumstances."

"Of course, Lieutenant Channing. It will be my pleasure," Horvat smiled. Jack noticed that he had pronounced his name correctly.

The meeting had ended by mid-morning. Jack and Chauvin joined their small contingent in the square outside and left instructions as to which section of wall they were to occupy. The sun was now warming the day, and the wind had dropped making a perfect example of Bohemia's finest autumn weather. The two comrades walked the main streets of the city, gauging that the mood of the people was generally positive, as Horvat had reported. Life appeared to go on as normal: a bustling market, busy vendors, children playing, carts rolling past. Their appetite, honed by the stroll, eventually led the men to one of the city's many inviting taverns for lunch. Before entering, they observed that the cathedral's belltower had been newly manned as agreed. As they settled into a comfortable corner over a generous plate of pork, cabbage and potatoes, Jack confided in his companion, describing in detail an additional plan that he had not raised at the meeting.

Before leaving for the capital at midnight, Jack intended to leave the city some hours earlier to make his own discrete observations of the enemy encampment and required a volunteer from Chauvin's team to accompany him. The corporal immediately offered his services, but Jack needed a younger, more dispensable man for support should they stray into trouble. Additionally, he reminded his friend that his job was too valuable here and that he needed to assist the other officers with the actions of the plan they had all agreed to during the discussions. If all went well, the pair would return by eleven, leaving Jack sufficient time to prepare for his own departure to Prague.

Chauvin's next suggestion, Julien Roberge, was rejected, and after some further open discussion, they eventually decided on Guy Vasseur. Jack wanted to rest during the afternoon and agreed to share a jug of ale at the tavern, knowing it would exacerbate his drowsiness. They sat in convivial discussion at the rough wooden table and soon called for a second flagon. At one point, Chauvin noticed a small dog asleep at the massive, fuliginous hearth.

"So, we've discovered the first to test our drinking water. We should enlist him and immediately promote him to the rank of sergeant," the Frenchman joked, pointing at the animal. "We don't want to make him a major, or he'll send the captains to the well every day." The pair laughed to a clink of glasses.

The tavern filled and became noisy—full of conversations punctuated by frequent bursts of laughter and boisterous outbursts—but the atmosphere was jovial and pleasant, and it was late afternoon before the pair reluctantly thought of leaving. Jack placed an amicable hand on his companion's shoulder, and when he had Chauvin's full attention, he began, "Alain, after tonight I will be riding home again, and you will be here defending this tavern, this city, this dog and your country's honour. They wish to steal our freedom from us like granivorous vermin." He squeezed the corporal's shoulder and continued above the clamour in the room after calling for another round of ale.

"Just remember who I am and where I am. I will always be in only one of three places if you need or want to find me. In Warszawa, I stay at the royal castle. In Kraków, I am with my family at the Channing estates; the locals will direct you. And if I'm not at either of these, I'm somewhere else in Europe on the king's business. Then wait for me in one of the first two until I return." Gulping another draught of beer, Jack hoped that what he had explained had made sense. "You know, Alain," he stammered, his cheeks flushed with passion and alcohol. "This fine drop was what brought me here into this bloody mess in the first place. I had planned to go directly to visit my friend and thought how a small detour would be insignificant in the scheme of things, and... well, here we are; you know the rest." He deliberated for a while, distracted by the serving wench at a nearby table, before adding, "Yet the positive side of all of this is that we two have met. Santé, my dear friend!"

Chauvin removed his cap and leaned across unsteadily to shake Jack's hand, spilling some ale with his elbow. He too valued the friendship that had developed between the two men in this short time. As they left the warm, good-humoured atmosphere, who would have thought or indeed cared that there was a large army up on the nearby hill, waiting to storm and occupy the city?

The corporal roused Jack at eight as he had been instructed. The fire in the presbytery had been rekindled, filling the large room with warmth and the smoky smell of burning wood. A cup of warm milk was ready, and he sipped from it as he dressed. Vasseur was waiting when Jack appeared in the nave.

Both men were without muskets, wearing only two pistols, their swords and their daggers. They donned fuscous cassocks to mute the jingle of their weapons and protect them from the cold, damp night. Accompanied by the corporal, they left the cathedral and walked briskly to the smaller of the two southern gates. There was only a pair of sentries, who had been forewarned of their arrival, waiting for them. As the gate was unlocked, Captain Horvat suddenly appeared from the nearby shadows.

"Forgive me, lieutenant," he extended a genial hand as he approached. "The corporal requested my assistance to arrange for this postern to be unbolted, and although I do not entirely approve of your strategy, I wish you and Vasseur every success and a safe return."

Jack and Horvat shook hands firmly. "Do you need an additional conspirator? I would eagerly join you," the captain added, eyes gleaming like sapphires in the rutilant torch light.

"Someone in authority needs to supervise the corporal," Jack countered playfully.

"We will be waiting here at eleven as agreed!" Chauvin added, side-stepping the jest. "See you when you get back. Keep him out of trouble, Vasseur. *Bonne chance!*"

The gate closed and was locked behind them by the guard. The pair made their way directly from the city, due south, across the overgrown and unkempt fields. The night dew saturated their boots. They moved slowly and warily. It was a dark and moonless night, but Jack had memorised the lay of the land from his observations this morning. They arrived at the curtain wall without incident, their eyes now adjusted to the darkness. They climbed over, one assisting the other, and then crept briskly up the wooded hill to the ridge. Turning left, Jack led them towards the main body of tents. All quiet—no sentries, no dogs—all well. The enemy forces were indeed very self-assured. Flanking the rear of the encampment, the two moved quietly from tree to tree until they reached the road that Jack was aiming for. This was a wagon track that ran in a north-south direction. They needed to complete their circular approach, so headed south along the grassy wheel-rut in the direction facing the now distant lights of Pilsen. Vasseur had shadowed Jack closely all the way.

Unexpectedly, the Frenchman caught the slightest glint of metal—a whispery movement ahead in the gloom. He grabbed Jack's collar firmly from behind, and the two men froze. Some 10 paces ahead was a soldier about to cross the dirt road. He had stopped by a tree to relieve himself. Jack turned around to Vasseur and pointed to the guard, running a finger across his throat. Vasseur nodded in comprehension and held Jack fast and then stepped away along the moist, silent grass. He drew his dagger and steadily crept towards the unsuspecting soldier. Without hesitating at any point, the experienced Vasseur approached his victim stealthily from behind, gagged him by locking his left forearm across the enemy soldier's mouth, and as he pulled the man backwards towards his body, thrust his dagger up to the hilt into the man's kidney. The sentry tensed with pain as Vasseur withdrew the dagger and ran it swiftly across the soldier's throat from left to right, like a seasoned butcher, severing the vocal cord and windpipe in one single effortless motion. The man went limp almost immediately. There had been no struggle, no sound, and no resistance.

Jack joined Vasseur as the latter dragged the body off the roadside into the woods. They would be long gone before it would be discovered in the morning. Grinning approvingly, Jack slapped the Frenchman lightly across the cheek and winked his endorsement. Vasseur smiled back, happy with his success. Remaining on the soft grass in the gloom of the woods, the two cavaliers continued to follow the road for another 150 paces, and there, beyond the edge of the trees, they came upon their goal.

Two ponderous cannons sat on level ground just out of the forest to the left of the road. Silent, execrable sentinels—sinister, one-eyed giants left unguarded. Vasseur squatted as Jack knelt on one knee both searching and listening intently for any movement or sound. They could plainly see the lanterns and campfires of Pilsen in the near valley far below them. The men, impressed by the guns' size, ran appraising hands over the cold metal of the two barrels.

Jack nodded as they produced assorted nails and a mallet from under their cassocks and hurriedly searched for each vent hole at the base. Stepping onto the truncheon of the closest gun, Jack located the vent and selected a nail of appropriate size while Vasseur mounted the other gun like a horse and fiddled with his nails. Jack tapped his spike to the end, covering its head with his coat to mute the sound, and handed the wooden hammer to Vasseur, who hastily completed his task. They then retreated into the forest and waited, listening. All clear.

They retraced their steps exactly the way they had come, stopping frequently to peer into the mottled darkness for signs of movement. It was imperative that the enemy gunners remain unaware of their visit. The return journey to the now familiar outer wall gate seemed to take half the time that it took to reach it initially. Jack cupped his hands and nodded to Vasseur to climb over the wall. Lying on top of the wall, Vasseur strained to lift Jack up next to him with one hand. They turned and sat, dangling their feet and facing the city. The two men were about to jump when the clouds suddenly drifted apart, exposing the full light of the moon. They had reached the wall a little further than before, and in the moonlight, they saw four enemy sentries asleep directly below them. Their fire had burned out, and all six men would have been equally surprised had the clouds not opened.

In spite of the sentries' presence, Jack and Vasseur jumped down. The former landed on one guard's throat, rolled off, stood up and withdrew his rapier in one fluid movement. The man did not move, probably due to a crushed windpipe and dislocated jaw.

Vasseur's victim groaned as the Frenchman rolled off his stomach. Without waiting, Guy had drawn his backsword and pierced the prone man's chest near the heart.

The other two sentries had now been roused from their sleep and were awkwardly but quickly on their feet, one with a pistol in hand. Jack rushed towards the man, who was aiming for Vasseur and drove his rapier into the man's temple forcefully enough that the tip appearing through the other cheek. The soldier lowered his arm and fired his pistol safely into the ground, already dead, before slumping forward.

The fourth stolid guard had drawn his sword, but Vasseur jumped over his comrade's body and dived with his own sword in full stretch. Too late to parry, the sentry was caught in the stomach. With Vasseur's full bodyweight behind it, the blade glanced off the sentry's spine and emerged out his back. He crumpled under the force of the impact and did not move.

Glancing up at the night sky, Jack uttered, "Bloody pistol! Who knows who else has been woken around here? Still a little more moonlight left. Run, Guy. Come on! Run!"

Sheathing their bloodied weapons, the pair ran wildly across the paddocks, not stopping until they collapsed in the culvert in front of the southern city gate. Panting for breath, Jack hammered at the door with his fist as small, distant fires began to appear at the curtain wall behind them where other sentries had been alerted by the stray pistol shot. *Too late for revenge this night,* Jack thought, as the bolts slid back and the gate opened on stubborn hinges to let them in.

"Après vous, s'il vous plaît, Monsieur Vasseur!" Jack hissed encouragingly, breathing hard, and the pair disappeared into the safety of the city walls. Chauvin and Horvat were there to greet them, and the four companions clasped arms in a ring and jumped ebulliently before swaggering back to the cathedral, laughing at the success of this evening's work. A bottle of red wine had appeared from somewhere back in the presbytery. The fire had been stoked, and the freshly added logs were crackling away midst the lambent flames, filling the room with warm and cheerful light.

"Santé, gentlemen," Chauvin grinned as they rammed their raised mugs together and drank with gregarious abandon.

"Why only one gun?" asked Horvat.

"We also spiked the second cannon for good measure, and they'll not fire either now." Jack's dirty face was grinning unreservedly as it gleamed in the golden glow of the fire.

"We could have rammed in powder charges, which would have split the barrels, but perhaps this siege will go badly for them, and we'll win the guns for ourselves," Jack ventured optimistically. Shortly before midnight and with a second bottle empty, Jack went to wash his face and packed his few belongings.

"Don't wake the others, Alain. Tell them in the morning what we've managed to do. I regret not being here to witness the enemy's disappointment or see Mansfeld's outraged face."

Laughing again, the men shook Jack's hand and walked with him to the small, covert northern gate.

"The other two riders packed hurriedly and left earlier," advised the captain. "You need to continue north from here and follow the left bank of the Berounka River all the way. Keep to the seclusion and shadows of the trees. It will lead you straight to the capital. Be careful, lieutenant!" He slapped Jack on the back.

At the gate, Horvat handed Jack the reins to his stallion. "This is my horse. I call him Abaccus. He's intelligent and will be faithful if you care for him. There's an apple and some sugar in this saddle bag. Now he's yours. Thank you for all your help. Pilsen will not forget."

Chauvin and Jack embraced. The crusty old soldier

kissed Jack on both cheeks and continued nodding his head. He was lost for words.

Jack turned to Vasseur and winked, "Goodbye, Guy. You're a brave man. Well done. It would not have been successful without you tonight. Look after this corporal of yours, and God willing, perhaps we'll meet for another drink sooner than later in much happier circumstances." To all of them, he added, "Good luck, gentlemen. This city is in fine hands. I will remain with you in spirit until we raise another glass together again."

The sentries opened the gate, and Jack walked out, leading his new mount.

"God speed, my friend," Chauvin called after him, and the gate groaned in protest as it was bolted shut.

Chapter 4

KING'S REGENT

Much like other prominent European cities, the streets of Prague bustled and throbbed with busy movement, crowds of people seemingly preoccupied with completing their own varied tasks and reaching their many destinations. Jostling in both directions along the stone-paved roads, the chaotic collection of people contained the full cross-section of the city's eclectic and interesting population.

The buildings, elegant in their Romanesque style and Gothic proportion, reflected wealth and order, some rising three or four storeys high. Founded in 1348, Prague was one of the most beautiful cities in Europe. With the shimmering Vltava River dividing the old town from newly-settled and expanding areas on the western bank, the steady sprawl of the capital was inevitable. The city had flourished during the reign of Charles IV, the Holy Roman Emperor and King of Bohemia almost 300 years earlier, and it was his foresight that transformed it into a resplendent imperial capital. It continued to be home to his son, King Wenceslaus IV, and then Ferdinand I of the House of Habsburg followed by King Rudolf II.

It was a prosperous age for the city, and Prague became the bourgeoning capital of European culture, attracting prominent astronomers, musicians, artists and alchemists. A thriving metropolis of over 40,000 inhabitants, Prague was a part of the world that Jack had heard much about during his years as a student, and he had sought any opportunity to visit and explore this marvellous city.

Jack had travelled through the night, and it was well into the afternoon when he arrived at the first dwellings and farms that formed the western outskirts of the city's precinct. To his left, the royal castle of Hradčany—the residence of Bohemian princes and kings—dominated the gentle hillside that overlooked the river and town centre like Poseidon silently surveying his vast watery domain. The road began to gradually descend towards the river, and Jack dismounted, slapping Abaccus's neck admiringly and allowing the horse to walk slowly beside him without the burden of a rider's weight.

Following the gentle curve of Mostecká, which led him to the imposing and picturesque Karlův Most (Charles Bridge) and its two end towers, Jack crossed the sedately-flowing river and made his way along

Karlová to the substantial cobblestone-laden town square. Surrounded on all four sides by stately buildings, the square reminded him of home in Kraków and absorbed by the culture and atmosphere around him, Jack felt very comfortable here. He recognised the Gothic town hall and its clock tower from earlier descriptions and made his way to the eastern perimeter, where he asked a local merchant for directions to a reasonable tavern. The burgher pointed to a rustic structure with a wide portico in the corner of the square.

A young attendant approached Jack to tend his horse as the Polish officer drew near.

"Can you ride, lad?" Jack asked the cheerful footman.

"Better than I can walk, your lordship," the youngster replied with a broad grin that revealed three missing teeth.

"Well, take my horse and ride to the Royal Palace across the bridge and pass on this note to the guard. I'll be waiting here at this inn." Jack eyed the sign, bemused. *Chlupate Prase—The Hairy Hog. Shows all the promise of decent lodgings*, he thought unenthusiastically to himself. He flicked a coin at the youth, adding, "When you return, settle the horse into the stable, if you don't mind. Make sure that he's dry, fed and watered, and you might also check his hooves. I'll be looking in on him later."

Jack stroked his horse's nose and mane as he passed over the reins. "Please hand me that saddle bag. I'll be staying here a night or two. My name is Channing."

Shouldering the bag that the boy had retrieved, Jack pulled a second coin from his pocket and handed it to him. "Here. Thank you. Take good care of him and see that he has fresh hay." He took a moment to regard the boy's dirty, freckled nose and uncombed hair. As an afterthought, he asked, "What's your name, boy?"

"Pavel, sir," the lad's grin widened. He bit hard on both coins before sliding them deep into his trouser pocket. *Perhaps that was what accounted for his missing teeth?* Jack pondered momentarily with a smile.

"How old are you?" Jack had taken a liking to the sprightly young man.

"I'll be 15 tomorrow, sir, and don't trouble yourself about the horse; I'll take extra special care of him. You can be sure of that."

"Well, Pavel, thank you again. I thought you looked like a trustworthy horse handler. Have you eaten lunch today?"

"No, your highness," the boy replied, "but I had a real good dinner last night."

"That's encouraging. Why don't you join me inside when you're finished with Abaccus?" Jack proposed, nodding towards the tavern. The boy became shy and continued to pat the horse's chest. Jack sensed his reluctance.

"The master don't like me in there disturbing his guests. He always reminds me that my job is out here tending to travellers and their horses and carts and the likes of gentlemen like you."

Jack smiled at the boy's brogue and replied, "Don't trouble yourself about that. I'll speak to the landlord. You just come in and report to me when you've done all that I've asked. Promise?" Bending slightly, Jack placed a hand on the boy's shoulder and stared him straight in the eye with an unrelenting look, forcing him to reply.

"Yes, your lordship. I promise, sir." The boy was unsure but agreed. Turning towards the door, Jack called back kindly, "Well, that's excellent. I'll see you inside later, then. Abaccus loves apples," and strode away.

The Chlupate Prase was a large establishment that gave first-time visitors a far better impression than its name implied. Jack stepped a few paces inside and looked around the expansive room. The tavern was warm, smoke-filled and cavernous, and its massive upright wooden posts were darkened with soot and the passage of time. Their immense size was designed to support the floor above. Many were draped with hanging coats and hats as well as the occasional sword or pistol belt, beneath which sat their owners—smoking, drinking or engaged in conversation. The low ceiling was comprised of exposed timber beams—bowed in the centre—that added to the aged, rustic charm. They had browned in the constant haze of staining smoke. Jack selected one of the numerous unoccupied tables with a view of the door and shuffled over to the serving bench after claiming a chair with his saddlebag and cassock coat.

"What can I offer?" asked the dour barman gruffly as he stepped across to where Jack stood and wiped the bench with a greasy rag.

"Do you have a lad named Pavel working for you out in the square, good sir?" Jack was polite as he inquired good-naturedly.

The swarthy, unshaven man peered at Jack with unfriendly eyes, tinged with suspicion. "Why? Has the rascal been rude? I'll pull his bloody ear," he countered. The bench had been wiped dry, and the surly publican leaned forward on his arms against the bar.

"Quite the opposite. You have a valuable assistant out there whom I have engaged in a number of small chores. He'll stable my horse after riding on an errand for me to the Royal Palace. I trust that this does not pose an inconvenience," Jack smiled and continued, "I have requested him to report here to me after completing these tasks, for which he has been paid handsomely." Jack inflected these last words as if seeking confirmation that this was acceptable. The old man dropped his shoulders in obvious relief.

"My son is a good, hard-working boy. I'm happy that he could be of service, and he'll come in to see you when he's finished if that's what you have asked of him. Sometimes I'm overly harsh with the lad, especially these last three years since his mother passed away from the fever."

"I believe I see the family resemblance. There'll be another copper coin for him when he returns, and a warm meal would not go astray to keep him happy against the autumn air out there. If you have a room for the night—something quiet, small and comfortable—you may add his meal to my bill."

The taverner's surliness disappeared as he replied, "I'm the innkeeper here, and thank you for your kind words. I'll fetch you a key."

Jack paid for one night's board—a modest room with a window facing away from the square. He ordered a jug of apple cider and pointed to his table, thanking the barman. After locking the saddle bag, he descended the stairs and made himself comfortable, draining a mug of the very palatable golden drink. He soon dozed against the wall as the effect of a long, sleepless night of travel, the warm environment and the alcohol took their cumulative toll.

After what seemed to be no more than a few minutes, Jack woke with a start as a gentle shaking of his shoulder brought him back to the present. Blinking and momentarily unaware of where he was, Jack looked up and grinned openly as he recognised the man shaking him. "Vilém! My old friend, Vilém Slavata! How good it is to see you after all these months."

The two comrades embraced warmly, swaying together like a storekeeper's sign in the wind. Inviting him to sit down, Jack helped his companion with his coat and filled both of their mugs from the ample wicker jug. Without speaking, the two stared at each other with watery eyes, barely believing that they were once again sitting at the same table. The middle-aged man before him had gained weight, Jack noted, since their last meeting. His forehead had become more prominent, and his receding light-grey hair sat neatly combed in abundant waves. Creases radiated from the corners of the regent's large, sky-blue eyes, giving him an aura of benevolence and bonhomie, like a child's favourite uncle. A grey moustache, curling at the ends, veiled his upper lip with tips that caressed his pudgy cheeks, and his double-chin was hidden behind a small, manicured, greying goatee. Dressed in sumptuous breeches of pastel violet and a matching doublet, Vilém carried the bearing of an educated man of title and authority burdened by the responsibility of high office. He had aged.

"I came as soon as your message was delivered, somewhat fortunate that the king is away today. Without his absence, I may not have been able to come—his industrious sense of duty and assiduousness absorb every hour of my day. When did you arrive? Ah, we have so much to talk about, Jacek; we may need a week to cover it all!"

"Not wanting to interfere with your imperial and aulic duties, I did not stop at Hradčany on my way past but sent word immediately on arriving here. I have taken a room for the night and can easily extend it to a week if that's what we need," Jack remarked, and the pair laughed convivially.

"How are your parents? And the king? How is King Sigismund?"

"I haven't seen them for over four months. The king ordered me to go to Paris to seek military support from the French, but that's another story that we can discuss a little later. There have been rumblings, especially here in Bohemia, that the situation between the Catholics and the Protestants is deteriorating rapidly every day. What is going on?"

Vilém's manner became animated; he looked briefly around him with darting eyes before replying in a hushed tone, "The bastards nearly killed me. Can you believe it?"

"They nearly murdered the king's regent!" the minister spat, taking another generous mouthful of cider. His face reddened with anger and incredulity, a vein appearing in the middle of his forehead. "In fact, two of us... and the secretary from the royal council," his voice took on an angrier tone. "Three of the king's representatives—on official business," he hissed, raking his hair back with a hand, his face still sanguine with rage. "We may not have—" he broke off as Pavel appeared at their table, oblivious to the tone of their discussion.

Jack looked up, summoning a smile. "Well, my young master. I see that my message was delivered successfully as my companion here has arrived at its request." He pointed at the regent with his eyes. "Vilém, this is Pavel, the innkeeper's son and the only man in Prague to whom I would entrust my horse. How is he faring?"

Pavel's face beamed unreservedly at the compliment and he bowed reverently to both guests.

"I have stabled your horse, my lord, and made him very comfortable with fresh fodder and water. As you asked, his hooves have been checked. I have also brushed his coat hard and inspected his legs." Pavel paused for a moment and looked up at the ceiling for inspiration, hoping he had covered every requirement.

"He's in excellent shape now and will rest well tonight," the youth reported proudly, "and I have caped him against the cold," he added as an afterthought.

"Just as I suspected, "Jack nodded, "and here's an extra coin for your trouble." He flipped a copper into the air with his thumb, and shifting in his seat to face the boy, he continued in a more serious tone, "I have also had a word with your father, who tells me that he loves his son very much and has a plate of something special for him at his earliest convenience. You should report to the cook and claim your meal."

Beaming with the news and the unexpected gift of an additional coin, the stable boy bowed again, thanking Jack repeatedly and backed away to head for the kitchen. Enjoying the happy interlude, Jack and Vilém emptied the apple cider jug and called for a pitcher of mead and a generous serving of boiled lamb with roast potato. The aroma permeated throughout the table.

"Where did this attempt on your life occur, and why?" Jack finally asked with concern. Between mouthfuls of food and honey wine, Vilém explained the events that led to the assault in detail.

Emperor Matthias had returned to Vienna last

year after attending the election—in Prague—of Ferdinand, the Catholic Duke of Styria, to the throne of Bohemia. In his absence, he left the duties of Bohemian government in the hands of a council of 10 regents, seven of whom were Catholic. The council was led by three senior imperial governors: Vilém Slavata of Chlum and Košumberk, Chancellor Zdenko Lobkowitz, and Jaroslav Martinitz.

Martinitz, in Emperor Matthias's name and with the assent of King Ferdinand, instigated and pursued a vigorous anti-Protestant policy. The three ordered the cessation of the construction of various Protestant chapels on Catholic land, which together with the closure of Protestant churches, raised a contentious issue as the Protestants claimed that the lands in question belonged to the realm and not the Catholic Church. This was viewed as a violation of the right to freedom of religious expression bestowed in *The Letter of Majesty* announced in 1609 by Emperor Rudolf II. The Protestants feared that all their rights would eventually be repealed and totally nullified.

Led by Jindřich Matyáš Thurn and Václav Budovec, angry Protestant nobles representing numerous Bohemian estates met on the 23 May 1618 to compile a strategy to remove the Catholic regents. A second meeting followed with a larger gathering of nobles at the Hradčany Castle, and from there, the incensed crowd moved into the Bohemian chancellery in the Ludwig wing. There, they confronted Slavata and Martinitz, and after a short, ill-tempered trial, found them guilty of violating the right to freedom of religion. At three in the afternoon, they seized and flung the two regents from the third-storey windows of the regents' offices. Their secretary, Filip Fabricius, remonstrated and was thrown out after the others. As the three fell 20 yards into the dry moat below, they were taunted by the frenzied nobles, who asked if the Virgin Mary would save them. A number of pistol shots were fired at them from the windows but with little accuracy. This retaliatory gesture unmistakably signalled open resistance to Emperor Matthias.

Miraculously, all three survived with non-fatal injuries. Protestant pamphlets alleging that the governors' survival was due to their landing in a drossy pile of horse manure were disseminated, and the Catholics counter-claimed that eye-witnesses had seen Christo Churmusian angels swoop from heaven to break their fall. Martinitz rose to his feet severely hurt, as did the secretary, and Slavata lay gravely injured. As Martinitz staggered to his rescue, he was grazed by one of the several shots from the window. Some servants quickly made their way to the fosse and carried off their masters. Fabricius fled the moat and reported the incident to Matthias after travelling to Vienna. He was later ennobled and granted the title *von Hohenfall—of Highfall*. Slavata, after being nursed back to health in custody, was eventually allowed to depart to the spa town of *Teplice* for convalescence and, from there, into Saxony. Martinitz escaped in disguise to Munich.

Jack had listened without interruption as Vilém concluded by adding, "We were most fortunate to escape with our lives. I suffered a bruised elbow and a broken collar bone, and the others complained of numerous minor scratches. Martinitz sprained an ankle and was immobilised for almost a week. The large shrubs and the incline of the ditch helped in breaking our fall—not to mention the feculent midden on which we found ourselves. You know, Jacek, that I approach my responsibilities with fervour and zealous determination, and I believe totally in our cause."

Their plates had been cleared away, and more mead was brought to their table. The serving maid curtseyed as she wiped the stained, wooden table-top between them and informed them that the inn master was most pleased to offer this jug with his compliments. As she departed, Jack began evenly, "There has already been a singularly emphatic, further response from the Protestants. I know not if news has reached you yet, but I had been delayed for two days in coming to Prague by Count Mansfeld's siege of Pilsen."

Slavata's overt surprise was unmistakable. It was now clear to Jack that the riders destined for the capital had never arrived. He related, as briefly as he could, the Polish king's business with Bishop Richelieu in France and his own adventures while returning from Paris. Their pensive and sombre mood deepened.

"Has Matthias been informed?" queried Vilém.

"Yes. Riders left for Munich and Vienna the same day."

"King Ferdinand will return tomorrow. I should organise an audience for you so that he can hear firsthand of Pilsen's plight."

The crowd had thinned in the tavern. Slavata had spoken of his wife, Lucie, and the young envoy shared what he knew of his own family, although the news was months old. Jack was yawning now, the long day finally taking its toll, and Vilém stood to let his friend retire.

"I will send word to you tomorrow morning after making arrangements with the king. He will without a doubt wish to hear details of your current distressing news."

"Let me walk with you to your horse," Jack offered,

summoning an attendant to fetch the chancellor's mount. They strolled towards the portico, absorbed in conversation, and as they reached the door, Vilém pushed it against an unseen cavalier who was about to enter the tavern.

The well-dressed stranger scowled at him with blatant contempt. "You clumsy oaf! Stand aside and let me pass," he snapped, pushing in on the pair.

Vilém, unaccustomed to this kind of treatment as a man in his position, lifted his hand and pressed against his chest to stop him, venturing emphatically, "Sir, your humour is as dark as the night that sent you here. Be so kind as to please step back and allow us to leave. Convention and etiquette dictate it."

The fastuous stranger stood his ground and glared sullenly at them.

Jack intervened by placing a restraining hand on Vilém's arm, offering graciously, "Our apologies, good sir. Please allow us to move aside for you."

They parted, and the ruffian barged in only to fall forward over Jack's intentionally extended foot. Barely containing his rage and embarrassed by his fall, the incensed aristocrat stood and turned on Jack, hand moving to the hilt of his sword. "You bloody blackguard!" he shouted, drawing the full attention of everyone in the room.

"I am unarmed, as you can see," Jack calmly raised

both arms, revealing that he carried no weapons—his sword and pistol still on the hook above their table. "You need a valuable lesson in manners, sir, lamentably something you seriously lack," he continued in a condescending tone, his tenor that of a chastising schoolmaster. "At home, we spank naughty children like you."

The stranger, controlling his emotions with the utmost difficulty, hissed through his clenched teeth. "Well, then, I invite you to meet me at six tomorrow morning, you insolent swine, behind the church on Karmelitská across the river," he snarled like a menacing wolf. "I'll bring my seconds; you bring the undertaker." His words dripped with minacious loathing.

Infuriated, the royal regent was about to intervene and threaten to throw the truculent stranger into the Daliborka Tower dungeon. Jack cut him short, not taking his eyes off the hostile cavalier for a moment. He was as calm as a monk at vespers. "I need the practice, Vilém. Let him be." Then he added, "It will indeed be my pleasure. Six it is."

The man stormed off, cheeks flushed with anger, while the pair stepped outside into the cool night.

"I will act as your second, Jack, if you're serious about this. I can have this impudence quashed by the royal guard with a simple snap of my fingers.

You need not involve yourself in this," the official offered.

Recognising the look of unchallengeable resolve in Jack's face, however, Vilém shrugged, beaten, and added simply, "How's your sword arm?"

"Never been better. I've been resting it too long and welcome this diversion. What better opportunity than with this obnoxious fellow?" Jack's eyes flared with anticipation for an instant, reflecting the flickering flames of the torches positioned along the terrace.

After the friends had parted, Jack moved to the stables to check on his horse and then returned to gather his belongings and arrange to be woken at five for a light breakfast.

The morning dawned grey and still, a heavy fog blanketing the river. *A perfect cool day for a little exercise*, Jack ruminated as he guided his horse at a slow walk to the appointed place. Calm, almost philosophical, he chewed on a wooden splinter as he approached the rear of the church grounds. He was the last to arrive, he realised, cheerfully bidding everyone, including his adversary, a very good morning. The sound, unbroken sleep had re-invigorated him; he felt vivacious, almost playful. Pavel had been in the stable tending to his usual chores when Jack entered that morning. Bidding the lad the very best on the anniversary of his birth, the officer handed him a shiny silver coin that he had polished over breakfast, and ruffling the boy's hair teasingly, he mounted and left for the bridge.

Nodding to Vilém, who had brought an accompanying captain from the castle, Jack dismounted and removed his cloak, flexing his arms and shoulders as he unsheathed his sword. He donned his father's fencing gloves, rapier under his arm. Jack quoted the capital's motto: *"Praga capot Regni"—Prague, Head of the Kingdom.* "A city with that responsibility relies on its good citizens. Our unfortunate and belligerent associate over there is not one of them," he added.

Jack's opponent appeared to be ready and anxious to begin, cutting the air with swishing practice cuts. His second introduced him simply as Lord Caravata and announced the few, straightforward rules. As his party was the aggrieved, it had been Caravata's choice to duel to the death or until either man could not continue through injury.

Caravata, of medium height, displayed the bearing of a self-important snob—thankfully a trait not frequently seen to this extent amongst the European nobility. Egotistical and abrasive, he was in the habit of being indulged by all around him. When not with prostitutes or playing cards for large sums of money, he frequently practised with the sword and considered himself a fencing celebrity. While physically strong, Caravata led an indulgent life that had softened the edge of his keen agility and well-honed reflexes but not his sense of self-importance. Brimming with confidence this morning, he believed that he would discard this young, detestable upstart like a soiled handkerchief and return to his estate in time to rendezvous with the neighbour's delightful niece, who was visiting from the country.

The duelling pair took their places, facing one another in their shirtsleeves at a close but manoeuvrable distance. At the command to begin, both saluted with their weapons, and Caravata immediately lunged forward with two sharp thrusts that were parried easily away. They circled on the even ground, staring intently into each other's eyes. Caravata advanced in short steps, swinging his blade like a scythe, from left to right and back. Jack easily countered each swing, moving his rapier like a pendulum and stepping back to maintain the distance between them. The blades sang like the strokes of a hammer on a blacksmith's anvil echoing in the empty churchyard.

Jack held his sword point close to the ground, bobbing the rapier lightly in his hand like a cork on a fishing line to feel its balance. It felt comfortable and delicate between his fingers yet secure against his glove. Caravata's sword was horizontal, stretched chest-high at arm's length and pointing at Jack's throat. Moving to his right in an arc, the man attacked again, this time cutting wide swathes through the air as if with a cutlass. Jack countered by lashing out to his upper right whilst stepping left. Blocking the sweeping blade, he took three swift steps forward, jabbing and driving and then slicing. His opponent retreated but not before his left sleeve was nicked and a short, thin red line appeared across his upper arm. The blood flowed freely from the wound, staining his sleeve like crimson ink spreading on blotting paper.

Profanity escaped the count's lips. The nostrils of his falcate nose flared visibly. He glared angrily at Jack, his brow wet with perspiration. When he regained his composure, he stepped to his left and took two practice swings with his blade. He continued circling and half-heartedly stabbing at Jack a number of times, testing. His eyes were filled with pure, pompous hatred and hostility.

Jack stood still with his feet well apart, breathing measured, and only his head turned as he followed the other's movement. Then, lifting his sword high above his damp curls, he advanced in measured strides, bringing the rapier down in mercurial sweeps and confusing his adversary, who retreated awkwardly. The onslaught continued with a frenzy of barely parried poking, feinting and cutting motions until Caravata tripped and fell backward onto the damp grass, his sword flying from his hand.

Jack paused, his rapier tip pointing an arm's length away from the man's heaving chest. Frozen for a brief moment, he lowered the blade and moved back to his starting position. He glanced up at Slavata and smiled briefly. Caravata picked himself up, retrieved his sword and walked slowly back to where Jack was waiting. Concern had replaced arrogance on his face.

Jack was now ready to direct the swordplay. He had allowed his antagonist time to show his cards and decided that it was time to end this. He felt calm in the cool morning, standing in the quaint but deserted churchyard surrounded by majestic trees. He breathed in the crisp air and allowed it to invigorate his surging confidence. It was not his time to die in some foreign land at the hand of this ignominious and supercilious narcissist.

Sensing the first spark of uncertainty in Caravata's posture, Jack focused his concentration on his opponent. Flexing his rapier mischievously, he peered obdurately into the other man's eyes and attacked. His first two sweeps were repelled awkwardly, but they were merely setting up for his third serious slash, which lacerated the full width of the nobleman's chest. Continuing to advance, Jack waved his blade in a 'Z' motion and then thrust it forward into Caravata's left arm muscle.

Withdrawing the blade, Jack blocked a sluggish stab and then drove his sword through the man's left shoulder. Caravata groaned and winced with pain, his left arm now effectively useless as a swordsman's counter balance. He had lost the will to fight and was stumbling backward, his left arm—losing blood liberally—pressed against his body for support. Unrelenting in his advance, Jack swept his rapier across the man's stomach, leaving superficial cuts in a chevron pattern. With one stinging sweep, he struck the sword from Caravata's hand and watched it pirouette in a large arc and land out of view in the long grass.

Enervated, Caravata was barely able to stand; he was swaying, his breath ragged, and saliva dribbling in a thin, ropey stream from his open mouth. Raising his right elbow above his ear and aiming his rapier like a matador, Jack drove his blade in a final unremitting thrust through Caravata's heart to the hilt, the bloody blade protruding from the count's back. A thin flow of blood dripped from the tip. Jack released his grip on the rapier and stepped back empty-handed.

"Adieu!" he snapped, devoid of any elation, and then turned and strode back to where Vilém and his escort were standing. Caravata stood motionless—a look of petrified disbelief on his face and his right hand holding Jack's sword as if intent on withdrawing it—and then his eyes closed and he crumpled backward without a sound.

"Well done, my friend," Slavata applauded as Caravata's assistant rushed to the stricken man.

"A cutting tongue deserves a cutting blade," Jack offered philosophically as he removed his gloves and drew an ample sleeve across his sweating face adding, "Our little splenetic acquaintance owned a long sword but a short life. His arrogant ignorance weighed a heavy purse." He allowed his adrenalin-induced determination to slowly ebb away.

"I know little of him," the regent volunteered, "and from now on will hear even less."

Jack threw his cloak over his shoulders as the captain retrieved his sword. He swallowed several generous mouthfuls of cider that the regent had offered him from a goat-skin bag. Wiping his blade clean, Jack sheathed it into the scabbard hanging from his saddle and mounted his horse as the comrades agreed on their plans to meet the king.

Chapter 5

THE KRAKÓW ESTATE

The carriage rattled along the muddy road at an even pace with Abaccus following on a long tether. Jack had opened the shutters on both sides in order to enjoy the fresh, cooling breeze and observe the passing countryside on the way to the Polish border. He was warm, wrapped in his heavy cloak and with a woollen blanket covering his legs.

Long stretches of forest enveloped the road in dark and sinister mystery. Low clouds, giving the appearance of fog, hung amongst the tall pine trees that obscured the sky, and the dampness accentuated the redolent, resinous scent that he enjoyed so much. The fragrance of coniferous trees filled his nostrils and brought back happy childhood memories of halcyon days outside Kraków.

Rows of verdant trees eventually gave way to open paddocks, some of these as cultivated farmland and others as green fields of swaying grass. Here he recognised the petrichor that hung in the moist air. Bucolic villages and small hamlets frequently followed these tracts of vast, cleared pasture, where carriages would slow to safe speeds allowing their occupants to observe fragments of the villagers' normal daily lives.

Obeying Jack's instructions, the driver had followed the Elbe River for some hours before crossing it and heading northeast rather than continuing on to Pardubice. The solitary hours in the rolling coach gave Jack ample opportunity to prepare for the meeting with the unsuspecting widow of his comrade who had died on the battlements in Pilsen. He toyed with the ring in his pocket, rehearsing the kind and gentle words he would use upon reaching her home in Hradec Králové.

It was dark when Jack left Hradec Králové towards the Odra River less than forty leagues away. He was eager to continue travelling during the night, and the coachman had arranged a light dinner at the inn and coupled a fresh team of horses. Jack would have liked to visit Vilém's wife, Lucie Otylie, but circumstances had forced him to alter his plans. Lucie was a remarkable woman whose keen wit and sense of humour always entertained and captivated him. He was fascinated by the contrast between her fun-loving spark for life and her husband's more austere and reserved demeanour.

The coach shutters had been lowered after night-fall, and Jack settled back comfortably, stretching his legs across to the seat in front of him. He recalled this morning's audience with the Bohemian king and pondered the outcome.

✠ ✠ ✠ ✠

Vilém had enlisted his captain to escort Jack to the palace. Jack had settled his account with the innkeep-er, and he turned to bid Pavel—who was waiting expectantly at the door—a sad farewell with the promise of the earliest possible return. Ignoring his station, the boy threw his arms around Jack's neck and hugged him tightly. He reminded Jack in a voice quavering with emotion to look after the horse until he could pamper Abaccus again himself. As the pair mounted to leave the inn, Jack turned with a final wave of his hand, and the two officers cantered off across the square.

Two immaculately dressed grooms appeared in the expansive forecourt to stable the horses on their arrival at Hradčany. Jack followed the officer down a number of long passageways until they reached a large, magnificent library, where they were asked to wait. Jack had purchased a new shirt, tunic and breeches and had left his hat and boots to be brushed and polished by a maid at the tavern. The girl had washed and pressed his scarlet sash and combed the plumes on his hat.

Eventually, he was ushered through the large doors into the room where Vilém was waiting. The two locked eyes and Jack shook his extended hand as he removed his hat. He followed his friend to a cluster of chairs arranged before a magnificent fireplace that radiated warmth from its smouldering logs. King Ferdinand was seated on the left, and Jack bowed obsequiously as Vilém graciously introduced him. The three were the only ones present in the room.

"Please, gentlemen. Please be seated and make yourselves comfortable." The king cordially indicated the chairs with a subtle sweep of the hand.

They obeyed, sitting on either side of him, Jack with his hat on his lap. The room was not large but contained a soaring ceiling and four windows overlooking an impressive garden. Beyond, in the distance, was an uninterrupted view of the river. Apart from an ornate table, the chairs were the only furniture in the chamber, but Jack was impressed by its simple yet opulent design.

"I have heard much of you, Lieutenant Channing, and I have been led to believe that you and my regent were students together at the University of

Kraków," the king opened warmly with a pleasing voice. "I gather that, with the misfortune of distance and together with the pressures of your individual ambassadorial and clerical duties, neither has had the opportunity to visit the other as often as you both would prefer?" He smiled politely as he posed the question, his voice as clear and melodious as a well-tuned instrument. "And although my minister has the obligations of marriage and you have not, that has not posed any obstacle to your friendship."

He's very well informed, thought Jack as he evenly replied, "No, Your Majesty. Although Monsieur Slavata is 18 years older than I, this was never a barrier to the friendship we formed as students. Similar interests and the pursuit of like philosophies and ideals were the clay that bound us together, sir." The king eyed the Polish officer with subtle respect as Jack continued. "The regent's wife is dear to my heart. We each have a mutually attractive personality, it seems, and had your chancellor not married her, I most likely would have."

The trio had laughed convivially before the king asked, "Your studies were of a medical nature?"

"Yes, Your Highness. The Uniwersytet Krakowski has a renowned and highly respected faculty of medicine. I practised my training initially whilst serving with the army, but eventually my interests attained a broader political agenda, and I have been privileged to occupy a diplomatic function in the service of King Sigismund."

"Jacek has been to France to make representation at the court in Paris," Vilém interjected with reduced formality, "and his intention was to visit me whilst returning to Kraków."

"I believe you had an unplanned delay at Pilsen? Would you care to elaborate?" The king leaned forward in his chair with obvious interest and clasped his hands together. Jack carefully offered a précised explanation of the situation surrounding the city's siege, emphasising the need for the urgent support of its inhabitants and defenders. The monarch listened intently, noting especially the limited supplies and the overwhelming imbalance in the sizes of the two armies.

Jack observed that the king was a thin, middle-aged man with intelligent eyes and Habsburg features. His hair was cut short, unusual for the times, and his narrow, angular beard exaggerated his large nose. He exuded amiable warmth, much like that of a father confessor. His erudition was breathtaking. The son of Charles II—Archduke of Austria—and Maria Anna of Bavaria, he was educated by the Jesuits and attended the University of Ingolstadt. A devout Catholic, Ferdinand II was not only the king of Bohemia but had also been crowned king of Hungary and Croatia four months earlier. The Protestant move on Pilsen, following the recent defenestration of the king's own regents in the chancellery here, was of profound concern.

The king interrupted whenever he needed further clarification, and when Jack had finally concluded his report, he issued a number of important and decisive instructions for Vilém to instigate promptly.

"And what of the neutralisation of their guns, my boy? I understand that you dared to believe that their cannons could be disabled and so you spiked them? This is a most warming chapter of your story and yet one that you have omitted. Kindly tell me what you did so we can all share a moment of success—a shaft of sunlight amidst a stormy sea of woe," the king beckoned with praise in his voice.

Jack obliged, and when he had concluded his story, the king applauded. "Bravo!" he called, lightly nudging Vilém's foot with his shoe and declaring, "Here we have our Jason and Mansfeld's large cannon his Golden Fleece."

The king leaned back into his chair as they continued to discuss other important matters and exchange intelligence imperative and significant to both countries. "Please remind your venerable king," he stated, looking at Jack after almost three hours had passed since their meeting began, "that our Catholic League has the support of the King of Spain and the Polish–Lithuanian Commonwealth. My current, inchoate efforts to appoint a suitable general to lead our armies will be escalated. Based on your recent exploits, I'm almost tempted to consider offering you the post, my dear boy."

Jack understood that the king was not serious but inclined his head in acknowledgement of the compliment.

"The fact that this Mansfeld has taken charge of the Protestant forces is a pogrom against us," the monarch continued, "and this requires urgent and solid countermeasures. Your intelligence is most helpful. *Ipsa scientia potestas est—knowledge itself is power,*" he added sagely. "Is there anything further that you wish to add?"

After a short silence, the king sat back and closed his eyes in concentration, like Kepler pondering the mathematics of an astronomical problem. "Tell King Sigismund Vasa that he also has our support should he require it and should we be in a position to grant it." He then roused himself from the pensive mood that this worrying talk had attracted and rose from his chair. He smiled thinly and thanked his guests as he retired, bringing the meeting to an end.

Vilém had organised for a carriage and horses with

a pair of experienced coachmen to take Jack home, and the two men adjourned to a small drawing-room where servants offered them wine and other refreshments while these accommodations were being prepared.

"He will be discussing specific tactics with his officers as we stand here," Vilém professed, sipping on his hot, honeyed milk.

Hungry now at the sight of this food and after the earlier exertion in the churchyard, Jack chewed on an appetising canapé. His thoughts were of Chauvin, Horvat, the mayor of Pilsen and the others trapped within the city. "Had I not the obligation to present my report in Warszawa," he insisted, "I would stay to assist with preparations to support Pilsen. I have left good friends there and am only happy in the belief that I have been able to offer assistance from outside the walls."

Jack reached for another piece of savoury bread, and looking squarely at the regent, continued. "From my observations, the primary advantages that General Mansfeld holds are the size of his army and its daily accretion. He has other minor benefits, of course, such as an uninterrupted supply of ammunition and provisions, but it's these very things that have made him complacent." Jack laughed aloud as he shared his next thought, "Because of some young, starry-eyed,

Polish lieutenant, he possesses two large cannons that he can't use immediately. He really has no other choice but to starve the city into submission, and if Ferdinand can counter quickly, von Mansfeld's smugness will be his Achilles' heel. I would attack him at first light from the southeast. Hit his flank—hard and decisively." Jack struck his palm with his fist.

A junior officer entered the room and caught the chancellor's eye. Vilém waved him across. "Thank you," was all he said after hearing the officer's message and then dismissed the messenger with a curt nod.

Jack continued after the minor interruption. "The Protestant troops are scattered all over the hill south of the city. This makes them even more vulnerable to an attack from the rear. Vasseur and I got in and out virtually without an issue. With their force split due to the companies stationed outside the city's gates, I would be taking their general, their 'king'—and checkmate! He's all but unguarded. I saw it from the belfry."

Vilém had been listening with keen interest. "I will pass on your comments to the king. I believe that some of the officers here have families that are affected by the siege. They will be able to assist with the topography of the surrounding terrain. Leave this with us, and your concern is sincerely appreciated. I have been informed that your carriage is now ready."

The two made their way through the labyrinth of Hradčany's many corridors and eventually arrived at the front steps overlooking the sweeping drive where the carriage had been harnessed and parked. By late morning, Jack was headed for Kraków.

✠ ✠ ✠ ✠

Jack crossed the Odra River at seven the following morning and expected to be on the outskirts of Kraków by late afternoon that same day. He felt a sting of boyish anticipation, like the feeling that accompanied opening presents on Christmas Eve, at seeing his parents again soon. As the carriage continued to travel east, little changed outside the windows. The road gradually became wider and was in better repair. Open to the sky and away from the occasional patches of forest, its surface was frequently dried by the sun and wind. The coachmen took advantage of this and encouraged the team into a faster gait. As the carriage rumbled over arch bridges across the many streams, Jack noted that the weather had gradually improved, and although still cool, it had turned into a very pleasant, sunny day.

He stopped at a pretty town shortly after midday for lunch. The horses were fed, watered and rested. Jack's appetite improved as he listened cheerfully to his own language. It had been a long time since he had last heard this dialect. Removed from the prospects of war, the local people exuded an ambience that was carefree and jovial. A saucy maid—an attractive young girl younger than he—smiled at him from the servery. The innkeeper, probably her father, laughed aloud, sharing a quip with a group in the far corner. Even the kitchen hand was happy as he sang to himself, albeit out of tune while sweeping the front steps. Sad to leave, Jack gathered his gloves and hat and left a few coins on the table. He shouted his appreciation to the publican, buoyed by the belief that the general mood would only improve as he drove deeper into his homeland.

The volume of activity on the roads increased as the carriage pushed towards home. In addition to farmers' carts moving hay and occasional herds of animals being driven by farmers from paddocks to fresh pasture, carriages travelling from their destination became more frequent. Recognising the villages the carriage passed through, Jack couldn't restrain himself as he approached the outer sector of Kraków and opened the door to peer out at the passing view. He yelled final directions to the driver and looked back at his horse, checking how he was faring.

The coach left the main road, turning towards the hills overlooking the Wisła River valley. Jack knew this country well. The vehicle slowed to ease the climb, and Jack noted that the vast tracts of spruce and pine forest it had entered were already part of the family estate. *Dulcis Domus—Sweet Home*, he mimed with rising anticipation. Paddocks of pastureland being worked by his father's people appeared on the lower slopes on the carriage's right. The country road had widened into an avenue lined with silver birches in rows on both sides after they passed the gates. The team pulling the carriage had slowed to a trot, the coachmen aware that the surface was dry and dusty as they approached the house.

Footmen and servants appeared on the main steps of the building as the coach finally rambled to a stop, level with the heavy timber portal. Jack waited impatiently for his door to open and the steps to be lowered. As he descended onto the gravel driveway, his father appeared at the top of the landing. Jock's expression, initially one of mild interest as to who this visitor may be, changed instantly as he was struck by sudden recognition. Without allowing time for a smile, he turned and yelled back into the house in a stentorian voice, "Janka, come here! Quickly! Andrzej's here! Our boy has come home!"

Jack rushed to embrace his father, who was descending the steps with outstretched arms, face beaming and eyes misty as he looked back at his only son. The two hugged for what seemed to be an eternity. The servants, whose bows had gone unnoticed, quietly gathered all of Jack's belongings and directed the coachmen to their quarters. For a moment, Jack stared over his father's shoulder as Abaccus was led away to the stables where the coach horses would also be rested and fed.

When the horses disappeared around the side of the mansion, Jack turned his head and saw his mother, Janina, appear at the door, where she stopped in disbelief. Huge tears welled in her azure eyes as she raised a hand to her mouth, which was open with blatant incredulity. Her head tilted slightly as she embraced the joy of knowing that her son was standing there, alive, unhurt, handsome and real.

Jack opened his arm allowing her to enter their embrace and the three of them stood together for an infinite moment, without speaking or moving while the servants waited respectfully in patient silence.

Jack recalled their parting on this very landing so many months earlier. When they finally moved inside at the urging of Jock's calm, quiet voice, Jack's mother continued to hold onto her son, not allowing herself to let go even to remove his cloak and hand it to the waiting valet. As they settled around the table in the kitchen, she gazed into Jack's eyes, her cheeks flushed with joy and asked, drying away her tears, "Why didn't you send word that you were coming?" Her tone was admonishing in a way that only a loving mother's could be.

This was followed by myriad more questions from Jack's mother, some impatiently thrust aside without receiving a reply as seemingly more urgent ones took their place. Jack's father tried to interject occasionally with questions of his own but without success. He eventually decided, with reluctance, to allow his wife to exhaust her stock of queries—which was more like an inquisition, with questions even regarding whether or not Jack was changing his stockings regularly. Instead, Jack's father relished this moment as a rare opportunity to watch and listen to his son. The cook and her assistant continued their work in the kitchen without interruption, listening to Jack's replies with equal interest. Both had known Jack all his life. The older woman had been present and even assisted as a midwife at his birth.

Transformed long before by the removal of the adjoining wall between the scullery and the washing house, the Channing family kitchen had become an enormous room. Despite the rambling proportions of Jack's stately house, his family's daily life revolved around the kitchen table as its hub. This was not uncommon in Polish households. Most important decisions affecting the running of the estate were made here. Jack's family members also ate their meals with their servants, encouraging a life of geniality and cohesion.

Adorned with many windows, the two-storey family home was larger than the Channings required. It contained 10 bedrooms spread across two small wings, much like a cathedral's transept. The separate, spacious servants' quarters were linked to the main house by a covered walkway. The stables and hay sheds were detached structures, all made from the same local stone gathered from nearby quarries. Beyond the sprawling 2000-acre property, the Channings had unrestrained access, by order of the king, to the extensive surrounding woods to hunt deer, boar, foxes and hares. Fish filled the streams. The land was rich and supported pastures of varied crops as well as the grazing of horses, cattle and other livestock.

With the exception of his bedroom, Jack's favourite room was his father's library. Many of the books in the family athenaeum had belonged to the house's previous occupant, who had abandoned it when he had returned to Sweden. Both Jack and his father had steadily added to the fine collection of tomes, charts and manuscripts attained during their frequent and extensive travels abroad. During his recent trip to Paris, Jack had assembled two chests of various texts in English and French that were due to arrive before Christmas. These included treatises on medicine, astronomy and mathematics as well as disquisitions on physics and alchemy and manuals covering more mundane but practical issues such as animal husbandry and improved farming techniques.

Having survived the family interrogation, Jack was eager to explore the palatial home and grounds for anything new after having been confined to the coach for over a full day and night.

"Let him go, Ninka," his father finally advised, soothing his wife as he noticed Jack's fidgeting desire to stretch his legs. Giving a thankful smile, the lad disappeared to inspect every room of the house with the inquisitiveness of a child before adjourning to the stables. Old Joseph—the family's gardener, blacksmith and stable master—had examined Abaccus and confirmed that a gentle ride would do him no harm.

A profound sense of ecstatic tranquillity washed over Jack as he cantered up the northern slope behind the mansion. He knew that he would have to leave for the capital soon but needed a short stay to revitalise his strained emotions. He rode into the wind, spurring the stallion into a quicker gallop. He wound the reins around the pommel and raised both arms, allowing the crisp, bracing breeze to make him feel alive. He stopped on the nearby ridge to survey the surrounding grassy countryside. Looking back, he saw Joseph at work in the eastern garden. The plot had grown since his departure. He would have to see what vegetables had been added.

Many years earlier, when Jack was just a boy, Joseph had taken him to plant a large section of lettuce and showed him how to tether the tomatoes to wooden stakes driven at regular intervals in the corner patch, explaining how the growing plants needed to be supported. Everything flourished under Joseph's care, and even his parents deferred to him—always giving the old man the last word. With the exception of one harsh season of unusually vicious hail, the kitchen was always abundantly supplied with healthy, succulent, home-grown produce.

Jack's father was at the stables, standing with his hands clasped behind his back while engaged in discussion with one of the servants. His mother was most likely in the kitchen. Jack smiled, imagining her supervising preparations for tonight's dinner. She would be fussing, always enjoying a social occasion, but today was special; they would dine formally as a family. Her amiable and gregarious nature would frequently have her eating with the servants. Jock would often join them, using these occasions to discuss general matters affecting the estate. At other times, particularly after a heavy lunch, Jack's father would seclude himself with a book or some important documents in the library. Occasionally a servant would be sent with a dinner invitation to the Channing's neighbours, and Jock would withdraw to play chess with Tadek Stachurski, also a retired officer, while Stachurski's wife, Wanda, would idly exchange local snippets of news with Janina.

Jack was a mercurial spirit, gravitating to all things new. Confined to a house with little to do was his ultimate boredom. To be restrained within the walls of an infirmary due to a debilitating illness was deemed to be acceptable only if he was unconscious or delirious or if his senses were incapacitated to such an extent that space and time did not exist. However, to be imprisoned within a library containing thousands of books was utopia to Jack. Each turn of a fresh page revealed something new and not yet seen—a voyage of discovery. It was not inconceivable for him to shut himself away and read three tomes in a single 24-hour sitting with only a pitcher of water for a companion. When stabling Jack's horse, Joseph would always find a book in his saddle bag, and his family members knew to start any search for him in the reading room.

Jack's ultimate release was to be out in the world, exploring a new paddock, a forest, a town, another country. Jack had familiarised himself with every cemetery for leagues around the estate, and he knew every tavern and inn-keeper in the region. He could select a particular ale-house to suit his every mood—not that he was a frequent visitor. Riding with abandon through the estate was his soul's refreshment, and it offered the opportunity to better acquaint himself with his new mount. Although they had travelled hundreds of leagues together in a short week, Jack was sparsely in the saddle. Horvat's gift would prove to be like an untapped reef of gold.

Abaccus was fast and responsive, his strength born from strict cavalry training—an advantage should Jack ever need to fire a shot over his head or wield a sword while on his back. Regarding the height of the autumn sun over the western hills, Jack observed that there was sufficient time to wander into the woods without pressing his horse. They trotted at a leisurely pace, weaving their way amongst the old forest giants in the coolness of the afternoon and cantered across the open, undulating terrain, lingering for a drink at one of the forest's many cascading streams.

They startled a small herd of deer at the edge of a large stand of spruce trees. Jack leaned forward until he was lying along the horse's neck, whispered a reminder into his ear to be still, and observed the group through his telescope, counting a leash of antlered stags. He was sure that his father hadn't hunted here recently and mentally noted the location. He knew from experience that a herd of does would be close by. Skirting the long line of verdurous timber, the two eventually made their way onto a granite outcrop. The prominent, windswept, grassy ridge ran from north to south, its backbone littered with spherical and egg-shaped boulders more than twice the height of a man. These ancient grey rocks had been weathered and burnished by an epoch of wind and rain. Known to some in the district as *Satan's Marbles*, their northern faces were covered with moss, a testament to their age and the dampness of the place.

Jack dismounted, leaving his horse to graze freely, and found a comfortable cushion of dense grass tufts on which to recline. He supported his head with clasped hands and gazed at the sky. A pair of eagles glided high in the breeze above him—majestic, outstretched wings soaring and tail feathers fluttering in their wake. They were hunting in the late afternoon, patiently searching for the opportunity to souse and seize an unsuspecting hare or unwary rabbit. Jack recalled a saying often repeated by one of his mentors: *Aquila non capit muscam—An eagle doesn't catch flies*, meaning that a nobleman doesn't deal with insignificant matters. Chewing on a sweet stem of grass, he envied the eagles' aerial dominance—powerful talons and superb vision—and marvelled at their regal beauty. It was no wonder that these powerful birds of prey were so often the chosen symbols of a nation, emblazoned on flags as well as the banners of aristocratic families.

Closing his eyes, Jack listened to the sounds of nature about him. Birds chirped as they flew past, and the breeze hummed its tune among the rocky crags. The bliss of solitude was a recuperating sedative. His mind drifted to the stories that his father used to tell him, and he imagined that the highlands of Scotland would be like this, serene yet wildly mercenary. A snort from his horse brought his mind back to the reality of the moment, and with great reluctance, he stood and slapped the grass from his breeches.

"What do you think of your new domain, Abaccus Channing?" Jack had pushed the horse's muzzle down with his shoulder so that the side of his face rested against the stallion's cheek, and he brushed Abaccus' neck with smooth, soothing strokes. "Will you miss me when I leave for Warszawa? Don't worry. Old Joseph will care for you. Don't get too fat because I have plans for both of us after I return."

The horse bobbed his head twice and stamped the turf with his hoof as if in agreement. Jack climbed up and turned him for home.

They arrived in the gravelled yard at the back of the house with less than two hours of light left in the day. The groom led the horse away to be stabled for the night, and Jack entered the kitchen through the rear door, reaching for an apple.

"Has mother been organising dinner with you wonderful ladies?" Jack asked, his question partly muffled by his bite into the fruit. The cook and her assistant giggled and curtseyed lightly, confirming that Janina's supervision had been relentless and that she had recently moved to the dining room to assist with table arrangements. Jack winked at them on his way out, asking politely over his shoulder, "Where's Father?"

He was directed to the front of the house. The front doors were often left open during these mild autumn days, and he stepped out onto the landing and gazed at the carpet of sweeping green lawns occupying the front of the estate. Taking a final bite, Jack tossed the apple as far onto the grass as he could, knowing that it would be gone by morning. The sound of distant male voices reached him from within the house, and he turned to investigate. It seemed that Father had a visitor in the library. Jack entered through the open doorway, and both men stopped to look in his direction.

"Volkov, you vodka-guzzling Cossack!" exclaimed

Jack with obvious joyful surprise as he recognised his friend. The two men stepped towards each other and embraced heartily, slapping each other's backs as close companions do.

"So, Andrzej, you're looking exceptionally well," the Russian observed with a hint of an accent, still tightly clutching Jack's extended hand. "Your father sent word that you were home as he knew that I was staying in Kraków and wanted to surprise you."

"Sit down, both of you! Come and join me. We have been waiting for your return, Jack." The Scot indicated the empty easy-chairs around him. "Tosiek! Bring the bottle and three glasses. And some salted herring with rye bread and diced onion, please," he shouted loudly into the hallway.

An hour had passed before their first break in conversation. The men had exhausted their questions and explanations covering the last month, Jock reminding them that there would be ample time to continue during dinner. "What about a short fencing session?" the fencing master suggested mischievously. "I'm keen to see whether my son remembers all that his father has taught him," he added, rising from his chair to fetch the foils.

Anton Volkov had been a family friend since 1605, when he first met Jack's father in Livonia during the Battle of Kircholm. Fair haired, he was taller and three years older than Jack. Lean and strong, he was a ruthless fighter and excellent swordsman, and he spent most of his life in the saddle. Although he was born in Kurgan on the Siberian plain east of the Southern Ural Mountains, his ancestry had been unequivocally tied to the steppes of the Zaporozhian Cossacks. He was a proud and fiercely loyal man, and his striking blue eyes reflected his heritage beyond the rapids of the Dnieper River. He had an easy laugh. Despite wearing the rakish uniform of a cavalry hussar and preferring the curved Cossack shashka, he possessed finesse with the fencing foil.

Jock produced two épées whose tips had been plugged with spherical wooden beads and turned the sandglass. Jack and Anton squared off and assumed the traditional en garde position, and when Jock gave the order, Anton teased playfully by repeatedly tapping the tip of Jack's blade. Advancing in small steps without crossing his feet, Jack pivoted his sword effortlessly from the wrist, moving his point in random sequences and forcing Anton to parry laterally and diagonally. Jack probed for a momentary weakness and lunged at full stretch, scoring a hit from a low level. The two men returned to their starting positions.

Still prepared to parry and defend, the Russian gradually gave ground. He realised that Jack preferred to attack from a lower blade-tip position, allowing him to constantly threaten his sword arm, and Jack's second strike found Anton's muscle just above the elbow.

At the third start, Volkov took the initiative with four successive thrusts. Jack's circular parries were successful, but not expecting the final flèche, he found Anton's point pinned high on his breastbone. The Cossack began the next round with a series of classical balestra—short, sharp, forward jumps. Although retreating, the younger man parried easily and was drawn into making an unsuccessful attack, which the Russian countered, scoring on the shoulder.

The Scot called a halt as the last grains of sand disappeared into the lower glass cavity and declared the win to Volkov—five to four. "A close contest, gentlemen." His voice full of approval, he turned to his son and added, "You still remember our classes well, and with continued practice and perseverance, you may beat Anton one day. You were always a sedulous student."

The men resumed their seats and accepted large mugs of water flavoured with lemon and honey from an attentive servant, who confirmed that dinner would be served in one hour. Their companionable discussion ended soon after, as Jock stood to return the épées to the rack and they parted to wash and dress for dinner.

The evening meal was a special occasion for the four of them—more formal than usual and without the house servants—to celebrate Jack's return. Jack's parents sat at the ends of the table, leaving the soldiers to sit facing one another. Following an initial serving of mushroom soup—Jack's favourite—the trestle was generously laden with fragrant, steaming dishes of pork, cabbage, potatoes and numerous boiled vegetables accompanied by various sauces and seasonings. Janina joined the men in a round of vodka, which was a rarity encouraged by tonight's singular event. Three striking candelabra adorned the table with mellow light. The diners passed bowls between them, helping themselves to the food and a selection of wines, cider and home-made mead, old Joseph's specialty.

Probed by additional questions and prompted by his and Anton's fencing performance, Jack described his recent duel in detail, drawing unanimous agreement regarding the provocative arrogance of Caravata. As the conversation inevitably turned and flowed, meandering and segueing across many topics and sliding into similar tangential subjects, talk soon reverted to the siege at Pilsen. Jack covered the salient points for Anton's benefit, recounting the fight on the walls, the cavalier and insouciant attitude of Mansfeld's army and the successful spiking of his cannons. The last accomplishment triggered another short, stiff round of vodka. Drawing on parallels from their earlier fighting days, the Cossack ultimately turned the discussion to the Battle of Kircholm on the Dzwina River in Livonia.

"Your father fought there Andrzej. Were you aware of that?" Janina began. "You were almost 15 at the time, and we were living in the city. It was before the king granted these estates to us. Your father would be away for months at a time; such is a soldier's life. I only knew that he hadn't been killed by the arrival of money from the royal purse. Payments were irregularly made in those days, making it very difficult to manage expenses."

Jack vaguely recalled the name of the battle, and turning to his father, asked, "What was the conflict about?"

Jock caught the eye of a servant and nodded. It was time to smoke. As he finished pouring a round of vodka, his favourite cherry wood pipe appeared at his elbow, packaged elegantly in a rosewood box. "Ah! Sharing fine tobacco with friends is almost as pleasurable as a good drink. Anton, would you care to light up this exquisite blend in my briar? Difficult to obtain, but admirable quality. Moist and mild—just try it," he explained, extending the offer to the other two men. Both declined as the servant brought a glowing, wax-dipped taper for the Scot to apply to his bowl.

"That indomitable pirate Raleigh has enticed the English queen to smoke dried, rolled tobacco leaves," Jack noted, arousing the interest of those around the table. "I was surprised during this recent visit to the French court at how widespread the habit has become among inveterate smokers," he added as his mother asked for the salted herring and dilled cucumber to be placed on the table.

With his briar glowing fiercely, Jock leaned comfortably back in his chair and began. "It was late September 1605. Riga, lying four leagues to the northwest of the village of Kircholm, was a strategic harbour city that controlled the region's trade routes and storage of provisions for the army of Lithuanian Hetman Jan Karol Chodkiewicz. The Swedish King, Karol IX Sudermanski, was keen to occupy the city and gain control of this major Baltic port, effectively reducing the operational ability of the Polish–Lithuanian Commonwealth.

"Some days later, 3500 men gathered at the Hetman's camp at Kircholm whilst the Swedes advanced their troops in torrential rain during the night. The Swedish forces consisted of 5000 veteran cavalrymen, 6000 infantrymen and 11 cannons. They arrived on a misty, autumn morning. On the heights above the village, four divisions in total were arranged in four ranks of alternating infantry and cavalry.

"From our hill, we counted seven small infantry tercios, all well-spaced, in the front line under General Anders Lennartsson as well as six in the third line commanded by General Henri Brandt and Prince Frederick Luneburski. Six squadrons of enemy cavalry under Frederick Joachim of Mansfield formed the second rank, and five squadrons formed the fourth. These were reiter cavalry commanded by Brandt and supremely directed by King Karol IX. The Swedish artillery was arranged in a line behind the first two ranks, and their troops were reluctant to lose their advantageous and elevated defensive position to begin the fighting.

"Chodkiewicz assembled his well-rested forces in the traditional 'Old Polish Order'. In the centre, under the command of Hetman Wincenty Wojna, were our elite, superbly-trained winged hussars. Although most of them were from the Grand Duchy of Lithuania, I rode with them. We were heavily armed, carrying lances, pistols and sabres—300 strong. About 1000 infantrymen and five cannons were with us, plus 300 Kurlander reiters arrived under Duke Friedrich Kettler just as we moved off to advance."

Jock paused, lifting his chin, and exhaled a thick plume of blue smoke. "Na zdrowie," he saluted with a raised glass. The others echoed the motion and emptied their glasses in one sharp swallow. Gazing at the upper wooden panelling, he continued, somewhat effusively after the drink as if reading from a history book.

"The left wing was led by Tomasz Dąbrowa and comprised 1300 cavalry, 300 hussars, 200 reiters and 800 Cossack light cavalry, with whom Anton rode."

"Dąbrowa had 900 hussars," Volkov corrected good-naturedly and continued with the story. "Four lines of 700 hussar cavalry stood in formation up on the right wing under Prince Jan Piotr Sapieha, including another 100 Cossacks. Remaining in reserve, Captain Teodor Lacki waited with 280 hussars and other small, voluntary cavalry units in mail armour. The Hetman's plan was to provoke the enemy by deploying numerous skirmishing parties and advancing our light artillery. We probed the Swedish position for several hours but couldn't lure them down the slope. Finally, Chodkiewicz feigned a retreat."

Jock and Volkov laughed aloud in unison as they vividly recalled this pivotal manoeuvre in their imagination. Jack sat as if in a trance, captivated by the detail. They drank another round in celebration of the occasion.

"The deception enticed the Swedish king into ordering his advance. The fight would finally begin!" the Russian stated animatedly. "Almost 4000 Swedish infantrymen marched off and proceeded first down and then up the hill to face a heavy barrage from our Lithuanian infantry muskets and artillery shot. Wojna was ordered to counterattack with his hussars down the centre."

Jock broke in enthusiastically to continue. "And off we rode, picking up considerable speed down the slope. Some fell from Swedish musket fire, but we rammed into the pikes like pushing the side of a hedgehog and broke through. I speared three musketeers before snapping my lance and resolved to hand combat with my sabre. Kettler's 300 reiters soon appeared in support, and the Swedish infantry broke. Our horses suffered the greatest losses; we lost 150 mounts. Our left wing moved in, finally crushing the last shred of King Karol's resistance."

Absorbed in the moment, Anton continued, picking up the thread. "Our light Cossack cavalry advanced with the river on our left, and we cut a wide path, slowly moving to the right with the hussars, hitting the rear of the routed Swedish infantry." His eyes began to flame like red-hot pokers. "We soon combined with the might of Wojna's hussars and Kettler's reiters. Their musketeers were unable to reload sufficiently quickly, and we cut them down with sabre and lance, our reiters shooting stragglers with their carbines. Complete victory, however, was not assured at this point," he noted with a pointed finger and raised eyebrows. He accepted a proffered cigar and leaned forward to light it from the nearest candle. Jack replenished his mug with refreshing cider and refilled the three glasses with vodka. Janina was happy to sit and listen, raising a hand to refuse both offers.

The Cossack lifted a fragment of tobacco leaf from the tip of his tongue with a moistened finger and resumed. "In response to Brandt's force moving to turn the flank of the Swedish left wing, Sapieha moved his cavalry and Cossacks simultaneously, severely splitting the Swedish reiters and pushing them into the wet marshes. In a countermove, the Swedish king activated his own force of reiters and the royal guard, weakening Piotr's position and threatened to cut him off from the main action.

"Chodkiewicz realised that Karol IX had committed his entire cavalry and ordered in Lacki's reserve hussars, who slammed the right Swedish flank at full force and crushed them completely. This definitive deployment ultimately determined the result of the battle. The Swedish reiters fled, exposing their left infantry's flank. Their fleeing force was in chaos."

The cigar wedged between his fingers, Anton had been illustrating his explanation with hand movements on the ash-smeared tablecloth. His eyes turned to Jack in a steely gaze as he resumed. "At one stage, your father and I collided on the field. We inadvertently backed into each other. I barely recognised him, with his face splashed in Swedish blood. We knelt beside discarded cannons and shared a joke, taking the opportunity to reload our pistols and rest. He produced a hip flask—I remember how bad the vodka was—but we shared it to the end. Shortly after, I saw him fire at blank range and kill their centre's commander, Lennartsson. This collapsed their retreating tercios. As a younger man, your father had a parlously cavalier attitude." He paused a moment and smiled. "The next day I celebrated my 18th birthday."

Anton turned to the Scotsman without a word but with a look that suggested he should continue. Jock met his gaze with smiling eyes. This story, he knew, would have a happy ending. Clearing his throat, he began. "The commonwealth cavalry surrounded at least half their infantry, and we pursued the remainder almost to Riga. The action, as we've described, took little more than half an hour. It was a complete victory.

The Swedes suffered losses of 6000—over half their original number—not including the few hundred we captured alive. Luneburski also died, and Henri Brandt was taken prisoner. Their king was severely wounded. In comparison, our losses were minor— about 100 dead and double that number wounded, including Dąbrowa, Wojna and Lacki. Remnant pockets of Swedish infantry managed to board ships at Dynemunt while some of their reiters retreated to the safety of Parnawy.

"As a result of the irremediable defeat, an emphatic rout, the Swedish king abandoned his siege and sailed across the Baltic Sea back to Sweden. Our campaign faltered at this point, however, due to the large loss of highly-trained horses, and there was no money to pay our troops—no meed for our fight. Volkov and I both returned to Warszawa as mercenaries in Sigismund's service.

"The Swedes continued to wage war until a truce was signed in 1611. Last year, however, they began harassing the commonwealth again, and the rest you know. That was the primary reason for your visit to Paris. Sigismund is seeking French support—that of another Catholic and powerful nation."

The Scot had been addressing his son and suspected that this fresh perspective further clarified what had been a mottled picture up until now. Janina bid the men goodnight, kissed her son and retired, leaving them to their own company. Jack confirmed his intention to leave for the capital the next morning, using the carriage provided by Vilém.

"A sound plan," confirmed his father, "and I suggest you take Volkov for company."

Jack's look for assent from the Russian met with a positive nod. It was agreed. They continued to sit, drinking and talking into the early hours of the morning.

Chapter 6

THE DINING HALL

The family embraced in the spacious hallway at the doors overlooking the drive of the house. Jack stepped out and climbed into the carriage, taking a seat opposite the Cossack. He called to the driver, and as the vehicle began to move off, waved to his parents until the curve of the road hid them from view. The two soldiers settled down as comfortably as possible for the journey north to Warszawa. They had talked long into the night yesterday after dismissing the servants to bed. Heavy-headed, they had emptied three bottles of good vodka and a couple of flagons of mead, eventually leaving the dining room filled with the smell of acrid pipe and cigar smoke.

Jack had been left to sleep for a time, but by mid-morning, his mother came up to wake him. She drew the heavy drapes and opened his window wider and then bent over his bed and kissed him fondly on the nose.

"Andrzej! Time to be up," she greeted softly, adding,

"breakfast is ready in the kitchen," and leaving, closed the door gently behind her.

Jack lay under the warmth of the eiderdown, hands clasped behind his head and stared at the ceiling. It was his habit to take these quiet minutes after a night's sleep to plan the order of his day. His father and Anton were well into their frugal breakfast when he appeared and joined them at the table, viewing the selection of food. After leaving instructions with the valet regarding what he wanted to be packed, he left to investigate the modifications to old Joseph's vegetable garden. The brisk, outdoor air refreshed him, and he walked the long way around the house to the stables in order to loosen his legs and check on his horse.

Abaccus greeted him with a snort and toss of the head. Jack fed the horse a handful of sugar and an apple, which disappeared—core and all—in two rapid bites. He then returned to his room, checked the clothes that had been laid out on his bed and instructed that they be packed and loaded onto the coach. At eleven, Jack and Anton rumbled out of the estate.

The coachman had been ordered to drive through the city and ignore the country by-pass road. Jack was eager to see any changes within Kraków, and after crossing the beautiful marketplace past Sukiennice, the carriage clattered over cobbled lanes and eventually made its way north towards their destination.

Anton was amused at his companion's boyish interest and suggested encouragingly, "We will stop here and visit some of our favourite haunts on our return. Kraków will wait for us!" He slapped Jack on the knee and settled back amongst the cushions to relax. The recurrent rocking soon had them both snoring, garnering much-awaited sleep.

Unsurprisingly, the condition of the road between the two capitals—the old one and the current one—was in excellent repair, allowing the carriage to travel at a quick pace. The change in rhythm as the coach slowed before entering the town of Kielce woke the two men. Jack sat up, stretching, and gazed through each window to determine their progress. His eyes, unfocused from the recent sleep, turned to the Cossack, who hadn't yet stirred. Gentle nudges from Jack's boot saw his companion blink awake then yawn deeply, rubbing his eyes.

The two sat without speaking, allowing their dulled senses to regroup. Both felt rested. Anton offered his friend his hip-flask, which Jack happily accepted. The spirit would revive them and dispel the final, remnant effects of last night's extravagant celebration. After agreeing that a meal would be in order, Jack and Anton were left at a respectable establishment as the carriage continued to the coach house to harness a fresh team of horses. They were soon on their way to Radom to stop for the night.

By early the following afternoon, the two officers were turning into the grounds of the *Zamek Królewski—The Royal Castle*. A sombre day with the threat of rain greeted the pair as they alighted. They were led to their suites by a senior valet, who had prepared bathing facilities and a change of comfortable and appropriate clothing for their audience with the king. Jack, as a member of the court, had a permanent room—including a complete wardrobe—at the palace. Volkov was ushered into a regular guestroom as he was a recurrent but less frequent visitor.

Clean, perfumed and refreshed, the two—who had been requested to dine with the king and his courtiers—made their way to the grand dining hall as twilight heralded the lighting of candles and lanterns throughout the royal grounds. As they entered, other guests, visitors and regular court attendants were taking their places at the generous table. Its thick boards were the width of a man's hand and had the reputation of once supporting a score of merry revellers, who in their inebriated state, had reportedly climbed onto it and danced for most of the night.

King Sigismund Vasa had pre-allocated a dozen

places for his formal guests to be seated around his chair at the centre of the table, allowing the remaining diners to select their own positions. The two comrades held back patiently, happy to be placed where a vacancy remained.

"Do you recognise any of tonight's formal party?" Jack queried, keenly eyeing the guests closest to the king.

"I believe they are ambassadors—the three Russians I know. The other four, I believe, have come from Courland and Lithuania," Anton replied, observing the delegates closely, "and I have it on good authority that discussions tonight will predominantly cover Swedish troop activity in the north."

Jack smiled at his friend's enviable ability to glean reliable and accurate information but didn't ask his sources. He turned to his companion with an apologetic look and volunteered in a low voice, "Why don't you organise two places for us while I find Colonel Krasinski? My father had asked that I hand him a note but was very clear that I should speak to him and hand it on personally."

With a faint, mocking bow and a broad smile, Volkov moved towards the table while Jack left the hall to complete his errand. The officer approached a servant for assistance and was directed to the barracks. The duty captain led him to the colonel's quarters, where he was admitted after a firm knock on the door. With their business concluded, Jack returned to the dining hall.

The capacious room was filled with a veritable army of servants meandering around the table while carrying dishes of food, gathering empty plates, pouring wine and catering to the general needs of the king's guests. The atmosphere was strepitous— with the loud hum of conversation spasmodically punctuated by raucous laughter and the cacophony of clanging cutlery against bowls and plates. There was a warm and inviting ambience that pervaded the grand hall.

Sigismund was totally absorbed in amicable conversation with the delegates surrounding him while his rows of guests were intent on their own discussions and food and even more so their wines and spirits. Jack observed the scene from the doorway through which he had entered. He had been approached by a retainer wanting to assist him but had waved the man away.

Had there been an expectation to dance on the table this evening, it would have been dismissed instantly. There was hardly space to leave a pair of folded gloves let alone space enough for dancing feet. Large, shining, metal dishes that held wonderful arrangements of meats were touching bowls of vegetables, which sat next to platters of juicy and exotic fruit. Glowing with gold, the intricate candlesticks were designed to hold tiers of smaller dishes containing viands and cheeses above the table but still within easy reach of the diners.

Engrossed in finding his friend, Jack approached the table with hat in hand and found Anton at the far side, next to an empty chair that had been reserved for the officer. He glanced to his left at the king as he passed, but Sigismund was absorbed in conversation with those around him, so Jack continued walking to the end of the table and casually claimed his place. A servant appeared discretely at his elbow and took his hat while pulling out his chair. With an appreciative nod, Jack sat down next to Volkov and turned to him contritely, saying, "Sincere apologies, my dear friend. Unfortunately my father's contact was quartered at the far end of the castle, and the whole business took longer than I anticipated. Many thanks for holding a seat."

Volkov leaned into him and tactfully remarked in a whisper, "My dear Jack. You must be blind! With you specifically in mind, I selected these two seats so as to place you opposite the most exquisite creature in the hall tonight." His words assumed a conspiratorial tone.

Jack immediately looked up—an impulsive and

involuntary reaction—and stared at the sight before him as if drawn in by Medusa's entrancing power.

Volkov simply whispered, "Close your mouth, Jack."

The face opposite the Polish officer was unbelievably beautiful. Jack's eyes were transfixed by a woman with a complexion the colour of milk, soft, seductive lips and a well-proportioned, finely-chiselled nose. The woman's hair, the colour of the candles between them, was parted along the middle above her forehead and fell in long, wavy tresses over her shoulders and below her elbows. A thin, green, transverse band circled her head, its colour enhancing her alluring eyes, which glittered like brilliant emeralds. Jack had never seen such piercing green eyes before; the gem didn't do them justice.

Jack and the woman locked eyes for what seemed like an aeon before the spell was broken. She suddenly realised that she had been staring and looked immediately away, her cheeks flushed like soft, pink roses. Jack's eyes wouldn't leave her. By his side, leaning away on his left arm, Anton studied his companion's rapt expression and smiled at his reaction.

The music began from the far side of the hall at a command from the king—a lively mazurka to which many gravitated from the table. Jack's paragon of beauty was approached almost immediately by a handsome nobleman and stood to leave at his invitation without a glance in the Polish envoy's direction. Jack's eyes followed her every move as she followed her partner, hand on his, onto the floor and fell into step with the other dancers. Jack was mesmerised. The woman's lithe, slender figure moved effortlessly, pale green gown flowing to the rhythm and pace set by the other dancing pairs as they made their way gracefully around the room.

"I would ask what you are thinking, but your brazen, speechless staring tells me—without a hint of doubt—all I need to know," the Russian volunteered with a muffled chuckle, feigned sarcasm in his voice.

Jack replied after a brief moment, still totally distracted, "What an extraordinary woman! I know I've never seen her before. That is something I would most definitely remember."

"You have forgotten to ask, but anticipating your question, my subtle inquiries tonight have put a name to that delightful face," Volkov continued in an imitation of mockery. "She is Lady Marianna Pomorska, daughter of Count Stefan Pomorski, a distant relative of the king." His arched eyebrows confirmed that he was pleased with his research.

A sudden gunshot stunned the room's occupants. The musicians stopped playing mid-tune, bringing the rotating dancers to a shocked halt. Hands muffled screams of alarm, and the men looked around in grim, uncertain scrutiny. The chattering crowd fell silent almost instantly. Officers immediately surrounded the king, restraining his attempt to rise from his chair.

Jack and Anton were on their feet. As they moved towards the doors, the captain of the guard appeared, eyes startled, but voice controlled. "An armed intruder has been shot in the adjoining foyer. He is unconscious but still alive!" he called into the hushed hall from the doorway.

Without a moment's hesitation, Jack replied, turning and looking to the king for assent, "As a physician, I can assist. Your Highness?"

Sigismund nodded curtly, his startled eyes mellowing with instant recognition.

The lovely lady with emerald eyes temporarily forgotten, Jack and Volkov strode out of the hall, their footsteps echoing in the continuing silence. In the foyer, Jack bent over the injured intruder and placed a finger against his neck confirming his pulse. He seized the prone man's collar, ripping it open in order to facilitate his breathing, and then began searching for the wound. Looking up to see Volkov's face, Jack asked in an even, commanding tone, "Please fetch my bag. It's on the floor beside my bed. Some urgency if you can!"

Anton nodded and was gone, taking the guard with him.

The intruder had been shot in the shoulder. Jack ordered a cloak to be placed under the man's head and slit his doublet and shirt open with a dagger. The bullet had left a neat entry point above the man's left breast, but the exit hole was gaping and bloody, marked with torn flesh and small splinters of bone. Jack pressed a swathe of cloth torn from the victim's shirt against the wound to staunch the blood and checked the man's pulse again. His confidence rose.

After Volkov had returned with the bag, Jack cleaned and covered the interloper's wound with a soothing balm and bandaged his shoulder firmly. A group of curious onlookers had gathered in a circle around the scene but parted as the assailant was taken on a stretcher under heavy guard to the palace infirmary.

The dining hall and adjoining rooms had been thoroughly searched for further signs of roguery and had returned to a degree of safe normality. Volkov carried Jack's bag as the Polish officer moved to a nearby table on which a basin of water had been placed to wash his bloodied hands. An officer appeared at the physician's elbow, requesting his return to the hall to speak with the king. The room buzzed with subdued voices, but the commotion subsided as Jack appeared and strode to where the king now stood. Silence fell as Sigismund turned to face him with outstretched arms, his face beaming. All eyes in the hall were trained on the pair.

"Andrzej, Andrzej... pivotal as always—here to aid the court in a crisis. Just like your father!" The king stepped towards Jack, who was bowing and placed his hands paternally on his officer's shoulders, pulling him up gently. "Good to see you again, my boy."

"And you, sire," Jack replied.

The king looked past his shoulder and signalled the music to resume with a flick of his hand. The disruption soon abated as people returned to dancing, conversing and dining in the buzzing great hall.

"What news, lad?" the king asked Jack, his voice serious and even.

"Whoever he is, whilst still unconscious, will live. I have tended to his wound and expect that he may be in a position to speak to us in a day or two. I will discuss the management of his condition with the resident military physician before retiring tonight, sir."

Sigismund smiled and nodded in agreement. Surveying the gathered group of officers, he replied gravely. "We'll need to establish his identity and motive as early as is practicable. Colonel, I will leave that with you and expect daily reports updating progress."

The colonel snapped to attention, bowing slightly.

The king turned to Jack and appraised him with one eye half-closed while studying him intently with the other. "What fares abroad? We have missed your wit and charm at court these months that you have been absent. Has your visit been endowed with any success?"

Jack scanned the circle of faces in the group around them, uneasy at the prospect of speaking openly.

"Your concern is unnecessary, my learned doctor. These are all trusted men," noted the king, who was nevertheless pleased with his officer's cautiousness and added, "You can speak freely here."

"Thank you, Your Majesty," Jack replied with a slight bow of his head. "The Paris court was pleased to grant me an audience with Armand Jean du Plessis, the secretary of state to Louis XIII and locally known as Bishop Richelieu of Luçon. An intriguing figure, sire, he represents the French king. Although he is a Catholic clergyman and the head of state of a Catholic nation, I was unable to secure an unequivocal agreement for military assistance for our commonwealth. I sense that he is mistrustful of the power of the Austro–Spanish Habsburg dynasty. At the time of my visit, I learned that he had audiences with numerous Protestant representatives. It is my belief, my lord, that we may have more success with a petition to the Holy Roman Emperor of the Catholic League."

The king listened attentively, his face impassive as the young envoy briefly shared the details of his meeting in Prague with King Ferdinand II and reported on the Bohemian king's desire and potential to reciprocate assistance to Sigismund Vasa if required. Jack also gave a synoptic account of the Pilsen siege.

When Jack had completed his report, the satisfied king thanked him and said, "Help yourself to a tankard, Andrzej, and lubricate your dry throat. Your news is not what I had hoped for; nevertheless, I will consider our options with my advisers." He swilled from his own vessel, spilling wine on his doublet, as he digested the salient points of Jack's account in silence for a long moment.

"I will speak with you again in a day or two. Make yourself comfortable and wait for my minister. He will make contact and direct you further. The palace remains at your disposal."

"You are most gracious, my kind liege," Jack bowed again. "I plan to monitor our uninvited and unidentified patient and am available at your pleasure."

The monarch smiled as Jack stepped back, saluting with his hand over his heart and head inclined. The Polish officer found the Cossack at the end of the table in discussion with a small group of officers.

"Ah, my friend!" Anton acknowledged Jack's

presence, swinging aside to include the young physician into the circle. Ensuring all were full with liquor, the Cossack reached for two small glasses and handed one to Jack, introducing him to the others. "Vashe zdorovie, gentlemen!" he toasted in Russian as they drained the vodka from their tilted cups.

Conversation continued, and there was general consensus that the Swedish king would accelerate his desire to further harass and invade Polish–Lithuanian lands. Jack listened patiently, agreeing generally with the flow of attitudes and opinions and realising that local sentiment in the capital of the Polish king was aligned with what he had heard and seen abroad over the past four months of travel.

Anton suddenly dug his elbow into Jack's ribs and stared ahead fixedly. Jack turned to him and followed his gaze, his attention ultimately captured by the young countess from earlier, who approached her chair across the table. The other officers, noting the distraction, fell silent and bowed to the attractive lady. Jack remained immobilised, managing only a faint, absent-minded smile after Volkov gave a second nudge to his ribs. Jack's mouth was hanging open again.

Easing her silk hand-purse from the back of her chair while avoiding Jack's gaze, the countess smiled apologetically at the inadvertent interruption. "Good night, gentlemen," she offered in a mellifluous, confident voice and turned to leave as the others reciprocated. Typical of his unashamedly incorrigible and guileless but well-meaning manner, Jack asked audaciously, "May I escort you to the door, or your carriage, or perhaps your apartment?" His starry gaze and hopeful words produced a laugh from the others.

"My father is waiting in the foyer, sir," the elegant noblewoman replied diffidently, her captivating eyes showing appreciation for Jack's frank boldness.

The young lieutenant moved hurriedly around the table to her side, spilling a goblet of wine in his haste. Ignoring it, he eased out an elbow. "The foyer it is, my lady. You never can quite tell what can happen in a place like this!" he joked, cocking his head. The countess accepted his invitation, and as she took his arm, he led her slowly towards the door.

"I believe that you are the Lady Pomorska?" Jack asked, looking for assent.

"Yes, I am. How did you know my name?"

"Ah, I have spies everywhere," Jack replied with feigned gravity. "And your father, the count, is related to the king?"

"Yes, he is. I am impressed with the diligence of your spies," the countess confirmed before adding, "And you are Lieutenant Andrzej Channing, a physician and envoy to the king?"

"How did you know that?" Jack asked with an admiring glance.

"I have spies everywhere," the countess reciprocated, her tone that of someone who had just won at cards.

The two laughed together as they reached the end of the hall and stopped at the doorway leading into the foyer.

"It would give me immense pleasure to see you again, my lady," Jack mustered all the sincerity he could for his request and looked beseechingly at her striking face.

After a brief moment of hesitation, the countess replied, "I live in the city with my parents. I am sure that you would be most welcome to visit my family. Are you staying at the palace?" Her stunning, anodyne eyes looked directly into Jack's for the first time, melting him away.

"Yes; for the next few days at least. I have further business with the king."

"Then I will send word," the countess replied with a disarming, insouciant smile and released Jack's arm. The Polish officer watched as she joined her parents and left.

Jack slept fitfully that night despite the distraction of his late-night visit to the wounded man. After he led Volkov to the infirmary, the two had met with the military surgeon and discussed the man's condition. There was no fever, and the intruder's dressing had been changed, although he remained insensible. They then made their way to their quarters where Jack bade farewell to Volkov at the Cossack's door and retired.

Restless and fevered, Jack dreamed of his countess. Her image appeared clearly in his mind. He marvelled at her breathtaking beauty, believing that she was modelled by the hands of ancient goddesses. Venus passed on her beauty, sprinkling her with prosperity and desire. Diana instilled the moon into her remarkable eyes and formed her lithe and slender body—that of a huntress—which was augmented by Feronia's gifts of health, abundance and freedom. Hecate enhanced the gems that were her eyes, through magic and witchcraft, rendering them with glittering green—nature's most tranquil and appealing colour. Minerva gave her wisdom—an intelligence and wit vibrantly plain on her face—while Athena prepared her for war with an unrivalled spirit, making her a defender of all that is good, and kind and gentle. Finally, the attributes of forgiveness and mercy donated by Clementia, were sealed with the peace and harmony granted her by the goddess Pax.

The morning activity outside Jack's window proved incapable of waking him, and it was Volkov's hammering on his door that finally stirred him.

"Breakfast, my friend?" the Russian called through the heavy timber, disappearing before Jack clambered out of bed and unlocked the door to let him in. The two ate sparingly, still content from last night's feast. As there was no need to hurry, they lounged at the breakfast table, sipping mugs of coffee prepared in the royal kitchen. Other officers came and went.

"I have a mind to visit that tavern in the northwestern corner of town. It's called *Złoty Miecz—The Golden Sword*. Do you know it?" Anton suggested as he chewed on a thick slice of ham.

"Yes, of course! We were there together, my Cossack friend," Jack replied indignantly. "You were so drunk that you couldn't remember if either one of us had been there."

Volkov slapped the table with an open palm, surprised at his own poor memory.

"You were keen on that serving wench, Gabriella, I seem to recall," Jack added for good measure.

"Absolutely! That's right. It was Gabby. What a woman! We both drank a lot that night. We staggered out after three in the morning and—"

"No. We stayed the night. The landlord showed me to a room with a comfortable bed, and you and Gabriella slept at the table. No one could wake either of you," Jack reminded the Cossack patiently.

"Then we came back the following evening and did

it all again," Volkov offered with confidence, proud of himself.

"You stayed. Gabby made us both a hearty breakfast. I came back to the palace to see the king and returned for you in time for dinner," Jack corrected, calling for another coffee.

"And did I stay the night?" Anton asked, obviously vague about the details and beginning to doubt himself.

"Yes. You fell asleep at the same table."

Volkov laughed, slapping his thigh. "We'll have to do it all again today."

The two men made their way to the infirmary to see the patient and stumbled on the physician in the surgery.

"Good morning, sir," they said, exchanging pleasantries, and Jack asked about the injured man's progress.

"He regained full consciousness soon after midnight, and I was called to examine him." The surgeon was a serious and dedicated man, circumspect in his views and sober in his judgment. Highly experienced, he had seen warfare first-hand while performing amputations and stitching and cauterising musket ball wounds in various field hospitals. He had seen action in the Polish–Swedish conflict of Kircholm—where he had first heard the Channing name—as well as at Kokenhausen, Biały Kamien, Rakvere, Salis and other campaigns in Livonia.

"His condition has improved markedly, and the swelling around his shoulder is beginning to ease," the physician continued.

"We have come to examine him briefly and—" Jack's vote of appreciation request was cut short.

"He was moved immediately after my examination by the night watch and taken to the dungeons for questioning, lieutenant," the surgeon interjected gravely.

The officers, surprised at the patient's early transformation into a prisoner, thanked the surgeon and made their way to the guardhouse. Introductions made to the guard, Jack stated their desire to visit the captive. Their request was transferred to the senior officer on duty, who recognised Jack immediately as the physician assisting with the outcome of last night's shooting in the dining hall foyer. They shook hands warmly.

"In my capacity as his attending physician and the king's envoy, we request permission to see the prisoner," Jack formalised his petition in a dulcet and charming tone.

"My apologies, lieutenant," the captain responded cordially, "but my orders are that he is to have no visitors."

"Yes, I understand, but we are not strangers, and I have a singular interest in the man's health," Jack continued with equal amicability.

"I can let no one through, sir, without written dispensation from the king himself." The officer was polite but insistent. "Those are my clear and strict orders."

It was a final word that Jack was not prepared to dispute any longer, so he thanked the captain, touching the brim of his hat and shaking his hand. As an officer, Jack understood the gravity of carrying out orders unquestionably. He knew quite well that he could approach the king for immediate approval but decided that he would play that card if he needed to later.

As they were about to leave, Jack half-turned to the senior officer and asked, "Can you recommend a decent tavern in the city, captain?"

"Of course, gentlemen," the captain replied with an amiable grin and a stroke of his moustache. "There are two that are very good: *Trzy Korony—The Three Crowns* and *Złoty Miecz*. The ale is better at The Three Crowns, but the other serves excellent mead— warmed if you prefer."

After thanking him, the two officers strode to the stables at a leisurely pace, enjoying the sunshine on what was a cool, autumn day. They agreed on the latter recommendation. It was almost midday when they entered the smoke-filled tavern. A fire blazed in the hearth, warming the far reaches of the cavernous room. The alcoves were empty with the exception of a couple of old men seated facing the burning logs, huddled in their own conversation. A sudden, piercing squeal shocked the new arrivals, forcing their gaze toward the kitchen. Out of the shadows near the serving bench, Volkov's favourite maid appeared. In typical Russian fashion, Anton half-crouched with extended, inviting arms—like a bear about to embrace its victim—and shouted, "Gabby, you voluptuous sinner! Come here and shower me with your erotic kisses!" Their theatrical greeting drew the attention of the two old patrons who peered across the room, perplexed.

Rapidly becoming a favourite and sentimental piece of furniture, Jack selected their usual table, settling into a comfortable armchair with his preferred view of the door. His sword belt, hat and cloak were hung on the hook behind him, but he kept his dagger hidden inside his left boot. Jack pondered the recent events surrounding the intruder in the dungeons, but as his thoughts drifted to the countess, Volkov appeared with his arms entwined around the barmaid, who was carrying several tankards of mead.

Anton dragged another armchair over, and Gabby

sat on his knee after he'd hung his weapons on the hook next to Jack's. She curled her arm around the Cossack's neck and hugged him affectionately, content as a purring cat.

"The captain was right. This mead is almost as good as Old Joseph makes at home," Jack observed, looking at his friend. Volkov turned to the girl and planted a seductive kiss on her milky neck, drawing a giggle. "Where are your customers, Gabby? The place is deserted. Perhaps everybody knows we're in town!" He laughed to himself.

"It's early still. The tavern will fill soon enough," Gabby replied, surveying the empty tables. "They'll start coming after three, and by six there won't be a spare bench in the room. We'll have another five girls serving by then."

Jack sat and nursed his mug after finishing an appetising lunch.

The Cossack, who was on his fourth drink, glared at his companion with mock anger from under a furrowed brow. "You're not in the mood to drink this wonderful nectar, my good friend? Don't be concerned; I'm drinking for both of us."

"No, I must keep a cool head. The king will summon me, but I don't know when. I sense that I'll be travelling far again—another diplomatic mission, I suspect." Jack's tone was pensive, his face sombre.

Gabby had left them earlier as patrons started to arrive. She had been correct; the inn was overflowing by nightfall. The ambience was relaxed and noisy, punctuated by frequent bouts of loud and hearty laughter. The barmaid joined the two men whenever she could, taking a healthy mouthful from the cup she left at their table.

Eventually deciding to walk back to the castle as he had no reason to make haste, Jack kissed the barmaid's cheek and slapped his companion affectionately on the back. The Cossack had plied himself steadily with mead interspersed with regular bolts of vodka, and when Jack stood to leave, he barely noticed, instead sitting slumped in his chair with one boot on the solid table and heavy head wobbling as if fixed to a metal coil.

It was a black, moonless night, the sky saturated with a sea of stars. The attendant retrieved Jack's horse from the stable behind the inn and happily accepted the copper coin the officer placed in his palm as he took the reins.

Although Abaccus had been left in Old Joseph's expert care at the Channing estate's stables, the physician had quickly reconsidered. Word had been sent home for his mount to be brought to the capital with the next available royal courier.

Jack decided to shorten the distance back to the

castle by cutting through a number of alleyways and led Abaccus over the echoing cobblestones at an ambling pace, turning into the first narrow, poorly lit row. Following this path led him past the rear access doors and loading ramps that fed the many stores and shops facing the main square. Crossing a number of intersecting laneways, he continued down the wynd until it opened into a quadrangle. This was fed by three narrow streets and surrounded by high walls and empty warehouses. A quaint water fountain operated by a hand pump stood at its centre, its small pool ringed by a wall two hands high. Two lanterns hung from wall brackets at opposite ends of the tiny square, casting a meagre, honey-coloured glow that barely illuminated the fountain.

Abaccus snorted, and Jack sensed trouble. He lingered at the edge of the yard, dropping the reins from his gloved hand. A vague movement from the distant gloom caught his eye; a gauzy figure stepped into the dim, golden haze, his naked sword flashing ominously. A moment later, a second figure appeared to the right of the first. Jack cursed the fact that there was insufficient time to fetch the pistols he had left in the saddlebag behind him before the caitiffs could reach him. *Spineless and aberrant thieves working as a pair,* he thought to himself.

As the shadowy figures advanced, Jack brandished

his rapier and stepped forward, away from his mount. The two cavaliers moved cautiously towards him, separated by the fountain. Their shadows, cast by the lanterns, were deformed and grotesque.

Jack knew that if he attacked one, the other would circle to flank him, and needing good light, he decided to stand and wait, aware of no danger from the lane he had just walked. Crouching slightly, he was ready for their move.

Both figures attacked simultaneously. They thrust at Jack's chest, allowing him to parry with a raised arm backhand sweep, pushing away their blades to his left. Pivoting on his front foot, Jack completed his block by rotating his body counter clockwise, further deflecting their swords. In the same fluid motion, he snatched the dagger from his boot with his left hand, and as he completed the turn, he drove the short blade deep into the groin of the assailant on the right. The man's guttural, hellish cry of agony momentarily distracted his companion, who retreated a few steps, disoriented by the sudden change in circumstances.

Jack faced the second man squarely; they were on equal terms now. Seizing the advantage, the officer advanced with his sword tip low. As the distance closed between them, he feinted with rapid, circular sweeps, pushing the dark figure back. His faceless opponent withdrew his dagger and lunged with his sword. Jack turned the blade aside with an open, gloved palm and countered, his thrust diverted by the man's dagger. They took a step back from each other and slowly circled a few cautious steps. Jack briefly glanced at the wounded swordsman; there was no movement.

As the second attacker jabbed at him, Jack flung his hat at the man's face and countered with an immediate plunge, stabbing at the shoulder of his temporarily distracted adversary. With a faint cry, the figure retreated, stepping hurriedly back, his sword arm clutching at his wounded shoulder. Although the man's features were hidden in murky shadow under his broad-brimmed hat, Jack imagined that there was a grimace of pain etched on his face. The place was silent, marked only by their heavy, rhythmic breathing.

The cavalier eventually withdrew to the far side of the font, never turning his back. He stood a long moment, his silhouette still and obscure, with the mellow meady glow of the lantern a halo behind him. He then raised the hilt of his sword to his lips in salute and vanished into the blackened recesses of the evening, returning the small square to the silence that initially enveloped them.

Sheathing his rapier, Jack bent guardedly over the

initial fallen figure and placed a firm hand over his motionless face. There was no reaction. He removed his glove and searched for a pulse; it was faint but unmistakable to a physician. Kneeling to one side to eliminate the shadow he had cast over the fallen figure, Jack withdrew his dagger from the man's body and whistled for his horse. The man's wound was serious, and blood had pooled onto the flagstones around him, but Jack was determined to keep the man alive. He hoisted him across the saddle, swathed with his blanket, and walked, hat in hand, the short remaining distance to the royal castle.

Attendants at the castle infirmary lifted the unconscious victim onto a bed and called for the surgeon. Jack ordered them to remove the man's clothing, and he inspected every piece, searching for the assailant's identity. He found no documents—only a lime-green scarf, which he hid inside his tunic. Taking the man's belt and weapons, Jack withdrew to his room, leaving the swordsman in the attendants' care.

A letter had been delivered during the day and thrust under Jack's door in his absence. The officer bent to collect it, and holding it to his nose, smiled as he flicked it onto the bed. The servants had lit a large, tallow candle in his chamber, which he used to light the other candles, filling the room with warm, silky light.

Hanging his hat and tunic in the passageway outside his door for the maid, Jack settled comfortably onto the bed in his shirt sleeves. He glanced at the letter on his right and then at his attacker's weapons on his left, hesitating. In the end, the decision was straightforward. No longer able to ignore the note, Jack broke the seal on the folded parchment and inhaled the perfume deeply, letting it pervade his senses. After reading the contents, he laughed aloud with a deep and involuntary stab of boyish excitement and rocked like a merry motley fool on the mattress. The anticipated invitation from the countess had arrived.

Laying the redolent message aside, Jack turned his attention to the rapier. It was a handsome weapon, and he immediately recognised the features of a German design: the curved knuckle guard was surrounded by a post arm at the base of the hilt arms, replacing the usual ring. The wire-bound grip had turksheads top and bottom, and sections of the pommel and guard were highlighted by raised acanthus leaf designs. Jack went on to examine the ricasso and then the forte of the blade. Closely inspecting either side of the fuller under the light of the brightest candelabra, he found the name *Johannes Mumm* unmistakably stamped in neat, tiny letters on the blade.

The assailant's dagger revealed similar design

aspects, and Jack guessed that both weapons had been made in Solingen at the turn of the century. The scarf, however, yielded no clues, remaining a mystery for now.

Jack stretched onto the bed and closed his eyes. Cupping the letter under his chin, his last thoughts were of the resplendent countess and her enchanting eyes.

Chapter 7

HOFBURG, VIENNA

Heavy rain had fallen overnight, and menacing grey clouds hung low, threatening further downpours. The early October days were becoming visibly shorter, and frequent cold gusts from the north signalled a bitter winter.

Wrapped in his heavy cloak, Jack shivered as he stepped out into the brisk, morning air. Puffs of vapour appeared like gossamer with his every breath. The smell of woody smoke from myriad chimneys hung in the damp air, reminding him of contented campfire gatherings in timbered forests with special friends. His steps echoed over the glistening flagstones as he sauntered to the stables and instructed the senior equerry to prepare his mount. He waited outside, back to the wind, pulling his hat down further and rubbing his gloved hands. His cloak flapped heavily in the biting breeze.

Abaccus whinnied with approval as Jack accepted the reins, and in accordance with the physician's request, was protected against the cold by a maroon caparison beneath his saddle. The officer patted the horse's forehead and slapped his neck before mounting him and then led him out of the palace at a steady walk. Metal-shod hooves rang in the courtyard.

As the address that Lady Marianna had given him in her letter was in the same district as the tavern, Jack retraced last night's route through the narrow streets and laneways, stopping at the small square with the font. Scenes captured at night seldom resemble those seen in the stark light of day, and the open space surrounding the fountain, which had seemed tight and cramped before, was somehow open and airy in the morning light. Jack dismounted to inspect the place in which his life had been seriously threatened fewer than 12 hours earlier. A solitary crow cawed sombrely as it passed overhead. All traces of blood had been washed away by the rain. The officer peered at the two lanterns hanging from metal sconces on opposite walls and then studied the alcove that had hidden his two assailants within its murky shadow. The buildings enclosing the courtyard stood lifeless even during the day. There was nothing to see.

Obtrusively situated along an attractive avenue, the countess' residence was one of many in a row of quaint three-storey buildings. It was well-maintained and had recently been repainted a pastel peach colour that enhanced its prominence against the two stark white structures on either side. This area of the city was well known for its high property values.

The count's valet appeared at the door in response to Jack's knock and invited him in, addressing him by name and bowing respectfully. The officer's cloak and hat were hung in the entrance hall and he was ushered into a warm, comfortable room, where the family was sitting. The count immediately rose to his feet, leaving a mess of documents strewn across the small table at which he had been busy, and thanking his servant, advanced with an outstretched, inviting hand.

Count Pomorski had a firm grip, and his hazel eyes exuded candid honesty as he warmly welcomed the visitor into his house. He was perhaps a year or two younger than Jack's father and was tall, lean and greying at the temples. He had retired from a distinguished military career and had been engaged by the king to gather and analyse intelligence—both military information and civilian data. Simply put, he was a spy.

With the limitless pool of resources available to him, the count had been researching the Channing family since the young physician had displayed his prominence two nights earlier at dinner with the king. The effect that his daughter had on the young officer had also not gone unnoticed, and the count was comfortable and satisfied with what he had discovered. He was a man with few true friends, but those few could trust him with their lives.

Relinquishing Jack's hand, the count swept an arm towards the two women seated beside him and stated, with overt pride, "May I introduce the two most important figures in my life? My wife, the Lady Barbara, and my daughter, Marianna—whom I believe you have already met." A hint of delectation touched the corners of his lips.

Jack bowed and delicately kissed both of the ladies' hands, lingering a fraction longer with the latter's.

"Please be seated," the count said, casually indicating at an armchair, "and make yourself comfortable."

Countess Barbara was a striking woman, and it was clear that her arresting green eyes had been passed down to her daughter. "We do not often receive visitors here that are as handsome and dashing as you, lieutenant," Lady Barbara laid the compliment at Jack's feet with the same candid sincerity that the officer had noted in her husband. "When Marianna suggested we invite you for refreshments, I was pleased to take advantage of the opportunity. I understand that your home is in Kraków?" Her voice was clear and mellifluent—laced with kindness.

"Indeed, my lady. I have unfortunately had little time at home of late but have managed to spend a number of days with my parents between engagements of duty," Jack replied.

Marianna's unrelenting gaze in Jack's direction was palpable. The officer glanced at her momentarily as he spoke, and she immediately averted her soulful eyes, blushing self-consciously.

"I am indeed fortunate," Jack continued, trying to maintain his concentration, "to have such a close and loving family. Our servants, who have been with us for many years, are my extended family. Many have been there since before I was born. As a boy, my education was broad and varied. Old Joseph taught me to fish and grow vegetables. I hunted with my father, and he passed on his fencing skills to me. He also tutored me in English. I learned to cook and sew buttons from my mother—and make my bed, of course," he added mischievously, drawing a laugh from his listeners.

The conversation flowed from there, and over an hour had passed before the countess remembered to bring in tea. She motioned to her daughter to summon the maid. As the clatter of cups and cutlery subsided, the count cleared his throat and gazed steadily at his young guest.

"Although we are both engaged in the king's

175

service, sadly there has been little opportunity in the past to become acquainted beyond the formal rigors of our respective professions. It is my responsibility," he continued in a tempered tone after a brief pause to choose the correct words, "amongst other duties, to support and protect the king's—and indeed the country's—security. I wish to tell you that, prior to this visit today, I had engaged a select small group to scrutinise your past, and I must tell you, my boy, that your record is impeccable."

Jack was stunned, unsure whether to be offended or pleased. Both women sighed audibly at this revelation, as surprised as he. The count continued, intent on fully clarifying his position. "The long-standing and utterly trustworthy relationship that your family has had with the king, through your father, is quite frankly irreproachable and rare. Additionally, this continued and laudable reputation carried on through you, his son, is as enviable as it is unsurprising. And I believe that this undivided loyalty has been justifiably and richly rewarded! You will appreciate that I must look after the interests of my daughter, my only child."

Jack's cheeks reddened from the unmitigated praise as the count's eyes held his without wavering. The count continued evenly. "As I was present during your report to the king following your journey to

Paris and have read the statements made by the intruder that you tended to, you must be aware that the king will charge you with the responsibility of another diplomatic mission, this time to Vienna. You will be advised imminently of the details of the next meeting with Sigismund Vasa and his council. I will be present as well."

Count Pomorski waited a moment, allowing the young officer to fully digest what was being said. Utter silence pervaded the room. "I was not surprised by the bland and guarded reaction that you received from Bishop Richelieu," he continued coolly after swallowing a mouthful of tea. "Our experience has led us to believe that he will side with whoever best suits his purposes at the time, be they Protestants, Catholics, or offshoots such as Calvinists and Lutherans." Approval crept into his smooth voice. "You suggested to the king that we may have more success in seeking Emperor Matthias' assistance and support, and he agrees. In fact, we all concur—hence your pending journey to Austria."

Jack's mind raced, his thoughts scattered, touching a score of possibilities at once. Finally, he levelled a question at his host. "Does a lime-green scarf hold any significance for you?"

The count stared at him with naked amazement, and Jack could see his thoughts play out. "Yes," he replied hoarsely. "Our friend in the dungeons carried one! It was found stuffed into his pocket."

The count struggled to follow the significance of the scarf. Jack immediately realised why he hadn't seen it as he dressed the man's wounded shoulder in the foyer that evening.

Replacing his cup on the tray, Pomorski rose and extended a beckoning hand to his wife. "We must leave and allow the two youngsters to discuss matters far less serious and melancholy." His face transformed, adopting a genuine smile. "We will have enough time to ponder these vexing issues later with His Highness. My daughter will see you out. Please take your time. You are most welcome in our home."

The count and countess took their leave as Jack bowed, thanking them for their hospitality. He welcomed the opportunity to be alone with the beautiful woman who remained a mystery to him. This had, ultimately, been the purpose of his visit.

Marianna met Jack's gaze, melting him away with her brilliant eyes. "Please sit down, lieutenant," she whispered with a disarming smile. Jack obeyed, docile as a puppy.

"I apologise for my father's brazen approach and must confess that Mother and I knew nothing of this. He is not easily a trusting man, a characteristic demanded by the draconian responsibilities of his astringent position," Marianna said smoothly, taking and refilling Jack's cup. "Yet he truly trusts you. This is abundantly obvious." Her dulcified tone gently pampered him and dissolved away any remnant, misconstrued feelings that may have lingered with him.She proffered the steaming cup, adding, "As his daughter, I know."

The two talked for many hours, time passing without the slightest care or consideration. There was everything to know about one other, and each one was as inquisitive as the other. They shared numerous moments in their lives—many filled with laughter, some tinged with sadness. Some were even moments that they had forgotten, that would have remained dormant. Greedy with a hunger for information, they asked—and answered—a thousand questions.

Suddenly, realising that the day had all but escaped them, Jack murmured in a sombre tone, his mood darkened with frustration. "It will be an eternity before I see you again if I must leave for the Austrian capital."

Marianna soothed Jack by placing a graceful hand on his. "I will be here when you return to Warszawa. And we can write," she added, seeking optimism. "Messages between here and Kraków leave and arrive daily."

With profound reluctance, Jack took his leave, mounting his horse in the steady drizzle. Marianna waved from the open doorway, ignoring the outside chill, and watched him disappear from view.

☒ ☒ ☒ ☒

The anticipated meeting to be convened by Vasa was held the following morning in the castle's spacious council chamber. The king sat in an ornately carved chair, resembling a small throne, raised on a dais, and his councillors occupied comfortable, cushioned armchairs spread around a large, polished table. Count Pomorski nodded a silent, cordial greeting to the officer.

Directing the proceedings, Sigismund began with the short, customary prayer and then introduced a small number of invitees, including his young envoy, to the regular members of the council. He summarised the current state of security and outlined a brief agenda for discussion. As a diplomat, Jack had only participated in a similar gathering once before, but the group had been smaller then and some attendees had remained nameless.

In response to the king's request for an updated report on the incident in the dining hall foyer, Colonel Lewandowski stood, firmly pushing his seat away from the table. As the senior officer of the king's guard, he was a formal, fastidious man of medium build with an irascible nature. A veteran of numerous campaigns, he had a penchant for garrison security, believing in rigorous and obdurately traditional methods.

In a gravelly, military voice, Lewandowski began. "The prisoner is Swedish and goes by the name of Halvar. He posed as a guest in an attempt to enter the banquet hall, and when questioned by my guard, he drew his pistol and was shot."

The colonel held his audience with a single, sweeping gaze, comfortable in the knowledge that he had performed his duty with proficiency and that his subordinates had prevented a disaster. "His upbringing was limited to farming life in a large Lutheran–Protestant family, and he has had no formal military training. His purpose here was to kill the king in defence of his own country's crown." Lewandowski paused as he looked up at the dais. A low rumble of indignant murmurs percolated around the table. "He has told us that he acted alone and confessed that his hatred was solely driven by Your Majesty's quest for the Swedish throne."

Sigismund, who remained thoughtful and unperturbed, waved at the assembly seeking questions. Jack waited out requests for details regarding the assassin's mental state, age and physical condition from various councillors and then asked, "What weapons did this Halvar carry?"

"A German-made wheel-lock belt pistol, a rapier and a dagger," Lewandowski replied stiffly after a brief examination of the sheaf of papers in his hand.

"What do we know about the origin of his sword and dagger?"

The colonel was perplexed by the question but stated that they appeared to be German in design.

"Thank you, sir," Jack offered in a mollified tone. "I trust that I may view them at the conclusion of these proceedings?" The senior officer smiled accommodatingly and resumed his seat after waiting a moment for further questions.

Sigismund looked to his head of security for comment, and Pomorski rose, confidently eyeing the wash of faces. "We believe, my liege, that an element has been formed to assassinate Catholic monarchs. Although the prisoner reportedly stated that his motivation was to punish Your Majesty's desire to regain the previously held throne of your nephew, King Karol IX Sudermanski, there could be more to this than a single, supposedly isolated incident of retaliation.

"The broad picture for the commonwealth is more complex in that we, unlike any other European entity, are at war with Russia and under threat from Sweden, the Ottomans and the Tartars. Central Europe may be on the verge of war. The continent is as turbulent as ever. We have heard the lieutenant's report on Pilsen and the ongoing and growing Bohemian unrest," the count pointed at the young envoy with an outstretched, open hand, "and we know that France cannot be relied upon as our ally. The Protestant Union has been dormant since its inception in 1608, but with Ferdinand carrying the Bohemian crown and pushing his aggressive, staunchly Catholic views, they may have become more militant in their endeavours to salvage their own religious identity. We must remain vigilant!"

The group immediately broke into a cacophony of debate until the king raised his hand, requesting silence.

"It is true and no secret that I refused to return to Sweden, after my dethronement by the Riksdag nine years ago, to become a Lutheran. I am a Catholic and believe that a Catholic crown should rule Swedish lands. I will continue to oppose my cousin, Gustavus Adolphus, as I did his father before him, to achieve what is rightfully mine. My envoy, Lieutenant Channing, has a question." Vasa stared at Jack with a raised chin, his face set in defiance.

Acknowledging the monarch, Jack began by

getting on his feet. "Gentlemen! I believe, and have it on good authority, that our prisoner Halvar carried a lime-green scarf in his pocket. On my return to the royal castle last night, I was attacked by two unidentified assailants after nightfall. One, I wounded, and I have him accommodated, under guard, in the infirmary; the other escaped. As yet, I know not why I was threatened and accosted nor by whom or on whose orders."

Jack reached into his tunic and produced the lime-green scarf. Holding it high for all to see, he added, "I took this from the wounded man. I have also closely examined his weapons. Both his rapier and his dagger were crafted in Solingen. He carried no pistol. I will shortly examine the prisoner Halvar's weapons to determine their make. We have already been informed by Colonel Lewandowski that he carried a German-made belt pistol. The evidence, thus far, appears to be pointing to a militant body of German origin. The Protestant Union is such a group."

The ramifications of Jack's logical, deductive sequence sparked a rush of incensed discussion, which the officer allowed to linger for some moments before raising a hand and calling for quiet so as to be allowed to continue. He looked briefly around the table before resuming. "We have to ask ourselves three questions. First, are those behind these attacks and who carry these green scarves, of German origin? Second, are they the Protestant Union? And finally, why?"

The chamber erupted once more into heated, garrulous discussion as Jack sat down, a frown fluting his forehead as he puzzled over the questions he had posed. Pomorski gazed at the young officer with bemused regard. Sigismund pensively pondered his remarks. Order was eventually restored in the council hall and a number of resolutions adopted, after minimal debate, including the young envoy's mission to raise a handful of important issues with the Holy Roman Emperor in Austria.

The count fell into step as Jack left for the guardhouse after the meeting. "I am interested to see what you find, Mr Channing. May I accompany you?" The pair marched across the open courtyard to speak with the captain on duty, who scurried off to retrieve the scarf and weapons belonging to the Swedish prisoner. Colonel Lewandowski joined them as the objects were placed on the table.

Jack laid his unfurled scarf next to the prisoner's.

"Made from the same cloth, it seems," the count observed. The swordsmith's inscription on the blades confirmed that both of the prisoner's weapons had been made in Solingen. Their design mirrored that of the weapons in Jack's room.

"*Cresit Eundo—the picture grows as it goes*," stated the count.

"*Domine Dirige Nos—the Lord guides us*," Jack responded.

A week passed before letters of introduction for the envoy's visit to the Austrian court were prepared. Compelled to wait, Jack looked to occupy himself in various productive ways. During days that were dry, he would fence with his Russian friend, perfecting his defensive and attacking techniques. One morning, he led the Cossack to the courtyard to show him where he had been set upon, but the scene offered no further clues to the second pair of scrutinising eyes.

Despite the severity of the wound inflicted to Jack's assailant, the man showed gradual signs of recovery, and Anton and Jack took turns questioning him at the infirmary.

The man told them that his name was Günter Hauf and revealed that he was born in Nuremberg, a strong Calvinist region in the Upper Palatinate. His weapons and scarf had been offered as the initial payment for accepting the task to kill "the black cavalier," although he could not explain the reason why or who wanted Jack dead. Further payment would be made in gold once the task was successfully completed, after submitting Jack's black hat and rapier as proof. When questioned further on the significance of the scarf, Hauf gave a feasible and simple explanation confirming that it was used as identification between the two swordsmen sent to murder Jack as neither knew anything of the other.

On days drenched in rain, Jack would spend time with Marianna or play chess with her father. The count proved a formidable strategist—shrewd and astute—leaving Jack struggling with the few rare opportunities he seized to win. The lieutenant treated these as invaluable lessons that later sustained his success in games against his father. Evenings were frequently lost at the Złoty Miecz, although Volkov became more prudent with his drinking. Gabby proved to be a loyal and genuine friend and all but Anton could see her love for him. She would often volunteer pieces of information that seemed insignificant in isolation but later proved helpful. Her perceptive eyes and ears were invaluable in obtaining this intelligence as she meandered throughout the inn serving loose-lipped customers and joking with boasting patrons.

Having prepared the travel papers, the king's secretary sent word on the sixth day after the meeting that he wished to meet with the Polish officer. In the administrative chambers, Jack received signed documents stamped with the official seal in red wax in addition to the final instructions regarding his journey to Austria and Bohemia. A leather purse containing a generous amount of mixed coins would cover his expenses.

The objectives of his assignment were simple: He would need to entice Emperor Matthias to pledge military assistance, both in troops and funds, against the commonwealth's enemies and to warn King Ferdinand of the existence and purpose of the Green-Scarf Fraternity.

Taking this opportunity to return the coach to Vilém and his king in Prague, Jack and Anton had their horses fastened at the rear of the carriage as it rumbled over the flags and cobbles on its intended journey through Piotrków, Częstochowa and Brno on to Vienna. Progress proved slow. Early signs of the pending winter were evident with roads becoming muddy bogs in heavy rain and the first light falls of snow.

Before leaving the Polish capital, the carriage made a scheduled stop at Jack's request to allow the officer to bid farewell to Marianna and her family. Aware of Jack's plans for some time, Marianna had prepared herself for his prolonged absence, but she found the parting difficult now that it had become a reality. Her mother left an affectionate kiss on Jack's cheek as she pushed a small, silver crucifix into his palm. The count squeezed his hand firmly and then pulled him in, slapping his back. He had grown to like and respect the boy and increasingly treated him with fondness, as though Jack were the son he never had.

On the verge of tears, Marianna hastened into his arms and buried her face in his shoulder. They stood trammelled in each other's arms, and as she moved away, she handed him a perfumed handkerchief, which he thrust into his sleeve. He kissed her cheeks tenderly, stroking her blond hair as she stepped back into his embrace and held him fast.

"We must away!" Volkov yelled from within the car with the sensitivity of a stampeding herd of cattle. "A few weeks and we'll return before the winter snows fall in Warszawa. It will be time to introduce Gabby to your countess, and the count can play checkers at the Złoty Miecz. There, we will carve our names into the table and will all drink vodka till we drop." His words successfully banished the sullen mood, causing everyone to laugh, and the two soldiers rolled away as the carriage driver cracked his whip over the team of eager horses. Abaccus and Volkov's rusty-black Friesian followed, bridled to the coach by long leather straps.

The journey was ambling, with progress impeded by long, alternating stretches of dank forest and open ground made marish by passing sleet and damp wind. The carriage's occupants slept for prolonged periods, lulled by the rhythmic swaying of the coach and were occasionally called upon to assist in guiding the wheels over particularly sticky segments of terrain. The coachmen often used their discretion in steering the team off the road for short stretches to avoid especially boggy patches of ground. Such inclement progress was not only a symptom of the poor road conditions but also of the subsequent drained stamina of the horses.

The tortuous odyssey took almost two weeks, and it was late October when the mud-splattered coach trundled into the walled city of Vienna. The capital of Austria—a remarkable European centre of artistic and scientific endeavour—thrived with the culture of royalty, diversity and scholarship. The circular, star-shaped city was protected by battlements containing impressive bastions and a formidable moat, and its walls were built in a circle that enveloped several monastic complexes and numerous Gothic churches, with the notable St Stephen's cathedral marking the city's precise centre. Cradled within two arms of the Danube and with the Viennese woods to the west, the city provided a nearby princely hunting ground for the local aristocracy. The metropolitan character of early 17th century Vienna was evident in the impressively tall buildings and intriguing narrow lanes, which brought a vibrant, urban quality to the lives of its residents. It lay at the continental crossroads of itinerant diplomats, scientists, artists and courtiers.

With the Hofburg Palace being the residence of the Holy Roman Emperor, building activity and leading architectural design within Vienna was heavily influenced by the court, church and nobility. Neither Volkov nor Jack had seen the city before. They marvelled at the impressive architecture, cleanliness and structured layout of this ancient seat of the House of Habsburg. Lodgings had been arranged for them not far from the university, an establishment that Jack remembered was almost as old as the Uniwersytet in Kraków.

Rested and presentable, the two officers were ushered into an ante-chamber in the west wing of the Hofburg Palace that contained an ornate sofa and matching chairs. Their wait was brief. The doors opposite them opened, and a palace servant bowed as he stood off to the side, implying that they should proceed. Jack and his companion nodded in acknowledgment as they strode past him into a larger room. It was bare except for a small desk and three sumptuous armchairs covered in soft, burgundy velvet that had been arranged in an intimate circle at the far end. Although no fire burned in the grand fireplace, the stately room was comfortably warm and strangely soothing.

A middle-aged woman of slender build stood beside the handsome walnut writing table, her hands, holding documents, clasped together in front of her. She was fastidiously dressed in an immaculate full-length tawny gown whose high neckline disappeared beneath a circular, starched lace collar. Conforming to the conservative fashions associated with contemporary royalty, she wore a matching long-flowing embroidered jacket, sleeveless so as to reveal the loose sleeves of her luxurious satin gown with its shoulder wings. Her laced cuffs matched the gown's reticella collar. A chain of office hung from her neck, and in her auburn hair, she wore the imperial crown.

The woman waited patiently, her sallow face serene and impassive, watching the officers' approach with large brown eyes. A woman of delicate features, she was not attractive, yet her regal bearing had a certain charming appeal. With plumed hats in hand, the two comrades stopped at an appropriately respectful distance and bowed. She studied each face for a moment, her placid eyes finally returning to and resting on the Polish cavalier. "Lieutenant Channing, I believe?"

Jack acknowledged her soft and even voice with a wordless smile.

"I am the Holy Roman Empress, queen consort of the Romans, Hungary and Bohemia; archduchess consort of Austria. To my people, I am known as Anna of Tyrol and the wife of Emperor Matthias, cousin to King Ferdinand II."

"Your Imperial and Royal Majesty, I am indeed Andrzej Channing, as you have correctly identified despite this being our first meeting," Jack replied courteously, introducing his silent companion and adding in a clearly impressed tone, "I detect an Innsbruck inflection. Am I correct, madam?"

The empress sparkled with amusement, momentarily disarmed and shedding her customary august manner. Moving gracefully to one of the armchairs, she indicated the others with a pale hand, her face fixed in a half-hidden smile.

"I have your letters of introduction," the empress said, briefly glancing at the documents on her lap, "and must sincerely apologise on the emperor's behalf. My husband is not well and has been bed-ridden for some weeks. I fear that his body is surrendering to God, and his mind also fails him often—more frequently now, it seems, than in the past. He is no longer young and finds it difficult to grasp the continuity of those daily tasks expected of his office."

The empress studied the men before her with profoundly sad eyes. "I am doing what I can in sharing his imperial duties." She averted her eyes, glancing down at the floor, and whispered, "Perhaps had we had children, our circumstances may now have been different." Her voice trailed off wistfully, leaving the thought behind in the silent room.

Her hand stemmed a sudden coughing fit, covering her lips with her handkerchief. "My apologies, gentlemen," she continued after regaining her composure. "How can Our Imperial Majesties assist your Catholic king?"

The desires and wishes of Sigismund Vasa and his council were explained in succinct but sufficient detail, supported by clarification of the Polish Commonwealth's vulnerability to continued ingressions from marauding neighbours to the east and north. The outcome of the envoy's visit to France and more recent discussions with King Ferdinand had brought on another bout of coughing. After struggling to restore her self-control, the empress hissed a vehement reply. "I told Ferdinand that I see clearly that my husband is living too long for him: is this the thanks he gets for having given him two crowns?" Her eyes were suddenly ablaze like two smouldering coals.

The Bohemian crisis had steadily deepened after the overt attack on Slavata and the other members of the Chancellery administration. Matthias, irenic and moderate, believed that an aggressive, hard-fisted approach was counter-productive and had requested that his head of the Privy Council, Cardinal Melchior Klesl, negotiate with the Protestant confederates.

Born into a hard-working, Protestant family in the city, Klesl had attended the University of Vienna and studied philosophy under the Jesuits. He and his parents eventually converted to Catholicism and at the age of 25, he received his minor orders. Two years later, he was ordained as a priest and became a doctor of philosophy and provost of St Stephen's in the capital, a prestigious position that carried with it the chancellorship of the university.

Klesl's inviolable faith caught the attention of Rudolph II, Emperor Matthias' predecessor, who channelled the priest's fervour in a successful campaign against Protestantism, making it the cleric's life's work. A short, intense man, Klesl ascended to the rank of Bishop of Vienna and was nominated cardinal, an apposite choice that recognised his dedication, two years prior to the Prague defenestration.

The bond between Klesl and emperor Matthias was immutable, and although the cardinal's staunch support of Habsburg imperial succession was unwavering, he was seen as hostile to the imminent candidature of Ferdinand II as Holy Roman Emperor.

His position with the Protestants was hardened and less flexible than that of his emperor, yet he was prepared to negotiate a mutually acceptable outcome.

Although the Protestants were offered generous terms in return for laying down their arms, they rejected Klesl's conditions. It was well known that the cardinal wanted to raise an army in order to force the rebellion into submission, and almost four months later on 1 July 1618, he became the victim of an unsuccessful assassination attempt when a bullet narrowly missed his head during the banquet celebrating Ferdinand's coronation as king of Hungary.

Although Klesl had the Habsburg Emperor's endorsement, his approval with the church began to wane, and he appeared to be so discredited among the Protestants that his continued presence as a strategist and negotiator was seen as inhibitive to reaching a satisfactory compromise. King Ferdinand became increasingly impatient with Klesl, and eventually the Papal Nuncio persuaded Archduke Maximilian to remove the cardinal from office and nullify his position of power.

A secret meeting was arranged at the Hofburg on 20 July wherein Klesl was seized by Colonel Dampierre and imprisoned at Schloss Ambras, a castle situated in the Tyrolean hills overlooking Innsbruck. His amassed personal wealth of 300,000 florins was taken by the crown. The bedridden, addlepated Matthias could do nothing.

Anna of Tyrol struggled to control her outburst and glanced apologetically at her young visitors. Her mood became pensive. "My lords, we understand your nation's position and the request of His Most Royal Majesty, the Catholic King of Poland and Lithuania, but with all honesty, our situation is..." She hesitated, searching for the correct phrase, "*compromised* by my husband's health and the removal of our trusted friend, Cardinal Klesl."

There was an urgent, albeit respectful, rap at the door through which the two soldiers had entered. Following a brief moment, a valet appeared, bowing without speaking, and approached the seated woman while carrying a highly polished silver tray. The empress took the note with a nod, and dismissing the servant, broke the seal with a slide of her hand. Her face became ashen after she read the letter, although she remained unsettlingly calm.

"Are you unwell, madam?" Jack's voice was saturated with concern. Both he and Volkov stared at the now frail woman whose dour demeanour heralded ill tidings.

"It is from Überlingen. My half-brother Karl, Margrave of Burgau, is seriously ill. His physicians do not expect him to live more than a week and suggest that his family and close relatives prepare for the worst. This is sad news. I must pray for him."

Uncomfortable in the awkward and private moment, Jack replied with forced optimism. "I am certain that his doctors are doing all that can be done for him."

Before the officer could continue, the empress was seized by another racking coughing fit, which she smothered with her white kerchief. Jack caught a glimpse of bright blood on the kerchief as she lowered it slowly, unaware, and cradled it on her knees, looking at them with controlled despair.

"You are not well, my lady." Jack was bold, speaking now as if to a patient. "Are you suffering from consumption? I see the blood blotting the material you hold."

The empress peered down with perfunctory eyes at the cloth in her hands and then looked back at Jack with resignation. "I am told that it has reached an advanced stage," she replied, visibly shaking off her vulnerable air and returning to her customary bearing of regal dignity. Then she stood, supporting herself with the arms of her chair, and the two men immediately rose to their feet.

"I must attend my husband and am sure that you will forgive this premature parting," the empress said. "It has been indeed a pleasure to meet you, and I can only suggest that you re-evaluate the matter with King Ferdinand. I will arrange for one of my marshals to minister to your needs during the remainder of your stay."

The officers bowed as their hostess left the room. The chamber fell silent, the lingering scent of perfume the only hint of their failed meeting with the empress.

Volkov dropped back into his chair, lounging with legs outstretched and crossed comfortably at the ankles. He was silent, with his fingers absently drumming the ends of the chair's elegantly carved arms.

Jack strolled slowly across the parquetry floor, studying the room with hands clasped behind him. The room's stark white walls and matching doors were ornately patterned, each bevelled recess trimmed in contrasting gold. He paused and gazed at the ceiling, impressed by the pattern of interconnecting timber panels, some protruding and others receding. He marvelled at the patience and detailed workmanship that the operose artisans had invested in this single, unassuming room and contemplated the time that would have been spent in the construction of such a magnificent palatial building.

Jack's distant thoughts were dashed by the sudden opening of the door behind him. He and Anton turned in unison as an immaculately uniformed officer entered past the bowing footman. The Russian sprang to his feet as the tall, thin soldier strode towards them. A man approaching 40, the soldier had dark hair combed back to reveal his broad, tanned forehead. Aligned with the current fashion at court, his triangular beard was neatly trimmed into a point below his chin. His most noticeable feature, however, was his enormous moustache, which was cropped meticulously under his nose but spread symmetrically in a luxuriant, bushy mass across each cheek, giving him the image of a hirsute boar with oversized tusks. The high-ranking officer wore the insignia of an Austrian cuirassier, his body armour replaced by a sombre, sleeveless tunic covered at the neck by a pointed gorget mirroring the contours of his beard. A stiff, plain linen collar surrounded his neck.

The soldier stopped in the middle of the room, his indurate gaze moving from Anton to Jack with the demeanour of an undertaker. Giving a curt nod, he introduced himself in an incisive tone of voice. "Colonel Henry Duval, Count of Dampierre, Cuirassier Commander charged with the suppression of the Bohemian uprising." His commendable German was tinged with a strong French accent. "Her Imperial Majesty has requested that I reinforce her apology for bringing your meeting to an early end and sincerely hopes that if your stay at the capital allows it, she would most cordially invite you to share refreshments, with the hope of arranging a meeting with her husband should his health improve."

Jack bowed and explained his and Anton's purpose in Vienna, confirming their hope that improved circumstances would permit a second audience with the empress. He omitted any reference to her health.

In line with the count's brusque and formal manner, the three officers continued their discussion while standing in a tight circle. Dampierre explained that King Ferdinand had taken up residence at the Hofburg a number of weeks earlier in order to prevent his safety from being compromised by the pervading uncertain attitudes of the Protestant masses in Bohemia, and especially in Prague. Vilém Slavata and a core group of the king's regents, supported by loyal administrative personnel and a veteran contingent of guards, remained at Hradčany.

Jack sought news of Pilsen. The colonel reported that his latest updated news confirmed that the siege was continuing and the city had remained resolutely firm. Písek, Krumlov and Budějovice remained the only other Bohemian towns under the empire's control. The rest of the country was more or less under Protestant governance.

Following a period of prolonged vacillation,

Ferdinand II had affirmed Charles Bonaventure de Longueval compte de Bucquoy to the post as commander of the imperial army. A Frenchman like Dampierre, Bucquoy had accepted the honour and responsibility a second time. Emperor Matthias had persuaded him into the role four years earlier, coaxing him out of retirement. He had moved from his birthplace of Arras in northern France and served with Habsburg forces at Flanders in the Spanish Netherlands as a young man. Quickly promoted to the rank of colonel at the age of 26, he had fought at the Battle of Nieuwpoort and the Siege of Ostend at the turn of the century and distinguished himself as general of the artillery.

Following Dampierre's return from Innsbruck after his incarceration of Klesl, Duval had been ordered to reinforce the three towns loyal to the king and secure the Linz–Prague road. He would be leaving within a matter of days. When questioned about any activity by a militant splinter group carrying lime scarves that may threaten the life of the king, Dampierre reacted with surprise and ignorance. Nevertheless, Jack pressed him to pass a hand-written note to his monarch warning of the group's possible danger.

As the three officers conversed in the comfortable Hofburg room, Bucquoy was making his way north to render long overdue assistance to the loyal population of the city of Pilsen.

Chapter 8

The inhabitants of the Austrian capital lay huddled and shivering, vexed by the icy fingers of a bitter north wind. Jack and Volkov had taken their leave of Colonel Dampierre, and eschewing the carriage drive back, made their way on foot from the Hofburg to the first inviting tavern that they passed in the direction of the university and their lodgings. They strode mercurially along the polished cobbles, holding their hats securely with one hand while clasping their cloaks tightly around their necks with the other. Their ruddy cheeks burned from the wind, which was laced with the memory of the Arctic snow that gave birth to it.

Anton leaned against the tavern's heavy, timber door and held it open as his companion hurried past him. A gelid gust of wind almost pushed them inside, momentarily drawing the sullen ire of those seated nearby. The fawning inn-keeper, girdled in a leather apron, ushered the two to a table that Jack had pointed out and promised that their meals and wine would be delivered from the kitchen presently. He lit the two squat candles on the heavy table with a burning taper and wiped away the remnant crumbs with a dampened cloth, inviting his new guests to make themselves comfortable with a gap-toothed smile.

Volkov slumped into the nearest chair and pulled at the fingers of his gloves as the physician slung his cloak over the back of an armchair that faced the doorway. They were tired, hungry and eager for a draught stronger than the wine that would accompany their food. This was the Cossack's specialty, and without wasting another moment, he cast around the vast, smoke-filled room and caught the eye of the nearest barmaid.

"Do you know anything about this Compte de Bucquoy?" Jack asked with raised eyebrows, fiddling with the wax that had hardened on the tabletop.

His friend thrummed on the trestle as he looked up at the smoke-stained ceiling, gathering his thoughts. "I have heard the name but will cast around the barracks for something more than what the colonel offered."

"It is pleasing to hear that he is on his way with a relief force to Pilsen." Momentarily distracted by a loud spate of gutteral laughter from the sweat-stained churls at the neighbouring table, Jack smiled tightly at Anton and then added, "I have a mind to join Dampierre and his cavalry. For the scenery, shall we say? From Písek, it's no more than a day or two on horseback. We could enter the city through the gate that led me out. Our presence could be of value to the mayor and his defenders."

The Polish officer sat quietly in thought, pondering the options as he tapped the wooden base of the antlered candlestick. "Or we could catch up to Bucquoy and assist from outside the walls?" he posited, looking for agreement from the Russian.

Noncommittal, Volkov dragged an empty chair closer with the toe of his boot and crossed his outstretched legs on the seat. He leaned back with hands clasped behind his neck as the buxom maid appeared with their schnapps. He watched her with admiring eyes as she set the tumbler and two small glasses in front of them, smiling alluringly at him. Wasting no time, he poured out two rounds and they drained them summarily.

Large plates steaming with hot pork and bacon-topped cabbage accompanied by generous slices of dark, fresh bread soon arrived. Nourishing their neglected appetites, the two men ate in silence following the clinking of their first raised glasses of dusky, burgundy wine.

Shortly after midnight, Jack rose from the table

to stretch his legs, comfortably full and relaxed by the alcohol he had consumed. Volkov waved him away with a dismissive hand, his discordant singing with the handful of other merry patrons unbroken. As the evening deepened, the Russian's drinking tempo inevitably increased. His solemn and laconic mood rapidly dissipated, and he was soon engaged in gregarious discussion with those at adjacent tables. Jack laughed at his friend and returned to his seat. The barmaids began to ferry larger pitchers of wine interspersed with jugs of vodka more frequently to their table. In true, inimitable Cossack fashion, Volkov managed, without once rising from his chair, to assemble a small choir around his armchair. The resulting repertoire of stirring military songs and emotive ballads spanned at least four languages.

The warbling group sipped from their bottomless mugs at the end of each tune, and at one point, the inn-keeper joined them for a lengthy German bracket. Jack embraced the amicable ambience, on occasion suggesting a Polish melody his mother had taught him. Like the other tunes, these were taken up immediately without interruption. Two of the serving maids, originally from the Dnieper valley, lent their mellifluous voices to a number of beautiful and haunting Russian folk songs, bringing a semblance of nostalgic melancholy to the silenced, scattered audience listening around the vast room.

It was late when Jack moved to retire, slapping his friend's cheek genially and leaving a handful of coins with the landlord. The innkeeper bowed as he pocketed the payment. Jack leaned closer to his ear and complained, "We have a problem with your liquor." Shock and disbelief immediately replaced the taverner's complacent contentment before Jack added, "There's too much of it," and he departed as they both laughed. His lazy stroll to his lodgings was uneventful. The cutting wind had died, making the short walk comfortable and pleasant. His restless mind gradually settled as he lay in bed, his thoughts eventually succumbing to the sleep his body craved.

Unrelenting, impatient banging on the door woke Jack from his deep sleep. Daylight strained through the gaps in the drapes around the window as the officer languidly rose to answer the door, wondering how long he had slept. The door swung open, creaking on its hinges, and the Russian appeared across the corridor, leaning against the wall. His arms were smugly crossed on his chest, and he eyed his sleepy friend through slitted, smiling eyes. His face was set in mock admonishment. Pushing off the wall, Anton strode into the room without a word, heading directly to the window to draw the curtain.

The sudden glare made Jack wince. He buried his contorted face in his forearm, shoving the door shut behind him with his bare heel.

"Good morning to you, sir!" Jack managed, squinting at the Cossack after warily lowering his arm. There was a hint of annoyance in his voice. "You smell like you've fallen into a vat of vodka."

Choosing to ignore the sarcasm, Anton put his left hand up behind his ear. He turned his head so that his fingers pointed to his earlobe in open view. "Do you like it?" he asked, proud of himself. "Lucy gave it to me this morning. It's pure silver—as precious to me as her lovely heart." A small metal cross swung from a tiny ring threaded through his pierced lobe, flashing as it caught the shaft of light streaming into the room.

Jack passed a hand through his hair, yawning. It was fashionable for men to wear earrings at court although strictly forbidden for military personnel. "Your head has always dipped to the right," he commented. "Perhaps this will help to even things out?"

Realising that the gift was wasted on his Polish friend, Volkov opted to change the topic. "As it is already past midday, your greeting is inappropriate," he corrected pedantically. "I have managed to gather some interesting news from the senior officer of the guard on duty at the barracks. He has Russian blood in him on his mother's side. It is unlikely that Dampierre chose to hide behind a deceptive cloak of ignorance. Apparently, quite simply and genuinely, he was unaware that two intruders had, on separate occasions, made attempts on the lives of the emperor and the king. He was at Innsbruck, after all, locking Klesl away. Interestingly, both assassins carried lime-green scarves."

Jack, who was pulling on his breeches, immediately gave his undivided attention to the Russian.

"One had posed as a cook in the royal kitchen and had revealed under interrogation that he was poisoning the food. As Matthias has been secluded in his bed with illness, the tainted food had gone uneaten. However, when the king's favourite dachshund succumbed after being fed the Emperor's untouched meal, the alarm was raised and the culprit apprehended. He is evidently Hungarian-born and had travelled to the capital from Pozsony, just up the Danube across the border. There have been recent anti-Habsburg uprisings in the city, and he cited a hatred of Catholic monarchists as the reason for his aggression." Anton further revealed that his name was László Szarka and that his pistol, rapier and two daggers had been confiscated. Although his family was Catholic, he considered himself an atheist.

The other, more recent attempt had been carried out by Kadir Tekin, a devout Mohammedian, who had been living in Budapest in Turkish Hungary. He wanted to kill men in power for political reasons and was not motivated by religious differences. His optimistic attack on the king's royal coach was easily quashed by the accompanying cavalry escort, and he died on the road outside Vienna without speaking or regaining consciousness.

"Anticipating your insatiable desire for detail, especially regarding the origin of their weapons, I was taken to the armoury and examined both sets myself," Volkov said. "All were crafted in Westphalia, as we've seen with the others previously. Their scarves, unsurprisingly, were identical."

Jack had donned his shirt and sat on the bed listening intently to his friend's news. The Russian had additionally discovered that following the defenestration, the Habsburgs had interrupted and deciphered every letter from the Protestant rebellion leaving Prague for a foreign destination. This revealed that, in August, the Duke of Savoy had offered Frederick, the Elector Palatine and representative of the Protestant Union, the services of the regiment that Count von Mansfeld had raised for him. Frederick had graciously accepted, and the troops were moved into the Principality of Ansbach, where they were quartered until September, after which they were ordered to capture the stronghold of Pilsen. Together with the attempt on Vilém Slavata's life, these were seen as the first distressing signs of a determined move to replace Ferdinand as king. Frederick of the Palatinate was the primary contender, but a list of other aspirants included the Duke of Savoy, the warring Bethlen Gabor of Transylvania and the Elector of Saxony—all powerful men wishing to expand the prominence and power of Protestant authority throughout central Europe.

Surreptitiously impressed with his friend's assiduous efforts at gathering information, Jack asked less caustically, "How is your voice after last night's performance?"

Chuckling to himself, the Cossack replied, "Splendid! It was well lubricated."

"You know, Volkov, your talents as a drinker are only partly utilised. With such a vast wealth of alcoholic experience, you could earn a handsome living by writing drinking songs and become illustriously prosperous," Jack ventured convincingly.

Seeking out the Count of Dampierre proved to be no straightforward matter. The colonel directed all preparations for the imminent departure of his cavalry himself. These included assembling provisions for his men and horses, obtaining letters from the king for the mayor of each destination town and taking advice on which routes to use from recently accumulated accounts. Jack finally managed to locate Dampierre leaving an assembly of officers at the Hofburg late that afternoon. After a lengthy and sedulous negotiation, the French officer gave his permission for Jack and Anton to accompany his force.

On the still and foggy morning of the second of November, Dampierre's regiment of cuirassiers, resplendent in full armour, rode out of the western gate of Vienna for southern Bohemia. The two officers accepted the colonel's request that they ride ahead of the column, immediately behind Dampierre and his own officers. Unimpeded by infantry, the cavalry unit was expected to reach Krumlov within five to six days, with an additional day to reach Budějovice, covering a total distance of 36 leagues. From there, the plan was to move the force to Písek and on to Pilsen.

The road between the capital and Linz proved to be in excellent repair, and progress was initially smooth and expeditious. There were long stretches where the road closely followed the river, and as they trotted along the embankment with the current, the officers were rewarded with beautiful sights of cascading water that boiled white over rocks in some places and flowed gently and peacefully in others. The river's surface was like a smooth, reflective sheet of azure and green ice.

Bucquoy had departed from Vienna over two months earlier, his objective to reach Prague and then Pilsen. His force crossed the bridge that led from the northern portal of the walled city and spanned the Danube, and then moved into South Moravia, fording the river Dyje at Znojmo. Passing the silver-mining village of Jihlava, his men continued through Chotěboř, intending to press on to Kolín along the meandering Elbe River and then advance west to Prague.

While Bucquoy's troops marched north, the head of the confederate Bohemian army, Heinrich Matthias Graf von Thurn, had abandoned his sieges of numerous Habsburg strongholds and entrenched his force at Čáslav, which lay on the road between Chotěboř and Kolín. There he blocked Bucquoy's advance into the Elbe valley, dashing the latter's plans to seize and bring Prague back into imperial hands. The ensuing stalemate created mounting pressure for Bucquoy, whose food and munitions supply lines were frequently broken by local Bohemian peasants loyal to the Protestant cause. Weighing his options, he eventually withdrew and moved his soldiers southwest towards Budějovice. Meanwhile,

Mansfeld's besieging army at Pilsen was augmented by the arrival of 2000 fresh Swiss mercenaries from Italy and Ansbach in addition to 3000 Silesians under the leadership of the Margrave of Jägerndorf.

On the fourth day since their departure, Jack and Dampierre's cuirassiers reached Linz. Founded and named Lentia by the Romans, the city was an important trading point, connecting several routes to and from neighbouring countries, as well as an important seat of provincial and local government.

During his visit to the French court, Jack had learned that Johannes Kepler—a prominent astronomer and eminent mathematician who taught mathematics at his home in the city—had determined the third law of planetary motion. Had he not been pressed for time and under different circumstances, Jack would have seized the opportunity to visit and meet the venerable philosopher as he passed through.

Dampierre's mounted troops entered the fortress of Krumlov on the morning of the sixth day. At Bucquoy's orders earlier in the year, Dampierre had installed a garrison of infantry there and at Budějovice. This bold stratagem had saved the two loyal towns from being overwhelmed by Thurn's army. Riders had confirmed the night before that the imperial count was marching towards Budějovice to make a stand against Thurn, who was in close pursuit. Jack advised the French colonel that he would be leaving to ride north to the next town with the intention of waiting for Bucquoy. After a scant breakfast, he and Volkov were gone within the hour. Dampierre was to follow the next day.

The two riders covered the five leagues comfortably, reaching their objective by early afternoon. They advised the commanding officer at Budějovice that the cuirassiers would arrive the following day. In turn, the officer informed them that Bucquoy's aide-de-camp had been despatched with news confirming that Bucquoy was less than half a day's ride northeast but would be quartered for the night near the village of Lomnice Nad Lužnicí.

As twilight on the eighth of November settled on the small hamlet on the left bank of the Lužnice River, the two officers cantered into Bucquoy's camp. His army was preparing to bivouac between two large lagoons near the road, leading southwest to the town from where they had come.

Easily visible in the fading light, a tall, canvas tent had been erected for the count, which directed the new arrivals to the general's quarters. An adjutant stepped forward to steady the two men's horses as they dismounted, heeding their request to report to the commander. The aide-de-camp, a captain, passed the reins to a junior officer and stepped up to the tent, requesting permission to enter. He re-appeared almost immediately, followed by a short man dressed in an open-necked shirt and army breeches and clutching a goblet of wine.

Bucquoy's French brogue was harsher than Dampierre's and reminded Jack of Chauvin and the way he trilled his 'R's. There was no doubt that long campaigns served in the Spanish Netherlands had influenced his dialect. A stocky man with dark almond eyes, Bucquoy had a flamboyant mass of medium-length curly hair. His upper lip carried a long, manicured moustache that protruded well beyond his cheeks, and his chin sported a stylish pointed beard.

The count sauntered over to one of the tent-posts and leaned on it with an outstretched arm, sipping his wine and studying his visitors definitively with his aristocratic gaze. Both junior officers, Jack and the Cossack, sprang to attention as one, and bowing with a sweep of their hats, waited for some form of acknowledgement. Chin raised, Bucquoy maintained a curious expression, clearly seeking the reason for the officers' presence at his camp.

Wanting to address that very curiosity, Jack fixed his stare past the count and offered succinctly, "Colonel Dampierre's compliments, my lord." He then explained who they were and why they had arrived.

Bucquoy's eyebrows remained elevated, but his sun-tanned face reflected an element of boredom—aristocratic detachment. Behind his moustache, his cheeks were ruddy from the wine. He emptied the last mouthful of drink and passed the goblet to his aide to be replenished. "Thank you, lieutenant. Your noble concern in wishing to assist us with the relief of Pilsen is noted. Although I have members of staff who know the city and its surrounding topography very well, your additional and recent intelligence may prove useful." His even tone matched his cheerless and indifferent countenance. "My captain will arrange your billet. We break camp and depart tomorrow morning at eight."

The count turned on his heel, taking the refilled wine glass, and without another word, disappeared through the canvas flaps into the soft, golden glow of his tent.

The town of Třeboň had risen over five centuries earlier from a ramshackle cluster of peasant huts scattered along the banks of the Lužnice River. Its vibrant waters provided inhabitants with a constant supply of fresh trout, eels and tench. This area of southern Bohemia was a large plain of gently undulating rich-soil tracts and low, rolling hills dotted with marshes and peat bogs. A patchwork of widespread verdant oak and short-needle pine forests shared the waterlogged land with vast fields of swaying grass and colourful wildflowers.

In mid-1366, the House of Rožmberk inherited the estate, and within three generations, the resourceful family began seriously developing and improving the land. They hired the services of a locally respected architect, Josef Štěpánek Netolický, to update and improve the fortifications of the growing town. At the same time, the potential for cultivating the paludal ponds was quickly recognised, and Netolický was appointed regent of the Rožmberks' domain and given the task of developing a fishpond system around the township. An educated man, he studied the contoured landscape of the neighbouring district and supervised the reshaping of low-lying, boggy fields into expansive, fresh-water lagoons. He engineered their inundation with water diverted from the Lužnice River via the freshly dug *Zlatá Stoka—Golden Canal*, an impressive channel spanning 10 leagues. Whilst supervising the excavation of a second canal, he managed the design and construction of a unique fortification system by adding a second defensive wall—with bastions, moat and ramparts—around Třeboň's walls. Two massive town gates were erected on the eastern wall, and a third, Budějovická Brána, was built on the western side. These massive masonry defences protected the Třeboň family castle, the Augustinian Friar monastery and St Gilles' Church.

Following Netolický's death, the pond builder's work was continued by Jacub Krčiń, another reputable pond builder and burgrave from Kolín. Krčiń further expanded the network to include almost 460 fishponds and installed an additional shorter, but equally important canal called the *Nová Řeka—New River*. This impressive network of man-made lakes and ponds augmented the prosperity of the district, defining it as a major source of carp for the tables of Catholic Bohemians on Fridays and Holy Days. The tranquil waters also harboured other varieties of fish—with pike, amur and bass available for trade to the surrounding regions—and attracted vast numbers of seasonal birds.

Every year, at the end of summer and in the autumn, magnificent flocks of thousands of ducks and geese as well as myriad white egrets and other migratory birds would flock to the area's mirror-smooth, shallow expanses of water. Cormorants would gather to nest with their chosen partners in the safe, sheltered environment of bucolic splendour.

The sleepy hamlet of Lomnice Nad Lužnicí—owned by Oldřich of Landštejn and his family—was nestled downstream, two leagues north of Třeboň. On 9 November, shortly after first light, the town's old proprietor was awoken from a dreamy sleep by insistent pounding at his front door. Irate and unaccustomed to such vulgar behaviour, Landštejn rose and shuffled downstairs with rheumatic limbs, his bony shoulders covered by a blanket. Shivering in bare feet on the stone floor, he threw back the pair of bolts and unlatched the door. A cool breeze wafted through the gap as he held the heavy door ajar. His eyes blinked into the brightness and focused on the silhouette of the source of his aggravation.

A peasant, cap in hand, stood hunched apologetically on the step, fawning nervously as his master and lord appeared through the opening orifice. Eager to explain his untimely affront, the crofter stuttered between bows, his wide eyes blinking rapidly from his dirty face. "Your Lordship will forgive this early intrusion, but many heavily-armed soldiers are marching through the town, and there are horsemen on the road."

Landštejn recognised Karel, a simple dairy farmer from a humble property just beyond the northern limits of the village. He would have interrupted the milking of his cows to bring the news.

Clasping the grey blanket tighter around himself, the landowner asked with irritation still heavy in his tone, "Who are they, Karel?" He looked past the farmer but could see nothing.

Continuing to bow, the peasant respectfully replied, "I have never seen them before, but the line is now south of Lomnice, and its tail is still passing my gate."

"On which road?" Landštejn asked, the picture still confused in his mind.

"Zámecká—in front of the old monastery, my lord." The landowner ordered the man to return home and lock himself inside and then shut his massive door with a resonant thud. He peered from the corner windows of his bedroom as he hastily dressed, but even from this elevated position, sight of the mentioned road was obscured by the two-storey homes across the modest and empty square.

The unwelcome tones of the bugle's reveille wafted intrusively across Bucquoy's sleeping camp. Jack opened a single eye from under the cloak that covered his head and peered at his comrade. Unmoving, but not snoring, Volkov was awake. Anticipating the coolness of the autumn morning, Jack was reluctant to move. With a protracted yawn, he rolled onto his back, rubbed his sleep-heavy eyes with both hands and then clasped his hands, with fingers intertwined, under his head. The marcescent leaves of the oak trees above him barely stirred. It was not windy—*a blessing*, he thought.

Jack let the camp stir slowly into activity, wishing

the freshly-lit campfires to warm the air before rousing his stiff body. He could hear the Russian rouse beside him, and the smell of wooded smoke motivated him to rise.

Anton sipped from his tumbler, the stirring aroma of hot, freshly brewed coffee lingering to intermingle with the scent of the crackling fire. He sat on thick, cushioning grass, leaning against a long fallen grey log, whilst Jack sat above him, straddling the same old horizontal stag. They drank in silence, enjoying the rousing flavour of the stimulating brew and the tranquil vista surrounding them.

The count had chosen to bivouac his army on two grassy fields between the large neighbouring lakes of Koclířov—to the west—and Velký Tisý—to the east—about a league south of Lomnice. A third smaller but still sizable pond, Služebný Rybnik, lay between the camp and the hamlet, its shores surrounded by dense, majestic oak forest. Each of the two larger lakes was over half a league in length and half that in width and would take almost half a day to circumnavigate on foot.

Over their steaming mugs, the two officers gazed out across the glassy water. The far shore was invisible, shrouded by thin fog, and the clacks of passing geese echoed in the distance, disturbing the otherwise quiescent countryside. The lake's mirror-like surface was randomly broken by jumping trout, spreading concentric rings that eventually dissipated, returning the water to a reflective plane. Jack observed the industrious labouring of an otter scurrying at the water's edge beyond the stretch of grassy tufts, ignoring the nearby movement of the soldiers. In the branches above him, the officer heard the chirking of a pink and blue chaffinch that remained invisible amongst the dry, browning oak leaves.

At the sudden, urgent blare of the clarion calling men to arms, an alarmed flock of cormorants took to the air like a rising cloud, signalling their dismay with frantic shouts. Anton and Jack both stood up, looking away from the water and towards the main camp surrounding the general's tent. As they had not been assigned to any company, they had no commanding officer; therefore, their actions remained utterly discretionary.

"Anton!" Jack's call was sharp and alert. "Find out what's going on. I'll saddle the horses." He bent to pick up the blanket and saddle as Volkov stepped off the grassy patch and trotted onto the dirt road that followed the shoreline. Soldiers were preparing to take up their battle order—dowsing fires, saddling and packing their gear and loading their wheel-lock muskets and pistols. Pikemen were hurriedly forming into squares under the direction of their captains. Within minutes, the count's tent was down and packed onto a dray, his main body of cavalrymen forming a line along the side of the road.

The Cossack returned, breathing hard, just as Jack led both saddled stallions by the reins out of the trees. "The sentries on the eastern bank of that rybnik have reported sighting an advancing Bohemian column," Volkov said steadily, pointing with a gloved hand in a northerly direction.

"Apparently Thurn, ahead of about 14,000 men, has been shadowing Bucquoy since abandoning his fist hold on Čáslav. Our general has decided that it's too late to withdraw and has ordered the troops to take up a defensive field position. He is deploying the infantry at the junction of these two large lakes at the stem of the funnel," Volkov formed an angle shaped like a wine glass with his hands in demonstration, "and the cavalry has been ordered to stand by here, in readiness, should he decide to instigate a charge."

The two expansive bodies of water were separated by the width of the single dirt road—which joined the towns of Lomnice and Budějovice to the south-west—along a length of almost 300 yards. Although the enormous size of each of the lakes made a flanking manoeuvre highly unlikely, Bucquoy wanted no surprises. A couple of dragoons had been despatched down the road to the southern tip of Koclířov, about a third of a league away, to observe and warn of possible unexpected enemy movement from the southwest. A second pair galloped southeast along the shore of Velký Tisý for the same reason.

From their position with the now fully-formed and waiting imperial cavalry, the two officers could see across the open waters of the western arm of Velký Tisý to the forest in front of the smaller Služebný Rybnik. Beyond that, their view was obstructed by the densely clustered trunks of oak trees whose branches were all but denuded by the last chills of autumn and the fog, which still hung silently in the morning air.

At Jack's suggestion, they two officers had advanced up the road between the two lagoons and joined the command post on the northern shore of Velký Tisý. They halted their mounts within earshot of Bucquoy, who had spread his charts over his field trestle and was surrounded by his officers and adjutants. The stern-faced men encircling their senior officer were deep in discussion, evaluating potential advance scenarios and defensive measures. They had chosen a flat and level position on the embankment of Velký Tisý, which by its design, had been elevated slightly above the surrounding plain. From there, the view up the road towards Lomnice Nad Lužnicí was impeded only by the cumulative blanketing effects of the fog. Thurn's confederate forces had halted on the southern outskirts of the village and had spread onto the fields to the right of the road.

The Polish lieutenant overheard one of the Bucquoy's senior officers giving an update on the situation as he peered intently through his leather-bound telescope. "The flow of troops from Lomnice has stopped. My estimate, general, is approximately 13,000 to 14,000 men. Von Thurn is placing his artillery east of the rybnik bank. There appears to be no flanking effort."

They were outnumbered. There was a buzz of discussion at the table. The terrain offered no topographical advantage to either army, and each commander would make his own choice regarding whether to advance or defend. Bucquoy motioned for a Jesuit chaplain with a tonsured head to bless his army, and the officers knelt for a short communal prayer—the general with them, tugging at his moustache while on one knee.

The imperial guns were positioned to the right and marginally ahead of the command point, their number slightly less than the enemy's. The first barrage of cannon shot was fired by the Bohemians, their guns spewing clouds of smoke. Each gunner fired individually in a line moving from left to right. A discordant whistling tune followed the sound of thunder moments later, culminating in ground-shaking eruptions of soil and stone as the cannon-balls completed their trajectories. The first volley fell short. It was just past nine on the morning of the Feast Day of St Alexander.

Bucquoy's retaliatory cannonade, belching fire and destruction, proved more effective, destroying one artillery piece and levelling at least 20 enemy soldiers. Elevation corrections were rapidly made on the enemy side, and the Protestant gunners' second discharge was accurate and deadly. Equally effective subsequent bombardment devastated pockets of troops and neutralised many Catholic guns and their cannoneers. The upper branches of the oak trees around them disappeared, carried a distance before dropping and crashing to the ground in pieces.

From his horse, who was snorting and tossing his head at the roar of the cannons and spraying clumps of dirt, Jack stood up on his stirrups and observed the carnage. He watched as a gun to his right disintegrated after taking a direct hit. Jagged slivers of hot metal tore indiscriminately into the three gunners manning the artillery piece. The man closest to the gun was decapitated; his head was carried 30 feet by the blast, an arc of blood trailing the lifeless airborne part. A spoke, splintered off from the timber wheel, embedded itself into his stomach and protruded past his spine.

Beside him, the unit officer was cut in half at the waist by a large piece of metal wheel-capping that had been torn off by the impact. His torso fell slowly backwards, his unfeeling arms outstretched. His face was frozen in open-mouthed and speechless surprise while his legs stood gushing spurts of blood for an eternity before he collapsed onto the blood-soaked earth beside the cannonballs.

The third man, who was holding the ramrod, was struck by a triangular shred of disintegrated barrel that severed his arm close to the neck and peppered his body with fragments of steaming metal pieces. His lifeless form fell limply onto the rust-coloured soil.

Jack gazed to his left at the files of infantrymen positioned at the base of the imaginary funnel. Cannonballs landed randomly amongst the congestion of pikemen, cutting swathes through their stationary ranks. The murderous decimation thinned entire lines of resolute veterans, dismembering, decapitating and maiming steadfast and obedient soldiers. Screams of agony carried above the roar of the guns as men fell—some killed instantly and mercifully while others collapsed, wounded but conscious, groaning and lying in shock in their own fetid excrement, bleeding onto scarlet-stained grass.

From his position, Jack had an unobstructed view of Bucquoy's infantry. The reek of scorched vegetation and flesh reached him as he scanned the field through his glass. The scene—with numerous pockets of men struck down, their blood splattering the faces of those beside them—gave him the impression of a chess-board, scattered gaps appearing among the remaining upright pieces.

Within 20 minutes, the enemy's position was obscured by an impenetrable blanket of thick, acrid smoke. With no wind on this still morning, the incessant fusillade had belched acerbic gun smoke across the entire battlefield. The guns fell silent one by one, an unsettling peace pervading the countryside. Only odd yells and commands were heard in the unseen distance, rising spasmodically from different points across the obscured battleground.

Both armies took the opportunity during the lull in the bombardment to gather their dead and tend to the wounded and dying. The priest joined the camp physicians, who moved amongst the fallen, wrapping superficial wounds with scarves and cloth bandages and carting the more seriously wounded to the rear, where a canopy had been temporarily erected to create a field infirmary.

Jack left his mount with Anton and moved amidst the injured on the front lines of the infantry squares. A grisly display met him: men were soaked in urine and vomit, blood pooling where limbs had once been. The mixture of abandon and dismay was palpable. He tended to the wounds as best he could, administering laudanum to alleviate the pain, often stumbling from one prone body to the next. A skirmish line of musketeers—each soldier spaced apart but within a visible distance to the next—was stationed before the front rank to fire in warning should an advancing enemy soldier be sighted from out of the smoke.

Jack lost complete track of time, totally absorbed in his medical duties. His blood hammered in his head. On occasion, he would call for the Jesuit, who would give a dying soldier final absolution, assisted by Jack's narcotic solution, which made the final moments of life physically comfortable and relatively painless. Often what lay before the officer was unrecognisable.

By late morning, the smoke had dissipated, leaving a fog that was slowly thinning. Despite the valiant and interminable efforts of the field physicians, supplicating groans and whimpers of pain contin- ued to rise from the field. On his knees beside a dismembered soldier who had expired, Jack placed his blood-soaked hands on his thighs, and closing his eyes, rolled his raised head from side to side to soothe the pain at the back of his neck. The small of his back ached from his incessant bending over dying and broken bodies. His mind had retreated into a silent, halcyon distance, relieved of the crushing trauma and despair confronting him. For a blissful moment, he was lying in a drifting boat with water lapping gently at the sides, looking up at a cloudless, blue sky with a zephyr gently cooling his face.

Out of the silence, Jack heard a remote voice repeatedly calling his name, gradually getting louder. He shook himself forcefully from his dream and followed the sound, realising that it was the inimitable Cossack. Opening his eyes, he recognised his friend standing between their two stallions and waving, calling for him to return. At the same moment, the enemy resumed the battle with their first booming salvo.

The valiant ranks of infantry were closing around the Polish officer as he stood and stretched his weary limbs. He began to jog towards his friend at the edge of the lake as airborne missiles hummed over his head. The coppery smell of blood wafted from his stained hands and drenched breeches. Doughty pikemen nodded respectfully in appreciation as he tramped past them, holding his small bag of medical instruments and vials in his left hand. He smiled back, hoping to leave some encouragement and reciprocated admiration for the brave and dutiful ones around him.

A cannonball struck to Jack's left, annihilating half a row of soldiers. He had reached the rear of the regiment, beyond which an unattended line of six small pieces of artillery had been positioned in reserve. He dropped to a brisk walk as he moved to bisect the placement and looked up at the Russian, who was smiling at him and waving in encouragement no more than 300 feet away.

Suddenly a smaller, stray cannonball from the nearest enemy cannon slammed into the line two guns away, shattering the piece into an unrecognisable mess. The ground reverberated. The gun exploded with an indescribable force, the impact hurling the physician through the air. Jack's medical bag flew from his opened hand and his ears droned, blocking out all other sounds. Prickles of hot pain seared his side and legs as his weightless body flew, arms and legs outstretched. He closed his eyes involuntarily, not wishing to see and believing that no harm would come to him as a result.

Jack struck the grass behind the guns like a limp rag doll. Fresh pain crushed his chest, making it difficult for him to breathe, and the impact immersed his body in a new dull and paralysing ache. He wanted to vomit, but the stress and punishment that had shocked his physical being overwhelmed him. He drifted effortlessly into Marianna's embrace, and she soothed him with caresses and whispery kisses. He must have fallen asleep in her peaceful arms as his world turned an inky black, and he remembered no more.

Chapter 9

CHRISTMAS

There were sounds. Distant sounds. Now drifting nearer and louder. The world had no light, only sounds. A chirping melody hovered above Jack's head—a birdsong, faraway yet strangely close and clear. Looking up at the sparsely leafed branches of the oak tree near the lake's shore, Jack searched for the source of the song, but he couldn't find it; he couldn't see the bird whose pretty song warmed him with its tune. *Open your eyes wider and look harder*, he thought, motivation growing more intense.

Jack's eyes snapped open suddenly and resolutely. His gaze did not find oak tree branches or a bird, however, but a stark white ceiling. He was staring at a ceiling. He caught the sounds of the song again and tried to ascertain the source, turning his head slowly to his left, where his eyes fell upon the window behind which an unseen bird was serenading him with its mellisonant notes. His thoughts confused him. If he was not at the lake's edge in the forest south of Lomnice, then where was he? He had slept well, he remembered. A sleep that was unbroken until the clarion call shortly after dawn. Volkov. That troublesome Cossack. Mischievous man. *Where is he?* Jack wondered as his eyes moved around the room in search of his friend. He couldn't see while lying on such a flat pillow. He needed to sit up and get a better view.

Jack abandoned his attempt to sit up after it resulted in burning, keening pain that racked his entire body in violent stabs of agony. Thinking, on the other hand, was painless. He was relieved to discover that the use of his mind, head and eyes brought him no discomfort. He tried his throat. First he gave a subtle cough and then followed that with a groan and a murmur. This was fine. Taking a deeper breath, he spoke aloud, counting to five. His ears worked well too. Despite some soreness in his chest, he could speak. He counted louder again without a problem.

"Volkov!" Jack yelled finally, repeating the name as loudly as he would dare after a short moment. The door to his right opened, and the wounded officer turned his head to follow an attractive young lady's entry into his room. She was a slightly-built young woman of around 20. Her long waves of sandy hair were hidden under a neat bonnet of pale blue, not dissimilar in colour to her sparkling eyes. She wore a matching blue apron over a tawny jacket and full-length skirt that barely moved as she walked. Her voice was sweet and reassuring, like that of one accustomed to caring for ill or incapacitated people.

"Lieutenant Channing," the woman voiced in excellent German as she arrived, almost gliding, at the side of his bed. Her face beamed warmth and sincerity like a beacon. "It is truly good to have you back with us. How are you feeling this morning?" Her look of concern only slightly detracted from her genuine geniality. She placed a cool hand on Jack's forehead as she gazed down at him, waiting for a reply.

"My head appears to be functioning normally, but from the neck down, every movement signals to my nerve endings to scream with pain," Jack managed a strained smile. "Why am I here and... Where am I?"

"You don't recall what happened to you?" the young woman asked with renewed concern, arching her eyebrows as she poked at his pillow to make him more comfortable.

Jack frowned in answer without speaking.

"You were at the Battle of Lomnice and were severely wounded by artillery fire. You are now in the home of an acquaintance of Colonel Dampierre in Linz."

"But that requires a number of days of travel..." Jack's voice trailed off, leaving the words unspoken as his mind tried to work through the machinations involved in transferring him the many leagues from the lakes to Linz.

"You have been delirious for weeks. I will fetch the Russian officer," the woman quickly stated in a dulcified voice. "Herr Volkov will be very happy, and abundantly relieved, to see you awake and conversable. He will be able to answer all of your questions and has seldom left your side since your arrival. He must be a true and loyal friend to you, lieutenant." She left with a slight curtsy, leaving the door ajar behind her.

Urgent, striding footsteps echoed in a distant corridor, growing louder. Jack stared at the half-open door in wait for his visitor. Volkov finally entered the room, pausing momentarily at the door, his hand on the handle. A broad smile erupted across his face, and he stepped over to the bed with measured, confident paces. Mischief touched his eyes as he peered down at his friend. The Cossack looked tired and unshaven and had dull grey arches below his eyes.

"Welcome back to the living, my dear comrade. I have a flask of the smoothest Polish vodka in my coat. We'll have a draught later when it's safe and Margareta doesn't catch us." Volkov spoke in a hushed and conspiratorial tone, not allowing concern to replace his mischievous demeanour. "Do you know how difficult it is to find a good drinking partner? You have no idea how I have suffered drinking alone. It's just not the same, Jack. No one in the taverns to watch my back!" he admonished.

"I've been told that you haven't visited many taverns recently," Jack shared what the young woman had intimated. "It confused me, and I thought that I had misheard her. That seemed impossible!"

"Bah! Margareta has been extremely busy caring for you. She wouldn't know when I sneaked out for a quick snort. You know, if I was unwell, I would want her to look after me. She is so dedicated—so caring and meticulous." He stopped, catching the fixed, enquiring gaze that Jack threw at him.

"What happened to me, Anton? Tell me everything. The last I remember was saddling our horses at the lake while waiting for you."

Volkov pulled across an armchair and made himself comfortable, crossing his stretched legs. The piece of furniture had become his intimate friend due to his having slept in it so frequently. He sat facing the foot of the bed, his head in his hand like a priest in a confessional. Recounting the start of the battle and the devastating exchange of artillery fire, the Russian spoke of the lull in fighting due to the blanketing smoke and Jack's subsequent medical assistance to the dying and wounded. He expressed his own shock and then dread as he rushed to the fallen officer following the blast, describing the injuries and medical attention Jack had received.

Jack's limp, unconscious body had been placed onto a medical dray and carted past the lakes to the field medical tent, where the surgeon had removed the damaging pieces of shrapnel, bathed and cleaned Jack's wounds and wrapped him in bandages, effectively immobilizing his cracked sternum and broken ribs.

By mid-afternoon, Count Bucquoy realised that the counter-offensive with his infantry had compounded the imperial army's failure, and because of heavy losses of both soldiers and cannons as a result of Thurn's artillery fire, ordered a hasty but orderly retreat. *Amat victoria curam—victory favours care*, Volkov believed were his words at the time.

A line of smaller cannons had been deployed just south of the two lakes to cover the withdrawal of Bucquoy's troops and front-line artillery. As twilight fell over the battleground, the losses suffered by the Holy Roman Empire's army amounted to 1500 dead, wounded or missing, with Jack among them. Thurn counted only 80 dead and 120 wounded—a swift and laudable victory. The Bohemians did not follow Bucquoy's retreat to Budějovice. Twelve days later, Pilsen fell to Mansfeld.

At Bucquoy's request, the Polish officer, who was

still unconscious and gravely ill, was despatched with Volkov and a cavalry contingent to Linz, where he was quartered with a friend of Duval von Dampierre's family. Bucquoy was considering his own return to Vienna, and after meeting with Dampierre, sent him with a sizeable detachment to reinforce Písek. On the last day of November, almost three weeks after the battle, the young wounded officer regained consciousness.

"The field surgeon had initially performed miracles in stabilizing your wounds. Later his attention at Budějovice confirmed that infection was minimal except in your thigh, which he treated with extraordinary attention." Volkov laughed to himself as he added, in afterthought, "The crusty old bugger appreciated a fine drop. He was Russian on his grandmother's side and was born in eastern Poland. Not surprising, eh?" He looked at Jack as the young, prone physician stared quietly at the opposite wall, listening pensively.

"So, my dear, dear friend. You've been missing in action for three weeks, floating in and out of consciousness. The surgeon was confident that a young and healthy man such as you would recover. Your lacerations are healing well, and the broken bones will need their own time to come good. It will be some months yet before you lift your rapier again."

"Patience, patience," Jack repeated, half to himself, subduing his frustration. "What plans, Anton?"

The Cossack played with his moustache, thoughtful for a moment, before replying. "When you can ride, I suggest we return to Kraków, where you can recuperate fully under your mother's care. Perhaps we can request a visit from Marianna to accelerate your convalescence," he added with a twinkle in his eye. "We can arrange a letter to be delivered by rider to the king, updating his council in Warszawa with what we have found. It would be prudent to warn him as this Green-Scarf Fraternity appears to still be active."

"Perhaps you are right. I am impatient with these damned injuries. Life is passing slowly on, and I'm being left behind in this insufferable bed! A doctor makes the worst patient."

"That is what happens on battlefields. We put ourselves in harm's way, and at times we're fortunate, at other times not." The Cossack understood well the impatience and frustration that his companion felt.

Jack turned to Volkov, groaning as he adjusted his position, and asked after the pain subsided, "Would you mind arranging three things for me, please? Now that I'm awake, I will facilitate my recuperation starting with positive thoughts and accommodating deeds."

Volkov nodded as he leaned forward, resting his arms on his knees.

"Now that I am conscious, as a medical man, I will expedite my recovery. I have control again. First, please find out where Johannes Kepler lives in this fair city. That should be easy considering the skills you have in gathering information. When I am fit and able, I wish to avail myself of the opportunity to visit him for a philosophical discussion. Unlike our last visit when we passed through like a pistol shot, there's more time now, and it would be a privilege to be stimulated by this man's mind." Jack's eyes sparkled at the thought. "Perhaps you can plead my case to him and advise him of my intentions? I know not when we'll be back in Linz again."

The Russian nodded in consent again.

"Second, when she is free, would you request the lovely Margareta to scribe a note to my countess for me as well as a report for the king—and lastly, where is that bloody vodka you keep promising?"

A full week passed before Jack's wounds had healed enough to allow him to sit and turn comfortably in bed and another passed before his first tentative attempts to rise. Anton and Margareta stood at each side as Jack managed to ease himself onto the floor and take a couple of probatory steps. Within days, however, and with unbending resolve, he could walk without assistance to the door and back. By the end of the week, he was dressing himself, although actions that stretched his breast muscles were still difficult. He was now more ambulant, regularly eating at the table with the other members of the household, and could sit and stand slowly without too much discomfort. His emaciated frame was steadily mending.

The following day, Volkov sought out his friend with updated news. Jack was, unsurprisingly, sitting in the library and reading. With the gradual improvement in his health and his return to independence, the Polish officer was much happier. His friend leaned on the mantelpiece. It had been snowing heavily for the past three days, and the hearth was bristling with burning logs, inundating the book-filled chamber with saturating warmth.

"A journey home on horseback is unfortunately out of the question at the moment," the Cossack began, lighting his newly-found pipe from the large candle burning above Jack's shoulder.

"I know." Jack looked up at Volkov from his tome. "I had hoped to be home for Christmas with my family, but the weather and my slow return to health have plotted against us."

"There are good tidings, however." Anton smiled, continuing in an encouraging tone, "I have made the acquaintance of the venerable Herr Kepler, and he confirmed that he would be honoured to meet you. He suggested early afternoon on Christmas Eve day—tomorrow."

Jack nodded in assent as he was passed a note with the astronomer's address.

"I would offer to accompany you, but your scientific conversation would fill me with absolute boredom." The Russian cleared his throat, and with a more sombre tone, regained his friend's attention. He blew a grey cloud of smoke into the air above his head. "This household is in regular communication with the capital, and Margareta brings me news almost daily of the gossip and prattle at the Viennese court. You know my insatiable nose for intelligence. Her Imperial Highness, Anna of Tyrol, passed away in her sleep just over a week ago, on the 14th. Your diagnosis was correct. The royal physicians confirmed the cause was advanced consumption." Fumigating the room with pipe smoke, Volkov added, "Incidentally, the Empress' brother, Karl von Burgau, died at Überlingen the day after our visit and audience with her."

Jack returned to his reading while Volkov dropped into the nearest chair, leaning back and savouring his briar. The two men sat in silence, each lost in his own thoughts.

Predictably, winter settled in with a harsh vengeance. The city's inhabitants huddled under the thickening blanket of powdery snow, and additional labour was harnessed to spade and move the heavy dumps in order to keep the roads open for horse and foot traffic. The soft, crisp shroud of snow brought a sense of peace and contentment, dampening the noises of everyday life. Residents embraced and enriched the festive spirit with innovative and traditional window displays and the hanging of additional lanterns around the streets. The city was aglow at night, bathed in amber and golden lights. Snowmen of numerous sizes and curious designs appeared almost overnight at street corners and across market squares.

At one in the afternoon on the day before Christmas, Jack peered out of the dining room window at the quiet, lazy fall of snow outside. Large, puffy flakes floated noiselessly down, covering all of the city's sins. Margareta stood at his shoulder; like the Polish officer, she never had her fill of the mesmerising and soothing atmosphere these tranquil winters educed.

"You may wish to delay your visit, or perhaps we can summon a carriage? This fall is heavy and it seems to have set in with no sign of abating," the young woman voiced in a hushed tone, hinting her ever-present concern.

"No, my sweet and caring Margareta. I have been waiting anxiously for this day. I need to have the snow caressing my face and want to feel and absorb the freedom of the outside world again. I may not even take my hat!"

Jack's flippant taunt missed its mark; Margareta was horrified. "You must wear your hat in this heavy weather," she insisted as the officer chuckled furtively to himself. "And forget this parlously cavalier attitude," she chided, knocking his arm with her elbow to emphasise her displeasure and apprehension.

"I am intrigued by what this sagacious and erudite man will teach me this afternoon. Our meeting will be a singular experience. My wounds have imprisoned me these past weeks, my bedchamber a dungeon and my bed the manacles. My spirit and I belong out there," Jack nodded at the world past the window, "and you'll find me a reinvigorated man when I return." He smiled gently down at Margareta's frowning face and bent to kiss her cheek before departing. Her anxiety and thoughtfulness were not lost on him.

"Christmas Eve dinner at six tonight? I shall not be late, an occasion equally important and awaited! Now, where is that hat of mine?" Jack commented loudly with a sassy bluster and mischievous wink as he left.

The Polish officer rejoiced silently as he strode with measured steps through the crunching snow.

The rediscovered freedom permeated through his being, enlivening his very soul. He walked across the small cobbled square and turned, waving back to the face in the window that he knew would still be watching him, and then rounded the corner and disappeared down the wynd. A short distance past the cloister brought him to the house he sought.

Jack was greeted at Kepler's door by the master himself and cordially welcomed into the inner sanctum of the astronomer's home. The house was comprised of Kepler's library and study, laboratory, observatory and classroom. The kitchen was an appendage only—the dominion of his second wife of five years, Susanna Reutlinger. The smallest room in the house, it existed only out of necessity in order to provide the house's occupants with meals.

While Kepler was outwardly austere, his lucidity of thought and wicked and effervescent sense of humour were breathtaking. He and Jack discussed the mathematics of the universe, and the old man perspicaciously explained the basis upon which his three laws of planetary motion had been formulated.

A thin, reedy man with penetrating eyes, the revered philosopher was not tall. Greying and slightly stooped in stature, he was the consummate educator and academic. With remarkable clarity, he explained his use of logarithms recently conceived by Scotland's John Napier in his own description of the solar system. He also shared his colourful opinion, punctuated with comical remarks, regarding the sparring of astronomer Christoph Scheiner in Innsbruck with Galileo over the nature of sunspots.

As he led Jack on a tour of his house, Kepler espoused his considered support and respect for the revolutionary work and theories postulated by Copernicus, Galileo and Tycho Brahe. Both men were quick to agree on their invaluable improvements to the telescope, although for different purposes. Jack's guided expedition culminated in the esteemed philosopher's work chamber on the third floor. The musty, expansive room occupied the whole level and reminded Jack of the advocating needs and domain of the ancient alchemist. Copious shelves were crammed with books, parchments and charts, many more of which overflowed in crooked stacks onto the floor. The work table and adjoining trestles were equally heaped with dusty tomes and scrolls, yet Jack was certain that his august guide could recall the location of any one of these in an instant.

Dominating pride of place was Kepler's pièce de résistance: his telescope. Pointed at the heavens, the impressive instrument stood silent and functionless in the current inclement weather. It was supported by a massive adjustable tripod and faced a vast window. The scientist had had a large section of the roof replaced with glass tiles, now white with snow, to extend his view of the sky. Kepler fiddled distractedly with the telescope's knobs, his crippled fingers and impaired eyesight remnant effects of having suffered from smallpox as a child.

Immersed in deep discussion with his host, the young physician lost awareness of time. Jack realised the lateness of the hour only when the pendulum clock standing in the corner chimed five melodious strokes. With a promise to correspond, he departed, elated by what he had discovered at his new mentor's residence. All pain and discomfort were forgotten as he trudged blithely, retracing his steps through the deep snow, to his temporary home.

Christmas, white and memorable, had come and gone, and as the end of another year approached, Jack and Anton were deliberating a possible return to Kraków. Jack's health and mobility had improved rapidly, and he was keen to go home. His strength was steadily returning, bolstered by regular lengthy walks across the city. Some days after his visit to Kepler's home, he stopped by to leave a note of gratitude as he passed the house. The snow fall had eased, and a decision was reached to proceed to Vienna with the intent of reaching the Channing estate before the eve of the changing year.

Wrapped in warm clothing and shrouded by heavy cloaks, the pair rode east, leaving their dear newly-made friends in the fair city. Progress on horseback was steady and proved more expeditious than travelling by coach. Although it was still bitterly cold, the force of the winds from the north had subsided, and the officers' journey was not hampered by wild and intemperate snow storms.

The two men had planned a brief stop at the Hofburg at the outset in order to fulfil pending obligations. Despite the short notice, Count Bucquoy had interrupted his busy schedule—full of meetings and appointments—and agreed to meet his visitors within minutes of their announced arrival. In his brusque manner, he politely accepted Jack's gracious thanks for arranging his place of convalescence. Outwardly he showed little concern for Jack's improvement in health, but the two sensed a genuine latent regard for his wellbeing. Jack made it clear that the count could call on his services at any time in repayment for his debt.

The two officers learned that Dampierre had been caught by the weather and was still in southern Bohemia, somewhere between Písek and Krumlov. Bucquoy confirmed the fall of Pilsen and explained that the city had not been sacked but that ransom negotiations were continuing. Mansfeld had demanded 120,000 golden guldens as compensation for his war reparations in addition to 47,000 florins for sparing the city's inhabitants and not burning it to the ground.

The mind and health of Emperor Matthias had deteriorated rapidly since the death of his wife, and all of the emperor's decisions were being made by the military under strict guidance from King Ferdinand. With leading support from Bavaria, the Holy Roman Empire was gathering forces that were destined to head towards Pilsen and Prague. Bucquoy seemed little affected by the defeat at Lomnice.

Another attempt had been made on the king's life at a public gathering on Christmas Day. The perpetrator had been apprehended, however, and Bucquoy promised to forward a written report updating King Sigismund of the situation. He agreed that the note would be addressed to the lieutenant as the king's royal representative.

By the fifth day, the mounted travellers had scaled the steady climb to where the road crested a ridge. The stormy, leaden skies ahead were ominous with the threat of rain and snow. The two stopped stirrup to stirrup on the grassy roadside, and from their high vantage point, peered with joyful relief at the sight of the magnificent buildings that made up Jack's home silhouetted against the threatening sky in the distance.

Chapter 10

Cavalier club

Jack's mending bones twinged in mild discomfort as he and Anton moved from a trot to a canter. He grimaced between gritted teeth but made no complaint, buoyed by the knowledge that he and his companion would reach their destination in time to greet the new year at home with his family.

Old Joseph possessed an uncanny sixth sense and waved to the riders from the front steps of the rambling house when they were still a long way off. Janina had always said that his gypsy blood had given him this remarkably accurate predictive power.

"How does he do that?" Volkov asked in a tone brimming with admiration and bordering on awe. He shaded his eyes from the glare with a cupped hand and waved back, still dubious that the old stable master recognised them. "How did he know we were coming? He must have the sight of an eagle. Even now, he's just a black dot in front of the house."

The venerable gardener, warmed by the heavy

fur-lined overcoat that he prudently wore each winter, stood motionless and watched the two men approach. Finally, he turned to the house to alert those inside. As the horses walked with graceful measured strides along the gravelled drive, Jack watched the old man's impassive face, recognising the latent joy of their advent hidden in his shrouded, enigmatic eyes. Snow lay on the rolling lawn and manicured gardens, and a thick cover surrounded the house everywhere that had been devoid of pedestrian activity. Janina—shoulders covered by a thick, colourful shawl—appeared from the doors, which had been thrust open, wide and welcoming. Moments later, Jock stepped out from behind his wife, carrying a tray laden with elegant glasses brimming with a clear and colourless liquid. Servants poured out of the house and spread across the landing.

This is Christmas all over again, thought Jack. Amidst the crowd of laughing faces and the odd happy call and whooping cheer, the riders dismounted. Interweaved amongst the hugging and kissing, Jock pressed forward, enthusiastically distributed the tumblers, and under his commanding lead, each person downed his or her drink. "Internal heating," he called it. This had become a Channing tradition and was reserved for the most important occasions and the most illustrious guests.

The celebration of greeting the new year was one that involved the whole family, including servants, and on occasion, an invited visitor. The Channings' heavy oaken table had been extended to accommodate everyone, and the dining hall was filled with massive candelabras. Both pendulous candle chandeliers were lit, flooding the room with warm golden light. Jugs of mead and ale stood at regular intervals along the board, interspersed with huge platters of food and carafes of vodka. Large bronze ewers had been filled with pristine snow should icy water be needed to drink or dilute the alcohol. Carvings of venison from a recently hunted stag had been prepared in various piquant sauces, the head and cape left with Old Joseph to convert into a trophy that would join other hunting mementos in gracing the long wall.

On arriving at the estate, the two officers had retired to their chambers to wash and prepare for the festivities. Several letters from Warszawa were left in a neat pile on Jack's bed by his mother, their fragrant, delicate perfume immediately revealing their source. With impatient hands, he tore them open and read each one three times, a pang of guilt pressing his conscience that he had managed to write only one since he and Marianna last met. Included amongst Marianna's parchments was one from her father, written two weeks earlier. Count Pomorski's note stated that an additional attempt had been made on Vasa's life, although the king had happily escaped with only a flesh wound. Under interrogation, the culprit revealed that he had been recruited in Prague. Additional details would follow imminently.

For the evening's celebrations, Jack and Volkov had agreed to dress in their officer uniforms. The young physician chose a jewelled doublet of royal blue with slashed sleeves to cover his starched, wide-sleeved shirt accompanied by matching breeches and a broad sapphire sash. His soft, black leather boots rose to his knees and were polished to a smooth sheen. He hung a sharpened dagger from his belt, leaving his rapier in its scabbard on a horn hook behind his door.

Volkov and his father were deep in conversation, standing by the hearth where a large log crackled, when Jack entered the dining hall. The Cossack was equally impressively attired, having chosen a velvet uniform of deep burgundy. Jock placed an inviting arm across his son's shoulders as the lad joined them at the fire. "Anton has been describing your Bohemian exploits in detail. You seem well recovered?"

"As someone who is familiar with medicine, I can confirm that I had exceptional care in Linz, father," the young man replied openly. Behind them, the servants quietly continued their preparations for the pending meal and long evening to come, directed as always from the kitchen by Jack's mother. The enticing fragrance of the numerous varied dishes filled the room and was difficult to ignore.

Jock prodded the burning log with the toe of his boot and then shoved it sharply with his heel, turning it slightly in a shower of golden sparks and bringing an invigorated blaze to life. "I'm salivating with the smell of this wonderful food," he admitted, voicing the thoughts of all three men as they stared absently into the lazy flames. "Your mother is such a wonderful cook; she even prepares my long-remembered Scottish dishes now better than I. It seems the apprentice has outdone the master. Her haggis is unrivalled."

The compliment provoked a laugh as the room filled with the household's complaisant servants, Janina shepherding them through the doorway from the rear. This was the signal to select a seat and sample the magnificent steaming feast. Jack took the initiative and distributed the filled goblets to all those standing. Prompted by the honoured head of the house, these glasses were raised to the call of "Na Zdrowie!" and summarily emptied. With a scraping of shuffled chairs, all took their places at the table. Old Joseph led grace to bowed heads, and the short, reverent silence was soon replaced by the dissonance of clattering dishes, glasses, plates and cutlery and the festal hum of voices.

Jack skewered a thick sliver of venison with his fork and sipped on his mead. He cast his eyes at the diners, absorbing the cheerful and carefree mood, and winked as he caught Old Joseph's eye acknowledging the extraordinary quality of this latest batch of fermented honey. The Polish officer revelled in the occasion, secure and content, surrounded by his loving family and closest friends. The Cossack raised his cup from across the table, appreciating the ambience, and they drank to each other's health.

Jock was keen to hear about his son's meeting with Herr Kepler, so the two moved to join his mother at the far end of the massive trestle, where Jack recounted his unforgettable meeting with the learned pedagogue. At one point, Janina hugged him tightly, relieved to have him home, and left a soft lingering hand on his cheek.

Ingrained in an immutable habit since before Jack was born, Old Joseph would routinely shuffle through the house and around the compound of outer buildings a number of times after dark every night. On more than one occasion, he would scare off a prowling fox or refill the water troughs and chaff bags. Often he would linger to talk to the farm animals; he had his favourites. His trips were more frequent during calving and foaling times, and he was invariably the last to retire. Tonight Jock asked him to stay and enjoy the special evening, so Joseph passed the routine responsibility to his younger protégé, Rysiek, whom he could trust with such a personal yet important task. Jack noticed the old man nod, reminding the younger of his obligation.

The young heir of the family slowly made his way around the table, conversing with everyone in turn. Interested in the daily business of the estate, he gained a broad perspective from his numerous discussions with the servants. As Jack moved to sit beside Old Joseph, the stable master cupped his face between his rough hands, a look of love and respect burning in his aged eyes. They spoke for a long time, and Joseph listened intently to the young officer's description of the unfortunate battle and his subsequent wounds.

"Don't tell your mother," the stable master warned, shaking a pointing finger. "Let her worry about less stressing matters such as her duties here at home. You are her life and her only son and must appear to be happy and safe for her sake. She frets enough as it is." They shared a drink, and Jack moved on, brushing aside a stray strand of hair from his forehead.

Jack pushed a chair between where Volkov and his father sat at the end of the table. Before sitting, he threw a glance at the grate to check the logs in the fireplace, and Rysiek's return caught his eye. He cast an enquiring look, and the servant nodded back with a brief smile, confirming that all was well around the buildings. The young retainer raised a hand with wavering fingers to indicate that it was snowing and resumed his position near the cooks and kitchen hand.

The young officer made his way towards the window but was stopped en route by a tug at his sleeve to share a quick round of spirits with a merry servant. When he eventually arrived at the window, Jack brushed the heavy drape aside, and in the glow flooding out into the darkness from the window, he could see the descending shower of soft white flakes, quiescent and opaque. He stood and watched the niveous display, mesmerised and soothed, and enjoyed the overwhelming sense of peace and security he experienced at being home. Once the restraining arm was removed, the released curtain fell back into place, and Jack wandered back to his empty seat.

Volkov was speaking, emphasising his point with his hands. "Central Europe stands at the threshold of a serious war. It is cleaved by opposing religious factions, each believing that it wields dominance and vested sovereignty while centres of political power remain vigilant and reactive. The Bohemian revolt is bubbling along steadily, watched by France, the German states, the Swiss, us and others. Vienna had been active in gathering troops to lift the siege at Pilsen, to reclaim control in Prague and the rest of the kingdom and to subdue Mansfeld and his force." He paused to lubricate his throat, his face frozen with passion.

Jock nodded silently in agreement and comprehension as his son flopped into the empty armchair. "The commonwealth is a formidable giant, Anton— a significant strength in Europe," the Scot began in response. "We have our own troubles at home with those around us nipping at our heels. The king is reluctant to concentrate on any one particular foe, although he would dearly savour regaining control of the Swedish throne." He gazed fervently at the two young men and self-assuredly continued. "I sense that we will be omitted from this conflict you describe unless we deliberately choose to be involved. Our size alone will deter our western neighbours; they will have other lands and territories to occupy their thoughts and satisfy their desires.

"The Ottomans are gradually receding," Jock went on, "their interest in us waning for the moment. The Tartars are merely opportunistic, raiding for plunder and wealth with no ingrained desire to subjugate us.

We have clashed with their marauding parties for more than four years; this last one proved to be relatively quiet. We have battered the Russians enough to keep them at bay, and peace is but a signature away. We hammered them, and the Swedes, at Klushino and later in Moscow. If I have a concern, it is from the north. Under their present king, Gustavus Adolphus II, the Swedes are consistently resolute. Our crown will have to watch them closely. Deep-rooted and long-standing animosity lies between Sigismund and his Protestant cousin in Stockholm."

"What you say is true, father, but we must, as Count Pomorski warned, remain eternally vigilant. The king is occupied with his northern boundaries and eastern borders. He is particularly sensitive to Gustav's activity around the Baltic Sea. I have been his eyes and ears to the west and hope to remain so. Volkov and I will watch his back." Jack looked at his comrade for a moment, gathering further thoughts, and continued. "These times remain troubled. Although France is a might to be reckoned with, her focus is on Spain and the Flemish lands. While there is mistrust of the Habsburgs, they will not involve themselves—by that, I mean commit religiously— unless provoked directly into self-preservation.

"With Jindřich Thurn stirring trouble in Bohemia, Bethlen Gabor scurrying around Hungary and

Transylvania, and Frederick waiting for his opportune moment in the Upper Palatinate, the commonwealth's southeastern flank must continue to be watchful." The young physician slapped Anton's knee playfully, receiving a grunt of agreement in return. "These are exciting days, father, and I relish the part that I have been dealt to play in this continental kitchen with many different bubbling pots on the fire, each on the verge of boiling over."

The room fell into sudden silence, and Jack and his companions raised their heads inquisitively, distracted from their serious and involved conversation by the hush. His shoulders and cap covered in snowflakes, Rysiek stood waiting at the door. He looked expectantly at his master and waited respectfully to speak.

Earlier the servant had returned into the bleak wintry night to inspect the security of the compound and had entered the stables to check on the animals. The large doors were secure and latched, and a goat bleated a short tune, seeking attention. He patted its head and knelt to reassure it, addressing the billy by name. He then passed by each stall before leaving; the horses stood asleep, peaceful, on three legs. Locking the heavy door behind him against the possible designs of a passing fox or sudden fierce gust of wind, he stepped outside. His steps fell silently in the soft, ankle-deep snow as he made his way down the side of the main house and headed for the front drive hidden to his right. The lantern cast a circular golden halo around him as he gripped his heavy cloak, pulling it tightly about his thin frame. Although the snow continued to fall, it had eased and was less dense than before, and in the white starkness of the night, he would have managed his tour of the outbuildings without the candle.

Rysiek rounded the front corner of the house. A loud, startled cry escaped his lips as he suddenly blundered into an unseen shadowy figure that had unexpectedly appeared from the murky darkness. Terrified, his breath caught in his chest. His cry of alarm was reciprocated by the faceless stranger, who had been equally surprised by the abrupt apparition of the servant. The two collided, almost extinguishing the flame from Rysiek's swaying lantern.

Now, in the subdued and quiet dining hall, the servant's pavid eyes danced from Jock to his son. He was oblivious to the other faces staring at him.

"What is it, Rysiek? You look like you've seen an apparition! Is everything as it should be?" Jack's voice was tight with concern as he stared back at the pale man.

A small snowflake dropped from Rysiek's eyelash as he blinked, and the young officer was not sure whether the man trembled from fear or the cold. Pointing through the door behind him, Rysiek managed to utter a reply, colour slowly returning to his pallid features in the warmth of the room, "This man says he knows you. He asked for you by name and has come to leave his sincere compliments with you, sir."

Seeing no one past the stile, Jack rose to his feet and answered, "Well, please bid him enter. If he knows me by name, he must be welcomed."

Rysiek looked back through the doorway and gestured with a beckoning hand. A cloaked stranger covered with snow, his face shadowed by a generous hood, stepped into the glowing hall. The visitor turned to face the young physician and slowly lowered the cowl onto his shoulders, exposing his gaunt face.

Jack's jaw dropped as he stood there like a gaping harlequin. "You crusty old bastard!" he yelled unreservedly, eyes ablaze with disbelief. "Chauvin!"

Jack rushed to the sinewy figure as the Frenchmen stepped towards him, and the two met in a bearish clasp, swaying and holding each other tightly. Smiling, expectant faces stared at the two friends from around the table. Jack motioned for an additional chair. Breaking the silence as they eventually separated, the corporal began fervently,

"How good it is to see you, lieutenant. Many a night in the cathedral, I dreamed of this moment, and now here we are." Jack attempted to take his cloak and pointed to the seat, but the old soldier declined and stopped him with a pleading look. "I hope you don't mind, sir, but I've brought some friends along. We apologise for this unheralded intrusion at this late hour, but I insisted that we come as the one group that we are. Some you will remember, others have joined us since our parting."

The physician looked up as Chauvin waved a hand through the open door in a gesture of invitation. Stepping back to make room, Jack waited as the Frenchman's companions entered the warm dining chamber. Julien Roberge was the first to appear, a broad, sheepish smile filling his face as he dragged his snow-covered felt hat off his head and peered happily at Jack. The two men hugged briefly as Chauvin introduced the others.

Kristian Blixt, a blond, clean-shaven man with the build of a tall Greco-Roman wrestler, stepped in behind Roberge, whom he dwarfed. He was closely followed by Candelario Montejo, who had the swarthy look of a Mediterranean man about him. Next was Marco Scrolavezza. Handsome and well-groomed, Scrolavezza was sure to provide some competition with the ladies. His long black locks and manicured moustache further hinted at his Veronese origin, which was confirmed after he bowed with a flourish and shared his greeting of "Buona sera". Finally, the corporal introduced Andreas Ritner, a stocky Bavarian with a cropped, russet-coloured beard. Ritner bowed with a formal click of his heels. Jock and Volkov, also on their feet, shook hands with each visitor in turn.

Space was quickly made at the table to accommodate the six newly-arrived visitors and clean settings placed before them.

"Please eat your fill," the old Scot encouraged them munificently whilst his wife arranged for a generous platter of roast chicken and pork to be brought forth, followed by another trencher of appetising venison. A plate of thickly-sliced brown bread and two liberal bowls of warmed roast potatoes were also left within reach. The most experienced at fussing around the house, Janina had these tasks prepared and completed with simple, regimental precision. It was Volkov who inevitably took it upon himself to ensure that the men's cups were filled.

The group of visitors occupied one end of the table, and Jack seated himself opposite his old comrade from Pilsen. There would undoubtedly be many things to talk about since the Polish officer's departure into the night from Pilsen's clandestine city gate. The Russian had taken an instant liking to Blixt and the brawny Bavarian, Ritner—perhaps because they appeared to be the most likely to enjoy the same measure of liquor as he. His instincts were indeed correct as the trio managed to empty a carafe of spirits before they finished their meal. Sensing that the two Latin visitors preferred red wine, Jock sent Old Joseph scurrying off to the cellar, and the stable master soon returned with a pair of dusty bottles.

Determined not to wait any longer, Jack posed his ever-pressing question to the corporal. "What happened at Pilsen, Alain? I am aware that the city fell over a month ago."

Wiping a layer of sauce from his plate with a slice of bread, the French soldier looked up with tired grey eyes. He wiped his fingers on the cap that lay in front of him, and Jack recognised the same knotted crimson scarf still encircling his tanned neck.

"We managed to hold the city against two assaults, repulsing them without much of an effort. Our spies reported Mansfeld's vehement anger at learning that his prized pair of cannons had been spiked." Alain shook with laughter at the memory, adding, "The general reportedly demoted the captain of the guard who was on duty the night that you and Vasseur infiltrated their defences. Our food supply was rapidly dwindling, and Hritek tightened the rationing to extreme levels. We were desperate. We netted the Mže River for fish over the northern wall at night, which helped, but a raid on the enemy's supply tents and wagons failed decisively. Horvat led the party, and Vasseur acted as a guide as he was familiar with the lay of the land from your successful sortie. Both are now dead. Only one man returned, wounded and barely conscious, to tell us what happened. The guards were reminded to do their duty, unreservedly, on pain of death. Mansfeld's patience had truly evaporated."

The grim pair sat in silence while Jack digested the devastating news. He had been extremely fond of both the now deceased soldiers.

Chauvin rubbed his furrowed, weather-beaten brow and stabbed with his fork at a plate of well-seasoned, wild mushrooms. "The confederates moved up and deployed their smaller cannons, probing for weaknesses in the walls. All three of our heavily-reinforced gates held, but they managed to hit and destroy the main city well, more by good fortune than design, and cracks appeared in the battlements. The Protestants eventually breached the ramparts and entered the city in two places just as our supplies of drinking water were about to become exhausted. Our strength was insufficient to beat them back."

Blixt had just finished sharing a bawdy yarn, educing loud laughter from Volkov and Ritner. This motivated the trio into downing another round of drinks. Chauvin looked back at his friend after the momentary interruption and continued. "The mayor surrendered on the 21st of November, and the city was inundated with rebel troops. Mansfeld maintained our meagre rations despite having plentiful supplies of food and fresh water. The well was repaired while we waited for a decision affecting our future. Wild rumours were rife around the city. Sadly, reinforcements never arrived."

"Bucquoy was on his way to you after I met with the king and reported the dire straits of the siege. I arrived in Prague soon after leaving through the northern gate," Jack replied, his fingers raking at his hair with frustration as he gazed tragically at the Frenchman. "A large detachment of Mansfeld's force blocked his advance at Čáslav; Bucquoy's contingent retreated in an attempt to regroup at Budějovice, but we were overrun and overwhelmed at Lomnice Nad Lužnicí less than two weeks before your capitulation." He stroked his moustache and asked, "Do you know of Duval, the Count of Dampierre?"

"Never met him, but I've heard of him. From Metz I believe. Has a good reputation in the field amongst our soldiers. In fact," the Frenchman added in a lighter tone, "Besson, Garreau, Maguiere and Paillard left to join him. Frenchmen usually like to stay together. I'm the odd one out."

"How did you get out of the city?"

"For soldiers with our experience, lieutenant," Chauvin winked cheekily, "it was easy. I informed Hritek, and we walked out of the same gate that you did. My companions headed south towards Písek, and Roberge, and I travelled east to Kraków in search of you. And here we are."

The two shared a laugh, Jack lifting his mug while the corporal fidgeted with his pipe.

"This is Julien's pipe," Alain explained. "He allows me to use it until I get my own. His tobacco rasps the throat like ploughing a rocky field, but it keeps my hands occupied."

"Well, pick at some of these," Jack suggested, sliding across a large wooden tray containing an assortment of tangy and poignant cheeses. "Dampierre is either at Budějovice or Krumlov—snowed in, I believe—and your men will find him if they're moving to Písek. And Bucquoy, I left him less than a week ago in Vienna. There has been an attempt on Ferdinand's life, and Sigismund's, but we can discuss that later. With anticipated support from Bavaria, the count will be pressing north again soon. Meanwhile, negotiations are continuing for Pilsen's release."

The two friends continued their discussion, savouring one another's company until Roberge called for the old corporal to join them at the far end of the room to settle an issue. The wiry old soldier excused himself, leaving the young physician to ponder on their conversation.

Jack had become restless. A mild throb of pain in his thigh began to niggle at him, and he decided that a short walk to stretch his legs would ease the discomfort. He noted that Chauvin was in deep conversation with his father as he looked across at the wine bottles in front of the Italian. Both were empty.

Jack nodded at Rysiek to join him, and the two made their way down the narrow stone steps into the bowels of the Channings' spacious cellar. The subterranean cavern had been cut deep, creating an immense chamber solidly walled with large rocks and a resinous mortar impermeable to water. Cold but not frozen, hundreds of bottles, jars and clay jugs lay in pigeonholed wooden shelves secured to the masonry walls and arranged in parallel rows of shelving, like books in a library. Some were ageless, covered in dust and with faded labels that were barely decipherable. Sausages, smoked hams and cured meats hung from hooks above sallow cylind-rical blocks containing ageing slabs of cheese, some covered in cloth and green with mould. These occupied a long, narrow bench next to the steps.

Multi-candle lanterns hung unlit from iron brackets around the vast space. A musty, acerbic scent pervaded the room. Asked for his opinion on a suitable wine, the servant suggested a number of possible candidates. He had been Joseph's wine-making apprentice for at least a decade, and Jack valued his judgment. Their final choice was a rich and robust Spanish Garnacha from the Penedès region in Catalonia and an admirable partner in a Sangiovese Chianti from Tuscany. Rysiek was left with the task of delivering the bottles to the table as Jack made his way outside to face the wintry darkness.

There was sufficient open sky to light the way under the gibbous moon, so the young physician moved out onto the thick snowy blanket covering the lawn and stopped, fleetingly, refreshed by the cold and crisp night air. A gentle northwesterly wind heralded the promise of more snow, and Jack turned in the vast open expanse of the yard to face its whispery frozen fingers. He shivered as he stood there for a moment, flexing his leg to loosen the aching thigh. Reinvigorated, he then sauntered into the stables and ambled across to his horse's stall.

Abaccus greeted his rider with a throaty nicker of recognition and stepped into his open palm as the latter stroked his horse's forehead. Jack entered the stall and refilled the chaff box. After adjusting the horse's blanket, he closed the barrier, fed him carrots hidden within his pockets and wished him a happy new year. He checked in on the other freshly-installed mounts belonging to Chauvin's party, and seeing that Old Joseph had done his job well, stepped back out into the compound. Light snowflakes began to fall as dark clouds drifted languidly across the face of the moon, dimming the night. He returned to the house.

The dissonant sounds of myriad conversations filled the dining hall. The drapes had been drawn back and the window left partially open to help dissipate the cinereous haze of pipe and cheroot smoke that permeated the room. Cheers greeted Jack's reappearance, the loudest ones from those fuelled by the most alcohol. The table had been replenished with fresh food, and Jack was pleased to see the happy, smiling faces and hear the laughter of the revellers. No one had slipped off to sleep.

Janina, the self-ordained timekeeper, announced that midnight was imminent. Responding to Jock's authoritative command, servants, guests and family filed out of the hall with drinks in hand and assembled in a large circle at the side of the house. Blixt snatched the vodka jug and winked at Volkov.

Blazing torches were issued to the men as they passed the doorway and stepped beyond the landing into the inky night. The mistress of the estate began the countdown, with others quickly joining in. Pockets of laughter rose from some in the circle due to the discordant counting in different languages—Polish, French, Russian, Swedish and others. Every second the loud chorus bellowed in unison, reverberating with increasing intensity around the snow-hushed, open grounds of the estate.

At the stroke of midnight, the revellers erupted into cheers and wild yells, and Jock trudged into the centre of the circle. A curious, straw-stuffed wicker figure in the shape of a man, like a scarecrow, stood fixed to a stake. The Scot lowered his torch, touching it to the feet of the effigy. The woven twigs instantly burst into flames that rapidly spread to envelop the whole figure. As the blaze took hold, Jock discarded his torch into the fire and resumed his place in the circle. More cheers and light-hearted hoots rose spasmodically from the assembly. Jack stood at the edge of the group, flanked by the two Frenchmen. Averting his stare from the mesmerising flames, Roberge half-turned to the young physician with a question, "What is the significance of this?"

"It is a long-standing custom, perhaps not widely spread throughout our country, but performed by many families." Jack paused to acknowledge and reciprocate Volkov's handshake as the Russian made his way along the line. Others hugged and kissed, exchanging New Year's wishes. "The straw figure represents the old year. By burning it, we are bidding farewell to the old and acknowledging the arrival of the new. With this transition comes the hope for better things: improved health, continued happiness, growth in prosperity and peace. *Annus mirabilis—a wonderful year*; we pray for this." Torches were cast randomly into the burning heap as the merrymaking crowd dissipated, gradually returning inside.

The women gravitated to the hearth, giggling and chatting as they warmed themselves after coming in from the cold darkness. Chauvin sought out his young friend, replenishing his empty mug with frothy beer. "When do you plan to travel north to your king?" the Frenchman asked between sips.

"There is no great urgency right now, although I am concerned about his welfare," Jack replied. "I despatched my report from Linz to his council and have nothing further to add for the moment. The Green-Scarf Fraternity continues to remain active. I must formulate a plan to uncover their source and understand their motives. Once we find the nest, we can capture the birds. I am expecting further details from Pomorski in Warszawa, and Bucquoy promised me an update."

Straddling the arm of his chair casually with one leg, Jack had settled into a comfortable position, the ache in his thigh forgotten. Old Joseph's apple wine was smooth and easy drinking, relaxing him further with every mouthful.

"Where did you meet your new friends, Alain? Tell me more about them."

With heavy lids, the corporal sat hunched over the table, leaning on his elbows. The pipe and tobacco-filled leather pouch had been returned to their owner. "Julien and I reached the central square in Prague late one evening. Our journey had been harrowing. Leaving an occupied city presented its own obstacles, and we travelled in fear, constantly alert for a sudden attack and peering regularly into the night behind us. Our spirits rose only when the lights of the city appeared in the distance and we reached the bridge leading into the capital." His face brightened with the memory. "Tired, cold and hungry, we chose the most roisterous inn, but there was space enough inside for us. We felt like fugitives, but nobody gave us a second glance. We ordered three teeming plates between us to dispel any lingering thoughts of rationed meals. You can well understand how ravenous we were."

The corporal stopped to refill Jack's mug and poured himself another ale, sipping at the rising froth before it overflowed. Wiping his chin with his sleeve, he continued. "A group had gathered by the fireplace, listening to a medley of Spanish songs. The harmony that the two caballeros shared was only surpassed by the guitar accompaniment. Our view was partially obstructed, so we didn't see what actually caused the uproar, but the song was suddenly interrupted and replaced by loud shouts. A fight erupted. As punches were thrown, somewhere from the far side of the room this blond giant of a man strode in, picking up a chair as he approached the brawl. He splintered it over the back of one of the ruffians. He managed to avoid a fist thrust from the fray as a stocky, red-haired cavalier with Germanic features stepped in to jerk the culprit back by his long black hair."

A barely visible smile touched the corners of Jack's eyes as he listened to the trilled 'R's in Chauvin's increasingly excited voice.

"The sight of these two sturdy strangers calmed the ruckus, and the crowd dispersed. The fair-head-ed man motioned in our direction, and the four of them ambled over to occupy the empty trestle next to us. We were soon in conversation with them. They were strangers merely brought together by the disturbance—by chance."

Chauvin looked across at Blixt. Catching his eye, the Frenchman invited him to join them with a sideways nod of his head. Blixt brought Volkov with him, and the pair eased into a couple of empty chairs. The Russian was red-faced but appeared to have sobered up.

Jack began smoothly, asking, "My guess is that Blixt has Scandinavian origins?"

"Common enough in the north—three generations of gunsmiths outside Stockholm," Blixt replied, looking up as his other three companions joined them. Chairs were shuffled to accommodate the enlarged group. "Three years ago my decision was made to leave home and travel. On the day I crossed, the stormy Baltic was like a boiling cauldron, and I was relieved to see the end of the voyage and set foot on land again at Rügen on the Pomeranian coast. Making my way gradually south through Brandenburg and Saxony, I found work as a civilian attached to various military contingents, employed as a gunsmith and explosives expert." He worked his strong square jaw as he peered with bright cerulean blue eyes at the faces around him.

"A most useful trade—with the direction Europe appears to be taking," Jack suggested evenly.

"Teplitz proved to be a comfortable stop. A talented local craftsman occupied a store off the town square. He was a kindly and tireless old man who knew his trade well, and we developed innovative designs for hunting pistols and long arms. His brother, a twin, owned a sister business in Klostergrab, and my work took me between the two towns regularly. The local country was ideal for deer and horned-sheep hunting, and the two brothers ran a profitable trade. That's where I met Ritner. We were the same age and shared similar interests. I was the handsome one with brains, and he was the better shot."

The Bavarian's hand paused, his goblet halfway to his lips, as he grinned and took up the story. "We hunted throughout the vast primeval, timbered area for 16 months. Known to the locals as Krušné Hory and to visiting hunters as the Ore Mountains, this elevated range was home to immense stretches of diversified deciduous forests." Ritner spoke with a typically strong, guttural Bavarian accent. "I worked with the brother as a hunting guide and knew those hills and the surrounding timberlands intimately. There was abundant and varied game for the serious and keen shooter: enormous red deer stags with magnificent racks, shy and elusive European fallow deer and plentiful packs of roaming wolves as well as copious wildcats, bears and the common fox. Fleet-footed, ruddy mouflon with spectacular curved horns populated the steeper, less-accessible slopes and were considered an equally-valuable prize. We established a chain of small gamekeeper lodges where hunters were quartered and the movements of the best trophies were monitored."

Ritner held everyone's attention with additional stories of muddy stalks by zealous hunters in drenching rain, falls and broken necks on slippery, sheer cliff faces and the blissful delight of a successful kill.

"Back at home in Augsburg, my trade as a trained cartographer proved very useful as I prepared charts of the shooting areas around Klostergrab. My passion for hunting was insatiable, weaned in the ideal Bavarian outdoors." Ritner paused momentarily as he proffered his cup to be refilled by the Cossack. "These North Bohemian mountains were also home to the golden eagle and numerous species of hawk, feeding my assiduous interest and study of birds of prey. I was fortunate to be a frequent visitor to Jezeří Castle, and Jan Mikuláš—the castle's most-obliging and benevolent owner—allowed me unrestricted access to the chateau grounds. I spent many long hours observing a convocation of eagles and a cast of goshawks soaring majestically in wide circles from the outer castle grounds as they searched for prey with ultimate patience."

Ritner was scratching at his reddish beard when the Swede interrupted. "Not only is Andreas an excellent marksman but the only man alive who can subdue me at arm-wrestling."

"Volkov also has a strong arm," Jack noted. "We must organise a contest."

"And a bottle of Joseph's superb cherry vodka will be the prize!" Jack's father, suddenly attentive, threw in as he arrived at their end of the table. "No better time than here and now. Jack and Anton will compete first; Mr Blixt will take on the winner. Andreas and any others will follow. Sudden death—no second chances." The old Scot had extraordinary organisational talent in setting impromptu contests such as this in motion. The rules were simple, and they were clear.

Seated at the corner of the table in their shirt-sleeves, Jack and Volkov locked their right palms together, thumbs entwined as they set their elbows against the timber boards. Jack decided to ignore any pain if it returned. With a short bark of "Dawaj!" from the old Scot, the two men leaned into each other. Their arm muscles bulged with the strain, and rivulets of veins appeared under their taut skin. Their faces reddened with effort. Urged on by their enthusiastic spectators, both contestants breathed in short, laboured rasps.

Neither man gained positive ground during the first minute, but then Jack's arm was slowly forced backwards. With renewed resolve, the young physician held and regained the lost inch, holding his friend in a neutral position for a long, persistent moment. Volkov snatched his vodka glass with his free hand and swallowed the spirit in one sharp movement as he held Jack's pressing arm steady. With a final strenuous heave, the Cossack pulled the physician's arm down, finally banging his whitened knuckles on the planks. A loud cheer applauded the pair. Red-faced, Jack slapped his dear friend good-naturedly on the shoulder and said, breathing heavily, "The only time I can beat you is when you allow me to win, and that has never been when alcohol has been the prize. Well done!"

The Polish officer rose from the table amid the group's laughter, and the Swede settled into his seat. "Be gentle with him, Kristian," Chauvin ordered as the struggle began on Jock's command. Little appeared to separate the strength of the two men; both were of the same height, although the Russian was leaner and a few years older. With an audible gasp to fill his lungs, Blixt concentrated his whole body's effort through his forearm and wrist, and Volkov's arm was forced backwards, an inch at a time, until he knew he was beaten.

The two men shook hands, and the Bavarian replaced the loser. He stared intently into the Swede's eyes after the signal and, with little apparent exertion, pulled Blixt's arm gently down in victory.

"Ah, you always do that, Andreas," the Swede complained. "I can't beat you!"

"I thwart you with my mind, Kristian; not with my physical strength." The winner accepted his prize graciously and lifted the bottle to study the transparent, ruby-coloured liquid. Old Joseph appeared, producing a tray of small glasses filled with the same spirit, and said, "Herr Ritner, try this. It's from the same vat as your prize. I am especially pleased with the way it turned out—more fruit and less sugar."

Following Andreas, each man took a glass, leaving the last for the spirits' master. "To our health and absent friends!" Old Joseph saluted the band with his raised beaker.

"Health and friends," the companions echoed.

"Señor Montejo has been sharing some of his exploits with us earlier. Introduce yourself to the covey, Candelario," Volkov suggested.

Somewhat shy, the Spaniard from Salamanca looked down at the floor, deciding where to start. "I come from a humble family of candlestick makers. In fact, my Christian name means 'candle wax'. Earlier generations of my forebears settled in Segovia, and my family name is translated to mean 'little mountain'. Segovia is a beautiful town in the Sierra de Guadarrama mountain range, and perhaps our name was inspired by Mt Peñalara, which is truly an imposing and majestic peak."

The Spaniard was of average height, his tanned

complexion barely bleached by the dreary autumn months. His thick black locks hung down in waves, framing his boyish face. It was because of his face that he looked half his age, which was nearing 30. He seemed the epitome of Narcissus. While his dark, beguiling eyes held a deceptive innocence, the Spaniard possessed a skill with a dagger and sword surpassed by few. Disproportionately long fingers at the end of soft hands had given rise to calloused fingertips, a symptom of long, regular hours of guitar playing. Years earlier, a flamenco master from Madrid who holidayed in his hometown had taught him to play. The boy had a keen, unquenchable interest in music, and his singing voice developed into something as beautiful as his strumming.

Montejo peered at the faces around the room in search of his Veronese friend. His wordless instruction—a cheerful nod and a cheeky wink—was immediately clear to his companion, and the Italian reached for the Spaniard's guitar, which had been safely left in the corner. He leaned against the table as he passed the instrument to the guitarist. Resting a raised knee on the chair, the Spaniard plucked absently at the guitar strings to test the key. He cocked an ear as he waited for a suggested melody and began strumming an introduction to the song he and his companion had silently chosen between them. Their plangent, velvet voices blended in matchless harmony as the room fell silent and embraced the mood of the mournful ballad.

Marco Scrolavezza could well have been the Spaniard's brother. His dark, swarthy looks complemented his manicured, ink-black moustache, and he was a constant favourite with the ladies, his vivacious manner endearing him to all around him. His deceivingly innocent and brooding olive eyes, surrounded by a mass of black curly locks, served as an unchallengeable magnet to all members of the fairer sex who came into contact with him. While the Italian's angelic countenance could easily mislead an unwary foe into believing that the youth was easy prey, the gracile lad was actually one of the best swordsmen in his native Verona—a sublime master of the rapier and dagger. He spoke fluent Spanish, which was not a difficult task for an Italian, especially as his mother hailed from Seville.

The final euphonic chords of the two men's plaintive melody faded, returning the room to a long, silent pause before the hypnotic enchantment was broken by clapping and smiling nods of approval. When the applause finally abated, Candelario lowered his guitar and pointed at his companion with an extended arm as he deferred the praise. Marco accepted a couple of playful shoves and back-slaps, and Volkov ruffled his hair as the Russian stood and grasped the bottle to refill the tumblers.

Many of the servants had retired. It would be dawn soon. Nina had taken her leave an hour earlier, bidding the company a cheerful good night. Old Joseph added another sizable log onto the smouldering coals and coaxed the fire back to life with a firm stab of the poker. Lazy tongues of rutilant flame appeared, flaring with the sudden flow of fresh air. He too bid the remaining cavaliers goodnight and withdrew to check the barn and stables one last time before seeking the comfort of his bed. He was followed by Rysiek, whose unfocused red eyes showed the effects of more drink than he was accustomed to.

The hall had dimmed as numerous candles snuffed themselves out, leaving behind smoking wicks and the sweet scent of burned beeswax. Only the thick, hexagonal pillar candles continued to burn with calefacient flames. Jock dug at the stalactites hanging from the closest candelabrum and grasping a handful of candles recently purchased from the chandler in Kraków, fitted them onto the arms, lighting their wicks with a taper. A relaxed ambience encompassed the chamber and its peregrine and disparate band, whose members were inebriated and mellowed by the ataractic effects of the liquor and replete with food.

Jack lazily scanned the faces before him, study-ing each individually, and it struck him how affable and homogeneous this small company of men had become together—nonchalant yet unified, stolid yet dependable. Chauvin's motley band had wandered into his home from the uncertain darkness and cold world outside. The men were essentially mercenaries without a cause or a master, each bringing specific skills and talents paid for by no man's purse. He was sure that his family would agree to give them a bed and feed them until a viable future course present-ed each with a satiable opportunity. Yet, as a single strength, there was a synergistic merit in keeping the group together—like a pride of lions hunting more effectively and successfully together than a solitary rogue.

Volkov had warmed to the visitors immediately. Although alcohol had been the initial, fervent magnet, the Russian had been lost in deep and considered conversation with every one of them over the course of the night. As had Jack's father. And then there was Chauvin, the most senior of them all, a stalwart of dependability and trust. Jack conferred unreserved confidence in him. The weather-beaten, gnarled veteran was an excellent judge of character, and he was happy to call the men his friends, otherwise Roberge alone would have remained his travelling companion. Jock and Anton too were relaxed and comfortable in their company, sharing their feelings and thoughts unguardedly. What fate had smiled on him and brought them to his door, Jack wondered?

Suddenly the young physician sensed the prickling feeling of eyes upon him, and from the wash of faces, he perceived his father's piercing gaze. Their eyes locked and held for an incalculable moment, and Jack realised that the old Scot instinctively knew what his son had been thinking. With a corroborating blink, the master of the estate averted his astute eyes to seek the Cossack's attention. Anton quickly acquiesced to Jock's silent request and ensured that all of the goblets, glasses, tankards and mugs were full. The conversation around the table dissipated spontaneously. Faces looked to Jack's father as he slowly rose to his feet and raised his glass high, level with his brow.

"It is an honour indeed, on behalf of my dear son and his beloved mother, to have you all as our worthy guests in my house. I know not if I should thank the bleak snow-filled winter outside or Monsieur Chauvin's friendship with my son, or perhaps both, for assembling such an august companionship under our family roof tonight." Jock's wrinkled eyes gleamed clearly in the flickering candlelight as he blinked away the misty traces of candour and emotion before continuing. "This special occasion has marked the greeting of the new year with singular significance— the forging of new and lasting friendships and the augmenting of old, deep ones. My unqualified and free-spoken wish is that all of us in this hall this morning—this camaraderie of soldiers, this cavalier club—remain as one, unified and dear in friendship and mutual respect for eternity!"

"To the cavalier club," Jack's repeated words were echoed in harmony as the first nascent slivers of grey dawn appeared against the stormy eastern horizon and distant, guttural grumbling warned of a pending snowstorm.

Chapter 11

Despatches

The noblewoman locked Jack's gaze with her alluring, ocean-green eyes. She flashed him an impetuous, radiant smile as she and an elderly gentleman—undoubtedly her father—promenaded along the busy cobbled footpath. The debonaire, grey-haired man guided his daughter through the chaotic oncoming stream of pedestrians as they manoeuvred their way past the tobacconist, arm-in-arm. The girl's pretty, sweet face finally turned away from Jack's as she and her father disappeared from view behind the trader's cart and down a nearby side street.

Never one to ignore an attractive, young pair of eyes, Jack had smiled back innocently until his father reclaimed his attention with repeated exaggerated coughs. They had come to Kraków together with a list of items to purchase, amongst them a suitable pipe and some mild tobacco for Chauvin. They were happy with their ultimate choice: an elegantly-carved, long-stemmed briar piece and a block of fragrant imported tobacco chosen with the assistance of the knowledgeable and helpful storeowner. Jack was sure that the willowy corporal would enjoy the gift. More importantly, the specially selected and diced tobacco leaves were blended in France. The two had also negotiated an attractive price for a second block—a sharper mixture—that would be for Roberge's enjoyment.

It had been a week since the New Year festivities. Heavy rain and regular snowfall had made it impractical to venture far from the Channing estate. Lazy debates and discussions, lengthy chess tournaments and idle reading in front of glowing hearths alongside culinary classes on the preparation of Spanish and Italian cuisines occupied the Channing family and its visitors. The first promising signs of clement weather had appeared late yesterday morning, and by mid-afternoon, the angry and threatening clouds had been replaced by light grey billows of sparse storm clouds soughed by a temperate breeze from the southwest.

Perhaps seeking the gentleness and experience that accumulates with the years, Chauvin was happiest when he was busy assisting Joseph with the latter's many interminable projects. The pair had discovered a respectful amity in each other's company. The sagacious stable master remained keen to ensure that his young apprentice was not idle despite the recent addition of Chauvin's helping hands. Late in the afternoon, all three were at the stables, checking the state of the horses' hooves. Rysiek had been instructed to fire the furnace and prepare 10 sets of new horseshoes.

Shafts of sunlight had cheered the morning, reinforcing the promise of improved weather, and with it, a surety that the climate change would remain stable for some days. This was reason enough to delay no further the visit to Kraków planned by the two masters of the Channing household. As Jack and his father rode out on farm mounts, Chauvin and Rysiek were shoeing the warhorses under Old Joseph's watchful eye. In the horseshed, they were shielded from the bone-chilling icy flurries swooping in from the north. Volkov supervised the loading of a large wagon and carted the remaining cavaliers to the far paddock to repair the northern line of fences and dismember any fallen trees. These would be chopped, stored and used for next winter's fires.

Having had ample time to write to his beloved in Warszawa, Jack left two sealed parchments with the rider at Wawel Castle. As was customary, the courier would be paid on receipt of the letters. Long shadows fell across the main city square as father and son mounted to cover the three leagues back to the estate, their business done and their saddlebags full with the items they had procured.

During the evening meal, Old Joseph confirmed that the mounts had been shod, and Chauvin tabled his plan to hand-stitch a special set of saddlebags to a cut that had caught his eye years earlier while on duty in Spain. With Montejo's innovative input, he had settled on a unique design that he believed would be more practical for the rider and less burdensome for the animal. The corporal was presented with his gift after the meal and happily filled the new pipe, offering no end of praise regarding the choice of tobacco. Roberge was equally eager to try the fresh mix that the masters of the estate had purchased, and the kitchen quickly filled with the wisping mist of blue, aromatic smoke. The women soon forced the men from the scullery as the clattering of washing dishes made quiet conversation impossible. The companions retired to the dining hall for their post-prandial liqueurs, cheroots joining smoking pipes as the men settled comfortably in a wide curve around the hearth. Jack was happy to refill glasses and cups as Volkov reported on the progress they were making with the fences.

"I am yet to ride and inspect the quality of the work of these artisans, but I must admit that they hauled back a heaped cartload of storm-damaged trees from the northern sector of the estate," Joseph offered with mock antagonism.

"We'll ride out together tomorrow morning," noted Jack, looking askance at the old gardener. "Did you see any wolves beyond the far paddocks, Anton?" he added with interest.

Ritner replied in the Russian's stead, his voice laced with subtle respect. "Two small packs but shy enough to keep their distance. Roberge dropped one with a remarkable headshot at over 80 paces, and the rest scattered after that. We left the carcass, but the magnificent winter coat is now with Joseph for curing."

"Rysiek has it to start on tomorrow. Alain offered to help him with it," Joseph retorted, sipping on his Cognac brandy.

"We've salted it thinly and left it cooling in the barn. Rysiek and I will flesh it tomorrow, and when it's cured, I can see it gracefully warming the Lady Janina's shoulders," Chauvin added lightly.

"Perhaps my wife and I will share it?" Jock added prophetically, coaxing a murmur of laughter from the assembly. "How long will you need to complete the repairs?" he asked, gazing enquiringly at the Russian.

"Less than half a day. The weather should hold

tomorrow, and my plan is to allow our visitors an opportunity to see the sights of beautiful Kraków when our work is done. How does that sit with you?"

"The change will do them good," Jock agreed. "But make sure that they see more than just the inside of a tavern or a whorehouse." More laughter concurred with the obvious, and Kristian offered to report on the extent of the tour. He was as incorrigible as Volkov. Neither gave any indication when they would return.

"My son and I have been discussing the need to erect an additional barn. It would be opportune to take advantage of the extra hands we have here now. However, the frozen ground will be impossible to dig so we can prepare to lay foundations after the thaw."

Nods of willing and open assent met Jock's proposal. Prompted by Old Joseph's quizzical stare to share his news, Ritner broke the silence after some minutes. "Whilst we were at the northern fence line, I watched a pair of hunting eagles circling nearby. Not surprising as this country provides an ideal habitat for birds of prey."

"There are numerous aeries here," Jack interjected. "Separate families of eagles and hawks co-exist happily on and beyond our estate. I see them often as I ride across the distant hills and surrounding countryside."

"Well," the Bavarian continued eagerly, "I joined Roberge to retrieve his wolf and to pace out the shot. As we began skinning the animal, a movement caught my eye, and I discovered a fledgling eagle straddling a lower branch nearby, studying us with interest. The dogs had not troubled it. Leaving Julien to his task, I approached the beautiful bird, cautiously and slowly, to identify it. It stared at me with regal eyes from behind that falcate beak, uncompromised by my presence. Although young, the magnificent specimen remained wary yet unafraid as I studied it from this proximity," he indicated with a movement of his finger between Blixt and himself, "but it sat still and silent, watching my every move. Careful not to frighten it, I pulled my hand back, hiding my fingers within my coat sleeve. Cajoling the majestic bird by gently rubbing its belly with my outstretched arm, I was elated as it stepped guardedly onto my wrist, one taloned leg at a time, head moving from its new perch to my face and back again. Raising it slowly, the weight surprised me. Willing it not to fly off, I carefully carried it back past Roberge, who handed me a couple of slivers of raw meat, to those working at the fence line. We fed it more there and again when Julien joined us with the coat and further collops of meat. The eagle travelled back to the house with us, quite comfortable and apparently unperturbed. Joseph and I watched it awhile, and we believe that it has a broken wing. Perhaps you would examine the bird and confirm our suspicions?"

Jack nodded back at Ritner as Joseph added, "The eagle raises its right wing freely but will not unfurl the other. It was fortunate not to have been taken by the wolves considering where Andreas found it. We should examine it tonight if that is not inconvenient."

"Why wait?" Already on his feet, Jack indicated that he would fetch his bag and join the others in the barn.

Jock assumed that the procedure had been accomplished satisfactorily from the men's smiling faces when they returned to the room 20 minutes later. "Successful?" he asked, cocking an eyebrow.

"We hooded the bird and fixed a splint to its left wing, which had a minor fracture. As long as we feed it regularly, it will be comfortable in the barn and safe from harm. It can be released when it's ready to fly—my guess, in about four to six weeks," Jack explained.

The men dispersed an hour later as dying embers smouldered in the fireplace. It was to be an early night. Physical work in the cold made for a good night's sleep.

As agreed, Jack rode out in the cool late morning to inspect the fence repairs, spanned on either side by horses carrying his father and the stable master.

The men had breakfasted at daybreak, and the others had driven out in the wagon, eager to complete their task. Volkov's supervision had not been misguided, and the quality of their work impressed the admiring inspectors.

Ritner pointed to a large, gnarled tree standing naked in the distance. "That's where I found our feathered friend. The wolf's carcass is gone, but it lay over there not far to the right." His pointing finger swung in a light arc to the right of the tree.

"Not a bad shot then," Jock responded, approvingly calculating the considerable distance with his eye. "The wolves or foxes would have taken the wounded bird eventually. There is little out there for them to eat during winter."

The old Scot looked down at the wagon, noting that it was half-filled with limbs and branches that had been collected from the broken fencing. "We won't want for firewood next year," he observed, airing a large leather pouch that sloshed with liquid and offering it to Volkov and his team. "Some internal heating, lads, for a job well done. We appreciate it."

Shortly after midday, the repairs had been completed, and the cart was turned towards the house. Eager to stretch his mount's legs, Jack wished the others a profitable time in town and galloped west, climbing to the nearby ridgeline from where he would decide which terrain to explore. From the high line of boulders, the young officer was struck by the breathtaking beauty of the country transformed by a blanket of snow, and in the cool northerly breeze, he scanned the distant rolling hills through his telescope. Abaccus twitched beneath him, mists of vapour condensing from both nostrils. He was eager for the run. Jack stroked the base of his horse's neck and spurred him into a slow canter, wary of the dangers of travelling across snow-covered ground. They traversed rocky stretches and found that the snow had melted in patches on the southern-facing lower slopes of the valleys. Here the forests stood in dense rows, and twice they startled small herds of red deer and a pair of marauding foxes covered in thick, rich coats of russet and white and socks of black. Soon after climbing to a clear, rocky outcrop, Jack traced the track with his eyes leading from the estate, a thin serpentine line. He recognised the small group of half a dozen horsemen riding steadily south to join the main road leading to Kraków, which was hidden behind the hill and lying to the east. *They won't return today,* he mused as he guided his mount towards the western extremities of the vast estate and beyond.

It was mid-afternoon by the time Jack galloped

into the compound and the waiting hands of Chauvin, who held the reins as the young officer dismounted.

"A good ride, sir?" the old Frenchman asked between puffs of his new pipe.

"Exhilarating! This is wonderful country, Chauvin. You should join me next time." Jack's cheeks were flushed from the cold.

"It would be my pleasure. I have been preparing some sketches of the saddlebags. Candelario cast an approving eye over them, so soon we'll begin the cutting and stitching. Joseph found some appropriately thick leather pieces—perfect for the task. You will be the first to trial the finished product."

"You'll have my honest appraisal, my friend. Believe me. How's the patient faring?"

Chauvin laughed, lifting the pipe from his mouth. "That eaglet will never fly again."

Jack turned his full attention to the Frenchman, eyeing him with a concerned and questioning frown.

"His wing will doubtlessly mend soon" Chauvin continued, "but he has been fed by Joseph, Rysiek and me—none of us aware of the others. He'll grow so fat that his body will never lift off the ground. We have delegated his care to Rysiek, who is now to be his sole guardian, and I'll advise Ritner when they return from their visit. By the way, the despatch rider was here about an hour earlier. Your mother may have some fresh news for you."

Relieved to hear about the bird, Jack thanked the wiry soldier and strode to the house as Chauvin led Abaccus away to be brushed and fed. Several letters lay on a small credenza by the front doors, and Jack sieved through them, recognising Count Pomorski's hand. He carried the others into the kitchen, where he was sure to find his mother. After kissing Janina's cheek, he asked for Jock.

"Your father is somewhere outside with Joseph. I'll make sure he gets these," Jack's mother replied as her son handed her the bundle of sealed missives. "Don't forget to wash your hands, Andrzej," she called after the young officer as he made his way to the library.

Settling into a chair by the fire, Jack broke the cachet on Count Pomorski's letter and unravelled the parchment, quickly casting a perusing eye over the whole document. He crossed his legs as he read the bold, flowing script in detail.

7 January 1619
Warszawa

My dearest Lieutenant Channing,
You will guess the unprecedented dismay that news of your injuries caused our household, especially Marianna,

whose distress and shock were augmented by the lack of knowledge as to their extent and severity. I personally understand and appreciate your reasons for keeping this from her directly, and it was of course made known to us from your despatch to the king, who alerted me privately to your incapacitated circumstances and recuperation in Linz. We trust that your recovery is all but complete and that these words find you convalesced and back on your mount. Be assured that you have our prayers and thoughts of support with you constantly.

Your letter to Marianna arrived some weeks earlier and informed us of your plans to join your family in Kraków at the earliest possible opportunity. I hope this letter finds you there, safe and mended, and that your family is enjoying the return of their only son.

As the bearer of tidings from around the capital, I fear that misadventures are reciprocated, and I can share the following with you, happily all of which is not disheartening and sour. In my previous, albeit succinct, correspondence, I advised you of the fact that the king's life had been endangered by another callous attack. Vasa's wound was superficial as the culprit was being overwhelmed by the king's guard as he took his shot, which was fortunately deflected by a pillar before tearing at the monarch's left sleeve. The physicians attended to the king's minor wound, a shallow lateral gash traced by the ricocheted pistol-ball. We thank God that the king's spirit has not been dampened by these events. It may not surprise you to know that his first reaction was to call for a goblet of wine.

Upon initial questioning, we discovered that the shooter was in his late 20s, a zealous anarchist who had spent time with the Saxon infantry as a musketeer and had been recruited for this task in Prague. After pressing him further, we now know that his family's background is Lutheran, yet he claims that he holds no single religion in significance and his motivation was solely based on political, anarchistic precepts. He has made puzzling reference to "Elbflorenz" in passing and claims that he met his recruiter in a darkened building to which he was led blind-folded and that he would be unable to identify him, or the premises, again. Their communication has always been in German, which is his mother's tongue. He has offered his name as Jürgen Schkirt, and we are holding him as our guest in the dungeons of the royal castle sequestered from other prisoners.

Due to the profound ramifications had this attempt proved successful, the king wishes the investigation of this matter expedited and has elevated its importance to the highest priority. I hope that I have not transgressed my station in putting forward your good name, my boy, as my primary choice in one to lead this inquest in uncovering the source of this most worrying vipers' nest. You have previously expressed to me, and to the king, a sincere *desire to expose this craven and contemptible plot, and should you choose to accept this important mantle, I will lay at your feet all of my resources to assist your venture.*

In your reply, I look forward to encouraging news. Should you report an ongoing or complete recovery, I will advise my concerned daughter. And should your reply to this paramount project be positive, I will advise the king. Both would be most pleased, but no more than I,

Your obedient servant and trusted friend,

Stefan Pomorski,

Count, etc., etc.

The letter dropped absently from Jack's hand and rested on his lap as he considered its contents. Impulsively, his initial reaction was to accept the task—one that he would relish and that would absorb his entire interest, energy and time. Yet he was not inherently impetuous and decided instead to consider his options carefully and seek the opinion of his family and closest friends.

The matter of his health, Jack had dealt with in the letters that left Kraków yesterday. Enthralled with the mere prospect of the chase, he moved to the nearby writing table. Withdrawing a fresh piece of parchment, he dipped his quill into an inkwell and listed in a logical sequence everything that he knew of the Green-Scarf Fraternity. A plan was forming gradually in his mind, and he was sure of the ensuing steps that needed to be taken should he decide to proceed. The beat of anticipation began to pulse through his veins.

There was no sign of the garrulous and merry band of mischievous reprobates that night. Dinner was rather a quieter and more intimate affair than usual, and the household members left for their beds earlier than would have been expected. Joseph was the last to retire to his chamber after completing his customary nocturnal review.

Shortly after breakfast the next day, the regular beat of a galloping horse bore a despatch rider to the Channing estate. Compensated for the delivery, the messenger touched the rim of his cap with two fingers and spun his mount around, leading him back down the drive in a smooth trot. Janina sought out her son, cradling the packages she had received in her arms.

The heavy larger parcel was bound smartly in a leather pouch with tight leather thongs, and Jack recognised that the markings it bore were from the town of Linz. Cutting the cords that bound the package's well-protected contents with his dagger, he noticed a small note discretely inserted into the cover of a manuscript. His surprise turned to delight as he read Herr Kepler's introductory words and perused his gracious gift of a signed copy of the astronomer's complete set of perceptive documents covering his beloved laws of planetary motion. The young officer grinned as he thumbed through the miscellaneous attachments, which included a minor thesis on sunspots and notes describing the mathematical calculations of elliptical orbits of mutually influencing heavenly bodies. A separate sheet provided a diagrammatic analysis of the passage of the moon around the earth alongside jotted notes explaining the earth's inclination and rotation. He and Kepler had discussed these matters during his short but memorable visit to the latter's home, and the astronomer had remained true to his word, wishing to maintain an ongoing correspondence.

The other letter bore the regal Habsburg seal of Vienna. Jack read Bucquoy's comprehensive report slowly, careful to consider every important and ostensible detail. He was both surprised and relieved by the host of coincident facts that mirrored those in Pomorski's text. The attack on King Ferdinand had occurred on Christmas Day; the count, on the other hand, did not specify a date or time as to when the attack on Sigismund had taken place. This would need to be clarified.

Retrieving his earlier notes regarding the Green-Scarf Fraternity, Jack quilled the additional relevant details below his list of facts and slid the document back into the bureau drawer. He then composed two letters of gratitude to the senders of the two packages and sealed them with the Channing crest in wax. His third and final note contained his reply to Pomorski, accepting the role and thanking him for his concern and proffered support. Sealing the letter, Jack bundled it with the others, still proposing to discuss his intentions before sending it. It could always be destroyed if his mind or circumstances changed.

The young man immersed himself in minor chores for the remainder of the day. While Chauvin worked diligently in preparing the deer cape and puffing happily on his pipe, Jack climbed onto the barn roof to assist Rysiek with the replacement of cracked and loose masonry tiles. Other retainers were chopping and stacking firewood, careful to leave ventilation gaps that would allow their pile to dry before next winter's use. Beyond the stables, Old Joseph had slaughtered a sow for the larder, and the cook assisted in butchering, segregating and parcelling the meat. The stable master would be smoking the hindquarters, gammon and hock as well as strips off the collar and backbone for the remainder of the week. This was a slow process, requiring a great deal of diligent patience.

A second night passed without the cavaliers' return. Jock struggled with a chess game against his son as the young officer employed the newly-learned tactics he had painfully acquired in Warszawa. Chauvin sat closer to the fire, polishing his pistols as he and Old Joseph reminisced about their happy, youthful days as musketeers in the infantry. Janina and the two cooks fixed the visitors' clothes, stitching on absent buttons and repairing frayed cuffs, as well as mending collars and torn sleeves. Rysiek had stoked the fire and joined the remaining servants for a bout of checkers in their own quarters. The young officer's wounds had healed well, and he felt better due to the lengthy rest than he had before Lomnice. He retired earlier than was his custom, wanting to re-read the letters that had arrived in the past couple of days.

Chapter 12

QUESTIONS

Jack found the cavaliers holding a firm line across the flagstones that paved the rear courtyard of St Mark's. A spacious, open area, the quadrangle was bordered by large elm and oak trees, their branches now denuded in the middle of winter. Their horses were nowhere to be seen, and their cloaks, doublets and other obstructive outer garments lay discarded on the cobbles or hung over the empty water trough.

Facing the cavaliers with grim determination stood a larger group of militiamen, their swords drawn and waiting for someone to cast the first thrust. Jack sat astride his mount, his right leg lying comfortably across the front of his saddle as he crunched on a juicy apple. He was clear of any possible action as he reined Abaccus in at the open gates that led to the rear of the church. *The odds seem reasonable*, he thought—nine against Volkov and his five companions.

A tall, dark-haired officer spat a curse in Ruthenian

across the drawn blades, to which Anton replied with equal and deliberate vehemence, pretending to bite on his thumb. This was sufficient provocation for the tall, burly man to shout back angrily and advance with his sword.

Duelling in Kraków was still legal. The whole line of Ruthenes attacked, yelling obscenities to goad their opponents. The courtyard erupted in a metallic cacophony of clashing steel. Blixt, Volkov and Montejo each took on two opponents. Roberge, at the far end of the line, was perhaps the weakest with the blade, and the Italian duelling next to him was eager to despatch his mark and assist the Frenchman.

Montejo was toying with his pair, enjoying the duel as if it were a game. Babbling happily to himself and throwing the odd Spanish remark at his two adversaries, he soon realised that Julien was struggling. On his right, Marco shouted "Basta!" and with a swift, elegant lunge, pierced the right shoulder of his own foe, who collapsed with a groan, his rapier clanging as it rolled away across the cobblestones. Seeing that Montejo was coping well against the swordsmen, the Italian interjected with his blade to parry a stab that was being levelled at Roberge's left breast.

"Take a drink, my French friend, from the fountain that bears my name," Marco jerked his head towards the small shrine that cast a short, curved stream of water into the stone well. "It will revive you while I take care of this Belorussian comrade of yours." His smile appeared more like a grimace as a result of the effort he was exerting, but a final, well-rehearsed flick of his wrist disarmed his opponent and a solid blow to the face with his finger guard shattered the man's jaw. With a nod of thanks, Roberge moved with Marco to assist the Spaniard and even the fight.

Montejo backed away as his companions took over. Earlier he realised that Ritner had taken a cut to the forearm that was clearly causing him some concern. Seeking the right moment, he stepped to the side of Ritner's opponent and slapped him firmly with an open hand across the cheek. The Ruthenian, astounded by the unexpected blow, broke his advance, momentarily disoriented. Candelario smiled as he planted a heavy kick to the man's groin, and Ritner, more by impetus than intent, pierced the Ruthenian's shoulder with his rapier.

"Roberge may need some assistance, Andreas," the Spaniard commented smoothly between breaths, "and I'll check how these two are going." He eyed Volkov and Blixt, both of whom were tiring. The odds were now even.

The Spaniard stepped next to the Swede's right and waved his sword tip under the nose of the closest of Blixt's adversaries, attracting his attention. The momentary distraction was seized by the big Swede, who disarmed his opponent and stabbed him through the thigh, pushing his blade deep into the man's meaty flesh. The wounded swordsman fell sideways with a loud cry of pain, clutching at his leg. Blixt's rapier swayed like a pendulum as it stood embedded in the disabled man's muscle.

Kristian aired his dagger and advanced to assist Volkov. With a fluid movement, he strode forward, bent surprisingly low for a man of his build, and swept his dagger's keen edge smoothly across the knee of one of Volkov's opponents, slashing cartilage and sinew and saturating the man's breeches with a growing stain of crimson blood. Volkov disheartened his remaining opponent with a deep gash to the cheek, and the man surrendered, dropping his sword to the ground.

At the far end of the line, Marco and Roberge were still sparring with the remaining two militiamen, who quickly lost heart as they realised their comrades had been vanquished and escaped on foot through the churchyard gates. Neither cast a glance at the mounted officer, who smiled as they ran wildly past and tossed his apple core after them.

Anton, bleeding from a nick to his neck, sheathed his blade and inspected his badly torn and bloodied sleeve. Breathing heavily, he leaned on Blixt's shoulder and thanked Jack with a touch of haughty sarcasm in his voice. "We would not have been victorious without your timely intervention."

"The fight was not of my making. You did reasonably well for a man your age," Jack replied, his tone silky smooth.

Volkov turned back to face his conquered opponent, who stood with his head bowed, swaying from side to side from fatigue. The Russian gripped the man's jaw firmly with a sweating hand and raised his head so that their eyes locked, only inches apart.

"Here you now stand, abandoned by your loyal friends and humbled by my cavaliers," Volkov spat in his own rasping tongue. "We accept your apology."

The man had not spoken and dared not blink, blatant fear frozen on his weary face.

"You and your rabble should consider leaving this city. Preferably with minimal delay, for if we meet again here or anywhere within the boundaries of this magnificent commonwealth, I will separate you from your manhood and fry your cowardly eyes for breakfast." Volkov glared intently into his opponent's crushed face, catching the acerbic smell of his foul breath. "I am ashamed to have you as my countryman. Return to the steppes and tend your pigs. Do not ever return here." He released his grip and pushed the Ruthenian away.

The cavaliers sheathed their weapons and gathered their belongings as their once arrogant adversary staggered from the courtyard, leaving his wounded companions behind. The band gathered around Jack's steed, and the young officer looked down at them, speechless.

"How did you know where to find us?" Volkov asked good-humouredly. He donned his jerkin as he peered out through the gates, his eyes following the disappearing figures.

"Quite simple, really. I came to Kraków to arrange the despatch of some urgent letters. I was later told at the tavern that you were at church. Knowing you not as a pious man, I intuitively understood the innkeeper to mean churchyard, and here I am." Jack spread his arms to emphasise his obvious and simple deduction. Glancing from face to face, he added, "Well done, gentlemen!" and then replacing his foot in the stirrup, he turned Abaccus with a tug of his reins and spurred him away at a trot through the gates.

Earlier, having no inkling of the time of his friends' possible return, Jack had drawn his parents aside, eager to move on with his decision to help the king with his investigation. Away from the servants, the three settled into the couches in the library, and Jack explained the content of letters he had recently received and his subsequent intentions. Without reservation, Jock voiced his support immediately, seeing it as his son's duty to protect the king. Janina was happy with any decision that the men in her life agreed to. Buoyed by the outcome, Jack had left for Kraków to arrange for a courier to disseminate his letters.

The sorry-looking, duel-weary cavaliers returned to the Channing estate as snow began to fall in earnest. Jock looked on without a word as his wife brought her hands to her face in dismay at the state they were in. Jack leaned nonchalantly against the far doorway in the kitchen as the hungry men entered in search of food. Ordering the dishevelled group to go away and wash, Janina instructed the cooks to prepare hot tea and bring in plates of sliced meats, bread and cheese.

Jack had said nothing of what he had seen behind the church as the sheepish men sat around the table and heartily attacked the food like wolves around a sheep's carcass. They had survived on little more than alcohol for almost three days. Old Joseph and Chauvin appeared briefly, breaking from their chores in the barn. A single thorough look at the men's haggard faces told them all they needed to know. With a snigger and a thick slice of cheese, they left to return to their work. Volkov sensed the heavy, pressuring silence and finally shared their story with his expectant audience.

After three nights at the tavern, the group had thinned the patience of many of the other customers, yet the innkeeper knew Volkov and was happy with the sum the cavaliers had spent at his establishment. Late one morning, a small contingent of Ruthenian infantrymen, acting as escorts to a merchant from Kiev, entered in search of a meal and refreshment. As was their way, the Ruthenians had rapidly become boisterous and vocal even before their food arrived and, fuelled by liquor, began bullying the staff and demeaning other patrons. Much of their lewd and offensive remarks were not understood by the locals, but they were not lost on Volkov, who spoke their dialect. Starved for sleep and enervated by drink, he retaliated with his own angry string of curses and derogatory truths. His patience was exhausted, and he was swayed into action by their interminable assault on the country's politics, religion and populous.

The exchange escalated to include personal threats and drawn rapiers. The leader of the swordsmen—a tall, well-built man with dark, menacing eyes—snatched a nearby serving wench and held her forcibly to him, pinning her neck with his arm. He licked at her cheek in long boorish strokes as her eyes bulged and her pursed lips struggled for air.

Both Montejo and Scrolavezza jumped to their feet, bristled at his treatment of the terrified girl. The leader's reference to her as a whore and Volkov's description of him as a mindless peasant set the scene for a duel. They had the sense to move the quarrel to St Mark's churchyard, which was a quiet, unassuming spot sufficiently distant from the busy market square to attract little attention and outside interference. Jack had arrived as the incensed scrappers were preparing to settle their dispute.

After hearing the story, Jock was about to herd the men into the compound, but his son stayed his request with a raised hand. "Gentlemen, with your broad and varied experience, you may be able to indulge me with a solution to my minor problem. Has anyone heard the term 'Elbflorenz' before?"

The initial silence from expressionless faces was eventually broken by Ritner, who offered an explanation. "I believe it refers to the town of Dresden, in Upper Saxony." He looked blankly at the others, catching a nod of agreement from the Veronese before continuing. "'Florenz' refers to the beautiful north Italian city, and 'Elb' is a shortened form of the river Elbe. The walled fortress of Dresden, which lies on the Elbe River, has on occasion been referred to as the 'Florence on the Elbe', implying the mirroring of Florentine beauty by the Saxon town."

Jack's assumption had been correct. "Thank you, Andreas," he responded. "I would ask that Chauvin and Volkov stay behind with me and the rest of you please follow my father outside. Thank you."

Chauvin, Volkov and Jack remained as the others left the table with a scraping of benches and chairs on the stone floor. The women had departed earlier to complete unfinished tasks in other parts of the house, so Jack had the undivided attention of his two friends. "Recent letters from Vienna and Warszawa have reinforced the continuing threat of the Green Scarf Fraternity, as I refer to it, and its ongoing activity has forced Sigismund's hand in wanting to totally quench it. Documents being couriered from Kraków as we speak confirm my acceptance of his royal delegated authority and request. My task is to uncover the perpetrators and neutralise them. The bones of a strategy are etched in my mind, and I will be departing for the Polish capital tomorrow morning."

"Excellent. When exactly will we be leaving?" asked Anton with open delight, always one for action. This new venture posed the promise of more travel and additional excitement, not to mention the sweet thought of Gabby's willing arms.

"I am sharing this with you as my dearest and most trusted friends," Jack replied squarely as he gazed from one face to the other. "On this occasion, I will need a companion whose mother tongue is German; someone familiar with the intricate nuances of the language; someone who has lived there. I doubt that the good Count Pomorski will have such a staff member on hand, and for that reason, I propose to invite Ritner to join me."

"Under the circumstances, lieutenant, I believe Andreas to be your best choice. He travelled in and around those parts for some time," the corporal concurred.

Jack ignored the Cossack's obvious disappointment. "I have my parents' blessing, and beyond them, you are the only ones who are aware of my fresh responsibilities. I would appreciate your discretion in the matter and will have a quiet word with Andreas shortly."

The three rose together and made their way to find the others. The young officer pulled the Bavarian aside from the rest of the group, and they walked away from the house as Jack shared his plan.

The two were gone early the next morning. With one overnight stay, they arrived at the king's palace the following day. Jack settled into his usual room, and Ritner was given Volkov's chamber as the two were located conveniently proximate to each other.

As always, the king was pleased to see his young

officer. "You should be appointed as my primary leech, Andrzej. You would undoubtedly do no worse a job than that morose streak of misery I have looking after me at present. How is that feisty Scotsman? Is your father well?"

Jack ignored the offhand proposal to change medics and simply answered, "Of course, sire. He's as fit as a bull. You know yourself what these Highlanders are like. He presents his compliments and shares my misgivings and concerns regarding Your Majesty's safety."

"Excellent! Tell him to visit me here. I miss him at court. I have plenty of palatable mead to share, and it would do me good to see an old, trustworthy face around the palace again." The king was in an unusually jocular mood. "I understand that you have accepted the task of uncovering the plot against me. Pomorski showed me your correspondence."

The young man bowed his head in assent, saying, "I have travelled here to Warszawa with an assistant for that very purpose. We have only just arrived. I will meet with the count shortly as he may not be aware of our arrival. Then I wish to spend time with the prisoner to clarify a number of pieces of information that vex me."

"You seem to have a firm direction in your mind then, lad, and I'm happy to say that you appear fully recovered after the unfortunate incident in Southern Bohemia." Jack nodded as Sigismund continued. "What is this I hear that the Lady Marianna has taken an affectionate interest in you?" The old man winked, not seriously expecting an answer to his question, as his envoy blushed. "Don't let her distract you far from your duty, although I was young once and know how difficult that may prove. She is a wonderful girl—a good family, fine parents. Look after her, my boy."

The monarch slapped the young physician's back and added as a parting comment, "Ensure Pomorski is aware of your progress, and good luck. May God open your eyes and guide us with his infinite wisdom. You have my confidence and my blessing to use whatever you need to halt this blight."

The young officer bowed, taking his leave of the king.

"Please join us for dinner in the grand hall tonight. Wander in at the usual time. You are always most welcome!" Jack heard the monarch shout after him before the doors to the council chambers closed softly behind him. On his way to the royal stables, he passed by Ritner's room and explained that he would be with the Pomorski family for a while and that he and Ritner would visit the guard station upon his return.

Jack hoped that an unheralded visit would not

pose Pomorski an inconvenience as he led Abaccus out of the palace grounds. He had stated in his correspondence that he would arrive imminently, so he was sure that the count expected him.

Marianna must have seen the officer arrive through the window because as he was about to knock at the door, it swung open, revealing her beautiful, ecstatic face. She crushed him with an unreserved embrace before he could remove his plumed hat or utter a word. They stood in each other's arms, swaying and laughing, and she finally stepped away and led him inside, guiding him with her hand. Hearing their daughter's earlier squeals of delight, Marianna's parents joined the two, both sincere in their warmth and happiness to see Jack recovered. The young countess pushed him into an armchair and forced him to answer what seemed like hundreds of questions. The count stood silently, listening patiently to Jack's account of Lomnice and his recuperation at Linz and at home. Jack had to swear that he had read all of Marianna's letters a dozen times, and she admonished him for writing back so infrequently. Countess Barbara's genuine concern was not wasted on him, and the older woman squeezed his arm as she left to arrange refreshments.

With her interrogation complete, Marianna sat in the chair beside Jack and left it to her father to update him on their own news. When he had finished, Jack briefly outlined his own proposed tactics for the investigation and noted that he had already had an audience with the king. The count was informed of Ritner's planned involvement and nodded frequently as the young officer chartered his intended line of questioning. Pomorski confirmed that he had no one with the specific German background that Jack required available to assist him and agreed that Ritner had been a logical choice.

With the reunion concluded, Jack returned to the palace some hours later and called in on Ritner in the mid-afternoon. The two men strode across the courtyard to the guard house. The officer on duty recognised the Polish lieutenant from their earlier meeting, and when requested, arranged for the prisoner to be escorted from his cell for interrogation. Jack and his companion were led into a small stone vault where three chairs had been placed, one arranged so as to face the other two. The room was otherwise bare and cold. No fireplace existed in its walls. A small barred window set high up one wall provided the only natural light, and an unlit, half-burned candle stood in a small candlestick on the floor in one corner, its sides turreted with frozen streams of previously-melted wax. The two waited at the rear of the chamber, behind the two plain chairs, and Jack donned his gloves against the cold. Rodent droppings dotted the unswept floor. He cast a furtive, sideways glance at his companion, who stood apparently outwardly comfortable with his hands clasped behind him.

Advancing footsteps reached the two from behind the studded door, which was suddenly thrown open as the prisoner was led manacled into the room. The leading guard stopped him with a lowered halberd while the soldier at the rear stepped back out and swung the heavy door shut on squeaky hinges behind him. His armoured back was visible through the small rectangular grate in the door. The remaining guard nodded as he stepped back against the side wall, where he stood at ease should he be needed.

The man in chains looked like a mere youth. His grizzled, curly hair had long remained uncombed, and nascent traces of a reddish beard appeared along his jaw and chin. He had tidy, albeit dirty, features accented by a sallow complexion, and his piercing eyes were glazed with arrogance and disdain as he stared briefly at the two cavaliers. He was of the same height and build as Jack, and his feet were bare and unwashed. He stood facing the two in torn fuscous breeches, his soiled shirt ripped at the collar beneath his yellow, sleeveless vest, eyes now downcast and sullen.

Jack motioned for the prisoner to be seated, voicing his request in German. The youth moved morosely into his chair. Without looking up, he leaned back, resting his chained wrists on his thighs. The guard caught Jack's glance and snapped to attention as the young officer requested a mug of water and a woollen blanket in Polish. The two cavaliers took their seats and waited, and when the guard returned, Jack signalled that the items should be given to the prisoner. The lad refused the blanket but gulped down the water and dropped the empty mug onto the stone floor with a hollow thud. Jack asked Ritner to cover the boy's shoulders with the quilt, and with this done, Andreas resumed his seat. The lad glanced momentarily at Jack and then he let his stoic gaze retreat back to the ground.

"Please tell me your full name and age," Jack began evenly, producing a scribbled parchment from inside his coat. There was no response—indeed no reaction—to indicate that the request had been heard and understood. He asked again with the same result. He nodded to Ritner, who repeated the request. The prisoner had obviously heard, looking up at the Bavarian with an emotionless stare, but he said nothing. Jack asked a third time. His question stubbornly ignored, he stood and calmly walked over to the youth. Removing his glove, he felt below the lad's sternum with his fingertips and suddenly thrust his thumb deep into the hollow below the boy's ribcage. The prisoner snapped back and howled in sudden pain, his face now contorted and devoid of insolence and contempt.

The physician resumed his seat and faced the lad squarely. He repeated his question, which was met with continued obstinate silence. When Jack moved to rise, however, the lad replied hurriedly, although in a subdued voice, his eyes remaining downcast like a captive with no will to resist.

"Jürgen Schkirt. Twenty-seven."

"And where do you live?"

"Prague," the lad replied curtly.

"How long have you lived in Prague?"

"Six months."

"Where is your family?"

The question troubled the youth, so he finally offered a general response. "Saxony. Upper Saxony."

"Is that where you were born?"

"Yes. I was born in Radeburg."

"Do you go home to visit your family?"

"No."

"And what do you do in Prague?"

"I am employed as a stable hand."

"Where?"

"At the royal stables, Hradčany."

"What is the name of your master—the stable master?"

Jack asked the guard for ink and a quill and a pair of leather shoes, pointing at Schkirt's feet. The guard eventually returned, dropping the shoes next to the youth's bench and then proffering the other items to the officer.

"Put them on, Jürgen," Jack ordered. "And please repeat the stable master's name." He made a note of the name, but the lad ignored his instruction to don the shoes. Jack pointed to them with his quill, throwing the young man a threatening glare. Intimidated, the prisoner thrust his feet into the shoes, and although they appeared a size too large, Jack was pleased with the outcome. "Why did you attack the king?"

"I hate him and all his kind."

"You don't even know the monarch. How can you say that?"

"I hate what he stands for."

"So you're an anarchist?"

"If that means I hate the king, then yes, I am."

"What religion does your family follow?"

"They're all Lutheran."

"And you? What is your religion?"

"Nothing. I follow no religion."

Jack was ticking off lines against his notes, adding

additional points where he needed to complete his records.

"What is 'Elbflorenz'?"

"Dresden."

"What is important about Dresden?"

"Nothing. I once lived there—for a short time only." Ritner's gaze met Jack's.

"Who recruited you?"

"I don't know. I never saw him."

"But you met him?"

"Yes, I think so, but I was blindfolded and don't know what he looks like or where I met him."

"What is his name?"

"I don't know. He never told me. I never asked him."

"Do you realise the seriousness of your attempt on the king's life?

"It's like killing anyone else. Where I've failed, others will follow and succeed."

"You will most likely pay with your life for what has been an unsuccessful effort. You are only 27; such a waste of a young life, don't you agree?"

The lad's head remained bowed, eyes averted and voice monotone and morose. "So be it," was all he replied.

"Do you wish to have more water?"

Jack's question met with a silent negative shake of the head.

"What were you given by the man that recruited you?"

"A scarf, a dagger and a pistol."

"Why were you given these items?"

"The green cloth was a form of identification within the group, the pistol was to be used to carry out my task and the dagger was for protection or suicide if I was caught."

"Would you have killed yourself?"

Jack's question met with a simple shrug of the shoulders.

"And what were you to do with these gifts had you been successful in your endeavour?"

"They were mine to keep."

The interrogation continued in this manner for another 20 minutes. Some questions were repeated in a different form, but it was obvious that the flow of useful information had all but been exhausted. Jack rose to his feet, saying finally to the young man, "We will be back again for another discussion. Think hard about your cooperation. It may save your life." He nodded to the guard, adding that it was his wish, with the absolute support of the king, that the youth retain the items he'd received and be fed adequately and kept in good health. It was vital that this prisoner remained alive and isolated from all others. He was also not to be questioned by anyone without Jack's prior consent or not in his presence. In short, the youth completely belonged to the young physician.

Springing to attention to confirm that he understood, the guard escorted the sullen captive back to his cell. Jack was pleased with what he had discovered and what could be inferred. "Let us leave this cold and miserable place," he stated with a shudder, and Ritner gladly followed him out of the dour and unwelcome chamber.

Chapter 13

··

THE FORTRESS ON THE ELBE

J ack and Ritner had accepted the king's invitation and dined with him that night in the great hall. While this was a less formal affair than the extraordinary evening Jack and Anton experienced during their last visit to the capital, the vast table was nevertheless comfortably occupied with many guests and invited visitors. The king invariably expected great things, and the kitchen did not disappoint. The cooks pressed the servants to maintain a steady flow of steaming dishes and platters, wary of avoiding any reason for a complaint to arise from one of the fickle dining courtiers.

The count attended the dinner with his daughter, Lady Barbara having conveyed her apologies through her husband; she had caught a winter's chill and retired early with the hope of eluding a fever. Pomorski was seated near the king in response to the monarch's request earlier that day. A number of envoys had been invited, and Sigismund required his minister to be close at hand to fulfil the role of interpreter and adviser. Marianna sat between her officer and his companion, and Andreas, enchanted by the beautiful young woman, occupied her attention with endless stories and amusing snippets of conversation.

This suited Jack well as he was distracted by the details and information he had gleaned from the prisoner and he wished to complete the plan that was being structured piecemeal from these facts in his mind. The evening meal, always of the highest culinary quality and featuring a diverse selection of dishes, proved uneventful, although this was to be expected as the guard throughout the palace grounds had been tripled since the recent attempt on the king's life. Senior officers around the table had been additionally requested to come armed, and all were required to carry loaded pistols. Before leaving the royal kitchens, all food was tasted as an added measure of security, and supplementary pairs of guards patrolled the expansive gardens and surrounding grounds with hounds.

Ritner had refilled everyone's liqueur glasses and was sliding them across to their intended recipients as Pomorski strode self-confidently over to join the group. He bowed and smiled broadly, obviously pleased with the outcome of the evening. "The ambassadors are about to retire, Andrzej, and I expect that Vasa will have no further need of me tonight."

The young lieutenant looked up at him, as did his two companions, and nodded his comprehension.

"When I extricate myself from the inner circle, I'll wait for you in the foyer behind the first lancet arch," the count said, and with a quick, stiff bow, he was gone.

The three sipped on their sweet, creamy Advocaat, a new arrival from distilleries in the Netherlands that had graced the tables of the eastern European aristocracy, where it was widely adopted with the lively enthusiasm of self-ordained connoisseurs. Marianna in particular had warmed to the delectable taste of the easy-drinking digestif. She leaned towards Ritner, sliding her empty glass back to him, and was about to request another when Jack intervened to report that he had seen her father leave the table and stroll towards the adjoining foyer. She nudged the Bavarian conspiratorially, momentarily ignoring her handsome envoy. Ritner hastily refilled their two crystal tumblers, and the pair emptied the yellow fluid as furtively and quickly as they could. Marianna turned to Jack as he pushed his chair back and kissed him softly, lacing his mouth with the liqueur. Momentarily surprised, he smiled affectionately at her and stood, nodding at Ritner as he drew back the young countess's chair.

Marianna leaned unsteadily against the two men, walking among them with arms interlinked for support to where her father stood waiting—*thankfully preoccupied*, she thought—in conversation with a royal staff member. Dismissing the subordinate, the count turned to face his guests with a rising smile, his humour undiminished. "So, Andrzej, you and Herr Ritner are most welcome to join us back at our home for a drink. What do you say?"

Interrupting with as much subtlety as she could muster, Marianna proposed that they adjourn to the tavern—Volkov's tavern, she called it, as she couldn't recall its name although the Cossack had mentioned it frequently to her.

"Złoty Miecz," Jack announced, supporting her suggestion enthusiastically. It would be a worthwhile introduction for Ritner as he had not been to Warszawa before nor tasted its nightlife. The count grinned in agreement after a brief moment's thought, and Jack suggested that they first change into more comfortable and less obtrusive evening wear. The count's ministerial uniform and his daughter's sumptuous, low-cut gown were not compatible with the nefarious patronage regularly visiting such taverns, especially at this late hour. Pomorski agreed to meet them after detouring home.

"Ritner and I can go as we are. We'll make our way

there directly, and you can ask for Gabby to bring you to us when you arrive. We'll look out for you from our table," Jack said, and they parted.

Gabby was pleased to see Jack and his companion, meeting them at the door as they entered. She hugged the officer affectionately, planting a firm kiss on his lips, and smiled at Andreas as she curtsied. "Where's Volkov?" she asked expectantly. "Is he coming separately?"

The barmaid's deep disappointment was evident when she was told that Anton had remained in Kraków. She led them to their usual table, which happened to be unoccupied, and pulled across an additional pair of chairs after Jack explained the situation. He stopped her by the hand and clarified that they would order after everyone arrived and then added, with a shade of guilt and sympathy, "Anton misses you and wanted me to remind you that you are his favourite barmaid. He promises to be back soon and will make this his first port of call when he returns to Warszawa." Gabby smiled and bent to kiss Jack's cheek, consoled by the white lie.

The two cavaliers settled themselves in the quiet, familiar corner of the semi-filled darkened hall. "I hope Marianna has the sense to put her hair up under a cap and come dressed as a man," Jack confided, half in jest. He was nevertheless unsettled as he noticed the roughish and minacious clients seated at and huddled over the many tables. The two men hung their hats and rapiers on the antler fixed above their heads, and Jack slid his dagger into his boot as he took a seat facing the door.

Figures moved at the dim entrance, and Marianna and her father, transformed by their subtle and modest garb, arrived in good time. The young countess's beauty, however, was insuppressible. Heads turned as Gabby made her way to greet the two and lead them to Jack's table, meandering past the many scattered tables and benches. A middle-aged soldier—a musketeer judging by his clothing—gawked brazenly at the countess as she glided by his stool. Her passing perfume filled his nostrils and his empty head, and he rose drunkenly to follow.

Marianna and her father slid into the high-backed seats as the uninvited guest arrived at her side. He snubbed Gabby's requests to return to his own chair. Leaning forward, instead, he placed his two hands on the board and belched, smiling mischievously at Marianna with a gap-toothed grin. Gabby's persistent tugs at his sleeve went ignored. Pomorski looked up at the scoundrel, speechless and more shocked than incensed by the scoundrel's bold behaviour. Marianna recoiled at the smell of the soldier's vinegary breath as his weathered face looked down at her.

Before Andreas could fully rise to his feet, Jack leapt from his chair. Blood drained from his face in seething anger, he stretched forward with his head close to the rogue's and plunged his dagger into the man's left hand, impaling the tabletop underneath. The victim's hellish scream was silenced abruptly as Jack slapped him forcefully with the back of his hand. Before the intruder could fall backwards, Jack held him fast with an iron grip on his throat. He peered unrelentingly into the musketeer's bloodshot eyes, rasping at him with a throat that felt as though it was full of salt. "Don't you ever show your face here again!" Shaking him once, he added, "Do you understand me?"

The man's steady drinking had reduced him to maudlin tears. Without averting his angry eyes from the pained face, Jack withdrew his blade and wiped the tip on the soldier's ragged sleeve. The group watched as the man limped away, nursing his wound, myriad eyes following his shuffling retreat in the silenced room. The innkeeper escorted him to the door and returned to their table, apologising obsequiously.

Pomorski covered his daughter's shoulders with a supportive, comforting arm as Jack looked at her with genuine concern, his anger abating slowly. Ritner offered her a beaker of water. With resolve evident in her fiery, emerald eyes, she returned her defender's gaze and asked, "Will you teach me to use a dagger like that, lieutenant?"

The men's initial incredulity melted away, replaced first with tentative and disbelieving grins and finally with a round of hearty laughter. Even Marianna's father had been taken by surprise. She joined with them, adding, "The whole tavern witnessed what you did. I could walk in here naked now and no one would dare to touch me."

Wanting to put the unsavoury episode behind them, Jack pointed to the flask of distilled rye spirit, and Andreas filled their glasses. The natural, light ambience soon returned. Marianna looked away to search the hall and summoned the barmaid with a raised finger when she caught her eye.

"Do you have a yellow liqueur, sweet and delicious, with a taste like egg-rich cheesecake?" the young countess asked when the girl reached her side.

"Advocaat; it hails from the western lowlands of Europe, Gabby," Jack assisted with the description.

"Not yet," Gabby replied in a sprightly tone, nodding knowingly. "The owner has ordered 10 crates, but they haven't arrived here yet. We know the ingredients and have our own version of it. We call it 'Ajerkoniak'. The brandy has been substituted with vodka, but the taste is almost identical. I adore it. I'll fetch some for both of us." With a sly wink, she added in a softened voice, "The innkeeper has instructed us not to charge you tonight. He feels responsible for what happened. It'll taste all the better."

Returning with a medium carafe, Gabby filled two small glasses, and the women saluted and drank.

"You may have more of a son in your daughter than you may be aware, Count Pomorski." Jack eyed his lady with open pride.

"It seems most certainly to be the case," the older man concurred, and Ritner added, "Dress her in breeches and doublet and give her a pistol and sword, and she will fit nicely into the Cavalier Club."

Humoured by the thought, the group ordered herring with onions and a bowl of cucumbers dilled in vinegar alongside a plate of smoked ham and various meats. In a more serious tone, Pomorski leaned forward and asked, "What of your interrogation today? Have we learned anything new?"

"It was a session of mild probing. We confirmed all that you had previously discovered, and it is obvious that he is carefully avoiding the issue of the identity of his master." Jack flicked a stray lock of hair away from his brow. Marianna playfully pushed it away again as it fell back over his eye.

Undistracted, Jack added, "We believe he knows who he is, where he met him and what he looks like."

"Torture will drag it out of him," Ritner suggested blandly as he skewered a slice of sausage with his fork.

"No. Brutal and archaic." The young officer scowled with disapproval. "We need a lever with which to threaten him. Not physical pain but something equally effective that he is not prepared to lose. People will admit to anything under torture." He reached for a slice of brown bread from the stack that had been placed on the table and laced it with a collop of ham.

"His behaviour during questioning confirmed that he is inwardly terrified with his incarceration and fears death above all, although he tried hard to conceal it. He also has a low tolerance for physical pain." Jack scratched his cheek, looking for agreement from Ritner. "There may be truth in his claim that he has been a stable hand in Prague, but I sense that Dresden is the fundamental key. He tried to avoid discussing the place for some reason. My guess is that this 'Elbflorenz'—to use his own word—is the important missing piece in his story."

"Where is his family?" Marianna joined the discussion.

"Dresden, we believe," the Bavarian replied in an axiomatic tone.

"Any siblings?" she added.

"A sister." Andreas nodded.

"Well, if we can find where she is, bring her here and use her as the lever." Marianna made the idea sound logical and simple.

"What—ask her to convince him to tell us all? I doubt it will be that simple." Ritner scratched his prickly chin.

"No. I believe what Marianna is suggesting is that we convince his sister—kidnap her, if necessary— to aid us and pretend to threaten her with death or torture until he speaks," Jack interjected.

"Exactly," Marianna concurred as she leaned her head on the back of her chair.

"Sounds like a task for our cavaliers," Andreas suggested semi-seriously through a broad grin.

"Perhaps not, my friend. Normally Volkov and I are inseparable and travel everywhere together, but I chose you for this particular task. You know the Saxony district and speak fluent German. It is your mother tongue." Jack pulled lightly on his moustache, curling one end around his finger. "Although Warszawa and Kraków are more or less equidistant from Dresden, we would lose at least two days waiting for our support to arrive. There may be another attempt on a European monarch in that time, so speed is crucial."

"And how are you so certain that the root of this

evil lies in one of the German provinces—Saxony in this case—and not in Bohemia or France or Sweden?" Pomorski asked.

"Because all the arms carried by these assassins were of German manufacture." Jack glanced from the count to the Bavarian and asked, "How well do you know Dresden?"

"I know the region immediately to the south like my own home and have visited the town there a number of times. It is small and well-fortified, and its streets are relatively few and form an uncomplicated grid."

"Yes, that is as I expected. We will need to locate the home of the Schkirt family and hope that his sister lives with them," Jack replied.

Marianna was curious. "Are you indeed going to take the girl by force?"

"We may have to. She won't trust us; we're strangers. I am hoping that she is unaware of the incontrovertible trouble that her brother has created for himself and will ultimately be willing to help us change his mind, expose the source and save lives."

"She may know what he's been up to. He may have taken her into his confidence. She may even support his actions," Marianna noted.

"Yes, that is certainly a possibility. Even if that is the case, however, I sense that their parents are oblivious to all of this. We may need them as a secondary lever if our original plan fails. Still, I believe that she is ignorant of his errant ways." Jack sounded convincing.

Pensive during the dialogue, Pomorski gave them something profound to ponder. "Your plan will succeed only if our prisoner values his sister's absolute safety."

With actions clear and a plan in place, a carriage was hailed to return the count and his daughter home. Jack and his companion retraced their journey to the castle on foot, and shortly after dawn one day later, the two companions left the Polish capital.

Dresden wallowed in a wintry gloom. It was almost the middle of January when the carriage carrying the two cavaliers rumbled through the Wilsdruffer Gate cut into the eastern wall of the fortified town. The coach joined a steady stream of carts and wagons making their tortuous way to the town's market square. At Jack's request, Pomorski had requisitioned an unmarked vehicle pulled by a team of four stallions under the control of an experienced coachman. The cavaliers need not have worried about attracting attention as the badly mud-splattered cab would have remained anonymous after the slow and boggy ride from the capital. They did not know how well Schkirt's sister could handle a horse.

Although their route was clear of the European Alps—where the journey would have constantly been marred by deep, soft snow and frequent fallen trees—the path was nevertheless slippery and was safe only at a slow and patient speed. In the summer, the passage would have taken less than half the time it took to traverse in the winter. Ritner proved a good travelling companion; he slept virtually all the way there.

At the main market place, farmers and traders drove their wares in what appeared to be a random and chaotic fashion across the square, each claiming a small space in which he would erect a temporary shelter and trestle table and ply his goods. Ritner, finally fully awake and hopefully well-rested, directed the driver to turn left into Kreuz Strasse, in front of the small church that bore the same name, and rein in the team at the doors leading to the Rathaus. The coach's two occupants alighted, cloaked against the chilly air in their heavy coats and relieved at the opportunity to stretch their shaken limbs.

Comfortably seated at his writing desk on the evening prior to his departure, Jack had sealed a letter to his family loosely advising them of his intentions. He had also prepared an additional document stamped with the official royal seal to support his quest to locate the whereabouts of the prisoner's family. Armed with this very parchment, he and Ritner climbed the few low steps and entered the town offices.

The clerk, a fastidious and knowledgeable man, was eager to assist the two. With a pair of thin-rimmed spectacles hanging discarded from a sombre leather cord around his neck, the scrivener peered at his visitors beneath grey, bushy eyebrows. Under the pretext of having to deliver important documents, Ritner regarded the short, thin man with querying eyes and asked for assistance. The notary wrestled with the request for a moment and then raised a solitary finger, indicating that he had discovered the most appropriate place to begin his search. With a courteous nod, he stepped up to a polished wooden bench containing a row of thick tomes arranged in alphabetical order. He reached for the pertinent volume and ran his ink-stained finger down the column of names until he arrived at the one he sought. Proud of his expeditious effort, he returned to the cavaliers with a smug smile and directed them to Schloss Strasse, number 14, located diagonally across the market square.

"Would you be so kind and confirm the woman's full name please," Ritner asked. Prompted by Jack, who prodded him from behind, he hastily added, "so that we can be sure of delivering the letter to the correct person."

The wiry, bookish man smiled briefly, happy to oblige and reveal how keen an eye for detail he had. "There are two female entries at that residence, gentlemen. Gertrude Schkirt, aged 45, and Anka, aged 23. There is only a single entry under that surname in our records."

"Thank you most kindly," Andreas replied affably. He and Jack returned to the street and instructed the coachman to stable the horses and arrange a single night's lodgings. They explained that they would wait for him at the address they had been directed to.

Dresden was a compact town, and a brief stroll brought them to a narrow, slightly leaning two-storey house clearly marked with a metal plate displaying the number 14. The street was one of the town's major thoroughfares. Wider than most, it followed a gentle gradient down to the Elbe River and the multi-arched stone bridge that spanned it. Aptly named, it linked Dresden Castle—the residence of the Saxon Elector—to the town's central district, through which the two visitors had walked. Schloss Platz overlooked the northern façade of the castle. Crossing it would take one through the *Elbtor—the bridge gate*—across the shimmering river to the northern outer sector of the town and beyond the safety of the walls.

After completing his duties, the coachman rejoined

the two cavaliers as they stood across the street from the Schkirt residence. Wanting their surveillance to be as inconspicuous as possible, Jack suggested that Andreas return with the driver to rest at the inn and then come back to the house to relieve him in three hours. Left alone after their parting, the physician studied his surroundings. He entered a small cake shop located conveniently across the street that offered an unimpeded view and purchased a hot mug of cocoa and some fluffy pastries. It was warm and comfortable inside the shop, which was filled with the aroma of freshly baked bread. He settled into a seat by the window and spread the pages of a thin broadsheet across his knees. His mind wandered, eyes seeing but not reading. Pomorski had confirmed that the attempt on Vasa's life had taken place on Christmas Day.

Is this a coincidence, or was it pre-contemplated? Jack wondered. He glanced up and peered out through the window. His wait had not been long. A sombrely attired, svelte young woman—possibly the sister they sought—entered the house less than an hour after he began his watch. Re-appearing not long after, perhaps after a brief lunch, she pulled the heavy door shut behind her and stepped blithely up the gradual slope towards the market place.

Jack nodded politely to the baker as he left the shop.

Turning up his collar, he followed the girl at a discrete distance. Skirting the stalls crowding the northern end of the square, she trailed the line of shops along Wilsdruffer Allee and entered a small building above which hung a green dressmaker's sign. The square was heavily trafficked with itinerant pedestrians and locals milling around waist-high braziers, and Jack blended in easily among the townspeople. He huddled within a small ring of others, warming his hands at the glowing fire. It was late afternoon, the town sinking into the fading light of a winter's dusk, when the young lady emerged. She passed the officer within a hand's touch, brushing his shoulder, and he was sure of her identity from her resemblance to her older brother.

Jack followed the girl home and found Ritner loyally waiting for him well beyond their agreed meeting hour. They moved into a darkened alcove and settled there to maintain their ongoing vigilance. The Bavarian would stand and watch for the next six hours, and Jack was to return shortly after midnight.

After two days, the two were confident that they had constructed a pattern from the girl's repetitive movements. It would be least difficult, they agreed, to take her during the dimming light of twilight. As this was their best option, they finalised a plan to be put into action the following evening. Its execution was met with an uncanny and coincidental stroke of good fortune. As the cavaliers waited at the edge of the old market for their mark to appear, a nearby cooking stall caught fire and quickly flared into a serious blaze. The vendor negligently splashed the flames with pork fat, spreading the fire along the trestle and onto an adjacent wooden cart. In the excitement and panic to extinguish the spreading conflagration, a nearby brazier was knocked over, spilling its burning contents and exacerbating the mayhem. Distracted by the confusion, the girl had no time to scream or cry for help as she was bundled, her head buried in a cloak and thrust into the waiting carriage. The slamming of the door signalled to the coachman to drive, and when he cracked his whip over the skittish horses, they careered down the cobbled street and left the town through the same gate they had entered days earlier.

Anka Schkirt's frantic struggles were futile. Jack subdued her kicking legs as Ritner engulfed her in a bear hug, pinning her arms and immobilising her torso with the weight of his body. They only risked loosening their hold on her more than a league out of the city, where even her loudest scream would not be heard.

As they bounced down the lonely road to the border, Jack attempted to mollify the girl's writhing form, explaining that they wished her no harm. The straining, twisting figure eventually settled, though more with fatigue than trust. Her nodding head confirmed that she would cease her wrestling, and the two men extricated her from the heavy cloak. Tousled hair and wild eyes met their gaze as the terrified girl sat speechless and still. She stared at the Bavarian next to her and then at Jack on the opposite bench.

Jack repeated that they intended her no physical harm. Speaking slowly as he had rehearsed it many times in his mind, where Marianna was the would-be captive, he began to explain. He knew that he desperately needed to gain her trust. The circumstances were incalculably detestable, and the young physician was aware that the forcible taking of a person against her will was illegal, but he gradually revealed the capture and imprisonment of her brother, hoping to continue to hold her attention if nothing more.

Jack's story unravelled logically and methodically, and the girl's hysterical, frightened glare slowly gave way—initially to a self-enforced composure and eventually to a look of comprehension. Her bewilderment gradually faded as well. He was not surprised that no one in the girl's family was aware of the decisions that Jürgen had made or of the background that led to what he had done. She needed to understand that Jack wanted to help her brother—the lad's life was at stake—and more so to bring an end to this attempted regicide and flagrant anarchy.

The girl sat and listened without interruption, occasionally looking at Ritner, who would nod in confirmation. On reaching the end of his explanation, Jack outlined the scheme that would induce her brother to confess all he knew, and she ultimately understood the part she would need to play to assist them.

They three ate a simple, cold meal as the coach swayed well into the night, and somewhere in the final, dark hours before dawn, they crossed into Poland, asleep and unaware.

Chapter 14

THE RUSE

Footsteps shuffled rhythmically along the cold, damp passage. They were accompanied by the unbroken sound of metal dragging on stone. Tethered at the ankles, Jürgen still wore the boots given to him by the man who owned his body and soul. The chain did not impede his regular steps along the subterranean corridor but was of a length short enough to restrict any movement faster than a trot. The prisoner's recurrent, sporadic dreams of escape were simply that—spurious vagaries dismissed almost as quickly as they blossomed in Schkirt's feverish mind.

The lad's outwardly impassive face harboured all the features of his surroundings; his expression was as raw, dank stone—bleak and melancholy. Jürgen glanced briefly at Jack with sunken, dark eyes as he passed the physician with a heavily-armed guard following at each shoulder. Without moving, the young officer turned his head to follow the sad escort. The corners of his lips rose in a wisp of a smile as he noticed the blanket covering the man's shoulders. Although he was the epitome of wretchedness, the unhappy inmate appeared to be in good physical health and had not lost weight since their previous meeting. Less than a dozen steps later, the sombre trio halted at an opened doorway cut into the left wall, a low entrance in the shape of a Gothic arch wide enough for three men to pass comfortably through. The stout, studded portal, which had been opened for the occasion, was made of broad timber planks secured vertically together. It was shaped to fit snugly into the frame and bore no window or grating but was fitted with a solid latch and three massive hinges ornately fashioned in heavy steel.

Jack moved to fill the space vacated by the two guards as they followed their ward into the gloomy interior. Naked torches emitted a rutilant glow from brackets spaced across the walls, yet much of the vast room remained in shadow. A brazier glowed in the far corner. Stale, damp air carried the unmistakably feculent stench of fear and agony. The realisation of where he was suddenly dawned on the youth in chains, who stopped abruptly, recoiling like a fugitive at the edge of a cliff, and swallowed noisily in the obscure silence. His sallow face was beaded with sweat and his eyes wide with unabated terror as his pulse hammered at his temples. The guards steadied him after his involuntary stumble backwards, holding him firmly by each arm. Standing in the doorway, Jack choked at the fetor, covering his revulsion with a raised, gloved hand.

A soundless movement in the distant shadows caught the trio's attention as a masked figure moved languidly into the circle of torchlight nearby. His eyes glistened with menace from behind the eye slits cut into the hood that covered his head and neck. A scarred and stained leather apron girded his squat, corpulent frame. The man's muscular, hairy arms hung exposed from a short-sleeved tunic while his fists, hidden in leather gloves, lay clenched at his side. He blinked at the prisoner without emotion as the guards urged the lad forward.

Jürgen stumbled reluctantly towards the lurid jailer, fully aware that he had arrived as a guest of the torturer in his gruesome domain. The hooded man waited silently as the guards prodded their charge further forward. The quailing prisoner staggered on, unwilling and intimidated, overcome with dread. The torturer folded his arms as Jürgen arrived next to him, and their eyes locked for a brief moment before the torturer's cowled gaze strayed to land upon the ominous table beside them. With a shudder and an audible gasp, the youth recognised the rack. A long wooden bed, it was fitted with a cylindrical timber barrel at each end around which ropes had been wound, their free ends fixed to adjustable leather cuffs.

The aproned torturer shuffled past the shimmering brazier to a plain metal table on which an assortment of instruments lay in two tidy rows. The captive was forced to follow by the guards, having stood by long enough to appreciate the pain that would be inflicted on him as his limbs and joints were systematically and forcibly separated. With stooped shoulders, the lad gazed at the array of tools and shut his eyes, turning his head away from the horrifying display. One of the guards jerked Jürgen's head back with a firm tug of his hair, forcing the prisoner to look at and consider the contents of the table. The collection contained a variety of cutters, nail pullers, knotted whips, blinders, extractors and pokers of numerous sizes and designs, each tool with its own specific way of extracting information through subtly applied pain.

The torturer reached for a nearby set of pincers and turned them menacingly in his hand, demonstrating their use. Returning the instrument, he pivoted on his feet and indicated the brazier behind him with an extended arm. The frightened youth recognised a number of iron pokers and grippers embedded in the white-hot embers, and he suddenly bent forward and retched violently onto the stone floor next to the jailer's feet.

The dour party moved along the far wall, stopping at each instrument of torture and allowing the pitiful prisoner to view and appreciate the numerous implements and ingenious devices available to the seasoned tormentor to perform his grisly task. Pale and obviously shaken by the gruesome tour, the lad—supported by his sentries—returned to the doorway in which Jack was waiting. With a nod from the officer, the guards escorted Jürgen to the small room where he had been previously questioned.

The prisoner slumped into his chair, his head bowed and chest heaving for air. Spilling the tumbler of water with a trembling hand while attempting to take a drink, he struggled to contain his fear. Ritner sat waiting, staring impassively ahead as the young lieutenant occupied the empty seat next to him and the guards resumed their places in the cell and outside the door. They waited in silence for the prisoner to regain his composure and give them his full attention. With an almost imperceptible nod from his companion, the Bavarian leaned forward, arching his eyebrows and asking in an even, emotionless tone, "Are you ready to tell us what we seek to know?"

After a pause that seemed to last a millennium,

Schkirt raised his bedraggled head and mumbled an incoherent reply. Dried vomit clung in patches to his mouth and chin. He stared with an unfocused, far-away look at the wall behind the two cavaliers and then dropped his head to gaze back at his feet.

Ritner repeated his question. Receiving no reply, he peered at the guard, who stepped forward and shook the slouching figure sharply by the shoulder. The youth seemed to wake as if from a daze and looked at his interrogator with a furrowed brow, implying that he had not understood. The question was posed once more, this time louder and enunciated one word at a time.

"I know not who my master is or where we met. He values the anonymity of his identity above all else. No one knows him. Even his voice is distorted by the scarf he wears beneath his cloak," Jürgen replied.

"If what you say is true, can you not describe him—his general appearance, height, size?" Ritner asked, almost benignantly.

"The chamber was dark, and he was shrouded in shadow. He revealed nothing that could describe him."

After a moment's pause, the questioner continued. "You have seen what awaits you in the chamber beyond this corridor. Why subject yourself to such intolerable pain and mutilation?"

The youth replied without hesitation, sincere tone overflowing with the desire to assist his interrogators. "I will admit to anything—even tell you lies and answer with fictitious responses—to convince you to believe me." He shouted back the words, shaking his head with frustration, and covered his face with his soiled hands.

On the verge of believing the wretched youth, Ritner glanced at Jack with a look of resigned supplication. He merely received an obtuse nod in reply, the physician indicating the door. Jack was obviously not convinced by the prisoner's earnestness, or perhaps he possessed less compassion than Ritner had believed. Had the choice been his alone, the Bavarian would have returned Schkirt to his cell and further pondered his next move. He had been sure that torture would break the lad's spirit completely, but now he was no longer confident and almost believed that the lad was speaking the truth and was indeed totally ignorant of his master's identity. The next step in their predetermined plan was clear, however, and he had no choice but to take it.

"Bring in the wench!" Ritner ordered with stern resignation, caught in the confluence of his own many conflicting thoughts and feelings of indecision. Retreating strides echoed in the nearby passageway as the guard left to fulfil the cavalier's bidding.

Ritner looked down as a prod at his elbow attracted his attention. Jack, holding a small flask, proffered the uncorked vessel to him. He took it gladly. Eventually, the sound of approaching footsteps reached the silent room. The door to the chamber was pushed open and Anka ushered in, her hands and feet manacled. Her strained face was smeared with dirt, and she stood behind her seated brother in a thick and warm but soiled gown. From their chairs, the two interrogators eyed the new arrival with expressionless faces as the guard indicated for her to step forward and then resumed his place against the side wall.

Jürgen lifted his head and turned in his seat to look up at the woman beside him. An initial moment of uncertainty immobilised him, but when recognition replaced disbelief and confusion, he staggered to his feet and embraced his sister as warmly as their restraints allowed. The siblings shook as their tears flowed freely, sobbing and speechless with their heads buried in each other's arms. Jürgen cried openly without holding back, not caring in the slightest when the blanket slid from his heaving shoulders. The two hugged and stared at each other with relief, tears carving streaks into their faces and smudging their stained cheeks. Then Ritner snapped his fingers, and the siblings were forcibly separated by the guard. They stood together, and Anka searched for her brother's hand.

Looking from one to the other, the Bavarian raised his chin to remind them of his authority and began. "Your stubborn resistance and blatant refusal to assist us have forced our hand. Persistence has rewarded us with the capture of your sister and the deaths of others in your misguided and anarchistic group. We will not rest to achieve what we need to put an end to this ruthless madness." He was in full flow, surprising even himself with the apparent conviction of his own oration and growing more confident that his words would bring this play to a satisfactory conclusion.

Ritner fixed his attention fully on the youth and continued. "You have been given every opportunity to reveal what we have asked. With your haughty and deceitful replies, you have chosen to delay and thwart our efforts to seek the truth in order to destroy those who wish harm to our monarch and eradicate the very fibre of our nation as well as that of our neighbouring supporters." His eyes bore into the prisoner's with as much venom and austerity as he could summon.

"Our diligence, despite your obstinate lack of assistance, has rewarded us with this prize," the Bavarian turned to momentarily look at Anka, "whose implication in your sordid plot will be borne out. The time for leniency is past. You have yourself nominated the course that we will now embrace. We will extract what we require, and death will not be a deluge but simply a slow stream of unimaginable pain. Take her to the torturer!"

With the assistance from the sentry beyond the door, Anka was prised from her brother's arms and led away. Jürgen turned to follow her, still struggling to retain his grip, but a blow from the guard's metal gauntlet knocked him reeling back into the cell. When the sentries returned, they bundled the semi-conscious youth into his chair, shaking him awake. Both guards remained in the chamber, standing behind the prisoner on either side of the open door.

"You can stop this by speaking the truth." Ritner's voice was hoarse and even.

Jürgen stared at his interrogators with a pallid face, eyes brimming with contempt. A red welt was beginning to appear where he had been struck. The desperate prisoner's glare reminded Ritner of his imagined perception of Satan, but the Bavarian turned his attention to concentrating on the gravity of their task and his hope—no, his belief—in the success of their grim work.

"Think hard, boy, on the decisions you make this moment." Ritner's eyes drilled back at the captive.

Breaking the silence that followed was an abrupt, blood-curdling scream from the torturer's chamber. It was followed by another scream moments later. A short pause, and there was another shrill howl, this time louder and unmistakably racked with agony. Schkirt's eyes turned wild, and he covered his ears, rocking frantically in his chair.

Ritner leaned forward, stabbing the frenzied youth with his rasping voice. "End this now, or your sister will die... eventually. Those are our instructions."

The rocking figure gave no indication that he had heard. He continued to sway back and forth, eyes shut tightly, humming and maundering unintelligibly to himself. His ankle chains scraped the floor beneath him, where a puddle began to form as he urinated onto the chair. A long shriek followed quickly by agonised, hellish pleading broke his low-pitched droning. Jürgen shook his head violently, racked by his sister's tormented appeals.

"Stop!" he yelled plangently. "Stop immediately!" He finally added in short, grating breaths, "I'll give you all you want."

Ritner nodded urgently at one of the sentries, barking, "Stop—for now—and wait for our further directive."

Jack reached for a parchment and quill as the broken man began speaking in a barely audible whisper. He told them that he had never been to Prague and had never been taken into the employ of King Ferdinand's stable. Instead, one evening during late autumn, Jürgen had wandered into a tavern in Dresden, the town that he and his family now called home. Cold and dispirited due to the abandonment of the butcher's daughter, a girl whom he had dearly loved, he stood at the serving bench intent on burying his grief in ale. After emptying the first pitcher, he promptly ordered a second when a tap from behind brought him face-to-face with a stranger. Oddly familiar but with a companionable face the lad did not fully recognise, the man called himself a friend. Paying for the ale, he invited the heart-broken youth to a small table in a quiet corner of the inn. Two others, also strangers, were already seated there. One of them was a youth like Jürgen, and the other, perhaps the oldest of the group, appeared to be the brother of the first. Their conversation—initially light-hearted and general—covered religion, politics and the disintegrating situation in Europe. The oddly familiar man and his supposed brother, who were later confirmed to be siblings, shared their belief in the removal of authority at a national level. They were of the opinion that all religions were equally avaricious and all governments invariably corrupt. They were adamant in their intent to destroy authority, both secular and spiritual, for the immeasurable benefits to mankind and were seeking fervent disciples to assist in their crusade.

Both young men backed the cause, convinced and driven by the belief that kings, popes and those in power were greedy and pernicious beasts. They vaunted their philosophy wherever the brothers directed them. Further meetings were held informally at the tavern, but the training of the youthful volunteers was conducted at the lair of *Einsamer Wolf—Lone Wolf*, as the leader of the group, preferred to be addressed. This was a three-storey gasthof located on the corner of See Strasse and Kavalier Gasse in the southwestern quarter of Dresden, not far from the gate installed in the southern wall of the fortified town.

Lone Wolf, also known as Arndt Krämer, was an enigmatic figure—tall, lithe and with a strong fighter's build. He was clean-shaven, and his straight, shoulder-length blond hair made him obviously notable in a crowd. With powerful shoulders and square jaw, he was a redoubtable fighter, furious and imposing in a scuffle. His prominent brow and menacing eyes had many cowering before him, yet he spoke with an uncharacteristic intelligence as one who was well-read and erudite. A persuasive and amiable man, his talent for recruiting committed followers was dazzling.

Originally from a family of candle makers, Arndt had been educated by Jesuits and was initially destined for the cloth but decided to follow in his father's craft instead. He often disappeared from the store, however, and his parents would find him sitting alone and reading among crates and kegs of wax or sparring with his own shadow, using a stick for a sword. They gave him his current pseudonym, which remained with him into adult life. Arndt's twin brother Burk, younger by three hours, was nearly identical to him in appearance, distinguished only by the scar that ran across his left eye and bisected his eyebrow. As a young boy, Burk was teased mercilessly by other children, who referred to him as *Krummen Narbe*—*Crooked Scar*—because of the disfigurement.

The sons of a dominant mother and overbearing father, the brothers were mentally and physically abused. It was rumoured that Arndt had plotted their parents' murder and Burk had put the plan into effect, but this was never proven. The boys eventually lost their interest in the family business, and it was taken over by their bombastic mother's brother. They began devoting their time—especially Arndt— to building a steady, seething hatred of authority, believing it to be an excuse for misguided power over the members of the weaker and more vulnerable strata of society.

Lone Wolf initially focused his hatred on powerful monarchs, especially those in Eastern Europe, a loathing that he planned to shift later to the west—to the kings of France and Spain and ultimately across the channel. Now, however, he nurtured a particular disdain for Ferdinand—the most likely successor to the frail Emperor of the Catholic League—and also Sigismund, the king of the largest commonwealth in Europe. The brothers funded their lifestyle with the sale of the family business and regular subsequent raids on religious institutions—including churches, monasteries, mosques and synagogues—selling the appropriated gold trinkets, precious artefacts and altar ware. They employed the protection of a number of mercenaries—mainly fugitives, deserters and those once employed as soldiers in Upper Saxony. The bodyguards were truculent drunkards who nevertheless performed their duty well and knew to obey simple orders.

The guesthouse that the brothers occupied had come to them through iniquitous and unlawful means, although they had pleaded that the resultant rumours were a calumny. The body of the prior owner was later discovered in the swollen waters of the Elbe River, entangled with a fallen branch and floating face-down near the embankment. Although the authorities harboured their suspicions, no one was ever brought to justice over the murder. Despite being old, the building was in good repair and had been well maintained by the previous landlord. Unlike similar establishments that were located in the more popular and scenic district by the river, this inn was quiet and was frequented by a small regular, recurrent following of patrons who enjoyed the relative peaceful ambience and the opportunity of a discreet, concordant palaver with comrades. This had undoubtedly influenced the Krämer brothers' choice of site.

The substantial building remained unaltered at ground level and served as a tavern, as it had under its previous owner. A network of shoulder-high alcoves filled the capacious hall, offering privacy without diminishing the effect of the centrally-placed hearth, which was vital during the bitter winter months. Simple meals could be procured from the kitchen, although a significant and exotic range of alcoholic beverages complimented and enhanced the basic menu. In the presence of their attentive mercenaries, divided into two vigilant shifts, Arndt and Burk held less formal discussions to one side of the ample stone fireplace. More sensitive and intricate meetings were conducted on the floor above, which boasted two large rooms and sleeping quarters for the hirelings and kitchen staff. The uppermost level was the private domain and the inner sanctum of Lone Wolf and his scar-faced twin. Only carefully selected prostitutes and the most important guests were welcome there—but never unattended. It was rumoured that a French merchant, visiting to negotiate a trading arrangement at the invitation of the Krämers, had inadvertently strayed into one of the bed chambers alone. His body had been discovered in the main market square the following morning when the dense fog had lifted, trampled by a horse-drawn carriage and barely recognisable. Numerous loose-lipped whores had shared a similar fate.

"Describe in detail the means of entry into the gasthof," Ritner demanded of Jürgen after the prisoner's lengthy and informative monolog. The lad's hollow eyes and ashen face confirmed that he was tired and had been crushed by the gruelling events of the day. He thought for a minute before responding.

"The three floors are linked by a single staircase along one side of the building. Although I have never been summoned to their restricted haven, I understand that access is possible through the uppermost windows and that an attic above their private chambers houses an archive of confidential documents.

The roof is sealed with slate tiles and is not abnormally steep. It is guttered on all sides. Krummen Narbe boasted once over a flask of Transylvanian spirits—as was often his way—that they could escape through the attic if badly pressed. There are two doors leading to the ground-floor tavern, although the entry behind Kavalier Gasse is permanently bolted from the inside and never used."

Andreas turned to the officer with a blank expression; he had exhausted all of his questions and could think of nothing more to ask the drained prisoner.

"Summon the girl!" was all that Jack said in reply, speaking for the first time since he had entered the chamber. "No! Herr Ritner," he commanded as the guard moved mistakenly to comply.

Andreas left the room as Jack added a final entry to his parchment, which was now covered with scrawled notes and scribbles, some underlined and others circled. He rescanned the jottings, refreshing his memory as his mind formulated options for their next visit—possibly their most vital—to Saxony and the nondescript tavern in the quaint town of Dresden. *"Audeamus—Let us dare,"* he murmured to himself as a movement at the cell door distracted his musings.

As Anka entered the room followed by her Bavarian escort, Jack looked up and smiled warmly at her. He rose from his chair and extended a hand, inviting her to join him. Schkirt lifted his sullen eyes and stared, mouth open, at his sister. Sensing the lieutenant's mood, she smiled back at the officer. The captive stood up slowly with a rattle of his chain and a wide-eyed look of disbelief and confusion, not knowing what to think or say.

"Your sister is unharmed and in perfect health, Jürgen," Jack explained. "We are not a barbarous race and not in the habit of torturing women. Whether it was your zealous belief or inane stubbornness, we had no choice but to resort to unconventional means to persuade you to give us what we needed to save the life of our king. Your love for your sister serviced our need."

Hot tears flowed down Anka's cheeks as Jack requested that the chains be removed from the over-emotional prisoner. "What will happen to him now?" she asked quietly.

"We'll give you a moment with him, and he will be returned to his cell, where he will be treated humanely and await the pleasure of the king. You will appreciate that he cannot be released, but I will make a number of recommendations when I present my report, and I suspect my requests will be granted by the crown within the confines of the gravity of his case."

Jack cleared his throat and watched as the youth

was freed from his manacles before continuing. "With your most valuable assistance, your brother has provided us with vital information. This will be used to put an end to this insanity, and if we are successful, it is my hope that your brother's life will be spared."

With a click of their heels, the two cavaliers withdrew to wait in the passage outside the cell, leaving the siblings alone.

Chapter 15

THE WOLF'S LAIR

Dawn welcomed the mid-winter sunrise with spectacular hues of scarlet and mauve. Snow covered the streets and alleys from heavy falls two days earlier and was slowly turning into hazardous ice due to arctic-born blasts conveyed by the northwest wind. Even the graceful Wisła River flowed unusually white and sluggish through the capital, burdened by slabs of ice floating in its waters. Tendrils of pale smoke rose from chimneys across the city of Warszawa as people left their beds, sounds of commerce greeting the new morning.

It had been four days since the royal courier had ridden out with despatches to Kraków, and Jack and Ritner eagerly awaited the arrival of their contingent of cavaliers. At Marianna's suggestion, Anka had been taken in as a guest of the count's family, and the two cavaliers made lengthy daily visits to the countess's house to discuss and amend their plans with Pomorski. It was obvious from the outset that a small but strong force would be needed to accomplish their task successfully, and so the remaining members of the cavalier club were summoned, their timely advent anticipated with impatience.

As the two girls were of a similar age, the young countess quickly warmed to her charge. The visitor's initial reticence quickly faded as the friendship between the two women blossomed. Anka freely shared her considerable, laudable skills as a seamstress, attracting even Lady Barbara's curiosity with the interesting and varied ways that she worked with the cloth. From making practical repairs to mundane clothes to engaging in the intricate embroidery of exquisite fabrics, the women congregated for hours around the radiant warmth of the hearth in the front salon while the men drafted and honed their collective ideas regarding the Green-Scarf Fraternity. Despite her inherently timid and reserved nature, Anka shared her domestic secrets generously. She was an assiduous support to her own family, helping her mother with daily domestic duties and tending to her father's needs. She took delight in assisting the count's family cook, passing on simple and wholesome German recipes that her mother had taught her. The appreciative family relished in the variety of hearty dishes that now enhanced their table, and in turn, Marianna would entice Anka to visit the market, where the young countess would purchase boots, gloves, capes and even dressmaking fabric as meed for the thankful houseguest.

By early afternoon—shortly after dining on chicken and Anka's savoury, saliferous sauerkraut—the members of the count's household were interrupted by a rider in royal livery, who delivered a note advising them of the arrival of their much-awaited comrades. The men departed for the castle to make the final arrangements for the new arrivals. Rooms had been prepared in the wing housing the quarters of the royal guard for Chauvin, Volkov and the others to rest prior to their anticipated departure an hour before dawn the next day. Plans were discussed in detail during the evening meal, which was held in a small dining chamber at the castle away from the great dining hall. The arrangement had been prudently provided by the count to allow Jack and Andreas to share all the salient aspects of Jürgen's interrogation. The evening was not one for premature celebration but was reserved for circumspect planning and careful co-ordination. By ten, all were in their beds.

The next day, Pomorski's servant delivered Anka to the castle in a plain carriage for her to be returned to her parents in Dresden. The morning was still dark and laden with thick fog. Having come to

Warszawa with nothing, distraught and terrified, Anka was elated at the thought of returning home accompanied by two massive trunks filled with expensive gifts and clothing. She also took with her the friendship and love of a family that had cared for her since her unhappy abduction a week earlier.

In true military fashion, expeditiously and with few commands, the convoy consisting of one coach and five horsemen clattered out of the royal castle compound in the cold, pre-dawn gloom. Anka sat beside Jack in the carriage, facing Chauvin and Volkov, and she hugged the young officer's arm as she smiled up at him with relief. The old corporal covered her knees with a blanket and then leaned back to fill his pipe. Anton closed his eyes and mused on the pending success of their strategy with a mixed sense of impatience and excitement.

Arriving after an expectedly long journey, the cloaked cavaliers followed the swaying coach at a trot as it was waved on through the eastern gate by the senior guardsman. Ritner led the mounted escort to the tavern in which he and Jack had quartered previously, and leaving the troop of cavaliers there, the carriage rattled into Schloss Strasse, coming to a halt in front of number 14. Anka hurried into the house, and her luggage was hauled onto the cobbled path next to the door. Jack alighted and straightened his doublet and hat while his companions climbed back into the warm interior of the vehicle. Many minutes later, Anka reappeared huddled within the arms of her parents, both of whom were crying. She alone was overtly happy and smiling. The memory of what had happened was now simply seen as an adventure.

Jack bowed courteously as he swept his doffed hat in a broad low arc. Anka left her parents' embrace and hugged him tightly, kissing him on both cheeks before taking a step back. Her father approached him with an extended hand and then retreated to join his wife and daughter.

Anka's red nose glowed in the cold, and she lifted her arm in the semblance of a parting wave. "Thank you for all you've done. Marianna has promised to correspond and loves you very much. May your plan succeed," was all she said, sincerity shining in her glistening eyes.

"Take care," Jack replied quickly, and with a slight bow, he climbed aboard the coach.

The horses pulled away as the horsewhip whistled in the coachman's hand. Within minutes, the cavaliers were alighting at the main entrance to the inn where their accommodation had been arranged. As the driver steered his team down a narrow and unremarkable lane towards the stables at the rear of their lodgings, Chauvin disappeared inside to fetch

Ritner. The Bavarian accompanied Jack and Volkov on a casual stroll across the market square, wrapped in plain cloaks so as not to draw undue attention to themselves. They chatted airily and stopped occasionally at one or two stalls to give the impression that they were interested purchasers inspecting produce.

At the far end of the marketplace, Ritner veered off to the right, following See Strasse to the gasthof that Jürgen had described in detail and entering the tavern to confirm the layout of the ground floor. Meanwhile, the two officers strode nonchalantly up Schreiber Strasse, which ran parallel to See Strasse. They turned right into a short, narrow alley referred to as 'An der Mauer' by the locals and halted at the far end, where they were presented with a clear view of the multi-storied inn across the street.

Apart from the odd passing cart, this section of the town was quiet and received infrequent visitors. Jack leaned casually against the alley's only lantern while Volkov strolled across See Strasse to the front of the building and then down Kavalier Gasse to inspect its rear. Built from local stone and darkened mortar, the tavern's solid walls contained several windows fixed with square tablets of mottled glass that provided the interior with light but were too hazy to allow a proper view out onto the street. A pair of soot-stained chimneys, both exuding white plumes of rising smoke, protruded beyond the high ridgeline of the slate-shingled roof. Volkov could see no means of scaling the building's three storeys to reach the roof, not even from the adjacent structure, which gave the appearance of a disused granary. A merchant's open dray pulled by a stout chestnut mare rumbled past the alley as Anton appeared from the side street, his hands hidden within the folds of his cloak. "It is impossible to see through the windows," he told Jack, who had reached the same conclusion.

"There is a single doorway generously covered with spider webs on ground level at the rear," Volkov continued, "and further along, a large window services what appears to be the kitchen. Wooden crates have been stacked against the wall, which could provide possible access to the middle floor."

The door to the tavern suddenly opened, and a figure stepped out onto the street. Raising his collar and hunching his back to the wind, the client had obviously spent some time inside as he stumbled erratically towards the town centre, oblivious to the cavaliers' presence. Jack pulled Volkov with him into the obscurity of an alcove as a precaution. Two isolated figures congregating suspiciously in broad daylight might attract unwanted attention.

"What about the uppermost storey?" the physician asked.

"There is a small courtyard surrounded by warehouses and a makeshift stable at the end of this alley," Volkov pointed behind him to Kavalier Gasse with his thumb. "The stable contains little more than the usual blacksmith's tools but is empty of horses and offers a suitable place to hide if needed. From its loft, there is easy access to the adjacent storehouse's roof, which links with Krämers' building."

The Russian leaned out from behind the wall, pushing Jack's shoulder with him and, prompting the young officer to follow the direction of his arm, pointed to the chimneys. "A man could be lowered by rope, if he was foolhardy enough, from one of those chimneys and gain entry by bursting in through the top window on the left." His outstretched arm swung left and down slightly as Jack traced its movements. "It would be noisy and a little tricky, but an attack through their bedroom window would be what they would expect least."

Jack nodded thoughtfully. A chilly gust of wind swirled rubbish around the officers' feet, rustling discarded papers as the two watched a stray dog trot by and stop to sniff and urinate at the base of the lantern. It wagged its tail as it gazed at them and then continued to the corner and disappeared from view behind the building.

Eventually, the tavern door opened and Ritner

emerged, noticing the beckoning wave of Jack's arm from the secluded recess. He strode blithely across the street to join his companions. Volkov moved aside to allow the Bavarian to slide in, and the two officers looked expectantly at him.

"One of the finest establishments I have ever had the pleasure to inspect," Ritner began. "They carry an immense array of ales—some of the finest local brands and an unimaginable range imported from countless foreign breweries. Had I more time, I would have explored their selection of meads and spirits."

The Russian gaped open-mouthed as Jack buried his face in his hand with disbelief.

"Oh, I almost forgot," Ritner continued, "the rear door on this level is bolted firmly shut. There is no way of quietly sliding the bars back without drawing immediate attention. Apparently one of the brothers is away but is expected to return by early evening. The other has cloistered himself away upstairs with a scribe, examining the accounts no doubt. I had ample time to study the downstairs tavern."

Without interruption, the two officers waited for him to continue.

"The tavern occupies the entire ground level and, as we already know, is segregated into many private booths and secluded alcoves. These, however, do not obstruct the view of the whole vast chamber. The liquor servery is visible from the main doorway, and the stairwell is situated to the right, within five steps of the entry from the street.

"I offered the innkeeper a tumbler of his own preference at my expense and discovered that the regular clientele generally vacate the premises by ten each night. The door is bolted at midnight. Apart from the two of us at the servery, there were four ruffians seated at a nearby table, most likely the mercenaries we were advised of. The remainder of the hall was empty." The Bavarian stopped and waited for questions, having exhausted his report.

"Well done, my friend." Jack was satisfied with the detailed information he had received. Volkov slapped Ritner lightly on the back as the three stepped out into the wind and retraced their steps back to their own inn. It was almost time for dinner.

Now that the premises had been explored, the final plan was laid as the eight companions sat huddled around the table after their meal. Few drank, except for Volkov and Blixt, who followed a round of spirits with two mugs of weak ale. Agreeing to assemble next to the hearth at eleven, the cavaliers retired to rest in their rooms and prepare their weapons. Chauvin was given the responsibility of sourcing a length of sturdy rope, which he managed to obtain

from the stables with the assistance of their coachman.

Jack was pleased with the strategy upon which
they had finally agreed. Given the limited knowledge of the premises that they had to work with, he
was confident that the chance of success was tipped
slightly in their favour. The element of surprise
would be their greatest ally in their mission to kill
the twin brothers and anyone who stood in their way.
Taking prisoners was not an option.

The physician sat in the chair by the fire, honing
the blades of his rapier and two daggers to their
keenest edge. It seemed an eternity since he had last
aired his father's fine sword; it must have been prior
to the battle at Lomnice. He felt self-assured and
unconcerned, and sheathing the steel after wiping
the blades clean with an oiled cloth, he turned his
attention to cleaning and loading his two pistols.
Packing his few belongings, he descended the stairs
and settled the account for the entire group with
the landlord. He pushed across an additional silver
coin with a wink and moved to wait next to the fire.
Before the appointed hour, the rest of the cavaliers
descended and gathered around, chatting quietly. It
was time.

The men followed their lieutenant outside and
bundled what small sacks of belongings they

possessed into the waiting coach for the driver to stow away. Montejo relieved the corporal of the rope, hiding it under his cloak, and followed Volkov and Ritner across the square. At this late wintry hour, it was unsurprisingly deserted. A few candles illuminated the windows of the surrounding buildings. People had retired to the warmth of their beds hours earlier; many would be rising with the dawn.

The coachman was instructed to move his carriage and the five tethered and saddled mounts to the agreed upon location facing east along An der Mauer, and after a wait of 10 minutes, the remaining five cavaliers walked south towards Lone Wolf's lair.

When they arrived at the gasthof, Marco climbed onto Blixt's shoulders and snuffed out the lantern, throwing the immediate area around the alcove into darkness. A dog barked in the far distance—*perhaps the same one we had seen earlier,* Jack considered with a smile as the cavaliers slid into the surrounding shadows and waited.

Volkov, Ritner and Montejo were to scale the building adjacent to the tavern and, on reaching the roof, secure the rope to the chimney nearest to the uppermost window. The signal for Jack's group to enter the tavern would be the sound of the window shattering as one of the men on the roof swung into it feet-first, protected from the splintering glass by a readjusted cloak. The plan was to storm the guesthouse from the top and bottom simultaneously.

Blixt peered restlessly from beyond the wall that hid his frame, catching a glint of steel as a caped figure launched itself from the roof in a smooth arc and entered the Wolf's sanctum through the disintegrating window. "Move!" he rasped but having heard the breaking glass, everyone had already drawn their swords and begun running to the tavern door.

The latch opened smoothly in Jack's hand, and he flung the door wide open as he pulled a pistol from his belt. He moved half a dozen steps inside, allowing those behind him to enter.

Four heads appeared above the partition next to the central chimney. Jack fired immediately as another pistol flared behind him. Both shots found their mark as the heads of two of the mercenaries snapped back with the impact of the leaden balls.

"The stairs!" Jack yelled, but the reminder was unnecessary as Blixt followed the Italian to the staircase. Drawing his second pistol, the physician moved to his left, sensing that Krämer's ruffians would separate. Just behind him, Chauvin slid lithely to the right with the agility of a man half his age and crept along the length of the servery. He too had discarded his fired pistol and held his second ready to discharge. He had nowhere to hide as he advanced along the open area. A head appeared from behind the stone hearth, and the man's shot, although wide, struck the corporal's pistol, knocking it from his hand. His finger had caught and bruised in the trigger guard, but ignoring the sudden jab of pain, the wiry Frenchman sprinted towards the shooter. The ruffian was surrounded by chairs and had nowhere to go. Before the man could pull his sword from the scabbard, Chauvin had skewered him through the heart. The mercenary collapsed, taking the corporal's rapier with him.

Jack continued circling along the left wall, intently searching the cubicles in front of him. He turned around momentarily to see that Blixt and Scrolavezza were pinned at the bottom of the stairwell by pistol fire from above. As he peered forward again, a quick movement caught his eye. He fired instinctively, hitting a chair leg that had been kicked as a decoy. With no time to reload, he slid the empty pistol back into his belt and continued his slow advance. An adversary suddenly appeared, standing in full view only yards away and preparing to fire. Jack froze, peering into the barrel aimed at his head, but the shot never came. Instead, the man's mouth opened with a gush of crimson blood, his eyes open wide in surprise as the pistol slipped from his fist. Only the handle of Chauvin's dagger was visible as the blade, buried to the hilt, had entered the base of the victim's skull and pierced the back of his brain. The man slumped slowly forward, dead, his arms slung over the partition. Jack nodded a silent thanks to Chauvin as the Frenchman retrieved the blade he had thrown.

The corporal advanced cautiously towards the kitchen as Jack reloaded his pistol and then retraced his steps to recover the other empty pistol he had discarded earlier. Roberge, the weakest with a blade, had been positioned outside on the street to guard the door and had been instructed to shoot and kill anyone he did not recognise attempting an escape.

Pistol shots could be heard from above, and Jack was concerned that aside from those now dead in the tavern, there were still the brothers and at least four mercenaries to dispose of. The odds were far from even upstairs. He reached the two cavaliers at the stairs, and when all had reloaded, he made a bold dash to charge those above. Marco, not only vivacious but eternally impulsive and eager as well, climbed the steps ahead of him. Blixt jumped up to the Italian's left, and Jack hugged the wall on his right. A mercenary appeared above them and fired his pistol as Kristian loosed a reflex shot, hitting the man in the chest. The damage had been done, however, and the handsome Italian stood frozen a moment in mid-stride, his head arched back as if he were studying the ceiling and his arms spread out like those of a person being crucified. Jack saw a single trickle of blood roll down the length of his nose from the neat hole in the centre of his forehead, and Marco fell from the fifth step, dead well before hitting the landing.

Anger pulsed through the young physician's temples as he climbed the stairs, now two at a time. Kristian was one step behind him. On the landing above them, a pair of mercenaries knelt on one knee, reloading. The officer and the Swede fired in unison at point-blank range, splattering the wooden wall behind the reloading men with a spray of brains and flesh-specked blood. Stowing his empty pistol, Jack stepped over one bleeding, supine corpse while the Swede peremptorily pushed the other with his boot, leaving the body slumped with open, unseeing eyes against the handrail. Frantic sounds of clashing steel drifted to the two cavaliers from the floor above. Their work was not yet done.

The pair rushed up the final case of creaking stairs, hesitating and wary of a gunshot or sword thrust. The darkened corridors were empty, but dancing shadows played across the lambent wall at the far end of the passage in time with the wild clanging of metal blades. Blixt withdrew his rapier, throwing a quizzical look at his lieutenant and stepping cautiously towards the light. Jack followed. They peered around the stile and stepped over the unmoving body of the last mercenary, who lay inside the doorway to the large room. A thin line of blood oozed from the corner of his mouth, disbelief frozen on his pale face. A section of his head had been blown away above the ear.

A figure sat slumped in a throne-like chair next to the shattered window at the far wall, head bowed. Jack recognised the grip of Volkov's rapier protruding from the impaled man's stomach. The man was still breathing, laboriously and in obvious pain, a large, growing stain seeping through his shirt around the wound. Glistening shards of glass lay scattered around his feet, and sweat beaded his ashen face.

Anton stood leaning against the ornate chair with his arms folded, and Ritner tarried next to him, holding a pistol in one hand and a rapier in the other. Kristian remained at the door as Jack skirted along the wall to the sedentary figure, recognising him immediately by the lurid scar across his left eye.

Unless Chauvin had found an additional miscreant lurking in the kitchens below, Lone Wolf was truly alone now. The two swordsmen clashing in the middle of the room were tiring, the contest appearing to be evenly matched. Montejo was indeed a master of the blade, but Schkirt had described

Arndt Krämer's swordsmanship accurately. Well-timed thrusts were parried with consummate ease by both men, and each advanced and retreated in turn, constantly probing for the other's weakness. Jack was impressed by the standard of the swordplay. The elder twin was roused and driven by the sight of his dying brother and looked to be gaining the upper hand. The Spaniard needed to be spurred on, so the officer called out to him above the din, "Marco took a pistol ball between the eyes. We will take him back with us and not leave his body in this iniquitous den."

Renewed resolve strengthened Montejo's arm almost immediately, and his tiring body surged with revitalised vigour. He stabbed at his adversary, who managed to evade the jab, and then advanced with a series of swathing slashes that the haughty anarchist barely rebuffed. Detruded by two quick, successive lunges, Arndt was forced back and his shoulder lacerated by Montejo's sword tip. Retreating in quick steps, pressed on by the Spaniard's poking blade, Arndt tripped and fell backwards onto his bed. Candelario pressed the point of his rapier menacingly against the beaten man's neck, drawing a spot of blood.

"I yield," the supine figure pleaded with a hint of asperity, and Kristian strode across to the bed and snatched the blade from Arndt's outstretched arm. Montejo's chest heaved from the exertion of the drawn out duel, but he didn't withdraw his blade until Jack stepped up and placed a gentle hand on his sword arm. The pair backed away from the bed, and the remaining twin sat up and wiped his glistening brow with the palm of his glove. He was the first to speak as the room was chilled by the southerly breeze entering through the splintered window.

"I can only guess at who you are and can pay handsomely for the lives of my brother and my own. An unimaginable fortune lies sequestered in the adjoining room. It will be yours, entirely, if you leave us alive and allow us to withdraw."

"By the looks of him, your brother won't be long for this world," Jack sneered with unbridled hatred as he nodded at the skewered twin with the scar. "We have not come here for your riches, although your generosity will assist in covering our costs. The rest will go to burying our man and to the crown—into the hands of the king you so badly wanted dead."

"Who are you?" Arndt asked with genuine interest.

"The king's envoy and Sigismund's protector."

"I know you," he elder twin cut in, rubbing his chin. "Ah, yes, the black cavalier. You killed one of my disciples."

"Wounded," Jack corrected curtly. "He survived and remains a guest of the commonwealth—along with Herr Schkirt."

"I was wondering how you found me. Jürgen was the only one who could have led you to me. You tortured the information out of him?" the man asked irritably, seeing it as his own error.

"In a manner of speaking," Jack prevaricated.

"So you may have won this battle, but there will always be another potent replacement. I could give you my word and retire to a distant and innocuous corner of the world. I would promise not to trouble you again and leave the rulers of Europe to bring down their own empires like decks of cards. What do you say, my black cavalier?"

"Finish it!" Jack hissed tersely. In response to those words, Volkov reached for the pistol in Ritner's hand and shot Arndt through the eye socket. The back of his head exploded, the force throwing him back onto his bed.

"And what about this one?" the Russian pointed casually at the impaled man on the ornate chair with the smoking barrel of his pistol. Jack grasped a handful of the scarred man's hair and pulled back his head. He searched for a pulse at the man's neck and held a fragment of glass to his mouth to check for breath. He found neither. "You can reclaim your blade, Anton. The twins are dancing in the devil's den now. Gash his wrists for good measure!"

Blixt and Ritner were left to search for valuables as

Marco's body was wrapped in sheets and a blanket by the others and strapped securely across the saddle of his horse. Chauvin had found no one at the rear of the servery, and after slitting the throats of the four dead mercenaries, he waited for the others whilst sipping on an excellent imported spirit and puffing on his pipe. He slid a glass across to Jack when the young physician joined him. Volkov arrived soon after for a drink and handed a green scarf to his friend.

"A souvenir for you, Lieutenant Channing, for an excellently conducted campaign. As proof of your success, you may wish to also offer this to the king." The Russian passed a neatly folded piece of stained white cloth to Jack, who opened it slowly. Inside was a cleanly severed finger encircled by an enormous jewelled ring that sparkled in the candlelight.

"Krämer voiced no objection in parting with it and agreed that you should have it. And you should possess the sword of the vanquished as well," Volkov added, pressing a sheathed rapier into Jack's hand.

The envoy smiled as he studied the elegant weapon. He admired the wolf's head intricately carved into the base of the blade and the hilt, which was fashioned with parts of gold and inlaid silver.

Two heavy chests of coins and jewellery were secured with the cavaliers' luggage, and shortly after the town's clock struck the twelve monotone chords signalling midnight, the coach rolled away from the guesthouse. Having had nothing to do, Roberge was left with the solitary task of shutting the tavern door. He mounted and turned his gelding to follow the carriage as it disappeared into the gloomy reaches of the night.

Chapter 16

PAUSE AND PAYMENT

The final days of January were met with a welcome peace in the capital. Marco's body had been interred in the frozen earth of the cemetery on the hill behind the royal castle. The plot would be shaded by giant, scented lime trees in the summer, and it overlooked the silver waters of the Wisła above the west bank. The Italian was buried quietly with his few belongings. His blanched right hand held the rapier he had mastered so well entwined with his mother's ebony rosary beads. In his left hand, he clutched a crumpled lime-green scarf as a sign of his last honourable achievement. Marco's combed black curls contrasted with his peaceful, pallid face— still handsome in death—as his wooden casket was lowered to the mournful notes of Montejo's farewell ballad.

The day after the group's return from Dresden, Jack sought to arrange a meeting with Pomorski. The two met later that day in a quiet chamber, where Jack explained in precise detail the sequence of events that had culminated in the demise of the Krämer brothers in their tavern in Saxony. The count, absorbed by the unfolding events, listened intently and without speaking. Nodding frequently, he grinned unreservedly as he heard the successful ending to the lieutenant's captivating tale.

Within hours of the parting of the count and the cavalier, the king had been informed by his minister of the mission's success and had sent word to them, offering his sincere appreciation and gratitude together with a formal request for an audience with his envoy three days hence.

The count confirmed that Jack's news had been promptly passed on to the monarch, who was utterly delighted by the outcome and wished to hear the account directly from his officer. The young man dressed as he would for any meeting with royalty, and following a brief wait in the adjoining foyer, he was ushered into the regal council chamber by a uniformed guard at the appointed hour. The sight that greeted him was totally unexpected. A wash of faces stared at him and clapping hands accompanied him as he strode towards the dais where the king was seated. Jack's parents stood proudly next to the throne-like chair, and nearby, he recognised Volkov and Ritner, whose beaming countenances appeared a step below those of the count and his family. The hearty ovation subsided as the young physician reached the base of the rostrum and bowed. Arms open wide, Sigismund left his chair and descended the few steps to greet his envoy with a warm embrace. The rapier that Jack carried almost slipped from his grasp. Stepping back, the king held Jack by the shoulders, gratefulness glimmering in his benevolent eyes.

Without turning back, Sigismund addressed the assembled councillors and friends in a clear, stentorian voice. "I am proud of my own judgement and of my ability to leave the safety and protection of our vast commonwealth in the mature and capable hands of officers such as our envoy, Lieutenant Andrzej Channing. Like his father before him, he has shown his willingness to place his life above his own welfare for the good of the king and his subjects. All of us gathered here owe him a profound debt of gratitude."

The king raised a hand to quell the applause that his words had evoked and looked at the young man before him as he continued. "You may recall my desire, Andrzej, when we spoke last, to have your family at court, and it is your daring that instigated and culminated in their journey here. Your father and I had the opportunity yesterday to reminisce our past years together, and I am grateful to him and your mother for raising another faithful servant of the crown and for agreeing to come to share in their son's moment of glory; it is well deserved. Indeed, one moment of many I hope. It is fitting that actions such as yours be appropriately rewarded."

Sigismund gave a nod to the elegantly dressed senior statesman standing to his right, and the Secretary of State stepped forward and read from a large scroll of parchment that he had unrolled. He briefly described Jack's bold plan and the subsequent actions undertaken by the lieutenant and his cavaliers, and then he revealed the reward that Jack had earned. Titled in his own name, the lieutenant was to be granted 5000 acres of prime, forested land abutting the Channing estate at the northern and western boundaries in addition to a gift of five stallions and three mares from the royal stables. A handsome annual stipend was also added to the current retainer that he was receiving together with half of the chest of coins that had been seized in Saxony.

When the grey-haired statesman finished reading, the king added from the foot of the platform, "Your father has been sharing some of his plans with me regarding the improvements that he has in mind for the estate. I wish to add that the costs of these works will be borne by the royal purse as well as the provision of labour to complete them."

Before Sigismund had time to return to his seat, Jack responded in a voice that reached everyone in the hall, "Sire, your abundant generosity is humbling and most appreciated by my family. The coins will be distributed amongst my company of loyal friends, who in no small part contributed to the success of our assignment."

Resounding cheers—led by Chauvin and Blixt—erupted behind the young officer, and more applause acknowledged the munificence he showed in sharing the reward with his comrades.

"I, in turn, have a leash of gifts for Your Majesty, which may serve as a reminder of the esteem in which your subjects hold their monarch." Bowing his head, Jack offered Lone Wolf's sword to the king with extended hands.

The monarch took the sheathed weapon and studied it for a moment. He was then handed the dead insurgent's ring and a neatly folded scarf.

"These belonged to the man who called himself Lone Wolf, Sire. Europe will not miss his parting as he will not miss these."

Sigismund briefly examined the objects and replied graciously, "I will keep the ring and the cloth as a constant reminder of the enemy that could have been but was crushed. The sword, however, I wish you to keep—not only for the same reason but to hold and use against our ever-present foes. Thank you, my boy." He passed back the blade and, holding the remaining gifts in his fist, returned to his chair.

With the formal ceremony concluded, the assembly adjourned through a set of doors opened by the castle servants, who invited the guests to enjoy the refreshments that had been prepared in the adjoining hall.

Jack embraced his parents and kissed Marianna before being swamped by his remaining companions. The cavaliers milled around him with congratulatory slaps on the back and sentiments of praise and encouragement. The young officer would later see to it that Pomorski arranged the distribution of the coinage according to his instructions.

Volkov, with Blixt at his elbow, brought a tray of drinks. They were too impatient to wait for the servants. It seemed so long ago since the intensity of and scrupulous preparation for their brazen adventure had commanded their every waking hour. In time, a letter would be sent to Marco's family with the Italian's share of the coins, but for now, Jack's sole intention was to enjoy a relaxed life with his family and closest friends until once again called upon by the king.

That evening, the cavaliers continued their extended celebrations at Złoty Miecz. The enlarged group occupied over half of the tavern, and even the landlord and his staff joined in the merriment. Volkov did his utmost to behave himself. He realised that the night belonged to his friend and moderated his drinking, treating Gabby with a level of respect that she had never experienced with him before.

In the early hours of the morning, when the regular patrons had left and the place belonged to the cavaliers, Chauvin sought his opportunity to quietly capture Jack's ear. With reluctance and in a sheepish tone, he confided in his friend that he and the other cavaliers planned to remain in Warszawa indefinitely. They had been offered service—with excellent conditions and an attractive pension in view of their recent success—with the king's special Drabant guards. It was their intention to accept the very lucrative offer on the condition that they were free to be of service to the king's envoy and Count Pomorski, the minister of security, as required.

Noticing his lieutenant's initial disappointment, Chauvin produced a letter confirming the cavaliers' conditions, rank and pay as well as the special circumstances outlining availability as described in separate added clauses that clearly stated the king's agreement. The document had been signed by Colonel Lewandowski and carried the royal seal and signature of the king's chief minister.

Jack's moment of discontent was brief. He realised the many advantages this commission brought for his comrades. They would be comfortably housed and regularly fed, provided with modern weapons and uniforms. They would also enjoy the use of well-trained destriers while avoiding the deprivations of regimental warfare and remaining in the relative safety of the castle. Granting Jack and Pomorski instant access to their services was undeniably a magnanimous gesture on the king's part, and the lieutenant's regular visits to Warszawa would provide him the opportunity to see them frequently. Jack gave Chauvin his blessing, and with a twinkle in his eye, suggested that the cavaliers' military skills would occasionally be required at the estate. Chauvin was now much happier and promised to inform Volkov, who was not yet aware of this development.

The idle days that followed allowed Jack to spend time with his parents in addition to his 'other family'. The count quickly warmed to Jack's father despite their markedly dissimilar personalities, and Jock picked up some of Pomorski's valuable chess tricks during their long hours hunched over a board. Their games became involved and steadily more even. On the chessboard, their military strategies tended to extend into complex scenarios, but they both loved to play and often made time over a bottle of fine cognac. An instant liking between Jack's and Marianna's mothers rapidly flourished into a special and close friendship. This was not surprising due to Janina's rare gregariousness. The women would often disappear to the market for long hours and travel together beyond the city to visit Lady Barbara's relatives or see the interesting sights in and around the vibrant capital.

In addition to the opportunity for relaxation, this was also the time to discuss the rapidly changing face of Central Europe. Jack set aside a day for correspondence and organised a despatch of letters to Kepler and Margareta in Linz as well as Bucquoy, who he believed to still be in Vienna. Eager to finalise the case involving Jürgen Schkirt, the lieutenant also sought an audience with the king. Following a lengthy debate, Sigismund agreed, albeit reluctantly, to commute the death sentences of Schkirt, Halvar and Hauf now that the fraternity had been crushed and no longer existed. There was unanimous agreement that none of the three could be released should they work to replant the seeds of anarchy in others, and instead of wasting away idly within the damp dungeons of the castle, they were engaged as free labourers to be used when and wherever needed.

Pomorski's perspicacious sources of intelligence were active and operating as effectively as always in strategic locations outside the commonwealth. According to frequent if somewhat irregular despatches, the situation in the German states, Bohemia and Austria appeared to have settled into an uneasy lull, which was understandable during the winter months. Sources in Vienna reported that Bucquoy had taken a sizeable contingent of troops to reinforce Dampierre, but due to adverse weather, Dampierre had fallen back to Krems in Lower Austria and Bucquoy had languished in Budějovice, both losing over half their force to desertion and disease.

The rebel army was similarly not immune to these setbacks, and vague reports compiled from numerous informers seemed to indicate that its total strength had fallen over the winter to no more than 8000. These soldiers were spread across lower Bohemia and Moravia, allowing the Habsburgs to secure the Golden Path, the primary trade route from the Danube at Passau through the southern Bohemian mountains to Prachatice. This allowed a cuirassier regiment of 1300 Walloons through to reinforce Bucquoy.

His obligations and work accomplished, Jack returned with his family to the Channing estate. Volkov followed a week later, accompanied by the Pomorskis, who had been invited to stay with the Channings for as long as they wished. The count had arranged for a deputy to manage important matters of court and state as they arose, and despatch riders frequently arrived at the Channing house bearing letters with news and updates of national significance.

As the melting snow surrendered to longer, warmer days, various members of the Channing household took up the annual vernal chores, cleaning windows, scrubbing floors, airing bedding and manicuring gardens. This was a particularly demanding time for Old Joseph, and in truth, he missed the company of the craggy corporal. Fortunately, Rysiek proved invaluable in tending to the fruit trees and vegetable patch, and the venerable stable master could leave his apprentice to take responsibility for the outdoor work, freeing himself to concentrate on the cellar and the smoking of viands and marinating of fish, cucumbers and mushrooms.

Having spent her life in the city, Marianna had arrived at the Channing estate with a chest full of gowns. Jack was bemused by her lack of practical clothing and insisted that the women travel to Kraków to purchase a suitable equestrian wardrobe. He was surprised by the count's horsemanship skills as they rode out beyond the boundaries of the estate, but his father reminded him that Pomorski had served as a cavalry officer and that even the count's daughter was an accomplished rider.

Ritner's eaglet had grown, its wing mended under the servants' care, and Old Joseph had declared that the bird was ready to be released. The household gathered to witness the majestic creature's return to freedom. The bird's leather hood was removed, and it was coaxed into the air from Joseph's arm. Its outstretched wings lifted it to cruise high in the sky, where it circled in the draughts of wind above the house like a tethered kite. As the assembly began to disperse, the bird glided in a slowly descending spiral and landed beside them, its fierce talons stretched out to grip the fencepost in the yard. It furled its wings and blinked regally at its master. Repeated attempts to induce its liberty produced the same result. As such, the bird was christened *Ritnerlein—small Ritner*, and given the freedom of the barn and stables.

Volkov possessed many obvious talents, but convincing him to correspond with his friends in Warszawa proved a futile task. Jack put quill to parchment in the Russian's place and wrote to Chauvin, updating him of developments at the estate and adding that Ritner should be informed of the addition of the young eagle to the Channings' menagerie. The lieutenant was pleasantly surprised to receive an answer in the Frenchman's untidy, laborious scrawl, and the two comrades continued to keep up a regular correspondence despite Chauvin's limited school-ing. Although it had been temporarily put aside, the Frenchman promised to continue with his saddlebag stitching during subsequent visits south.

Well into spring, the construction of additional outbuildings, a byre and several extensions to the stable were completed. The responsibility of manag-ing the rearrangement of horses and farm stock was left to Old Joseph, and by summer, the stable master had the new compound in order and fully functional. The eagle was left to choose his own home within the enlarged complex. Near the trees beyond the newly erected structures, Old Joseph established a dozen beehives as part of his plan to increase the produc-tion of mead, and some honey, to sustain the estate's increasing demand.

By that time, Jack and Volkov had begun to grow restless. Jock sensed their increasing restiveness and suggested that Pomorski, who had returned home with his family, may have use for them in the capital.

Europe had focused its attention on developments in Bohemia, and King Sigismund's thirst for news intensified the need and advantages of having a dependable diplomatic presence at the source where the Bohemian cauldron was boiling most intensely. Numerous despatches left Kraków in late spring hoping to receive a timely and informative reply from Count Bucquoy. Although Sigismund was very supportive of his envoy's proposal to accompany the head of the Imperial Catholic army as an observer, he had not stipulated any urgency in the implementation of the role. Pomorski acted as Jack's mouthpiece to the king, and the two strategists were in constant contact by letter. Occupied on the family estate, Jack valued the count's unswerving assistance and support at court. The minister constantly had the king's ear; after all, the king had employed him.

Jack's suggestion to return to the Bohemian conflict had been received by Marianna with displeasure, but he knew that this was driven solely by her love for him and her ubiquitous concern for his safety. She struggled to understand the reasoning behind his apparent desire to place himself directly in the face of danger. She was acutely aware of the volatility within the troubled Bohemian state and felt helpless and frustrated by his absence in Kraków, although the Channing estate was only a day's hard ride away. Southern Bohemia might as well have been France or Spain or even the distant Americas.

Life at court was essentially the same everywhere, and it mattered little which regal entity or country was involved. Only the faces and the language differed. Endless meetings with court officials and the setting of constantly shifting strategic plans with military personnel at the highest level, left little time for the head of the imperial army. Jack understood this well from his own experience and travels and gave Bucquoy the benefit of the doubt in explaining away his prolonged silence. He was prepared to pepper the Hofburg with despatches until a response from the count finally arrived—and arrive it eventually did.

Jack tore the recognisable red Habsburg seal away from the parchment with the blade of his dagger and unfolded the document with anticipation. He read the scrawling script and was elated by Bucquoy's reply. The count had written that he was more than comfortable with Lieutenant Channing's presence as an accompanying observer due to the young officer's military and diplomatic background, an important factor as many postings would involve military action. Bucquoy also welcomed the constant company of an experienced medical officer, writing, "Your services would prove eminently useful should a shred of shrapnel temporarily disable my ability to raise a goblet of wine to moisten my palate in enjoyment." The count further added that due to sensitive field intelligence that had reached the Viennese palace he planned to depart on campaign by the end of the first week in June.

Jack folded the response and lay it aside. He and

Volkov would need to leave the estate before the end of May—preferably no later than the 30th, which would be tomorrow. Travelling the roads during the summer was less onerous than in the winter, and a pair of seasoned mounted soldiers could cover ground very expeditiously.

✠ ✠ ✠ ✠

A sunny, humid day greeted the two officers as they rode into the courtyard of the Austrian capital. It was late morning, and they dusted their breeches and doublets as grooms approached to steady the horses' reins. Jack and Volkov were greeted cordially under the shade of the grand canopy at the top of the steps by a liveried guard who asked their business and then led them to an antechamber, where they were asked to wait. An unfamiliar uniformed colonel appeared a few short minutes later and greeted them in a formal and imperious manner. He gave his name as Lieutenant-Colonel Pierre de la Motte.

"Baron de Vaux, Le Comte de Bucquoy has been expecting you. He is about to dine with his officers and has requested that you join him for lunch. Please follow me."

The count's reception of the two visitors who entered the elegant dining room was far more relaxed than that of his lieutenant-colonel, with Bucquoy acting less haughtily than he had been at their previous meetings. He even stood to greet them and bowed briefly as they approached, his starched white napkin dropping from his unbuttoned shirt front. Jack retrieved the linen serviette and handed it back as Bucquoy introduced the other officers at the table, all of whom had stood up with their commanding officer. He had obviously arranged for two spaces to be kept vacant so that the newly arrived guests could be seated next to him on his right. The food had been prepared in a French style, the aroma perfuming the table. This pleased Jack, who was partial to French cuisine and its subtly different flavours, spiced distinctively to dishes originating in Eastern European kitchens. Volkov, on the other hand, was indifferent; he ate everything.

The count occupied the authoritative position at the head of the table, and de la Motte sat stern-faced to his left, across from the new arrivals. Bucquoy resumed his response to a question posed by a younger officer who sat at the far end of the table. His explanation had been interrupted by the cavaliers' entrance into the chamber earlier.

"Supported by Spanish subsidies, our forces were travelling north to free Pilsen at King Ferdinand's directive. The Moravian estates gave us free passage through Moravian territory, but as we marched north, we were pushed back and significantly outnumbered by Thurn's army and his Silesian allies when we reached Čáslav. I decided to make a stand at Lomnice, on relatively flat ground, but we were outgunned." Bucquoy turned to Jack and asked plaintively, "When did we get pounded at the ponds? You were there; both of you."

"Last November; the ninth, sir," Jack replied steadily.

The count grunted, returning his gaze to the younger officer, and continued. "Thurn left us to retreat and lick our wounds within the walls of Budějovice. He posted Count Georg Friedrich von Hohenlohe outside the city walls to keep an eye on us. A curious little man, although an experienced soldier. Does anyone know of him?" His eyes flicked across the faces at the table, but when no one volunteered to speak, he continued.

"Quite a student, I understand. He studied at the Universities of Geneva, Siena and Padua. A veteran of campaigns in France, the Ottoman Empire and the old Hungarian kingdom, he has always fought Catholics and doesn't think much of our Ferdinand. He is the general commander of the Bohemian Estates, and I was tempted on more than one occasion to parley with the pudgy fellow, and although we slipped away from under his nose, I'm sure our paths will cross again. Gentlemen, you must all make an effort to know your enemy. Study him well. Scrutinise his undergarments and the wax in his ears and learn what accumulates between his toes. Above all, learn his weaknesses and his routine. You will then anticipate his moves and profit by it." Bucquoy shut his eyes and ran his fingers across his brow, adding, "Hohenlohe, I didn't entirely trust the fellow. He takes his wine in sips."

The falling of a birch-wood toothpick could have been heard in the silence of the courtly room as the officers around the table listened with the intensity of those watching a chess tournament. The florid, portly count refilled his goblet, studying the hue of the wine in the carafe before replacing it. He then fixed his junior officer with a kindly smile and continued. "Meanwhile, boosted by the fall of Pilsen and his success at Lomnice, the overconfident Thurn crossed the border with the intention of attacking Vienna. He returned to Moravia not long after, but his progress was impeded by the fierce winter and a shortage of supplies. At the same time, the Moravian Diet assembled in early December, and despite the pressure that Thurn and his cavalry applied to them, Karel Žerotin used his considerable influence as a prominent and highly respected nobleman to urge the Moravians to remain loyal to the Emperor. God bless his soul."

Bucquoy sat back in his plush armchair and combed his greying curls with his fingers.

"Nothing happens during winter, especially a harsh one. You're a soldier. You should know that. There was no campaigning, no activity, and we believe that funding and troop support from Savoy and James I of England fell silent for the Protestant union.

"Then as an added complication," the count continued evenly, "albeit one that was expected, Emperor Matthias died on the 20th of March this year here in Vienna. His designated Habsburg replacement was Archduke Albert VII of Austria—Matthias' brother—but at 58, in poor and deteriorating health, and with his profound interests deeply rooted in the Netherlands, he lasted only a matter of months, and we are now without an Emperor. Albert has returned to the Habsburg territories in the southern Low Countries, where he has lived for the past 20 years. His heart is there—always was."

Bucquoy leaned forward and reached for his wine, emptying the beaker. He dabbed his mouth with a napkin and left it within reach in front of him.

"So, gentlemen, the chaos continues." The count was now speaking to everyone seated around him. "The Protestants are arguing amongst themselves, and the Union is beset with internal strife between its Calvinist and Lutheran constituents. But they are united in their desire not to have another Habsburg Emperor. The Upper Austrians have rebelled, the government placed in the hands of Protestant noblemen allied with the Bohemians. Now Lower Austria has become restless and nervous, and—with the exception of Carniola, Styria and Tirol—Austria is rebelling against the Catholic League."

Bucquoy eyed each of his guests steadily, wanting to impress upon them the seriousness of what he was saying. "Only six weeks ago, Bohemia despatched Thurn with 10,000 men into Moravia to slap the vacillating Moravians' wrists for giving us free passage. Žerotin and his supporters have unfortunately been removed, and Moravia has now joined the rebellion." His speech was becoming impassioned, and he reached for his wine glass, forgetting that it was empty. He cast around the room impatiently, and a servant stepped over to refill all of the empty cups.

"Wallenstein fled to Vienna with a handful of soldiers and Moravia's treasury," the count went on. "Unsurprisingly, Thurn has followed him, strengthened by the Moravian army."

"Are they his troops around the city, sir?" Jack interjected, the situation being made steadily clearer for him. "We passed through many companies bivouacked beyond these walls and were questioned by the guards before we reached the city gates."

"Absolutely!" Bucquoy's brow furrowed, and his face reddened further. "Thurn advanced into lower Austria a month ago. He took Laa an der Thaya and crossed the Danube at Fischamend only four leagues to the southeast from here. The Protestants have demanded an audience with Ferdinand. Thurn's presence is their war hammer with which to beat and intimidate us."

The count downed his wine and smacked the empty cup on the table. "You have heard the history; now wait for my orders. I am expecting Dampierre with a detachment of cuirassiers and news of reinforcements from Archduke Albert to arrive any day. We will reconvene when that transpires, and I will seek my revenge, first on Mansfeld, then on Thurn. If any of you must leave the palace, ensure that your officers know where to find you."

The count's guests were beginning to rise from their chairs when he stood and added, "Please resume your seats and finish your meals, gentlemen. I have an appointment with the king. I recommend the claret that he is currently holding." Bucquoy pointed to a servant standing across from the far window and strode out of the room.

A number of the others finished their wine and left

to attend to unfinished duties. De la Motte remained, apparently in no hurry to leave. He signalled for the tobacco box with a curt snap of his fingers and asked for his glass to be refilled.

Scrupulously attired in the style of a cavalier, de la Motte sported a neatly-trimmed moustache and small, angular beard. His immaculately combed hair was greying at the temples, giving him the appearance of a man around 40. He peered at Jack over the rim of his glass with hazy grey eyes and asked in heavily accented German, "The count has informed me that you will be travelling with us?"

"Yes, lieutenant-colonel, we will. He has graciously allowed us to accompany him as observers," Jack replied in French, ensuring that Volkov was included in his response and was charged with the same duty.

De la Motte was surprised and impressed by Jack's eloquent pronunciation, and when next he spoke, it was with less pretentiousness. "And you participated in the Battle of Lomnice with the count?"

"That's correct; we both did," Volkov interjected as Jack was distracted searching for a suitable sandwich. "Again, our presence was unofficial, and we participated in an auxiliary role. We were not attached to the command of any company or regiment. The lieutenant was badly wounded after entering the field in a medical capacity."

The Frenchman nodded, pursing his lips, and drew thoughtfully on his pipe. Before he could pose another question, Jack asked, "How long have you been under the count's command, sir?"

De la Motte exhaled a gauzy curtain of dusky grey smoke that temporarily veiled his face. He coughed lightly before replying, "Not long. I currently hold command of the cuirassier regiment of Count von Wallenstein and have known Colonel Dampierre for many years. I was a young soldier when Count Bucquoy served in Flanders, and I cut my teeth with the military in the Lowlands."

A polite knock on the door interrupted the conversation as the senior officer was called away to preside over an altercation between some of the officers in his command. He bowed as he strode from the room, leaving the two companions alone. They finished their meal and adjourned to a smaller room, where the view over the sun-washed gardens complemented the choice of digestif they had requested.

✠ ✠ ✠ ✠

The fifth of June 1619 began as an unremarkable summer day—warm, pleasant and pervaded by a gentle, cooling breeze. The court of Vienna was continuously occupied with formal and royal functions, many involving both the emperor and king and some requiring the presence of either one or the other. Ferdinand II had little time to spare since the death of Emperor Matthias, which had resulted in the king shouldering the emperor's responsibilities in addition to his own; responsibilities which he devoted appropriate time to as a monarch of numerous kingdoms and principalities. His schedule today was filled with various meetings and a particularly unwelcome audience with an irate representative from his own countrymen.

All of the officers who had dined with Bucquoy yesterday attended the session in the throne room, which was expected to occupy most of the morning. The vociferous Protestant nobility of Upper and Lower Austria was impatiently waiting for its turn to present its grievances, interjecting sporadically and heckling the speakers as the king conducted the list of preceding audiences with numerous delegates and ambassadors. The nobles had been requested to observe proper civil behaviour a number of times, but their discontent had been escalating for many months, and today's conference with Catholic authority was viewed as the culmination of badly strained emotions and clashing fervent beliefs.

As the Protestants' turn arrived to state their case, it was soon obvious to all present that things would not go well, and anticipating trouble, the captain of the arsenal despatched a rider to put a pre-arranged plan into action.

Word had been sent a week earlier to Krems requesting the immediate return of the Florentine Regiment. Dampierre, the Colonel-Inhaber, had crossed the Danube by boat with his troops and marched into Vienna with much fanfare and ceremony. With him came two cuirassier companies and five companies of mounted harquebusiers—a total of 500 men—who entered the grounds of the palace through the Fisherman's Gate when the noblemen were threatening the king in his own throne room. The parading of additional Habsburg cavalrymen was enough to persuade the monarch's hostile adversaries to withdraw.

Bucquoy was now prepared to activate his plans. Knowing that Dampierre's force was in Vienna and having received confirmation that reinforcements were approaching Budějovice, the count marched his own troops out of the Hofburg to intercept Mansfeld, who was on his way to reinforce Hohenlohe. Jack and Volkov departed with them. Bucquoy's scouts and messengers, his ubiquitous eyes and ears, conveyed regular reports to their chief commander, and four days after vacating the barracks behind the palace, Bucquoy was informed that Mansfeld's force had arrived at Záblatí, awaiting the arrival of three companies under the command of the Count of Solms-Braunfels. At Krumlov, Bucquoy turned northwest and headed for the little-known village to confront Mansfeld's troops, the germinal plan for an ambush crystallising in his mind.

Chapter 17

BATTLE OF ZÁBLATÍ

The unmistakable smell of wood smoke drifted in the languid breeze. It hung in the air like a woman's perfume, teasing the villagers' noses before their minds reacted enough to search for the source. Following the smell, dense plumes of ashen smoke billowed in continuous, rolling bulges that rose into the sky as if escaping the very womb that created them. The sound of guttural crackling, like distant echoing volleys of gunfire, could be heard many heartbeats after the first spewing tendrils of orange and scarlet flames were visible.

Volkov watched from a safe distance as the fire took hold among the tinder-dry straw and summer-scorched timbers of the stable. He heard the wild whickering of terrified horses. Their distressed neighing alerted a villager, whose panicked cries of alarm could be heard above everything else. Other voices joined in as anxious villagers absorbed the gravity of the scene. The fire spread quickly. In the dry air of the summer morning, the flames rose high beyond the rooftops and travelled with a vengeance from building to building, engulfing all in their path like ravenous rodents. The sound of barking dogs and the pealing of the village bell added to the cacophony and chaos on the streets.

Responding to orders shouted by Dampierre—who sat astride his skittish white mount—officers and cuirassiers moved about, torching nearby homes, stores and the bakery. Hysteria spread as fast as the flames, turning the populace into a stampede of wild stallions. Driven from their houses by heat and smoke, people lurched wide-eyed and spluttering onto the street. Those who strove to organise a water chain or ran with buckets to the well were pushed back or cut down by the soldiers. Within 20 minutes, more than half of the village of Netolice was engulfed in indefeasible flames that relentlessly devoured rows of tightly-huddled wooden structures.

From a wooded knoll rising across the furrowed meadow, the Russian officer looked on despondently as a vast cloud of grey smoke filled the sky above the hamlet, blocking out the sunlight like a giant parasol. Lurid shapes danced across the breadth of the hazy little settlement, wavering like a mirage. Standing in his stirrups, Volkov could see men cut down by hacking swords and screaming women dragged away by their hair. Within an hour, three-quarters of the bourg was destroyed or well ablaze, including the quaint church of the Virgin Mary that overlooked the stone-paved square. Bodies lay where they had fallen; smoke mushroomed across the adjacent rolling hills.

Anton slumped back into the saddle and turned his mount's head northeast, towards the neighbouring village of Záblatí two leagues away. As his horse cantered across the grassy fields, the Cossack noticed three companies of rebel cavalrymen riding hard towards the stricken dwellings alight at the crossroads behind him. The diversion had been a success. Reining his horse under the shade at the edge of a stand of trees, he watched the detachment of enemy troops move like carrion to a kill. With his task successfully completed, Dampierre gathered his cuirassiers and rode away from the smoking ruin that once was Netolice to rejoin the main army that had assembled to the northeast only an hour's ride away.

It seemed unnecessary and wasteful to the average burgher to build a church in Záblatí. This was not a reflection of any lack of piety or abandonment of God by the local population but merely a logical belief in preserving communal resources for the provision of the little village's other, more practical needs. The small community was indeed profoundly religious, and worshippers were more than happy to stroll along the peaceful, level track that cut through the intervening paddocks and fields to the quaint church less than 10 minutes away in the neighbouring hamlet of Záblatíčko.

This place of prayer, the Church of St Peter and Paul, stood like a sentinel on the southeastern perimeter, where it overlooked the marshlands bordering the lazy, meandering Radomilický brook and the main earthen road that led south through Radomilice to Netolice.

Replacing the original humble shrine, the church was built in 1300 in the Gothic architectural style that predominated the time. It was a modest chapel that served the local community of 50 families of farmers, shopkeepers and fishermen. The church's square bell tower stood higher than any other building in the village and accommodated the main twin doors through which worshippers entered to pray. A single aisle, dividing neat rows of austere wooden pews, led to the altar and the sacristy beyond. It was an unassuming sanctuary, comfortably catering for the small, closely-knit and God-fearing citizenry. Although humble in its proportions, the church represented a cohesive hub, geographically and metaphorically, for the villages' congregations.

Shaded by a random sprinkling of birch and maple trees, the little church boasted stark, white-washed walls and a second smaller steeple that symbolised the unity of the two neighbouring hamlets. To cater for the old, infirmed or odd passing traveller, a kaplička had also been erected at the main crossroads in the centre of Záblatí.

The countryside surrounding the two villages—a serene and picturesque carpet of lightly undulating, rolling hills—contained a mixture of dense forests of oak and pine dotted with shallow lakes, streams and narrow canals. Záblatí lay amongst ponds brimming with fish for more than a century and was part of the Vodňanská Basin and its sprawling fens.

Count Bucquoy directed his force to assemble on the elevated field beneath the linden trees a short distance south of Záblatí. To his right lay the sleepy hamlet of Dubenec and immediately behind it the spectacular, metallic waters of Blatec lagoon. Over his right shoulder, the huddled houses of Dívčice shimmered in the summer sun on the southern Blatec bank. Directly in front of their position lay the road linking the two villages with Radomilice, off to their immediate left. Záblatí was clearly visible straight ahead, less than half a league away.

It was late morning—Monday, 10 June 1619. A gentle breeze fanned the faces of the waiting rows of imperial troops from the northeast. Excessively cautious and prone to procrastination, Bucquoy had slept well and was feeling unusually exuberant and confident—almost impetuous.

Three companies of mounted harquebusiers and 300 musketeers from Bucquoy's army were ordered out of the woods. They were directed to stand within the shade of the forest but in full view, while the remainder of the count's 5000 men rested comfortably behind the tree line. Waiting for Dampierre's return, Jack listened as Bucquoy conferred with his officers, seeking agreement on the strategy that would guide them on the battlefield later that day. The Frenchman was a master of defensive warfare, but today would be one of aggression and visceral initiative rather than defence and hesitation.

Jack's attention was drawn by Volkov's arrival. The cossack jumped from his lathered mount as a groom came forward to take the reins. Respectfully touching the brim of his hat, he informed the count that Colonel Dampierre's torching of Netolice had succeeded as a distraction, drawing the assistance of Mansfeld's cavalry and splitting and weakening the latter's force as planned. He added that Dampierre's return could be expected within the hour.

Bucquoy was visibly pleased by the observer's report, and the success of his tactic further buoyed his optimistic mood. He nodded as Volkov stepped back to join Jack and then searched the faces surrounding him for de la Motte. On being summoned, the lieutenant-colonel snapped immediately to attention.

"Sir, you will organise a chamade and take a couple of officers with you to parley with Mansfeld. You will inform him that we are awaiting his pleasure. We will accept reasonable conditions for his army's impendent surrender or else look forward to meeting him on the field between us." Bucquoy gave his orders and dismissed his lieutenant-colonel with an aristocratic gaze. As de la Motte disappeared to undertake his task, the jingling sounds of approaching cavalrymen reached them, and their circle was soon augmented by Dampierre's arrival.

Jack and Anton watched from the shade of the trees as de la Motte and his small party approached the village on the distant rise under a white flag. The lieutenant-colonel halted as a small contingent of riders appeared and trotted towards his party. Jack observed the sombre discussion through his telescope, as did most of Bucquoy's command. It was a short encounter. Both parties saluted as protocol required and separated. When de la Motte returned, he handed Mansfeld's scribbled note to the count, whose lips curled into a wry smile as he shared the short reply from the rebel commander.

"Our pikes, cannons and muskets," he read aloud, "will carry my sentiments to the field below Záblatí this day. Your blood will soak the grass, and your final gasps will choke on the smoke of our guns." The note was signed '*Servabo fidem*'—*Keeper of the Faith*.

There was a murmur of laughter as Bucquoy added, "We have time for lunch, gentlemen. Please dine with me before we take the battle to this arrogant cur and teach him a lesson in humility."

The sun had reached its zenith when the first signs of enemy activity appeared. Bohemian infantry regiments marched out of the village along the main road, leaving a translucent cloud of dust hanging in the air behind them. A small number of artillery pieces drawn by pairs of horses followed, and after them rode Mansfeld's cavalry. Two roads branched out from the southern perimeter of Záblatí; one led southwest towards the settlements of Záblatíčko and Radomilice, and the other ran southeast and avoided a number of ponds before crossing over a narrow, moss-dappled stone bridge and continuing on to Nákří.

The field that lay between the two armies dipped like a shallow bowl, rising where Záblatí sat elevated at one end and climbing lightly to the southern edge of the road where Bucquoy's force nestled out of the sun. The opposing troops were now separated by a distance of less than a quarter of a league.

Bucquoy observed with interest as the contending general placed all his available regiments on the gentle, grassy paddocks between the two roads. He noted that the Catholic army had two minor advantages. The enemy was waiting in the stifling heat of the early afternoon and would be facing and fighting into the sun. Additionally, he had received no reports from his many scouts confirming that the detachment sent to aid Netolice had rejoined the main body of troops, and the anticipated support from John Albert Count of Solms had not arrived yet. Mansfeld's questionable tactics reflected a carelessness that could only have arisen from the inflated ego he gained from his success at Pilsen. Bucquoy believed that he outnumbered his opponent—albeit marginally—and was sure that he possessed a far greater cavalry strength as he studied the Bohemian cuirassier numbers waiting on the far rise. He peered at Mansfeld through his glass, surrounded by his confederate company and regimental officers and flanked by colourful banners and pennants.

The first salvo of cannon fire broke the bucolic tranquillity a little past one in the afternoon. Bucquoy delivered his orders in an even tone, without shouting but loud enough to be heard by his circle of colonels. Jack and Volkov stood to one side of the count and were well within earshot. The artillery was not to be used but remained aligned in a row amongst the trees, pointing away from the battleground. Bucquoy asked for the exposed harquebusiers and musketeers to be joined by companies of pikemen, and all were to move forward immediately at a slow pace. They were to protect the left flank and provide support in containing enemy stragglers and deserters after the main cavalry charge. He asked de la Motte to lead 10 companies of Wallenstein's Walloon cuirassiers on his left and Dampierre to command a similar force on his right. He would lead the remaining mounted troops directly through the middle.

As the Bohemian soldiers adjusted their guns' direction and range, Bucquoy looked momentarily at the two observing officers and smiled. Then he mounted his charger and took the reins from his aide. A trumpet echoed his hand signal to advance, and his cavalry moved in a series of wavy lines at a walk towards the village of Záblatí and the foe that stood before it. Brimming with a cool confidence equal to the imprudent brashness of his adversary, Bucquoy had mobilised all of his troops. There was no reserve. The regiments—containing a total of almost 4000 cavalrymen—presented an awe-inspiring spectacle. Metal jingled, and the thud of 16,000 hooves almost blotted out the sporadic groans of the distant guns. A sudden glare of sun reflected from the riders' glinting helmets and cuirasses as the entire mounted body moved into a trot down the subtle slope.

When the cavalry reached the effective range of the enemy cannons and isolated pockets were being hit, Bucquoy ordered his force into a canter. At first the Protestants responded with their own advance, the regimental colonels leading from the front. Mansfeld positioned himself behind his main body of cavalrymen, squares of pikemen and musketeers behind him. The two armies slowly converged. When the imperial troops fired their first volley of carbines and broke into a gallop, a tremble of indecision reverberated through the Bohemian ranks.

The first to break formation and retreat like terrified sheep from a hungry pack of wolves were the pike and shot tercios on Mansfeld's right flank. De la Motte's cuirassiers had surged ahead and led the charge. The effect this had on the enemy was unmistakable. Many of their flags and standards had disappeared, their bearers dropping them in their haste to escape the onrush of charging cavalry, leaving the flags to be crushed under foot and torn under hoof. The Walloons gave no quarter. With their harquebusiers spent and holstered, they fired their pistols into the backs of the fleeing, panicked soldiers. When these were empty, they slashed and cut with sabres, hacking off limbs, cleaving heads and splintering shoulders.

De la Motte ordered his trumpeters to signal the cavalry to divide, and he turned six companies right into the side of the marching squares following Mansfeld. The remainder trailed the soldiers deserting the field and continued their inexorable slaughter without resistance. Those trying to escape the mounted pursuers shed their muskets and pikes and dropped even unfired pistols—anything to lighten their load. The cavaliers' swords fell in deadly arcs, gashing unremittingly, and their horses trampled anyone who appeared in their path, their headlong gallop unbroken. The infantry behind them reached the first line of those who had fallen and skewered any wounded soldiers who were unlucky enough to still be alive.

At the same time, Bucquoy's contingent overran the enemy's guns. Most of the gunners had been shot by pistol fire, and the imperial cuirassiers slammed into the first walls of Mansfeld's infantry. On the right, Dampierre's dragoons had engaged their mounted opponents and gained the initiative after the first volley of musket fire. The tide of the battle had swung decisively in favour of the Catholics. The units surrounding Mansfeld held on grimly and gave away no ground, but both rebel flanks were either being pushed back or fleeing desperately for their lives. The senior officer of the count's personal regiment realised that the path for escape was rapidly closing, and Mansfeld fled the field surrounded by a score of his mounted guard. Within minutes, the infantry's resistance crumbled under Bucquoy's frontal assault and de la Motte's pressure from the side. With no general to command them, the Bohemian cavalrymen and foot soldiers began to surrender. Many were shot as they discarded their weapons until orders from Bucquoy confirming that prisoners could be taken reached his soldiers.

The rout had been absolute. Captives were cordoned into designated areas while the badly wounded were mercifully despatched. As a matter of haste, Dampierre was ordered to occupy the village and seize Mansfeld if his capture was possible. Sporadic gunfire could later be heard from Záblatí, culminating in a booming explosion when the ammunition depot was ignited to increase confusion.

Jack led Abaccus down the grassy slope as he and Volkov moved away from the birch-studded knoll to inspect the battlefield. Imperial casualties were scarcely evident, yet the number of enemy dead was in the thousands. Piles of collected weapons were being stacked on the wagons that followed in the wake of the count's force. The pair acknowledged

Bucquoy as their mounts moved to avoid the bodies of the dead, and they made their way slowly up the opposite incline until they reached the outskirts of the village. Signs of minor skirmishes were evident from the occasional bodies of lifeless enemy soldiers that dotted the empty streets. Civilians, traumatised by the nearby battle, were afraid to leave their homes. Although the fighting had stopped, the sight of soldiers was sufficient to keep the villagers' windows shuttered and doors barred. The pair made their way along the tidy abandoned streets to the small market square. Black smoke continued to billow from the destroyed armoury in the distance. A junior officer bowed obsequiously as Jack and Anton dismounted and entered the council chambers, where half a dozen aides studied documents and collected books and sheaves of records.

Dampierre, who stood leaning against a bench below a window at the far side of the room, looked up from a wad of parchments as the two officers approached. He had discarded his hat as it had cast a shadow over the pages he was perusing.

"Gentlemen, good afternoon to you. I believe we have found ourselves an invaluable library here. Take a look at those." Dampierre indicated a pile of thick tomes on the trestle beside him.

Jack whistled through pursed lips as the

significance of the find dawned on him. "These records form part of Mansfeld's field chancery abandoned in the bastards' haste to save their lives," he commented incredulously. "They are more valuable than the venerable and dusty scrolls once housed by the ancient Library of Alexandria."

In addition to journals detailing accounts attributed to the cost of provisions, soldiers' pay and other recurring entries, the pages contained recurrent references to the financial support and involvement of the Duke of Savoy—an embarrassing record of his supply of troops, money and patronage of the Bohemian cause. Letters in the Duke's own hand appeared frequently among the documents.

The Protestant village played unwilling host to the celebrations of the imperial army's victory at Záblatí that night. With unreserved humility, the mayor tendered his official surrender to Bucquoy in return for guaranteed security and the count's promise to leave the village unmolested and intact.

The battle of Záblatí proved to be pivotal for the success of the emperor's Roman Catholic forces. Mansfeld had fled the field with his life but in disgrace. His army had been decimated, and only a remnant handful had managed to escape with him. Most of those who had survived and been taken into captivity joined the Habsburg army. Mansfeld's reputation had been eroded as much as the size of his regiments, and with his communication with Prague now cut off, Count Thurn was forced to abandon his siege of Vienna. Hohenlohe, learning of the decisive defeat, withdrew from the walls of Budějovice to Soběslav, where he waited to be reinforced by Thurn.

Exactly one month later, Colonel Christian Illow, who had commanded a regiment of cavalry at Záblatí, was ordered by Bucquoy to seize Vimperk Castle. The castle was being held by Volf Novohradský of Kolovraty, who had sided with the Bohemian Protestants. Overlooking the Volyňka River and the city of Vimperk, the castle was crucial in protecting the golden trade route between Bohemia and Bavaria. Illow occupied the strategic stronghold and further reduced the flow of intelligence between the pockets of remnant rebel ranks.

Savoy, now totally exposed as an opponent of the Habsburgs, ceased all fosterage of and involvement in the war. He was already brutally aware that his dream had evaporated and that he would not be elected King of Bohemia.

Bucquoy gained control of southern Bohemia with his victory and sent Dampierre to quell Moravia, with Jack and Volkov following as keen observers.

But that's a separate adventurous tale.

Cast of Characters

THE CAVALIER CLUB

In Order of Appearance

Lieutenant Andrzej Hiacynt 'Jack' Channing:	Physician and envoy to the Polish King
Corporal Alain Chauvin:	French musketeer
Armand Besson:	Musketeer in Chauvin's contingent
Emile Garreau:	Musketeer in Chauvin's contingent
Guillaume Maguiere:	Musketeer in Chauvin's contingent
Tristan Paillard:	Musketeer in Chauvin's contingent
Guy Vasseur:	Musketeer in Chauvin's contingent
Julien Roberge:	Musketeer in Chauvin's contingent
Jean Legard:	Musketeer in Chauvin's contingent
Michel Arbois:	Musketeer in Chauvin's contingent
Matthias:	Habsburg Holy Roman Emperor and King of Germany
Ferdinand II:	King of Bohemia, Hungary and Croatia

Sigismund III Vasa:	King of Poland
Vilém Slavata of Chlum:	Bohemian nobleman and Regent to Ferdinand II
Graf Ernst von Mansfeld:	Mercenary and Lieutenant-General of Protestant Bohemian rebels
Jock Channing:	Jack's father
Jaroslav Hritek:	Burgomaster of Pilsen
Captain Emile Horvat:	Officer in Pilsen's defence regiment
Captain Zdeněk Svoboda:	Officer in Pilsen's defence regiment
Captain Miroslav Kovar:	Officer in Pilsen's defence regiment
Janina 'Janka' Channing:	Jack's mother
Old Joseph:	Manager and caretaker of the Channing Family Estate
Anton Volkov:	Cossack officer and Jack's loyal friend
Lady Marianna Pomorska:	Polish noblewoman from Warszawa
Count Stefan Pomorski:	Relative of Sigismund and responsible for his security. Marianna's father
Countess Barbara Pomorska:	Marianna's mother
Halvar, Günter Hauf, László Szarka, Kadir Tekin, Jürgen Schkirt:	Members of the Green Scarf Fraternity

Colonel Henry Duval, Count of Dampierre:	Commander of Imperial Cuirassiers
Charles Bonaventure de Longueval compte de Bucquoy, Baron de Vaux :	Commander of the Imperial Army
Heinrich Matthias Thurn, Graf von Valsássina:	Commander of the Bohemian rebels
Margareta:	Nurse
Johannes Kepler:	Astronomer, mathematician and philosopher
Rysiek:	Servant and Old Joseph's protégé
Kristian Blixt, Candelario Montejo, Marco Scrolavezza, Andreas Ritner:	Members of the Cavalier Club
Anka Schkirt:	Jürgen Schkirt's sister
Arndt Krämer:	Einsamer Wolf, Lone Wolf
Burk:	Arndt Krämer's twin brother
Lt-Colonel Pierre de la Motte:	Imperial cavalry officer
Count Georg Friedrich von Hohenlohe:	Bohemian General Commander